Kitty Wilson lived in
Recently she has moved t... the understanding that she and her partner will be returning to Cornwall to live very soon. She spends most of her time welded to the keyboard, dreaming of the beach or bombing back down the motorway for a quick visit! She has a penchant for very loud music, equally loud dresses and romantic heroines who speak their mind.

www.kittywilson.co.uk

🐦 twitter.com/KittyWilson23
📷 instagram.com/kittywilson23
BB bookbub.com/authors/kitty-wilson

EVERY DAY IN DECEMBER

KITTY WILSON

One More Chapter
a division of HarperCollins*Publishers*
1 London Bridge Street
London SE1 9GF
www.harpercollins.co.uk

HarperCollins*Publishers*
1st Floor, Watermarque Building, Ringsend Road
Dublin 4, Ireland

This paperback edition 2021
First published in Great Britain in ebook format
by HarperCollins*Publishers* 2021

2

A catalogue record of this book is available from the British Library

ISBN: 978-0-00-840542-7

Printed and bound in the UK using 100% Renewable Electricity
by CPI Group (UK) Ltd

MIX
Paper from
responsible sources
FSC™ C007454

FSC
www.fsc.org

Dedication. For Netty.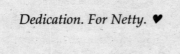

So long as men can breathe, or eyes can see,
So long lives this, and this gives life to thee.

New Year's Eve. Five years ago.
Belle.

I roll my eyes but stay silent as Luisa rants about how I need to grow up and look for a person who will respect me – instead of constantly sleeping with Lost Boys, who contribute nothing and make my car smell bad.

But truth is, she may have a point. The car smells heinous and I do deliberately pick the most god-awful men that I have no intention of committing to. I know my experience of relationships is not to be relied upon – she is definitely the one winning at life – and today she can say anything she wants and I'll happily suck it up, but ouch.

'Oh Jesus!' She bends over, reaching out with her hands, and grabs the dashboard as she does so. That's definitely four minutes since the last contraction. She nods her head up and down as she breathes in and out, swear words falling over themselves in a hurry to get out of her mouth, in between the panting and the life advice.

My best friend is the picture of the perfect wife – she asked for (and received) pearls on her birthday and Boden is very much on her bookmarks tab but my God, she can curse. She is turning the air blue around us. I expect we'll be flagged down by Environmental Health any minute now. And whilst I am dressed head-to-toe in the hospice shop's finest, she is currently wearing a pale pink cardigan, and a grey and pink frou-frou maternity skirt that is pushed out with the merest hint of netting. We know who will be blamed for disturbing the peace.

'Let's breathe together. In … out … in … out … in … out, you've got this,' I say.

'I was looking forward to the gas and air. If I breathe in here I'll be too stoned to find the maternity ward,' she spits. Pregnancy has not made her meeker.

Her breathing regulates and she relaxes her hands before bowling straight back in to the personal attack. 'Maybe try celibacy, work out who you are. Because the you I know shouldn't be doing this, sleeping with men like Sam. The you *I* love gave that sort of behaviour up years ago.'

'Aren't all relationships just trying to find someone to sleep with regularly who you don't want to murder? I'm simply— Out of the way!' I beep hard on the horn as some bloke misses us by not much more than a millimetre.

Luisa winds down the window and hollers abuse.

'You won't be able to swear like that when you're a mum.'

'Which is why I had better fit it all in today.' She grins as she rolls the window back up before turning back to me and starting again. 'I get that you have issues – dear God, if I had your parents, I'd be institutionalised by now – but you need to take charge. Stop letting their view of you shape who you are, start to believe you are worthy of more. You're about to be a godmother, any minute now, and Belle, I need my best friend to be a grown-up.' She grabs hold of the dashboard and starts breathing manically again.

We career into the car park of the hospital and I screech

to a stop in the parking bay outside the main entrance. Today I am going to be the best friend on earth. I can let her say what she wants to, coach her through her breathing, and make sure everything goes as smoothly and as stress-free as possible.

I race around to the passenger door and help her out.

'I'm not convinced you're listening.'

'I am, I am. I should definitely get rid of Sam. You're right. But honestly, Lu, I spent my whole childhood waiting to be an adult and now I am, it's not all it's cracked up to be. It's bills and chores and complicated personal relationships. More adulting at this point doesn't really appeal.' We shuffle towards the main doors and she gives me a look that would scare killer wasps. 'But obviously, for you and your baby I am willing to be the best grown-up possible. I'll just let the desk staff know Remi isn't too far behind us.'

She stops walking; her hand grips mine suddenly, so tightly I think she may well pop the fingers out of their joints. She starts to swear at the top of her voice again, drawing disapproving looks from the elderly smokers clustered outside the main door, who have no issues smoking next to their portable oxygen tanks but who presumably have never seen or heard a pregnant woman say fuck before. I fix them with a stern glare and join in her chorus as we walk past.

'This will all be over soon and you are going to have the most precious, the most amazing little bundle of gorgeousness. You're doing so well.'

'Pfft.'

'We're nearly there and they'll pump you full of Entonox

and all will be good,' I say, hoping I have developed the skills of an oracle during the short car journey. Childbirth terrifies me but letting on how scared I am to the woman I love more than anybody else in the world won't be helpful. My own anxieties don't have a place right now. Right now it's her day.

We're inside, the maternity desk is in sight, our pace is slow and my fingers no longer have any feeling left in them.

My attention is distracted, just for a second, by a man on some chairs by the A&E reception. He has his head in his hands and is sobbing and sobbing, while a couple – I assume his parents – sit on the ground beside him, trying to offer comfort. My heart goes out to him. That is what truly broken must look like. I have never really seen it before. I thought I had seen a lot, but this man, the keening noises that are coming from his covered face sear into the very core of you. It blocks out Luisa's cursing as I can't help but look at him and feel utterly forlorn that humans on this earth ever have to endure such agony. His mother leans forward and sweeps a lock of his hair out of his eyes and he briefly lowers his hands to look at her, eyes hollow with pain, revealing himself to be a man I know from a long, long time ago.

That is my home of love. If I have ranged
Like him that travels I return again.

December First.
Belle.

I love my goddaughter but she's like that baby in *The Incredibles*, just older, quicker, and more cunning. I have been looking after her for the week while Luisa and Remi are away and it's safe to say I am exhausted, on first-name terms with the Poison Unit in Birmingham, and I'm not sure how to tell Luisa that her downstairs bathroom is now covered in permanent marker, or, as Marsha would call it, Dalmatian spots. Let no one ever tell you Disney is harmless.

'And I'm not scared of the Gruffalo because I can roar this loud ... Rooooooaaaarrrrr! He'd be scared of me,' she confidently declares. I suspect she is right. The elderly gentleman crossing the road at the same time as we are certainly jumps into the air in shock. I smile apologetically, hoping he is an indulgent grandfather, and grip her hand tighter.

We are walking from the car park into Bristol Airport Arrivals, with Luisa and Remi due to land any minute. Marsha is holding my hand but is so excited that she's jumping up and down with an energy that should really be bottled and sold.

She may be exhausting but she's also next-level adorable. I mean it. There is nothing, no one in the world, that makes my heart beat as fast as this child does. She makes me feel all Mother Lioness – proud, maternal, and ready to rip any possible danger into shreds before I allow it within an inch of her.

However, I am more than ready to hand her back to her mother, get home and spend some time lost in *The Winter's Tale*, the last of Shakespeare's plays that I am working on and my absolute favourite. I have loved – no, been obsessed with – Shakespeare ever since I was a very small child. He represents all that is good in the world to me and all that is real as well. And whilst I could witter on in praise of his works for weeks at a time, I know my adoration stems from something far more simple than his skill in iambic pentameter. It stems from love.

I grew up in a house full of extroverts; drama was crammed into our house, flounces, sighs, screeching, all bouncing off the walls, the windows and the floorboards. It used to make me want to scrunch my shoulders up and fold my whole being into a teeny tiny scrap. I wished for a shell I could escape into, a small one in which I could hide and take up all the space, maybe with a fairy door attached to pull shut and keep the noise away.

Nana understood, she would swoop in with gentle grace and poise, a hint of lily of the valley in the air, and an unruffled tranquillity that made me wonder how my own mother could be related to her. She would spirit me to the garden or my bedroom, wrap me in a cloak of calm and ask what I was reading.

When I was about seven she bought a copy of *Midsummers Night's Dream* and suggested we start to read a part each, telling me it was a tale of fairies and donkeys, kings and queens and teenagers. I think most seven-year-olds are split between wanting to be a fairy and a teenager.

She'd been a wardrobe mistress for a theatre company for years, and was used to glamour and shrieking, but also recognised the value of quiet. Over the next few years she would bring over all sorts of props every time she visited, which we would wield as we each took a part. She died when I was eleven and we moved into her house soon after. Her loss impacted me greatly – she had been my touchstone, the one I belonged with and the one that made me feel I belonged somewhere. From that point on, I worked through every single play, every single sonnet and then went back and did it all again.

I still am. For the last few years I have been working on my Shakespeare project, gathering in one place all the knowledge I have sought out over the last twenty years. I have very little left to do but I am excited about wallowing in some last-minute additions to *The Winter's Tale* package that I thought of whilst on godmother duty.

Marsha is feisty like Paulina in that play, feisty, determined and focused. She's going to be a cracking adult, it just means she's a slightly terrifying child. The number of household incidents that have occurred whilst I've been looking after her are high – but Luisa (whom I've informed of each one over the phone) always laughs and reiterates that looking after Marsha is like driving abroad: with everything flying at you at speed from all angles.

As we enter the airport, Marsha spots the shop by the arrivals gate, wriggles out of my grip and races towards it, hair streaming behind her as she screams 'Percy Pigs!' at the top of her voice.

For all Luisa's laid-backness about most things Marsha-related – which I suspect is born out of necessity as much as experience – she is a nutrition diva. Nothing but the highest quality of food is to pass Marsha's lips; if it isn't organic, free-range and farmed by nuns then she isn't allowed it. But the worst sin by far – as I discovered when she found me giving Marsha a Milky Bar last year – is sugar. You would have thought I was teaching her to freebase on the way to nursery school. The language Luisa used – that hasn't changed over the years – meant I learnt that sugar was the devil and was only allowed near Marsha's lips at Christmas.

I start to run after her, spying a display of wind-up musical boxes as I do so and I grab one on the way past. Persuading Marsha against the pink rubbery deliciousness of pig-shaped sweets will take next-level negotiation skills.

'Marsha! Wait!'

This is not going to be an easy sell.

Rory.

The flight from Australia was long, but I'm finally here, back in the UK for the first time in five years. I pull my phone out the second I'm through immigration and call my step-dad, Dave. For the preceding few days, my mind has been unable to focus on anything other than getting home. I am here now though, realising that I should have come before, that by hiding away and avoiding reminders of my grief I have neglected my responsibilities and become the sort of man I never wanted to be. I can't turn the clock back and undo that, but I can make good now. I'm keen to see Mum, to get all of this sorted.

'Hey, Rory, good to hear you.' Dave answers immediately and reassures me that everything is in hand. I love Dave for many things, his calm manner being at the top of that list. He manages to soothe every situation, possessing powers only known to Jedi Masters. Still, it's going to take more than a reassuring tone to put me at ease. From the minute I heard Mum's words last week, *the* word, my heart has been in my throat. I had immediately booked a plane and rented a winter let for a month in Bath.

Bristol is still a bit too raw.

I may not be the most self-aware man in the world but I know waking up every morning and seeing the skyline of a city I once loved is a step I'm not able to deal with just yet. But with Bath as my base I can sideline my own baggage, support Mum, talk to her consultant and make sure she's getting the best care possible.

'Your mum is so excited to see you. We can't move for quiches and cakes, biscuits and sausage rolls. She's made you a cheesecake in the shape of a heart!'

'Don't tell him about that, that's a surprise!' I hear Mum shout at him in the background before she wrestles the phone from his hand.

I laugh. I can picture it, both the wrestling (she'll stamp on his foot to take him by surprise and then grapple the phone from his hand as his indignation kicks in) and the mountains of food. Mum is a feeder, not in a lock-'em-in-a-basement-and-pipe-them-full-of-cream kinda way, obviously, but in a I-love-you-so-much-words-can't-express-it-so-I'm-going-to-feed-you-and-feed-you-and-feed-you way.

'It's a silly fuss you flying back like this...' She pauses before adding more quietly, 'But I'm pleased that you've come.' Her voice returns to its usual strength. 'And don't listen to him. I haven't made anything special.' Him, I imagine, is jumping around on one foot and looking pained. Whereas she will be half overjoyed at the thought of me flying back, and half terrified – not just of the diagnosis but of being burdensome.

'It's important to me. *You're* important to me, so of course I was going to come home. I'll be here for a month, I've a few business contacts I want to chase up as well, see in person whilst I'm here. Let me get involved, tell me how I can help.' I knew if I pitched work opportunities, she'd feel better.

Mum has made it clear my whole life that I am *her* whole life and she won't have it any other way. I can't be on the other side of the world when she has news that will rock her very being, shock her out of a future she imagined she had years before she had to face the disease that had taken her mother, her grandmother.

'I don't want you making a fuss about the ... well, you know ... but you could come and help us eat some supper. I can't quite fit everything in the fridge and I'm The Mont's Jenga Champion you know, five years in a row.' She namechecks the local pub. She's lived in Montpelier since I was born, back before the area was as chi-chi as it is now.

'I do know that. Unbeaten, I believe.' I can practically hear her smile down the phone, picture the upwards curve of the corners of her mouth. 'Right, I'm going to jump into a taxi so, traffic willing, I should be with you within the hour.'

The loud shriek of a small child, haring into the Marks and Spencer outlet in Bristol Airport Arrivals, interrupts my thoughts.

'Perrrrcy Pigs!' It sounds as if she's about to launch a pirate attack, so firm is her intent and I can feel the grin cross my face. Small children are terrifying. I've always thought that if marauding hordes from days gone by had lots of small children with them they could have achieved their levels of destruction much quicker than mere battle-hardened men with swords.

I stand on the spot for a minute, the return to these shores after five full years away hitting me. I had always hoped for a life with children, lots of them, running around, playing football in the garden, barbecuing, helping them learn to read. A life where I would stick around, be involved as a father, prove myself a product of my environment not my genes. Turns out that isn't for me after all, and that's okay.

I hope the girl gets her Percy Pigs. I see a woman with dark wavy hair bomb into the shop behind her, calling her back and trying to persuade her to swap the seven odd packets of sweets in her hand for a Musical Biscuit Tin that's shaped like a Christmas tree. I can only see the back of the woman but I don't fancy her chances; that child has devilment shining from her eyes all the way over to where I'm standing.

The two of them are against a backdrop of poinsettias, and my memories resurface, causing my full Scrooge to break out. I am transfixed as I watch the child shake her head furiously, her grasp on the sweets tightening. There is something familiar about her.

I send an email to Nick Wilde, confirm I have landed and will be available tomorrow, and move towards the taxi rank. Standing and staring fixedly at a small girl is never a good look for a grown man.

An email whizzes back. Nick will be at home with family tomorrow but is happy for me to call in. An address accompanies the email, one that I am already aware of and unlikely to forget. A quick glance back at the store – I don't know why – leaves me surprised. The woman has won and the small girl is cradling the Christmas tree tin as if she has found a chest of buried treasure, its tinny rendition of *White Christmas* causing her to pause in bliss.

Belle.

I won. Marsha swapped the sweets for the tin and she was so full of joy with the music coming from it that she managed to wallop Luisa lovingly in the face with her jagged-edged gift the minute her mother came through the arrivals gate and scooped her up. And now I am home for a couple of hours. Blessed relief.

In theory.

'Yes, yes, like that, that. Oh my God.' I roll my eyes as the sounds coming from my flatmate's bedroom flood the living room. Again. This has been going on since I arrived home, with only very short breaks in between. She's in there with a pilot she picked up at work and I don't know what they feed them at British Airways but it obviously has an impact on stamina. My legs would have failed me by now, my vagina would be begging for mercy and I'd just want some sleep, whereas they seem to be back on for round three.

My phone starts to ring and as I glance at the caller ID I roll my eyes. I knew this would happen today. I may be over thirty, living independently and mooching through life in my own way, but my parents are still firmly of the belief that a) I'm still a child, b) I have absolutely no coping mechanisms or adult skills whatsoever, and c) I need reminding of every tiny thing. They'd message me to remind me to brush my teeth if they weren't so scared of encouraging any level of intimacy. Because of this they manage to limit their nagging to things that are important to them.

'Hi, Dad. How are you?' I answer the phone whilst scanning the laptop screen in front of me. My attention is really on Leontes, I love this final scene so much – *Turn good lady, our Perdita is found* – and I know why my dad is calling anyway. I tell you, Perdita had it pretty good with the whole foundling thing.

'Harder, harder, harder.' Chardonnay is a woman who knows what she wants.

'Oh, I didn't expect you to pick up so quickly.' No hello then.

'Uh-huh...' There is no point contradicting him. Passive neutrality is a great parental tool.

'I don't have time to chat. I just needed to remind you about lunch on Friday, your mother's birthday.'

'I'm going to... I'm going to... I'm going to...' Chardonnay bellows as she bangs on the wall.

'Yes, Dad. I know. I'll be there. Like I promised.'

'Where are you? Sounds like some sort of orgy.'

'Don't know what one of them sounds like. I'll have to take your word for it.' I smirk. Maybe my parents have a point, I do turn into a fifteen-year-old whenever I hear his voice.

'You may mock but when I was young... *Eyes Wide Shut*, I practically lived that. I know sex noises.'

I grimace and faux-vomit.

'Oh my God!' A scream follows and the walls practically shake.

'Goal!' Ooh, yuk. Not that one again. Clearly the pilot has some football issues.

'Yep, you've been telling me that since I was twelve. It gets no less disturbing.'

'Lots of people would be happy to have such glamorous parents. You've always been so resentful. But look, the other thing I wanted to talk to you about...'

Best not to speak. *Lots of people would be happy to have...* is one of his stock phrases, followed with a quick but low blow. It doesn't need a wordy response.

'...it's your mother. I just thought I should remind you that she's still feeling pretty vulnerable, so if we could not mention the thing then that would be great.'

Seriously! My dad is telling *me* not to upset my mum. I pick up a cushion and nuzzle it for a second and grit my teeth, leaving the phone on speaker on the table.

'I expect it's her age,' he continues. Remarkable. You think he can't get any worse and then boom! 'And because I know you're not very ... well, emotionally aware ... it is a difficult time for me too at the moment...' Yeah, because the whole nation is learning what I've had to live with from a very early age – that my dad may be a national treasure but he is also a complete arse. Plus, he is a man that should never use the words 'me' and 'too' together, never ever, ever. He lost those rights some time ago.

Neither a borrower nor a lender be,
For loan oft loses both itself and friend,

December Second.
Rory.

Should I admit to enjoying spending time with my parents? It has been a while and I hadn't realised how much I missed it. Yesterday was great, we did *lots* of eating and catching up, reminiscing about childhood – we always skip uni as if any mention of my time there will cause some kind of catastrophic meltdown – and silly giggling.

Inevitably, Mum talked at length about how well I look, how tanned I am and how I must be beating off Australian women with a stick. I managed to side-step it this time but know an interrogation won't be far off. I hate it. As much as I love my mum, this constant assumption that I should start dating again makes me angry. Angry, misunderstood and somehow at fault. Jess and I may not have stood in front of a vicar and made vows – although that had always been the plan – but we whispered vows to each other, our heads side by side on a pillow, her hair fine as silk stretching out and weaving in with mine. Those vows do not lose power because she has gone, and to break them would disrespect the bond we shared, the lifelong commitment we made to each other. I know there will be a time in my life when I can both honour Jess and move forward but that time is not now.

But morning is here, Mum, Dave and I have done the

nice catching up bit and Jess and my refusal to date are not on the agenda. Now we need to discuss reality. I love my mum but this is serious and I cannot indulge her. I'm not taking any prisoners. I need to focus and take control of this.

'Thanks, Mum, I needed that.' I drink the tea she has made for me. 'No, thanks, I really don't need another biscuit. Will you come and sit down?'

She puts the biscuit tin on the table and takes the lid off, of course she does.

'Now, can we talk about the elephant in the room?'

'That's no way to talk about your father.' She has always referred to Dave as my father rather than step-dad and I'm happy with that – he's earnt it far more than the man that walked away before I was even born – but she isn't getting away with deflection, no matter how big the grin on her face.

'Right! I know this is unpleasant and you would probably rather not talk about it, but I love you and I need to know what exactly is happening.'

'Of course, I'm so grateful you're here but you mustn't worry. We can't always change the hand life deals us but we can choose how to deal with it.'

'Hmmm.' It is true but I'm not here for philosophy. 'Look, I've lined up an appointment with a consultant and thought we could maybe all go along together.'

'That's good of you.' Dave pulls out a chair and joins us at the table.

'But not necessary. I have a perfectly good doctor on the NHS,' Mum answers.

'Yes, but this one is good too. I did some research, she's local to Bristol and one of the leading oncologists in the country. Here, take a look.' I pass her the details of the appointment I've booked and she scans it quickly.

'She's already my doctor. We don't need to pay a fortune to see her again. I don't believe in private health care, never have, never will, and it seems stupid to me to pay out for something I'm getting just the same and for free. My surgery is lined up for the week before Christmas and that timing suits me really well. The NHS have been very quick to respond and I have no need, or desire, to queue-jump. I won't do it.'

'I just want to help. I didn't realise it was the same doctor. It's not a crime for me to be concerned is it?'

'No, it's not, and I love you and I understand your need to have things go the way you want them, I do. But this, this you can't control and you need to stop trying. Let me do this my way, I promise I'm going to do it right and I'm not going to take any risks. Having you here is lovely, but you can't come home and take charge. Come to my appointments, spend time with me but let go of the reins. You can't control the world, love, you just can't.'

My sigh, although unintentional, is so forceful it ruffles the piece of paper with the doctor's details on it. I know that since Jess's death I have been trying even more than usual to control the world around me. That maybe I need to relax a bit more, let go. But the thought of losing Mum as well... Now is not the time to chill.

'But what you can do is tell me all your news. I noticed you dodged my question last night.' She scrunches up her shoulders, and her nose, her brow furrowing with excitement and she shoots me a broad grin. 'So any young ladies on the horizon?'

'Mum ... please...' I don't know how to say it clearly without snapping. I don't know how to say that even looking at a woman makes the guilt rise up in me, gurgle in my throat, bitter like bile. That even thinking of it makes me feel as if I'm cheating. I don't know how to say that I don't believe it's possible to find someone else who will understand me like Jess did, that being that lucky twice in life wouldn't be fair. I certainly don't dare tell her that I can't risk falling in love with another woman and disappointing her as I did Jess. I can't say those words out loud and I can't listen to her tell me I can do no wrong. I want to tell her all the whirls of feeling scooting around inside me but I cannot tolerate the answers I know she'll give. The lies she believes to be true.

I hope to God she can't see the tear pricking in the corner of my eye as, pasting the fakest smile ever across my face, I beam at her and reach for the biscuit tin and try again to explain how busy I am with work.

Belle.

Three more times. Three more times that night. *Goal* has been followed by *Score*, and most alarmingly *Boot it*. I'm not surprised the pilot hasn't found his forever partner yet. I really hope it's not going to be Chardonnay.

20

I hadn't got to sleep until gone four and by that time I was considering hacking the pair of them to death with the set of kitchen knives my dad had bought me when he realised we were being followed into Harvey Nichols and getting papped. One of the good things about my father's utterly shallow fuckwittery is that when the cameras are on him he is remarkably generous. When the cameras are off he struggles to remember my birthday and for Christmas one year I received his latest cookbook, complete with wine stain on the cover. But still, it was better than the chlamydia he had lovingly gifted my mother.

I have a big meeting at work today and as it's common knowledge that the company is in trouble and as I was the last person in, I'm nervous about what today may bring. I'm not married to this job, I'm an office assistant and do little more than answer phones, respond to emails, provide hot drinks and smile. But still, I'm both bleary-eyed and anxious as I fill my reusable cup and prepare to leave.

'Morning! Glad I caught you. That smells gorgeous.' Chardonnay nods at my coffee. 'So, just wanted to say that your rent came through okay and ... ooh, this is awkward, but no sign of that money I lent you a couple of months ago.'

Oh shit, I had forgotten about that. That is actually a serious fault. Pure me messing up right there. Again. Every month I mean to and every month something comes up or I forget. I hate myself a little bit right now, and my bad temper at her sexual meowings disperses as I realise I'm guilty of a far bigger crime.

'Oh, Chardonnay, I'm so sorry. I'll get to that.' I had

promised her she'd have it back before Christmas and now I am zero paychecks away from the happy day, my wages had all zoomed out pretty much as soon as they had zoomed in, and I have no clue what the hell I am going to do. I don't need to look at my banking app to know that I'll be making gifts again this year.

'Yes.' I can see her discomfort and am cross with myself for putting her in this position. 'Thing is, Belle, I really need the money.'

How much can you get for a slightly ropey kidney these days?

Hell is empty,
And all the devils are here.

December Third.
Belle.

I am now officially unemployed. The creditors have been pushing and pushing and the company I worked for has been forced to file for bankruptcy. Whilst I'm grateful that they managed to pay us this month, I have no idea where next month's money is going to come from.

I've spent the afternoon in the job centre, the evening on indeed.com and at gone midnight, when Chardonnay's pilot pitched up again, I had jumped in my car and driven back to my parental home, unable to face another night of football-themed aural fun.

I quite like sneaking into my parents' house in the early hours of the morning. There's something forbidden about it, but it also gives me a couple of extra hours to enjoy the house without having to say hello to them first.

I may struggle with my family but I love this house. It was Nana's and when she died it passed to Mum and we all moved in. It was before Dad had become super well-known and they were still besotted with each other. We have photos of moving day and the way he looks at her, and at the house, it's as if he can't believe his luck.

I particularly love my bedroom. It is tucked up at the very top of the house, where you have to twist and turn up narrow sets of stairs with aged, faded carpet, a feel of secret passageways and Agatha Christie novels accompanying you. A million coats of lead paint on the bannisters. It's the one part of the house that is pure me, its closest contender being the room that Dad pretentiously calls the library but is in fact the old dining room lined with books that he has never read, their spines unbroken by any hand other than mine and Nana's.

As you open the door to my room you see posters of epic performances blu-tacked on the walls, Fiona Shaw as Richard III, Jüri Järvet as Lear, Brooks' *Dream*, Gielgud's Prospero, and they make me smile every time my eye catches them. Nana had worked in the wardrobe department at the RSC before getting married and moving to this house. *The Tempest* in 1957 at the Stratford-on-Avon theatre had been the last production there she had been involved with, so the Gielgud print was close to her heart and thus extra close to mine. I haven't made it there yet, but one day I will.

I had toyed with moving the posters with me but until I have a permanent spot they can stay here. They help me when I have to come home and they keep some small part of Nana alive in this house, her house, where most evidence of her has been expunged, replaced with sleek surfaces and symbols of Dad's success. With the posters here in my room, it feels like an extension of her and me. Special, just to the two of us.

There are secrets in my room, obvious ones like inside the wardrobe doors where I had spray painted peace and anarchy signs. My old bear, One Eye, still hidden between the mattress and the fabric struts of my bed after my mother had given him to my sister and whom I had stolen back, withstanding slapped legs and a week of high dudgeon. Plimsolls I'd refused to throw out after winning the egg and spoon race in them at primary school – my only sporting glory.

Through some magical psychic luck, last night I had dreamt of a secret stash tin that I had lost as a teen. It is nothing short of a miracle that I found it upon waking today, exactly where my dream had said, in the plimsolls. I remember losing it fifteen years ago; many tears had fallen as I tore my room apart.

I stopped smoking forever ago, when Marsha was born, bar occasional but rare parties and moments of weak will, but with today being my mum's birthday and our first family get-together since the tabloid stories exploded, I reckon today constitutes both.

Tin in hand, I tiptoe down the stairs, in the most exaggerated fashion with arms wide, hands splayed, down through the front door and into the garden. If I avoid the kitchen I should be safe. My parents won't expect to see me until noon. One of the advantages of being subject to such low expectations.

I sit myself in the low-hanging curved bough of a favourite tree, an old pine that had proved my haven for years. Here I played *Peter Pan*, *Wind in the Willows* and *Fairy Kingdom* as a child, later becoming Ariel to the tree's Prospero, Banquo to the tree's Macbeth.

Currently though I am channelling my adolescence rather than my childhood and am wearing the most ridiculous short pyjama set that I had when I was sixteen.

I've grown a little since then and my boobs are spilling over my top, and my shorts feel like they are extracting a kidney. I'm completing this high-fashion ensemble by being wrapped in an ancient, scratchy check blanket that I think has been around since my great-grandma's time. It may still have smallpox.

I make and light the spliff and lean back against the trunk. Familiarity waves over me as I inhale.

My mind tracks back to yesterday. Any chance of paying back Chardonnay seems pretty weak right now. Am I going to panic? Thanks to my find – currently coursing in through my mouth and down into my lungs – probably not until tomorrow.

'*Still* smoking?' A deep male voice speaks behind me. The voice is vaguely familiar but out of place here. I spin around, my blanket slipping slightly with my movement, revealing a sliver of Snoopy chatting with Charlie Brown.

What the hell?

'Rory?'

'Hey, how you doing? I didn't expect to see you today, but one sniff of that and I figured you must be home. I had a feeling it wouldn't be Rose.' He smiles and I remember the last time I saw him and my heart cracks a little.

'Yep, back for the birthday.' I wave the spliff at him.

'Nah, you're okay.' He shakes his head, his dark red hair longer than I remember. He's allowed his curls to develop instead of shearing them back and trying to pretend they didn't exist as he had at eighteen. It suits him. He was always puckish but just a smidge. Willing to do as he was told, not go full carnival chaos. Mind you, Rory wasn't all

26

bad; from what I remember it was his girlfriend Jessica I had struggled with. She was one of those women that always seemed at ease with herself. A state of being I can only dream of. What must that feel like? To wake up every morning and not worry about whether you're adequate.

'Whose birthday? Not yours. Isn't your birthday in spring? March?' Rory's question interrupts my reminiscing. How the hell does he remember that?

I remember the pitch of his keen. That will stay with me for ever.

'Yeah, it's Mum's.'

'Your dad said he'd be home with family, he didn't say it was your mum's birthday. How is she?'

'Difficult. But still the better of the two.'

Rory smiles wryly. He saw them in action many moons ago. If he can remember my birthday then he can likely remember them shrieking in the driveway one afternoon as he dropped me back at the end of term, my mum throwing a tennis racquet at my dad's head. A beautiful snapshot of middle-class dysfunction.

'What you doing with my dad anyway?'

'Work thing.' He doesn't make any move away so I push for more.

'You're a chef? Or in media?' Both surprise me.

'Neither, reputation management.' He leans against the bough of the tree and smiles at me. Some men grow into their looks and Rory Walters definitely has, but if he's working with Dad, that doesn't speak well to his character.

'Ah, *The purest treasure mortal times afford / Is spotless reputation*,' I quote.

'Eh?'

'Never mind. Reputation management? I didn't know that was a thing.' I manage not to say it sounds a bit weaselly.

'Yep, I got in early but it has exploded as an industry now.'

'You're going to have your work cut out with my dad.'

'Yeah, I know. But we can get his optics back on track if he does what he's told to.' A laugh escapes my lips. Standing, I drop the end of my smoke to the ground and wrap my blanket around me, aware that I am far from decent and for some reason, caring about it.

'Come on then, I'll walk you to the front door, but do you mind ringing the bell and pretending you haven't seen me? It'll give me a couple of hours more respite.'

He grins again and nods. I'd never noticed all those years ago how green his eyes are.

Rory.

I hadn't expected to see Belle today. In fact, I haven't seen her for years. She'd been a funny thing at university, somehow managing to combine wild with aloof, party girl with snippets of intellectual brilliance – on the rare occasions she turned up.

I had been fascinated by her back then – she was everything my life wasn't. But for all of her privilege she had always reminded me of a world-worn baby fox on its guard.

I hadn't been able to put her into any kind of box. I was fond of boxes, assessing people and who they were, where they sat. It had given order to life. She had something of the indefinable. I knew even if I squashed her into that poor little rich girl box she would fight her way out, battering the edges down, refusing to be contained, screaming that there was more.

We had done the same course, English Literature, and our paths had crossed many times. She had been in the same halls as Jessica, they had shared a kitchen, but very little else, and I had found myself driving her home more than once. It had become a habit; with her parents so close to Bristol and mine living there it became an end-of-term routine we fell into. I would drive and she would moan about spending time at her parents, rhapsodise or complain about her latest boyfriend, panic over essays and later her dissertation. For all of her doubt she had a mind that worked so quickly, fair racing past mine.

I have often wondered what happened to her, and when her father's agent had reached out, curiosity had been awakened. What was she doing now? Who was she? Had she changed? Smoking a joint outside her parents' house whilst wearing some ludicrous outfit that merged both aging granny and pre-pubescent teen was definitely the Belle I remembered.

I was pleased to see her, but it was bittersweet. I had imagined her trotting the globe, capturing hearts and minds, pushing boundaries and opening worlds in whichever field she had chosen rather than getting stoned in her parents' garden. But then who am I to judge? And who am I to assume that because she's home on her mum's birthday she has not made something of her life, is not happy, successful? Judgement, that was the old me, putting-people-into-boxes me. The Rory that thought if you made the right choices, did the right thing, then you couldn't go wrong.

I should have been more Belle.

Having given Belle a good five minutes to make her escape upstairs, I press the buzzer.

'Hello, hello!' Nick Wilde flings the door open and flourishes his arms, welcoming me into his home. His trademark blond hair is sticking out at all angles atop his ruddy face. A large glass of red in his hand.

It's eleven in the morning.

Great.

I follow him through to a huge kitchen. The house itself is old and sprawling, a little neglected in places but squeaking with generational wealth, whilst the kitchen itself is new money, achingly modern. Sleek NASA-like appliances, razor-sharp lighting juxtaposes with a blazing fire encased by old stone, and a huge, worn wooden table that could have easily seated the Last Supper and had room for some more.

Cyndi, Belle's mother, is sat at the table, and her features fuse themselves into a generous welcome the minute she sees me. Performance art. Which, like the ridges, scrapings and stains on the kitchen table, I suspect has been perfected over the generations.

For two hours I sit there listening to why Nick isn't to blame for his reputation being in tatters. A whole bottle is downed as he talks, chopping vegetables at speed, caressing meat with its fat in marbled thick lines. 'Do stay for lunch.'

'Yes, do,' Cyndi echoes.

'You know how some women are – flighty, hysterical, will say anything for attention and especially for a payout.' He continues to prevaricate and my eyes flick to his wife, who is up and filling her mug from the boiling water tap. Her hand is tight on the mug handle, gripping it the same way she is holding her shoulders, taut, her rigidity at complete odds with the looseness of her husband. 'I could be the Archbishop of bloody Canterbury and the newspapers, that scum, will still find lies to print, to spread on fucking Instagram,' he adds.

'There *were* a lot of women,' I say. He arches his brow at my tone and I can almost hear his claws unsheathe. The lion disturbed in his den.

'A lot of women have problems. You're not naive. You've been around, you *know* that.'

I hold his stare.

I have worked with people I have disliked before, when their reparation serves the common good. Companies that need to suddenly greenwash and pour millions into environmental projects to make up for their previous misdemeanours, celebrities who I have believed were truly apologetic. But I have also walked away from people who were clearly manipulating optics with no intention of changing any of their underlying behaviour.

Nick is the latter. The only thing this man serves are his own appetites. On the phone he said that he is repentant, that booze had played a part. He told me he was knocking the drinking on the head, that his family were supporting him. So far, he has prepped salads, marinated meat, drunk nearly a bottle of wine and blamed womankind.

I do not need to stay for lunch.

I start to phrase my polite withdrawals when Belle pops into my head. The amber of her eyes. This man is no more an island than any of us and she is part of his archipelago. When the waters rise to flood him, push him down beneath the waves, then she will go too. I do not want to lie awake at night picturing her as the waves wash over.

It is the most uncomfortable lunch I have ever been to. Belle shrinks in front of me, a hermit crab hiding out in someone else's shell. Her parents are relentless in their put-downs. They do not allow her to finish a single sentence, not one.

To make it even worse, Rose is here and the sycophancy is off the scale. Any question of who is the favourite child is dispelled five seconds after she breezes in, with a huge bouquet of winter roses in one hand.

'Rose is married to Jack Sharp, you know, in the cabinet and only twenty-seven. So clever, the both of them. She was approached by GCHQ in school and again at university. Such a sharp mind and she's putting it to good use. The golden couple of politics. Perfect politician's wife, aren't you, darling?' Nick's pride in his youngest daughter spills over.

'Madly dyslexic though, Rory. Would have sold my soul to Santa if it hadn't been for Belle. Couldn't have got through school without her help, it was painful.' Rose smiles at me and I don't trust it for a second.

'You would have been fine. Belle barely bothered going to school so I don't know why you think she helped you. She's not the one rising high with a powerful husband.'

Both sisters cannot get away from the table fast enough.

Rose is practically in her car before the table has been cleared. I'm not going to be far behind. I'm just coming out of the loo when I pause, hearing Belle shout hello.

I push the door beside me open to see if she is looking for me. And realise it's merely wishful thinking. Belle is sat with her back to me, her legs crossed on a large leather chair, her laptop angled towards her, cutting out the edge of the door frame where I stand. On the screen I can see a familiar face waving back at her. Is that Luisa Fischer? It is. I want to wave and shout hello myself.

'How are you doing? Are they being hellish?' The German accent is still there. I wonder if she went back to Berlin after university.

'We had an extra for lunch so they reined it in a bit.'

Reined it in? That was them behaving? And I'm condensed to an extra. Belle Wilde, ever dismissive.

'But listen, I need to cut to the chase, um, I hate having to ask this and I know I told myself I never ever would again but um, oh God … um…' Belle brings her hand to her eyes, her middle fingers rubbing her brow, her elbow jutting at a right angle and I am shot with a memory of her doing the same during her dissertation stress.

'Do you need some money for Christmas?'

'Yes, no. Yes. I need some money. But it's not for Christmas. This year, like everyone else, you'll be getting a salt-dough snowman. I wish it was for Christmas. But I owe Chardonnay and I still haven't paid her and...' Her voice dries to a whisper and I find myself craning in. 'I'm ... um ... work laid us all off. They were hoping to get us to Christmas but...'

I know I should leave, I should have left about three seconds after I had opened the door, but I am stuck there. My legs have taken root.

'Oh shit, Belle. I'm sorry. On the upside at least, you were blameless this time.'

'Really...'

'Okay, tactless. But you have form.'

'I do. I did. I'm a good girl now, a stupid one though. I told Rose about losing the job before lunch; that's going to come back and bite me on the arse. But listen, I hate to ask ... you know how much I hate to ask ... but the nub of it is that I no longer have a job and Chardonnay reminded me I owe her for that time she lent me money to buy that costume.'

'Yeah, I still don't know why you didn't come to me for that.'

'Because I didn't want to ask you again. You've always been so generous and I would have rather gouged my eyes out with a spoon than asked you. Irony, huh?'

'Lear.'

'I taught you so well.'

'On a serious note, you know I don't mind. Plus, most people have parents who are willing to help out in a pinch. You don't. How much do you need?' My ears prick up. It had never occurred to me growing up that people born to families like Belle's had to worry about money. But then I suppose after today's display I shouldn't be surprised; they seem to begrudge her breathing, there was no way they'd shower her with money. They probably wallpaper Rose's house with fifties.

'Um … I owe Chardonnay £250.' It is a huge amount when you don't have it – I remember those days – but to Nick Wilde it would be the equivalent of pennies. I need to leave. This is so wrong. I head down the corridor and pause in my tracks again.

'You know what women are like.' Cyndi's voice mimics her husbands from earlier. 'You are such a piece of shit.' Her voice is raised, angry, I see her lash at him, her fist landing on his chest, the other following. He brushes them off and as she raises them again he grabs both wrists.

I step forward.

He drops them again and I pause. Neither have spotted me yet.

'Let's not forget you are not without blame,' he spits. He turns on his heel and walks back to the kitchen as if such an outburst is everyday.

Cyndi bends over and breathes deep. After her bravura performance at lunch, it feels cruel revealing myself, a further stripping of her dignity. But it's hard not to race over, comfort her, offer to get her out of this house. I take a step forward but as I do so she stands up tall, shakes herself out, fluffs her hair over her shoulder and heads back into the kitchen. I slide back along the narrow corridor, photos in frames of a happy-looking family on the walls. Nick and Cyndi besotted with each other, Rose being whirled above Nick's head. I search the photos and it strikes me that Belle is always on the periphery or in the background untended, her smile forced.

I tiptoe back to hide in the loo, give everyone five minutes' grace before I go in to say my goodbyes. Walking down the corridor again, I mark my way with a cough just in time to hear Luisa say, 'There, it's done. But it comes with conditions.' My good intentions pause; I really want to hear the conditions.

'Anything. I'm a whizz with nipple tassels, you know.'

'Oh, trust me, I remember. But this is not about your twirltastic nipple skills. I want you to stop messing about. I've given you enough money for next month's rent as well—'

'Wait. That's too much, I'll get another job. I promise. I'll keep trying for any seasonal work that's left going.' She lets out a hollow laugh. 'I will get you this money back, I swear I will.'

'Listen! I have had enough of seeing you live hand-to-mouth and work crazy hours to pay your rent and keep your head above water in these minimum-wage jobs.'

'That's how most people live. Those jobs, they give me time to work on my—'

'Shut up, for Christ's sake. Will you listen? I'd like you

36

to work for me for the next month. I mean it. Remi and I are doing all right at the moment. We've just had a huge contract come in from a major supermarket so this is fine. Spend the next month looking at how to monetise your Shakespeare site. That is now your full-time job...' Luisa carries on speaking but I have stopped listening. My ears had pinged up at the mention of a website. I'd forgotten that. Belle was obsessed by Shakespeare. Obsessed.

I remember a time, years ago, when we had sat up until four in the morning in Belle's student kitchen drinking and talking about how I was wrong to find Hamlet dull and something about folios and quartos that I don't quite remember. Is she still doing that? This makes me happy, I don't know why but it does. I tune back in to Luisa. 'You have created an amazing thing there, something that is going to help so many people. Get it out to the world, find a way to make money from your unique skill.'

An idea begins to blossom in my mind. If she has a literacy project that needs proper investment, that may solve a problem I've been trying to untangle all week.

There's no art
To find the mind's construction in the face

December Fourth.
Belle.

'Hey, how you doing?'

'Just heading out now.' Chardonnay is in her uniform, her hand resting on the extended handle of her overnight case. 'Thanks for sending that money through. I appreciate it.'

'Not a problem,' I say breezily. I sent the money across yesterday straight after my chat with Luisa and a weight had been lifted. 'I'm sorry it took so long and you had to ask.'

'We're all good, see you in a few days.' And that's it, she whizzes out the front door. This isn't a flat where we curl up together on the sofa, binging Netflix, eating ice-cream and examining each other's manicures. We have minimum human interaction and the quiet it affords me is exactly what I want.

I pitched up here after yet another desperate quest on spareroom.com and fell in love. I love the area, love the thought of living above the mini-mart and hearing all the chatter from the street below, and I love that most of the time I have it to myself.

I like my own company – there is less pressure, I don't have to worry so much about being a disappointment, that I'm constantly failing to meet people's expectations. Luisa has a lot to say on this subject and I'm aware I'm feeling extra insecure today because I've recently spent time with my family. I am resigned that things there will never change and know I am not the only person with a tricky parental relationship, but in the couple of days after the prolonged contact of a visit, I feel the anger well up in me. It really stings, the injustice of it. The fact that I have never known what I have done wrong, other than being born a little different, that I don't understand their codes, their behaviours, no matter how much I tried as a child before the fury and rebellion took over in adolescence.

December is always tough, with Mum's birthday and Christmas in the one month, but I am prepared this year. I will wrap a cloak of reinforced steel around me. I am an adult, I am not going to let my insecurities drive me, I'm just not. My parents have made me feel like shit most of my life but I can take ownership of it, I can stop allowing it to upset me. I need to stop dwelling and avoid getting sucked into a spiral of self-pity and injustice. Starting right now.

Pepped up, I fill a hot water bottle and pop on some lentils – it's a good job I like them, they need to be my primary diet for the next ... um ... for ever. I curl up on the sofa and grab a blanket before I lift the lid of my laptop. The temperature has dropped overnight and it really feels like December today. December without enough money in my account to whack the heating up.

The tap tap tap against the window is fast, heavy, relentless, reminding me of how cold job-hunting had been earlier. I had been buttoned up, my breath snuffling into a scarf as I wandered from pub to pub seeing if they had any spare seasonal work, the rain battering the outside of me until my very bones were ice-snap cold.

I had marched around all of Easton, most of Eastville and Greenbank too. There isn't much work being advertised, not even seasonal. But as ever with this community I found things that couldn't help but make me smile.

The wall scheme, for example, is one of the reasons I love this area. It's simple enough: if you have something you no longer need you pop it on the low wall that runs outside the front of your house and someone will walk past and pick it up and take it home – a neighbourhood freecycle scheme. And today I had found a pair of winter boots in my size and a style I like. Which is great because my feet were hypothermic and I have a pair of boots for best but the ones I'm wearing now are a little leaky.

I'd been so desperate to get warm, I had snuck into the mini-mart and huddled against their old Calor Gas heater, the ceramic tiles of which always reminded me of little fox faces. It looks old enough to be condemned but, my God, it chucks the heat out. This shop has stock piled up so high you take your life in your hands every time you enter. It's owned by Temperance, who runs it – and her son, Innocence – like a totalitarian dictator. Today, Innocence was free from maternal oversight and took the time to tell me I have the face of an angel and the ability to grant all of his prayers. His mother was out the back or his ear would have been cuffed so hard he would have flown across the store. She has Very Firm Views on flirtation and non-marital sex and these days I do too.

When Temperance did appear and heard of my job-seeking, she promised to include me in her prayers that night. That should do it. No short *Gentle Jesus, meek and mild*, for Temperance, no, that woman hurls up essays to heaven. With her on my side I'll be employed by Tuesday.

I've sent back the money Luisa gave me to live on. I appreciate the gesture, I really do, but it doesn't feel right taking it, it's bad enough taking what I had for Chardonnay. It isn't Luisa's fault that I am a total screw-up with zero savings and an inability to prepare for rainy days. And she had given me a bigger gift than the money, she had reiterated her faith in me, in the Shakespeare project. I had bravely – foolishly – told myself I would rather starve than take advantage of her offer. Forgetting that starving may actually be a reality and it was not such a sweet thought once the money left my bank account.

Still, I wanted to make it on my own. That she had faith meant the world but I wasn't going to take another penny from her.

Now I need to work out the best way to secure funding. I've been thinking about taking all the info I've collated, putting it into an app and making it free, raising revenue by adverts. Ads are annoying but the whole point is to make the information accessible to everyone, especially those who don't have a privileged life. Kids brought up very differently to my gilded bubble.

I could also look into funding from places like the Arts Council – there must be charitable funding out there for literacy projects – or I can go old-school and go via a bank, but I have a feeling any money I'm given will be because of my name, my connection to my dad. And that I do not want. I know it's precious of me and I know how lucky I am to be in a position where that is a possibility. I also know at one point I may have to cave, that maybe in this rare instance the product is more important than the process, but if I can, I'll do this on my own. I want to prove to myself – and to them – that I can make my own path for once.

So the whole of this evening is dedicated to researching funding. My mind slips, just for a minute, from my practical plan into my fantasy dream of raising enough money to go around schools and bring the magic of Shakespeare to those who traditionally struggle to access him. I picture myself walking among groups of kids in a school hall explaining why these plays are relevant to their lives today. Why the Capulets and Montagues could easily be played out on the streets of Easton. Why Hamlet's battles with his mental health are exactly the same as those faced by young men in the twenty-first century. Why we all need to keep an eye peeled for an Iago.

The smell of burnt lentils jolts me from my daydream. My hippy gruel bubbling on the stove is ruined and the thought of eating it for the next few days, meal after meal, makes my soul concertina in on itself.

Grrrrrrrr.

My phone rings, no caller ID. Yeah, I'm not getting that. Then I remember why my coat is still damp, why my nose may never feel warm again and why I am even contemplating burnt lentils. I take the call.

'Hey, Belle, it's Rory Walters here.'

'Rory?' Weird. It had been nice to see him yesterday, that

familiarity when a face from another era pops up. But I don't know why he's ringing *me*.

'Yeah, I thought I'd reach out. I wanted to talk to you but it's a bit sensitive.' Okay, he obviously wants to talk about Dad. That is shit I don't need right now. But then, Dad is my dad, I'm going to have to. Duty and all.

'That's okay, I understand sensitive. How can I help?'

'Could we meet up?'

'Meet up?' Jesus, duty only goes so far. 'I … um … I guess so.' I close my eyes. 'When were you thinking? Where?'

'You still living in Bristol?'

'Yep, I am. Are you staying here too?'

'Nope, Bath, but right this minute I'm at my mum's. I was about to head back but if you're free, maybe we could catch up now?'

'Now! Do people usually says yes to you in this situation?' He laughs as I ask and I like it. His laugh is deeper than I remember, full-bodied.

'Not usually no, but I was hoping you might. It won't take long.'

'Okay.' I look up at the window. Tiny ice balls are now noisily hurling themselves at the panes. 'If you're happy to swing by here?' I give him the address.

'Is that the street next to the street you used to live in?' He laughs again and the room grows warmer.

'Yep. What can I say, once I've given my heart to a place, I've committed.'

'You always had shocking taste. Is it still all piled-up mattresses and tyres on fire?'

'Eh, posh boy, less of that.'

'Ha. I don't think so. I'm not the one who had a silver-spoon education.'

'Just 'cos they paid for it doesn't mean it was any better. All I learnt at that school was underage sex, not to emotionally engage and how to skin up at an age I should really have still been into horses.'

'Were you ever into horses?'

'Nah, not really. Look if you're going to come over, come.' I know girls are meant to love chatting on the phone for hours, but I do not. Thirty seconds is ideal, three minutes if I love you. Other than that, nope. Luisa and Marsha are the only exceptions to this rule. I prefer video where I can see people's faces, decode their reactions as I speak.

'Ha! Okay, I'm on my way. I'll be there in thirty, Miss Wilde.'

———

Exactly thirty minutes later, the buzzer goes. I adjust my top as I hit the button to let him in. My tummy rumbles and I know the flat still smells of burnt saucepan. I hear his feet on the stairs and I pull down my top to cover my tummy a bit more. Then pull it back up in case I'm now showing too much cleavage. Argh. This is why I like to have my evenings to myself.

Then I remember his cry in the hospital.

Then I remember his laugh from half an hour ago.

He knocks on the door. Right by my ear. Hey, hello,

come in. I practise sounding calm and together in my head and then pull the door open.

He is there. Right there. Those green eyes. Are they contact lenses? No one has eyes like that! Is he that kind of man? Possibly. Grown-up Rory is kinda suave with his beautiful clothes, his accent now hinting at his new international life Way too urbane for a screw-up like me. I step back to let him in, stumbling over my feet as I do so, disconcerted that he is going to see my flat. That I haven't moved on that far from uni whereas he has crossed the globe.

'Come in, come in.' I try to cover up my embarrassment with a big smile and notice he is holding a brown paper bag, a grease stain like a small island on its side. Dear God, please don't make me sit here looking at takeaway food whilst sniffing eau-de-pulse-brûlée.

'I brought food, I hope that's okay.' That very much depends upon whether he has brought enough for me or whether I'm expected to sit and watch him eat it.

'No, no that's fine,' I say a little weakly as my tummy growls again. Thanks, body.

'Just in time.' He smiles. That has to mean we're sharing. I want to punch the air. 'It's from Thali.' He names the restaurant around the corner and my mouth waters. 'I love their food and this has been calling my name since I landed,' he adds.

'I can definitely answer a few questions about my dad in return for a Thali. Did you get their salad, oh, and their coconutty dippy thing?'

'Ha, yes, but it's not your dad I'm here about,' he says as I lead him to the kitchen.

'What?' I spin around and, in the tight space of the kitchen, send the bag flying. He keeps it secure in his hands as it does a round 360, then swings pendulum-like for a little while. I close my mouth and look at him, my heart beating loud enough to wake the dead. He smiles.

'I didn't come over to talk about your dad.'

'But everybody always wants to talk about my dad. Plus, you said it was sensitive. That can only mean him!'

'Shall we eat?'

'Before I successfully knock dinner out of your hands and onto the floor, you mean?'

'Yup.'

'I should have warned you coming into a kitchen with me qualifies you for danger pay.'

'I think I learnt at uni that generally being in your orbit qualifies for that.'

'Ouch.'

'Joke, obviously. Sofa or table?' he asks as I wave plates at him.

'I'm a sofa person but don't want to piss my flatmate off more than usual and we both know I'm going to spill this. Quite frankly the only safe way is to put a bib on me and make me eat on the front step.'

'Step it is then.' He walks over to the front door, turns, grins and then heads back to the table and starts unpacking the bag as I lay down plates and cutlery. 'We didn't get a chance to talk much yesterday.' He looks at me and I carry on faffing with forks, avoiding his eye.

'Yeah, they're big personalities. It's easier just to remain quiet, wait it out.'

We both sit at the table, my tummy shrieking in excitement. There is Keralan chicken, spiced potatoes, coconut rice, all manner of dips, and my favourite salad, lush!

'Tell me about yourself, what have you been up to?' Why does he want to know about me? His eyes are serious as he looks up from his food and catches me watching him. He doesn't break the silence, merely looks at me assessingly, waiting for me to answer.

'What do you want to know?' My tone is more aggressive than I intend but he doesn't acknowledge its harshness.

'What are you doing these days?'

Eating a delicious curry and shying away from questions I don't really know how to answer. What am I meant to say? I'm still being bullied by my parents at the age of thirty-one, out of work, desperate, and *really* grateful you bought food.

'I've just finished *The Winter's Tale*.' I smile across at him, my mouth can't help it when I say this.

'Spinach.' He nods at said mouth. Of course there is. I wriggle my tongue into where I think I can feel it and try to extract it as subtly as I can. 'You've just read it?'

I laugh. 'No! I mean I've finished all my work on it. For this project I do. Alphabetically, *The Winter's Tale* is the last of the plays. I didn't know whether to do them in date order or alphabet, but I thought date would make it tricky for those not so familiar with them whereas everybody knows the alpha— Never mind. It's a project I do.' Do not ramble. He is just being polite.

'Wasn't your dissertation on Shakespeare?'

'Yes, my nana instilled the love when I was little. How did you remember that?'

He smiles and shrugs. That's cute. No. No, it isn't cute, it is Rory Walters, he is all high-powered these days, do not get carried away.

'Actually, it was accidental but I overheard you on a call yesterday, talking about your project and I guessed it might be something about the Bard. I was interested.'

'Really?'

'Really. Have you got anything I could look at?'

'*Really?*'

'Really!' He laughs again. It changes the shape of his face, opens him up, makes me want to trust him. King Duncan's words from *Macbeth* come to me in that moment, a reminder I wish I had heeded many times before: You can't read the mind by looking at the face. Rory may be all handsome these days, and when he was young he was known to be a nice guy, but now he's working with Dad, and that speaks volumes.

Beware that handsome face, I tell myself. Resist. Is he just being polite? People are and I can never call it for sure. But someone wanting to listen to me as I talk about this, that never happens. Never. I suppose I can indulge myself for five minutes and then stop. Definitely do it for no more than five minutes.

I pull my chair closer and open my laptop.

'Oh my God. Are all these files ones you've written?'

'Yep. All mine. I started by taking each play and writing really easy-to-follow guides.'

'All the plays?' he asks, eyebrows raised.

'Yep and the sonnets too.'

'I remember the sonnets from uni. I used to think there was no greater love letter than someone writing a sonnet.' He looks embarrassed after he speaks. 'Anyway, back to the plays. Show me what you've done.'

'Okay, here, look.' I glide past what he said about sonnets to save his discomfort, although it's a pretty cute thing to say, and click open the *Midsummer Night's Dream* folder. 'Every play has scene-by-scene breakdowns, as well as summaries of the action in each act, literal modern-day translations for each line – proper translations that kids understand, not dated English-teacher waffle – and notes on themes and character, all of which can be cross-referenced. They're not that different from Cliff notes or such…'

I watch his eyes gallop across and down, across and down. 'I think they are. Your tone is a lot more inviting, conversational. You're definitely not dry. I love these literal line translations. They're funny in places, engaging…' His eyes don't leave the page. 'May I?' He reaches across to the trackpad.

'Of course.' As he scrolls down I find myself watching his face, his lips move at super speed as he reads. 'This is great … *Love looks not with the eyes, but with the mind,* … I always loved that.'

'*And therefore is winged Cupid painted blind.*' I quote back. 'Me too. It's what I need to remember, not to be a sucker for a pretty face, it's the mind that's important, character. See, he's always wise.'

Rory lifts his eyes from the laptop and looks at me. I feel the tingle of something fritz up my spine, whizzing past every bump of every vertebra. His hair falling slightly forward, a solitary curl dancing, his face lit as it was when he laughed. I feel myself glow; is this what winning X-Factor feels like? I gave up seeking extrinsic validation for the things I care about years ago. I am learning to be happy and to judge me myself, bar my little dips post-parental interaction. But honestly I never thought someone else's opinion would make me this happy. This is insane. I need to stop staring at him as if he has just brought me all my Christmases at once.

'You've got so much content here, I can't believe it. Is it all this good?' His eyes run down the files again. 'You've got maps of all of his settings, fictional and real?'

'Yep, all the ones it's possible to have.' I know I sound like I have just found penicillin, run the four-minute mile and landed on the moon all in the same second, but this is awesome. I shouldn't brag but I can't help myself. 'And there are loads of different levels of knowledge, so whether you come at it as a complete novice, say Key Stage Two in primary school, or someone who wants to really ease into these things like the everyday sayings that Shakespeare came up with…'

'*Neither a borrower nor a lender be.*'

'Exactly, that's a really famous one and *dead as a doornail*. Oh, and *bated breath*.'

'*Refuse to budge an inch*, that's one, isn't it?'

'Yep, and *brevity is the soul of wit*.'

'Okay, hint received. *Hoist with my own petard*!' Rory winks and I quirk my brows in return, as if he is a naughty schoolboy.

'I take it all the way up to graduate level studies, I signpost to academic works, JSTOR, CORE and so on. I keep them updated every week so it's always current. Then here...' I lean in closer. 'Here are the primary sources we have about the man and the plays, the primary texts he used as his source materials. For example, for *The Winter's Tale*, my favourite, he used *Pandosto* from 1588 and for *The Dream*, he had lots including Ovid's *Metamorphoses* which obviously dates back to 8AD.'

'Obviously.' He smiles. 'How long has this taken you?'

We are so close now I can feel his breath upon my face, our dinner surely cold and congealing on the plates to our side. This is too much, too many feelings coming at once. What is going on here? Distance, I need distance. I lean back to make sure my backbone is secure against the back of my chair, and breathe. Look normal. Speak.

'My whole life.' I hope my tone doesn't give away any of the tumult of feeling surging inside me. Feelings I am sure have arisen because no one ever shows this much interest in my work, not since Nana died. Plus good food makes me happy, and a little bit horny, and I'm not sure I trust myself not to try and take his top off. I've been intentionally celibate for a long time. Such a long time. I need to get control before I make a complete tit of myself.

'I can believe it. How have you found time to work as

well?' he says and I screw up my face in response. It may be fair to say I haven't always prioritised my jobs over this.

'What do you want to do with it? What now?' He clicks and scrolls through the files.

'What do you mean?' I know what I hope he means but with the exception of Luisa, no one has ever been bothered before. Will he laugh if I say?

'I mean do you want to become the UK's premier Shakespeare expert, get a doctorate?'

'Ha, that would be ace but no, no that's not the dream. I'm thinking of turning it into an app so its accessible to all and when that's up and running and I have a reputation because of it, I'd love to take it round schools, maybe do a podcast. Schools are the dream though. I think I've got packages that would appeal to each key stage. Like I said, I've tailored things into quite detailed levels. I'd like to reach out to communities that currently don't find it accessible, that get stuck at the language, take one look at the page and think nah, not for me. The majority of people write off Shakespeare before they even try it but the truth is … well, the truth is there is so much *truth* in it. How many of us have not felt like Desdemona, falling overwhelmingly in love with someone who our families are not keen on? I look at Leontes in *The Winter's Tale* and I see my dad. I'm sure kids here in Bristol can relate to the gang culture in *Romeo and Juliet*, to the death of Mercutio, him paying the ultimate price despite actively trying to avoid the skirmishes between the Capulets and Montagues. It should be on every curriculum because it's just so … so human …

and in that example, so scarily fucking pertinent to life today.'

My words are spilling out on top of each other, tumbling like striped acrobats in a circus from my mouth. 'It's helped me to know that every emotion I have possibly experienced has been experienced before, I am not alone, I never have been. All these people have come before me and felt these things too. And that helps me, it helps my mental health, it stops me spiralling when I find things, truth be told, people, a bit difficult. It makes me feel normal. Now I know that as far as normal goes, relating to Perdita or Ophelia or wanting to grow up and be Paulina – she's proper kick-arse – is not really usual. And I'm not sitting here thinking that everyone's problems, all the world's ills, will be solved with one swoop of Shakespeare's wand...' I stop and giggle, both at how carried away I have become and at the innuendo. I do like innuendo.

'Always with the filth, huh, Wilde? Always with the filth.' Rory laughs as I giggle, and before I know it I am telling him all my dreams, all my fears and all about my passion as the night rolls past.

He that is thy friend indeed, he will help thee in thy need

December Fifth.
Rory.

I had fallen into bed after chatting into the wee hours with Belle. She caught me up in her talk of Shakespeare, her passion contagious. My mind was fervid and awake, firing off ideas, links, possibilities, next steps. It was a relief to have something other than my memories filling my head as I hit the pillow but by the time my alarm woke me this morning I was groggy and thick-headed.

It's 4 p.m. now and I think I've found a solution. Belle's work is too good not to be up and running, she just needs the finance. Luckily companies with deep pockets and a philanthropic desire are something I have an excess of. It's merely a matter of marrying the right ones. I have a feeling Belle may be particular about where her cash comes from and it would have to be from a place that was happy to be pretty silent about its involvement, a few sentences on their website, but no desire to stick logos everywhere, corporate branding tattooed on her face, that sort of thing. Which meant that my initial idea, the problem I had thought she could solve for me, would not be a good match for her – they wanted lots of brand sponsorship to advertise their do-gooding – but I have managed to pair them with a phonics company, only too glad to have the cash input in return for some corporate advertising. However, after seeing her project for myself, I have the ideal pairing.

'Hey, how you doing?'

'Oh, hi, Rory.' Her tone is pleasant but I hear her surprise as she answers my call.

'Hey. I don't wanna freak you out but I think I've got something that will make you smile.' I realise that could sound like I'm being sleazy. Truly, sex is the last thing on my mind these days, the thought of any kind of relationship with anyone other than Jess leaves me all kinds of cold, but Belle doesn't necessarily know that.

A loud mechanical noise comes down the line at me.

'Sorry, couldn't really hear that.' Thank the Lord! 'Hang on... Marsha, come away from the chainsaw.' That sounds terrifying. I don't know who Marsha is but Belle within spitting distance of a chainsaw is a scary thought.

'Where are you?'

'Christmas tree farm, you should see it up here. It's proper old-school Christmassy. You can't help but have your heart lifted, your head filled with "It's beginning to look a lot like Christmas" and pictures of Bing Crosby, stockings, fireplaces, presents, the smell of cinnamon and orange and pine, the taste of mince pies...'

Oh my God. I thought she was obsessed by Shakespeare. Now it turns out she has a raging passion for Christmas too.

'Ah, I hate Christmas,' I say. I'm aware of how Scrooge that sounds, but it's true. Christmas and I are not friends anymore.

'You what?' Incredulity encapsulated.

'Um, nothing. Are you free later?'

'No. I've got Sankt Nikolaus.' What fresh hell is this? She

says it in a tone that implies everyone knows about Sankt Nikolaus.

'Eh?'

'Sinterklaas! Tonight we put out the shoe.'

'*So* much clearer.'

'I have to spend the night with Marsha. We get the house ready for decorating tomorrow, that's why we're getting the tree now. Then the shoe goes out and the best bit is waking up and seeing her face in the morning. It's the only time of year I'm allowed to go crazy with the sweets so it's pretty epic.'

'Ah, okay, I really hoped to see you today.' Was that too needy? Only I know that if I don't get to see her today, the opportunity I have for her may have to be shelved until goodness knows when.

'Well, come over, I'm sure Luisa won't mind. She's not seen you in yonks. Come and join us. It'll be proper Chr— It'll be fun.'

At six o'clock I am standing on the doorstep of what I presume to be Luisa's house. This is surreal. Within two days of being back in the UK I am completely in Belle Wilde's life. Years have gone by with no thought of her and now here I am.

The house itself paints a picture, a pretty accurate one of the Luisa I knew back in uni and how I pictured her to be now. Sage painted door, beautifully managed front garden, aesthetically pleasing ceramic pots full of tasteful plants, olive tree, bay, that sort of thing. I had googled her before coming over and she is a successful businesswoman, running an ethical, healthy and sugar-free cupcake business – very Bristol – with her husband.

Luisa opens the door and Christmas music floats out to greet me. Ugh. I hadn't really thought the ramifications of Sankt Nikolaus through.

I can do this. Admittedly, listening to Christmas music in Australia is easier with the sun beating down but I am not going to allow myself to spiral because of 'God Rest Ye Merry Gentlemen'.

Luisa is immaculate. As if she expects cameras to roll any minute. The perfectly groomed woman in her thirties. There is, no doubt, a slot on daytime TV opening up for her any minute now.

'Come on in, come in. I haven't seen you in ages. How are you doing?' There is no sympathy imbued in her welcome, no head tilt and brief furrow of concern. Just an old acquaintance from uni saying hello to someone she once knew. Thank God. It has been a hurdle I've been dreading from the moment Belle invited me. People's micro-expressions, their sympathy, that is partly why I had escaped.

'Yeah, good, thanks.'

We all move through to the kitchen, the most beautiful scent filling the room as Luisa does busy things at the stove. My eyes, though, are on Belle, sat next to me, colouring in reindeer with Marsha, asking the child her advice on the best colours to use for each part. I have seen a different side to this woman every day so far. I can't help but wonder what else there is to Belle Wilde.

'Would you like some mulled cider?' Luisa brings us over a pile of mince pies and clotted cream decanted into a china pot that would have looked perfectly in place in my grandma's dresser.

'Ah, thanks but no, I don't really…'

Determined eyes, almost black in colour and certainly black in their intensity, stare at me from the end of the table. 'My mummy makes the best mulled cider. The best. It's magical.' Marsha holds her glare as she finishes her sentence, and whilst I have never thought of myself as a weak man, I quail.

'Right then, that would be lovely. But just a little please, I'm driving.' I see Belle and Luisa exchange a smirk but what can I do? I'm not upsetting a small child on blooming St Nikolaus Eve or whatever it is. Plus, I was a child who had been fiercely proud of my mum and all she did so I can relate to Marsha.

With a flash I remember where I've seen that mutinous stare before. Of course – she's the child I had seen in the airport and the dark-haired woman must have been Belle.

Wow. The world is a funny place.

Marsha's eyes are still upon me, I take a sip the second Luisa fills my glass and brace myself.

I didn't think I would ever enjoy the taste of anything mulled, but the flavours of cinnamon, cloves, orange and nutmeg marry together beautifully, floating on my tongue.

Marsha catches my eye and nods with satisfaction. 'Told ya.

My mum…' It was cute the way she said that, possessiveness clear in her tone. 'My mum makes me mulled apple juice which is the same but won't give me a headache and it's my favourite drink in the world and I only have it when it's near Chrissmas and when you've finished that and we've all had a mince pie, my favourite food in the whole world, then we're going to bring in the Chrissmas tree ready for tomorrow, aren't we, Mummy, Belle?' She looks to them for confirmation.

'We are,' Luisa says and Belle nods, her mouth too stuffed with mince pie to speak. This is nice, sitting here at this table and it occurs to me this is probably the most relaxed I've ever seen Belle. Last night in her flat she had been fired up, passionate about her work, but here, here she is at clearly at ease and her whole body tells it. Her limbs are no longer taut as if waiting for the next attack, there's a softness to her.

'Rory, are you Belle's boyfriend?' Marsha asks. The question comes from nowhere and I feel my chest constrict. I should just say a simple no, it's not a tough question but the words are stuck in my throat. My heart is galloping, the very thought makes me panic.

'No, Marsha, they are just friends like you and Kye at playgroup,' Luisa jumps in, breaking the tension and causing me to be able to look across at Belle who is bright red and seems almost as flustered as me.

'Kye was my boyfriend last week, but he doesn't like *Paw Patrol*, so he can't be my friend anymore. Do you not like *Paw Patrol*?' Marsha asks me.

'Um … I just … um…' So much for being an articulate man.

'Marsha.' I can hear warning in Luísa's voice. Marsha ignores it.

'Is it because of your wall, Belle, the wall Mummy was telling you off about?'

'Enough!' Luisa stands up 'Sorry, she obviously wants to go to bed early.' Marsha shakes her head ferociously. 'Well, in that case stop haranguing our guests and we'll go get the tree in.'

With huge relief on my part, and I suspect Belle's as well, we collect the tree from outside.

'The man told us this tree is two years older than me,' I am informed by a very proud Marsha, 'but I'll probably live longer. Mummy says she kills everything green eventually but I'm pinky-brown so I should be okay.'

I find myself wrapped up in a cloud of comfort as we bumble happily through the evening, threading popcorn and giggling at the antics of *The First Snow of Winter*. I can't remember the last time I relaxed like this, not fretted about how I needed to get to the next thing and the next. It is only when Luisa and Belle are putting Marsha to bed – which involves her running up the stairs as if her heels are on fire shrieking, 'the biggest shoe, the biggest shoe' – that I realise I have been here for about two hours and, as yet, have not pitched my plan to Belle. So much for my focused professionalism.

There's a lot of kerfuffling and eventually the two women come down the stairs giggling.

'Another mulled cider, Rory?'

'No thanks, it was really good though. Your daughter was right.'

'Marsha is biased but flattery like that will get you almost anywhere. It's been lovely seeing you again, Rory, really nice to catch up. But now, tell me, what are your intentions with our Belle?'

Belle.

Oh my God. My mouth drops open. I love Luisa but there are times I could bloody kill her and this is one of them. Kill her!

What the hell is she thinking? It's been a really nice evening, and then boom! She has to drop a bomb into the mix. I'm amazed that Queen Tact here hasn't followed it up with *So, go on, we never got all the details about your girlfriend's death, tell us everything.*

Rory, to his credit, smiles and goes as red as I am and assures us it is merely professional interest.

I am too busy right now trying to get my face to lessen its massive flush of embarrassment, hoping that breathing regularly and plotting revenge on Luisa are the way forward.

'What is it that you want her for then ... professionally?' Luisa quirks a brow and truth is, had it been anyone but me and Rory frigging Walters at the centre of this I would be hard pressed not to giggle. That woman's facial expressions are comedy gold. I cock my head and hold my breath. It's a good point. What does he want from me professionally? Last night he told me he had something sensitive to discuss and came over, but then we got caught up in the project and he never really said anything further about why he was there. And at the time it hadn't mattered. Was this what that was about?

'Last night you showed me…' Rory began.

Luisa quirks her brow again and I go from crimson to scarlet.

'You're so bad,' he addresses Luisa as I nod in agreement. She is. 'Belle showed me her project and I was blown away. It's remarkable.'

'See, I told you!' Luisa claps her hands gleefully and points to me. 'It is, isn't it? I know she loves it and she's right to but I don't think she understands the enormity, the magnificence of what she's done.'

'It's okay, I know I've worked hard but you know that's the perk of not having a life.' I look down at my feet and then it dawns on me that with Rory's past that was not a tactful thing to say. Shit. Surely, he knows I didn't mean it literally. That I was covering up my embarrassment at the fulsome praise. I'd best just shut up. I scratch at something on the corner of my shoe, pretend I don't already know it's a scuff mark.

'I couldn't agree more, Luisa, and it seemed to me that it deserved a wider audience,' Rory says.

Luisa's nodding now with fervour. I'm trying to keep my eyes open. When I was a child, if something was uncomfortable I'd close my eyes, block the world out until it was gone. But adult me knows that it's neither Rory nor Luisa's intention to make me feel uncomfortable. It isn't their fault that this is so cringe for me. I just hate being the centre of attention, I'm uncomfortable with it and quite frankly it has never turned out well for me. *Belle, what do you think you're doing? Tut, it's always you, isn't it? You can be relied on to let everyone down... Why are you always so difficult? Why can't you just fit in?* I turn the voices off and focus on what is going on around me, tune into Rory's voice instead of those of my family.

'So I had a think and I don't want to be the twat that turns up with loads of suggestions of what are the best next steps to take, mansplain stuff to you, so if you think I'm doing that, stop me and I'll cease immediately and vacate the premises.' I look up at him through my eyelashes and see that he too feels a bit uncomfortable. I force a smile to my lips, one that I hope says *I know your intent is good, don't fret, please continue,* rather than channelling Joaquin Phoenix's Joker on an off day.

'We get that, come on.' Luisa is on the edge of the sofa now.

'I listened to what you said about how you wanted to get this to everyone, but especially to young people, and I knew I could help, I just wasn't sure how initially. I had a couple of ideas and have spent today chasing them. So I won't mind if you say no...' He looks at me intently and I know I have to raise my eyes to meet his. He needs the reassurance.

'Sweet Jesus, will you come on!' Luisa interjects.

'So, based on what you said about an app being the first step, I figured a good way forward was to look into actually getting your work made as a free app.'

'Yeah, that would be amazing. But I don't know how to

and I simply can't afford to get someone who does. I tried already.'

'Right. I estimate it's going to take a budget of twenty to thirty K to send it out to a developer, you need someone to design the UX, make it user-friendly, and someone else to do the heavy lifting, the coding, make sure there's a CMS in there, all that sort of thing, get it to the marketplace.'

'I don't understand half of that.'

'UX is user experience, and CMS is Content Management System, so they can make changes once it's set up, keep it updated, flexible, right?' Luisa interjects, less excited now, her serious business face on.

'How on earth do you know that?' I exclaim.

'I may make cupcakes but I also keep up to date with business and tech.'

'Right.' He nods at Luisa and then turns back to me. 'And then you're going to need a further budget of at least twenty K for a marketing campaign once it's up and running on the app store. I know that sounds like a lot, but for what you need, it's fair. You need someone hot on SEO.'

'Search Engine Optimisation,' Luisa offers.

'Oh stop it now, show off,' I say but the inside of me is dying. I've been waiting for years to finish this and get it to the next steps but this is insane. All that work and it's going to shrivel on the vine. Rory presumably knows what he is talking about, Luisa hasn't flinched at these numbers, but this is beyond any funding I can hope to secure from the Arts Council or from going around schools. I try not to let my face reflect the fact that my hopes are now dead inside, dust.

'Right, and then a social media marketer to implement it in a micro-targeted ad campaign, not just to attract the keen English students and teachers, but deliberately targeting kids that are not on academic or study aid sites. It takes a fair chunk of money.'

'Yep.' By this point I know the despondency is on my face.

'And of course, a salary for you. That's something you would have to think about. You can't implement the next stage, going into schools, meeting head teachers and so on if you're working a forty-hour week in something completely unrelated to pay the bills.'

'Right.' I nod. He can stop now.

'So we're looking at a start-up budget of seventy-five K and then ongoing running costs.'

'When you put it in black and white like that...'

'Right, it makes it more achievable, we know what we're aiming for.'

Seriously?

'Yes, that isn't what I was going to say. But thank you, you've obviously put a lot of time into this.' I rise to my feet, desperate to change the subject. 'I'm getting another drink, who's up for one?'

'Sit the fuck back down, woman. He hasn't finished yet.'

'Yeah, but I think it's clear I am. Can we not hack the corpse when it's already rotting?'

'Oh my God, sit down now.' Luisa grabs my sleeve from where she is sitting on the sofa and yanks me down again.

'I'd listen to your friend,' Rory advised, his green eyes twinkling.

'I listened to her in college and all it got me was a raving weed habit and an STI.'

'You forget I knew you in college.' Rory grins. 'And that was *no*t down to Luisa.'

'She was a nightmare!' Luisa smirks. 'When I made her godmother, I did it because she has the best heart, although the worst habits, of anyone I know. Belle is true and good.' I shoot her a look that says she can stop now. She ignores me. 'Heart, character, you can't change that but habits you can work on, so as she held Marsha when she had just been born and was shooting out crazy love-me-look-after-me pheromones, I told her if she was to have a place in my child's life she needed to be someone I could trust my child with without worrying about the next unsuitable boyfriend coming through the door, or the baggie left on the kitchen table.' Luisa switches her gaze from Rory to me and we exchange a look of love that only a decade plus of friendship can create.

'Yes, and I haven't had sex since.' I grin and flourish my hands very much like my dad does.

'You're so naughty. You know that's not true.'

'Practically true. But I knocked the smoking on the head, mostly, but never, never if Marsha is around or if I'm going to see her imminently. And I've completely sorted out the only dating losers thing by just not dating. In fact, right now, I'm off all sex for the foreseeable. All my love is for Lu and Marsha.'

'Good to know but I think you might love this too. I'll cut to the point. I have a client, well, friend, primarily, who is very keen on investing philanthropically into literacy projects. They want to target primary schools, address inequalities there, and this may shock you but 75K is a drop in the ocean to them and they didn't even blink when I ran the figures past them. They want to meet you, talk about how you deliver it in schools as well as develop the app. See if you could filter it down to primary schools when they're studying the Tudors and try and engage them with Shakespeare then. Get them learning early that old texts aren't anything to be scared of. Teach them about rhythm, cadence, rhyme in language. If you can do that he'll support you with the secondary schools and colleges too. And as luck would have it, he's in Bristol until tomorrow evening, and suggested a face-to-face tomorrow, what do you think?'

Think? I can't think.

Rory reaches across, places his hand on mine and very quietly whispers 'Hey, *all things are ready if our minds be so.*'

I don't dare look at Luisa.

No legacy is so rich as honesty

December Sixth.
Belle.

'Yaaaayyyyyyy!' I open an eye as Marsha's shriek pierces the air. I'm sleeping top-to-toe in her bed, a tradition that started when she was two with her first ever Sinterklaas night and one that I assume will end in a few years. Surely she won't want me sleeping in the same bed as her once she's in secondary school? I'm going to make the most of the joy now. But also, it *is* 5 a.m.

'Look at this, Belle!' she says, waving a huge bar of Milka around so excitedly it whacks me on the head.

Ow.

'That's huge, Marshy-moo!'

'I know. Huge-est ever. It didn't even fit in the shoe, it's like, one, two, three, four, six shoes long. It's going to last for ever.'

'You reckon?'

'Mmmmm … here, shhhh.' She breaks me off a chunk and puts her finger to her lip. Almost five years old and already skilled at getting me to collude so I can't rat on her. I know Luisa will make her make the chocolate last until Christmas Day itself, so I don't blame her for eating as much as she can before her mum wakes up.

'I've got Percy Pigs, and these…' She holds up gel pens. 'This…' A Beatrix Potter colouring book – the girl is obsessed, and who in their right mind does not love Mrs

69

Tiggy-Winkle? 'And look! A skipping rope...' I duck. 'And a huge bag of reindeer poo!' The chocolate raisins are a fairly large bag. We cuddle under the covers and both take a page of Tiggy-Winkle colouring, munching chocolate while we can.

I'm getting ready to go home when I get a text from Rory with an address and a time slot. It would seem this meeting is going ahead. It will be quick, he's a busy man, I am told, but not so busy he's prepared to give away 75K without a brief face-to-face. He can fit me in after church.

The address is in St Pauls, barely a fifteen-minute walk away from mine, through the underpass and then a couple of roads down. In fact, I think it's not far from an underground club I used to go to when I was younger, big steel metal door, sliding hatch, password, that sort of thing. Proper sketchy. The sort of place I don't think I could find sober and in daylight. And definitely not now I'm in my thirties.

'Don't fret,' Rory had said last night, 'the two of you have a lot in common. I've known him since primary school. He'll take one look at you and decide in an instant whether his investment is safe or whether you're a shyster. He always does business this way. I think you're going to like him.'

'I don't need to like him.' I had said at the time. 'I just need him to like me.' But inside I'm terrified. Should I prepare a pitch? I had asked, aware that twelve hours was not a long time to get ready. No need, I had been reassured, bring you as you are and answer any questions he has honestly and that will be enough.

Great, I'm going to meet some kind of psychic business savant, and bar being me, there is little else I can do to win him over. No pressure!

Before I allow my mind to go down into a poor self-esteem whirl I decide to reframe the way I'm thinking. Stop concentrating on my flaws and how this man will react to me. If he hates me I'm no worse off than I was twenty-four hours ago.

I also need to find a way to thank Rory for this. He had said last night it was his job but to me it's so much more than that. What can I do for Rory? He's financially secure, has no worries that I know of in his life and is only here for a short amount of time. I'm not sure why he has come back. I should ask him but I wonder if it has anything to do with Jessica. She died in December. I know this because it was the day before Marsha wailed her way onto this planet, red-faced and determined.

He had admitted to hating December whereas for me it is the most magical month. It is also the toughest. It's tough because I am required to see my parents twice, but other than that the sparkle, the magic, the thinking of gifts for those I love, the joy in Marsha's face, peaking not just once at Christmas but again on New Year's Day when she celebrates her birthday, all of that is joyous. The excitement in the air, the jollity everywhere you go, the anticipation. Maybe I can pass some of that magic on to him.

That is what I will do. I will teach him to love Christmas. I'm not going to be able to wipe away his pain, suddenly cleanse December of the tragedy he has experienced, but whilst he's here I can be his friend and show him the magic of winter. I can be his very own Christmas elf.

———————

It's noon and I am standing on the doorstep of a fairly average-looking terraced house in St Pauls. Not some schmancy-pants hotel or Clifton address. There's music blaring out from a house down the street and despite wearing the smartest outfit I can, borrowed from Luisa with the intention of reassuring Mystery Man his money is safe with me, my feet are itching to dance.

I love this area of Bristol, I'm a die-hard attendee of Carnival when it's on in summer and have actually clambered over Luisa once to get my hands on a cold Red Stripe and a bowl of goat curry. She hadn't minded. The houses here are all jammed together and as well as the music, I can hear people as they walk down the street, a stream of chatter bringing life to the place. All senses are awakened here.

Still, my love for the city doesn't stop me being nervous right now, in this moment. My hopes of getting my Shakespeare project out are pretty all-consuming and I've gone from zero to two hundred in less than a day. My dreams of wandering around schools sharing my bardolatry with keen minds have been over-inflating all the way here and I've worked out a pitch as I've walked. Shakespeare me is not going to let an opportunity like this slip through my fingers through lack of preparation. If it all goes wrong I need to know I've given it my best shot.

Deep breath. I ring the doorbell.

Breath in, breath out.

A lithe young woman with the most beautiful face opens the door. She's wearing some kind of gold mesh and has an afro that must be a good ten inches wide – that takes maintenance. She might have just walked straight off the cover of *Vogue*. She certainly looks like she belongs where 75K is pocket change. I'm intimidated and trying not to stare.

'Hi, come on in. Belle for Jamal? He's expecting you.' Her voice is pure Bristolian and I could kiss her; the intimidation has waned.

She leads me through a hallway into a kitchen.

Sitting at the Formica-topped kitchen table is a woman, probably about my mum's age, but where my mum exudes brittle sophistication twinned with cold desperation this woman is warm and dressed in her Sunday best. This kitchen feels like a hub of the home and there is a delicious smell pervading the house.

My gaze swings from my guide to a tall man stirring a pot. His shoulders are so broad that he looks as if he could be a warrior king. Even through his hoody I can see how beautifully built he is and I feel a pang of lust flood through me. Woah, that's not appropriate right now.

'Hello, hello, hello.' The woman waves me in. 'You are just in time for Jamal's brown stew chicken. It is the best, I tell you, the best there has ever been.'

I smile.

'Hello, that's quite some recommendation.'

'No word of a lie.' Glamazon gestures for me to pull out

a chair and sit at the table. This is not how I imagined my pitch meeting.

'He won't be a minute and he'll make you a cup of tea as well.' The elder of the two women says as if *he* isn't in the room with us.

'That would be lovely.' I sit at the table and decide to go with the general vibe. The man at the stove stirs the pot one more time, turns the heat off and leans over and flicks on a kettle. I'm hypnotised. He turns to face me.

Fuck me.

No.

Jamal is actually Jamal! The UK's brightest and best. The twenty-first century's version of Da Vinci, Aristotle and Helen Keller rolled into one, a polymath to rival all others. He started out in the music business, making a name for himself on the hip-hop scene before he was even out of school. He then went on to release an album that had gone mainstream and hit all the number one spots on every streaming service whilst he was still sitting his A-levels. He has since done some television, partnering up with Channel Four on a drama set here, in St Pauls, that then won a BAFTA – of course it did – and now he is releasing more music, running an ethical clothing company, campaigning against sweatshops and is rumoured to have something new he is about to announce. He's thirty. A year younger than me, way more successful than anyone could hope to be and sexy as fuck. Sweet Jesus Christ he is sexy. And currently making me tea in a kitchen in St Pauls.

I'm going to kill Rory. How could he not have warned me?

'Cup of tea on and you're welcome to a bowl of chicken…' He pauses as he turns and sees me. 'F—' He looks across at the older woman and makes a 'sorry' grimace. 'I know you. Rory didn't tell me it was you!'

I laugh. How surreal is this? Jamal knows *me*. I don't think so. There is no way this is happening to me right now.

'You know me? You must have me muddled with someone else. I didn't realise I was coming to see you, Rory didn't say.' I stammer. So much for my professional I-know-all-about-Shakespeare-and-am-well-worth-your-investment speech. I'm fairly sure *You know me* wasn't supposed to be my opening line. Neither is dribbling with open-mouthed awe. Yet I seem to be rocking it really well.

Jamal looks me up and down. Not in a sleazy sexual way, not at all, but in a way which makes me practically see the cogs in his brain whirring around at super speed, his eyes lit with an intelligence that is more than a little intimidating.

'Yeah, he's good like that. Loyal, tight-lipped, never talks much unless there's something to be said. I like him. He is the most honourable man you are likely to meet. We've been friends for years. That's why I took this meeting. But yeah, I know you…'

'He's always had a photographic memory, ever since he was a boy. He sees something, he remembers it. It was one of his superpowers when he was little. So where do you know this nice young lady from then, Jamal?'

'The papers.' His tone does not fill me with hope.

'Ooh, are you famous too?' the older woman asks me, a big grin on her face. The Beautiful One looks interested.

'No, I'm really not.' If he remembers me from the papers then here I am back on my dad's coat-tails. My least favourite place in the world. My heart sinks.

'Yeah, look, I'm sorry your dad's a dick, ooh, sorry, Nan...' Nan! No way, she does not look old enough. Jamal continued, 'Your dad is a ... well, you know what I'm saying. The papers are intrusive but still, must have been a shock.'

'Nah, not really.' He hands me a mug of tea and I take a slurp appreciatively before I look up and hold his eye. He's watching my every move, my every micro-reaction. 'I've known he's a di ... um ... a bounder?' I look over at Jamal's nan who nods. 'I've known my whole life. From about the age of five, anyway, when I caught him snogging my reception teacher after the parents' race.'

'Some men, they just can't keep it in their pants,' Jamal's nan says, her accent pure Jamaican, as she shakes her head.

Glamazon nods wearily.

'Not my Jamal though. He is a good boy. A smart boy. He won't see you wrong.'

'Let's eat before it gets cold. Stew, Nan? Alisa? Belle?' He serves the chicken into a big bowl and gives us all small plates.

'Nan came over with *Windrush*, so this reminds her a little of home. She taught me when I was small,' he says as we all sit there, cramped up together in the tiny kitchen polishing off our bowls.

'That was so good, thank you.'

'No worries. But why are you sat in my kitchen? Your

family is rich. Why won't your dad invest? Free up my money for people without your privilege?'

Ouch. It's a question I can't answer either. I go for honesty.

'Maybe you should give your money to people who didn't have my start in life. But I'm sat here now hoping you'll give it to me and that my project helps open up the world a little to people who may struggle to access parts of it otherwise. I'd like to do this without going to my father.'

'And I'd like to live in a world with more equality, where people don't have to go without food to make sure their kids eat. *Like* is a luxury in this life.' Again, I can't argue with that. The food had been delicious but nothing is going to remove the taste of failure, peppered with a sprinkling of humiliation, from my mouth now.

I desire you in friendship, and I will one way or other make you amends.

December Seventh.
Rory.

I had been wandering the aisles in the Tesco near Mum's, wincing at the bloody Christmas songs belting out – I swear they had managed to run through the whole gamut and start the loop again just in the short time I was in there – when I'd had a moment of seasonal madness and found myself putting a jar of mincemeat and a tub of clotted cream in the trolley. I picture Mum's face as I triumphantly present her with a mince pie, warm from the oven, the cream sliding off the top like snow from a warmed porch.

She had been exhausted yesterday, evidenced by the fact she let Dave cook the roast – I almost lost three teeth, how he did what he did to the potatoes was a mystery, and who, *who* burns peas? I saw the fatigue on her face, her eyes lacking brightness, a pallor hanging over her. I don't think this is the cancer, this looks like lack of sleep, and I can well imagine that after showing a brave face and a bright side throughout the day she is lying awake at night, consumed with worry about having to leave us should the worst occur. I know how struggling to doze off feels and it breaks my heart that I can't cast a magic sleep spell for her.

So instead I went to the supermarket, then batch-cooked a whole host of things for her freezer and was currently stood ready to slide out mince pies from the oven. I've done this once before when I was twelve, trying to make amends for something hideous I had done at the time, although now I can't remember the actual crime. I remember the feeling though, as I presented her with the plate. That. That was what I was aiming for today, for the both of us.

It isn't just my mum who will be surprised though; I have to tell Belle this. I'm itching to reach out to her and see how yesterday went but don't want to overly intrude. My intention had been to pair them and then step back. The fact that I haven't heard from either her or Jamal does not bode well. It's niggling at me.

The two of them are made for each other, I had been so pleased when I had thought of it. What I know and others don't is that Jamal is back in the UK for the next few months in rehearsals for the RSC's production of *Coriolanus*, scheduled for the summer. He's politically active with strong opinions on the state and its responsibilities, and this role, so he tells me, is a good one for making a statement about absolute power. Twin that with the coincidence of him being back from America, and in Bristol seeing his family this weekend... If this isn't the universe intervening then I don't know what is.

I whip out my phone.

You're not going to believe this but right now, right now, I am making mince pies. From scratch. Mince pies.

Send. There, that might make her smile, and she might tell me what happened yesterday. I put Mum's recipe book back on the shelf, an old red ring binder with all Grandma's recipes inside, handwritten and fading. Grandma had died of breast cancer but I had spent the morning trying not to think about that. Medicine is better now than when my mum's mum had first got ill. The oven timer buzzes at the same time as my phone.

Mince pies. Wow. I'm impressed. I was going to message you today but it's been hectic. What's caused the thawing of your frosty Christmas spirit?

She punctuates her texts. Of course she does. And she's been busy, that's a good sign. Maybe I should stop being so pessimistic. Maybe she and Jamal haven't been in touch because they've been up all night hatching plans, her enthusiasm for her subject captivating him as it had me. I feel a flash of something uncomfortable and turn to the cooker, opening the door and sliding the pies out. They smell amazing.

I think thaw is a bit strong. Trust me when I say I still loathe Christmas. But I love my mum. And she loves a mince pie.

Well luckily for you, I have decided to be your very own Christmas Elf and…

What does that mean? I picture her in an elf costume, hair in bunches, and shake my head quickly. For some reason that image has appeared straight out of *Playboy* circa 2002. Thirteen-year-old me would have been keen but adult me is rapidly trying to delete that mental picture right now.

81

This is Belle Wilde and a complication I do not need on my brief visit home. The list of reasons for avoiding that has to number a billion. I am still grieving, we would not be a good match, she is not attracted to men like me, she is not Jess. Mind you, I want to know what she means. My phone beeps again.

...and tonight I have tickets for a show on the Brunel SS. You know you love a boat ;-)

How did she remember that? I must have told her one of the times I gave her a lift home that I had always been fascinated by old boats, and a memory flashes into my head of the both of us giggling about how we could pinch one of the barges docked by the quay and sail away, leaving all of the panic over dissertations behind us. Well, she would have giggled, I probably said something terribly responsible. We'd had a funny friendship back then.

I haven't been on the SS *Brunel* since I was a boy. I did love it then. I suppose it would do no harm.

———

I walk through the car park and see her before I actually *see* her. I hope I'm wrong but know I'm not. I head towards the person wearing flashing lights both on their torso and head – a Christmas jumper with flashing lights on Rudolph's face and an elf's hat with flashing lights built in. I raise my brows.

'Just helping you get into the Christmas spirit.'

'I don't think that I need that sort of help.'

'Oh, I don't know, I think that's exactly the sort of help you need.'

'Hmmm. You do know there are several Christmas phobias, don't you? What you're doing right now could be cruel as cruel could be. Like locking someone who is afraid of birds into an aviary, that sort of thing.'

'Oh, calm yourself. You're making that up.'

'Am not. It's called "selaphobia" – the fear of flashing lights – and my selaphobia means that those lights wrapped around your hat are currently causing me trauma.'

'Pshaw.'

'Pshaw? Is that the best you can do?'

'Honestly, it's a bit of a relief.' She reaches up to her hat and pulls it off her head, clicking a button as she does so, and then reaches under her jumper and clicks another. 'I bought these cos I love Christmas and thought it would be fun. But truthfully, I have always been way too embarrassed to wear them. This will probably be my one and only time. And I did it because you need to know I take my elf duties to you very seriously. Very seriously indeed.'

'Okay, in that case, please keep them off.'

'Phew.' She shoves the hat in her bag. 'I shall take care not to take you anywhere with too many flashing lights.' Then she winks. She's different to the Belle I knew at uni. I like this Belle better. She's less brittle, less aloof.

'Any more Christmas phobias I should know about?' We walk towards the ticket office manned by someone in Victorian dress.

'Yes, but hang on… Thank you,' I address the person

83

who has taken our tickets and is waving us through as Belle nods her thanks. 'What have you got me into here?'

'Nothing to fret about. Let's get these phobias out of the way first.'

I do not trust that smile. If I end up having to take part in some kind of historical Christmas pantomime her elfing days are over. I'll chuck her overboard and let the River Avon deal with her. I give her an arch look, just to make sure she knows she's on thin ice. She smirks.

'Okay. There's also ghabhphobia – people who hate receiving presents because they can't cope with the social anxiety triggered by people looking at them as they receive it,' I continue.

'I can understand that one.'

'Really?'

'My social anxiety is off the scale unless I'm super comfortable with the person or, um … when you knew me back in the day, chemically aided. I have to talk myself into and through social situations because I don't want to let them control me. I think that's why I'm at my happiest at home lost in the Shakespeare project. I'm always second-guessing whether I'm responding appropriately to social cues rather than just responding. So yeah, even when I'm given a gift I worry that the way I have reacted may not be the way the person wanted me to. Don't get me wrong though, I like presents, and I'd rather feel uncomfortable than never have another present again.'

'Wow.'

'Wow makes me feel like I've made a right tit of myself.'

'You…' I stopped. I had been about to say you stood

there in those lights and *now* you're worried about making a tit of yourself. But seeing as she has just opened up to me about how deep her social anxiety runs, that would be a tad insensitive. It also makes me realise what a sacrifice of comfort the lights had been, and how badly I had misjudged the Belle I thought I knew. 'You have nothing to worry about. I'm sorry. Do you want to hear more phobias, Christmas elf?'

She nods and smiles. I'm forgiven.

'I have, with good reason "Christougenni-atikophobia"…' I pause again, but we're being honest. It's just that I'm not used to being this honest with myself let alone someone else. 'It's a mouthful and is a fear of Christmas in general.' There, I had said it out loud. And it was actually okay. I am scared of Christmas, the season at least, with my discomfort ramping up the closer we get to the day itself and then spiralling into oblivion in that ridiculous time people now call 'twixmas'. I flick a quick look across at her but she doesn't seem at all phased by what I said. Just accepting. As if it is both perfectly possible and perfectly normal for me to have some kind of overwhelming fear. I take a deep breath, nod and continue. 'Then there's "meleagrisphobia", the fear of turkeys. I don't know if people who have that phobia would be scared or relieved by a dead turkey but that is a thing.'

She laughs.

'I reckon you may understandably suffer from "syngenesphobia", particularly triggered by Christmas and for you specifically twice in December. This one I don't have. I have the others though.'

'I do not believe you are scared of turkeys, Mr Walters. But okay, syngenesphobia, um … let me work this one out, syn. Syn is not same, that's homo … syn is with?' She quirks her brow at me, not quite sure, and I nod. It sounds about right; she's way more likely to know than me. 'Um, genus, that's family. So I'm going to go with fear of family and hope my half-arsed attempt is actually one … hundred … per cent right.' She spaces out those last words, victory in her tone.

'Boom, you've got it.'

'This is fun. Another?'

'Probably only fun for us, you know. Others would think we're pretty weird.'

'You *are* weird,' she says, deadpan.

'I'm opening up, discussing medically rationalised fears about Christmas, and that's fun to you? Are you always this sadistic?'

'Yes.'

We're on the boat now and I'm excited, as if I were still a child. It has been years since I was here and I remember how much I loved those spooky wax Victorians that I was both scared and captivated by.

'Do we get to look around before you take me to whatever hell you're planning?'

'For sure. Hell doesn't start for another half hour or so in the first-class dining room so we can grab a bite to eat on the promenade deck, have a wander. I've actually never been here before. You can be my tour guide.'

'I am so up for that.' And I am.

We grab a mince pie, I say no to more mulled cider –

Luisa's batch had to be a stroke of luck – and we wander back through the narrow wood-lined corridors, the narrowness of them pressing us together. I'm aware of Belle's every breath as she peeks her head into cabin after cabin.

'They are so tiny! How did they get four people to fit in there? I can barely fit me in! I'll never bitch about the size of my flat again. Oh, but look at the ironwork on the corner, isn't that pretty?'

We go down into the cargo hold. 'Oh my goodness... This is how they'd get their horses across. I suppose I knew they would but never really thought about it. Although I should have. *The Tempest* begins with a shipwreck. Think of all the people crammed in, all the animals, all that life bouncing over the waves. 'But look there...' she points, '... look at how shiny they keep the hulls of the lifeboat. That wood is a thing of beauty, that must take so much work. Why have I never been here before?' Her delight at everything is making something I love even better, and her talk is some kind of stream-of-consciousness babble but I like it.

'Ooh, I don't want to leave. But the performance starts in ten minutes. You've got time to show me one more thing and then we'll have to grab our seats.'

'What exactly are we going to see in ten minutes?' I query.

'It's a Dickensian Christmas improv evening. They're going to make up a Christmas play on the spot with a bit of help from the audience.'

'You are joking me?'

'No, no I'm really not. It's going to be awesome, and besides, it's Dickensian so no flashing lights.' She winks and her nose crinkles with delight.

'We're never going anywhere together again,' I say as sternly as I can.

'Oh, but we are. I'm your Christmas elf.' She waves the elf hat out of the corner of her bag at me and I can't help but smile.

'I don't think I ever agreed to that.'

'Nope. It's magic. You don't need to agree, it just happens.'

'We live in an age of consent.'

'Not for the next two hours. I don't think consent is very Dickensian. Anyway, hurry up with your one more thing before we need to grab our seats.'

I push her through the corridors back into the promenade deck where I lead her into one of the booths where the waxwork doctor stands, his kit all laid neatly out in his bag – scissors, glass bottles, possible instruments of torture – working on a patient who is looking away from his wound with credible emotion for a waxwork, even better than Cyndi on her birthday. She oohs and leans over to stroke the saw with a ghoulish fascination. Then her eyes light upon the medicine cabinet.

'Ooh, look at this, they have everything. Laudanum, obviously…' She turns and gives me a grin.

'Don't go getting any ideas,' I say mock-seriously.

'I was thinking for you, not me, to get you through this performance.'

'Oh, well, in that case.' I open my mouth wide and she

giggles before turning back. 'Look, they've got everyday things too like cream of tartar, what medicinal use does that have? Epsom salts. Nitre... That sounds dangerous.'

Her exploration pauses as a bell sounds.

'We need to get our seats, come on.' She grabs my hand and pulls me out of the doctor's cabin. 'We need to be quick, we want to get the right seats.'

'You're not going to sit me at the front, are you?'

'Are you mad? It's audience participation, the thought of being called upon scares the living daylights out of me. No, I'm going to sit at the back and refuse to make eye contact, that's my plan. Then I can enjoy it in safety.'

I laugh and trip through the corridors with her up to the first-class dining area where she swoops on the chairs right at the back, next to a large column.

'Phew, that was lucky.'

'Who comes to an audience participation without wanting to participate?' I ask. She really is a contrary creature.

'I do.'

A thought pops into my head. I'd forgotten my intention for this evening. 'How did it go with Jamal?'

Everyone is seated now and the cast, all in Victorian costume, are gathered by the entrance to the dining room.

'Oh yeah.' She pulls a face. 'He didn't take to me but thank you for trying. I really appreciate it.'

A large man in very tight trousers, a long tailcoat and high narrow-brimmed hat strides out into the centre of the room.

'What do you mean he didn't take to you?' That's

ridiculous, these two are the perfect match, her project has to appeal to him on so many levels. There must be a mistake.

'Will you shhhh, it's starting.' She wallops me on my leg. I yelp and the couple in front turn around and give us furious looks.

'Ladies and gentlemen, thank you for coming tonight.' The actor adopts the Lord Flashheart pose and a hammy shouting voice. 'I am in dire need of your help. My wife has disappeared...' he pauses, '...so I am desperately searching for Fanny!' The audience guffaws. Someone starts making pig noises.

What has Belle Wilde brought me to?

Wise men ne'er sit and wail their loss,
But cheerily seek how to redress their harms.

December Eighth.
Belle.

The wind nips at my cheeks and my ears, making them burn one minute and numb the next as I walk briskly to my trial morning at my first new job. Today is a crazy day of new starts, lots all hurled into one day, and truthfully, I'm scared of how I'm going to manage. It's a lot. So, I'm going to break it down into manageable units and fret about one at a time. I may well resemble Crazy Eyes from *Orange Is the New Black* by teatime but at least by then I'll have got most of the day out of the way. And who doesn't like a little rocking in the corner by the time the evening is here?

Right now, I'm borderline hypothermic – despite my seven layers of clothes – which has a strange way of concentrating the mind. I may have to reconsider my decision to always walk to places within an easy distance.

However, my survival and determination to get somewhere slightly warmer than the current Arctic temperatures are distracting me nicely from whatever I'm about to walk into. These seven layers are intended to keep me warm but have the added bonus of making sure no one can get me naked easily at my next destination.

Not that I think they will try, but you can't be too careful. I have Luisa's number open and ready to press in an emergency and Find My Phone is clicked on with my location available to her all day. Not that I've told her what I'm doing. The ad I have responded to, a card in the window of Temperance's mini-mart, wants a cleaner who is hard-working, discreet and open-minded.

Being a bit of a loner covers discreet, and I'm way more open-minded than anyone should be. I'd once put on one of those human bridle things for Sam, an ex, and then cantered around his room neighing loudly – his flatmate had never been able to look me in the eye again. Luckily this story didn't have to feature in my phone interview, general assurances seemed enough, and now, at the crack of dawn and trudging through a wind that would have made Shackleton wince, I am going to do a trial shift at Hope House.

My psychic senses are telling me this will probably be okay. My bank statements are telling me this is definitely going to be okay. I have also reassured myself that as much as I need to pay rent, and as much as I don't want to take money from Luisa, I am an adult and will not be staying anywhere I'm uncomfortable, or suspect there is stuff going on that just isn't all right. With no real idea of what I'm walking into, I have both worst-case and best-case scenario expectations.

I arrive at Hope House. It looks fairly normal. A house typical for Bristol with its big Victorian bay windows and contrasting stone around the doors and the windows. Usually these houses are divided into flats but as the howling Siberian gale helps me up the steps to the door I can only see one doorbell.

There's certainly nothing from the outside that screams twenty-first-century bordello. I close my eyes and hit the bell.

'Hello,' a friendly enough voice says through the intercom.

'Hi, this is Belle, I've come for the trial.' And then I add hurriedly, 'The cleaning trial.'

This is going to be fine. This is a good job for me as it means that the rest of my day is free for job-hunting and dream-chasing and two hours every day is £140 a week, which is my rent just about met.

I push the door open and walk through the hall. So far so good.

'Come on through.' I follow the voice and push open the door. There's a very nice living room – bookshelves line the walls, there's a big screen in the corner and a drinks trolley that would not look out of place in a country house hotel. There are two sofas and on one is a large woman, a grin taking up most of her face. This is not what I had imagined.

'Come in, come in, you are early, this is good. Look at you, so skinny. I'm Dorothy and you're Belle, eh?' Dorothy looks as if she runs a Sunday school not a Community Collective for Female Sexual Safety, Welfare and Empowerment, which is how she described Hope House to me on the phone yesterday. I nod in agreement and she continues. 'Let me show you around and you can get started. We have everything you need, all the sprays, lots of gloves. I like to run a clean house which is why I need you here every day. The girls like to come to work and have it smelling good, you get me?'

'I do.' I nod. I may not be great at keeping my flat tidy but I do have a weakness for the smell of bleach. Somehow it makes the whole world right – ditto Dettol, Germolene and creosote. 'If your girls want clean, they shall have it.' I smile, channelling the love child of Doris Day and Mary Poppins. If I had a wand I would wave it.

She nods, slowly and about seven times, before leading me through to a cupboard under the stairs. A Hoover, a mop and bucket – four mops actually, each a different kind – neatly piled dusters and cloths, and every cleaning spray on the market stack the shelves. Mrs Hinch would be catatonic with joy.

'Green for the bathroom, pink for the bedrooms, blue for the loos and yellow for the kitchen. At this time of the day, things should be nice and quiet, so you can do a good clean of everything. I want it spanking,' she says this with no hint of irony and I battle to keep a straight face as she proceeds to show me around the bedrooms, every single one nicer than any room I have ever had. 'We take online bookings and run a 24/7 operation so if a room has a red light on outside, please do not go in. Come back and do it when it is green again.' I clock the discreet panel next to the door, point at it to confirm I know what she means and nod my head. This is going to be fine. The light system means I'm unlikely to accidentally witness someone's bobbing bottom.

'Oh, and Fat Alan will be in the basement every morning. He likes to sleep here at night. But don't worry about him, just go around him. He'll be fully restrained and his mask means he will be able to hear but not see you if he's awake, so he shouldn't be a problem. If he makes a noise just tap him with your feather duster and he'll settle down and wait for Ariana, our BDSM expert, to come in. Okay?'

———————

I'd cleaned the house from top to bottom, gingerly flicking Fat Alan with a feather duster as directed – he seemed to like it and very politely said a muffled thank you before settling back down – and I noticed out of the corner of my eye that he had a security guard's uniform folded neatly in the corner of the room, complete with his Dalton's swipe card on top. Did he not go home at all? I felt a little sorry for him.

Job One seemed to be in the bag. In fact, my trial shift this morning had been the most successful part of my day. I then visited two schools and I'm now on my final school stop of the day – the primary school around the corner from me. In the two secondary schools I started with, I had been diligently led in to see their headteachers. The first one listened to me for a couple of minutes before cutting me off, explaining I had picked the worst time of year to be coming in and that they didn't really have the budget for that sort of thing. When I countered that I was offering a free session in return for testimonials, she merely smiled, her attention back on some papers on her desk, and waved me out of her office.

The second Head had been much friendlier, although to get in I had to pass through metal detectors, and trek down corridors full of laughing, shouting children, past toilets that reeked of smoke. It was bedlam. If I got invited back I'd be rocking up in head-to-toe Kevlar.

He sounded interested, although, to be honest, it could have just been desperation – I never can tell the difference, ask Luisa – and said he was keen but it would have to go through the Head of English who was on a course. However, before we could arrange anything more concrete his secretary came racing through screeching that there had been 'another incident'. His face went green, and muttering apologies he shot out from behind his desk and raced out of the office. For the first time in my life, I questioned just how dedicated I was to Shakespeare.

This primary school though is lovely: everything is brightly coloured and scenes of winter and Christmas fill all the walls. The sounds of the children feel right – not as frenetic as the previous school. I like it here. However, whether the headteacher will see much need for Shakespeare is another matter. At least the secretary had sounded positive yesterday on the phone when I had called.

It was Jamal's rejection that had spurred me on yesterday, turning today into a crazed maelstrom of trial followed by interview, followed by interview followed by trial. It had reinvigorated me into realising, after twenty-four hours of blissful daydreaming about being funded, that no one was going to get this project off the ground if it wasn't me. So, I admitted I could no longer hide behind my computer mewling that the project wasn't finished and I called around to schools in the area.

I knew the run-up to Christmas was poor timing, but I also knew if I didn't do something immediately my self-esteem was going to take such a battering that I'd curl up for a bit and not take any next steps for a few months.

I take a deep breath as the school secretary waves me through to the headteacher's office with a smile.

'Hello, come in. Nice to meet you.'

'Ah, Mr Latham, thank you for seeing me.'

No one had mentioned Mr Latham is a dish. Somehow, I manage to articulate a sentence. The parents must be hurling themselves, panting, at the school railings. No wonder the school looks immaculate, they probably have mothers from other schools volunteering here. I imagine the PTA coffers are overflowing. They'd only have to auction him off for 'an evening with…' at the school fayre and that would be three minibuses bought.

He's like Orlando Bloom – you know, as he got older and all hot – with that flicker of naughtiness in his eye. I sit down in my chair, try to breathe evenly and use my most graceful posture, the one that is second nature to my mother and that I have never, ever felt the desire to emulate before.

'Absolute pleasure, how can I help? You mentioned something about offering workshops for the children?'

'Yes, yes, exactly that. I have developed a package for primary school children introducing them to Shakespeare at a young age to familiarise them with the language and story to help them access it both now and as they go through the school system…' And I'm off.

Twenty minutes later, I am panting a bit myself. Although not with desire, merely because I'd got a little over-excited discussing why I thought it was important that children were familiarised with a long-dead Elizabethan playwright.

'You are certainly passionate about your subject area.' Mr Latham smiles.

'I am.'

'And I would love to have you.'

'I would love that.' I wink.

Mr Latham smiles again. I can't decode it.

I had winked!

What the actual hell did I think I was doing? Way to go, Belle. Is my self-sabotage now at such a high level it has crossed from merely making shitty decisions in my personal life into making them in my potential professional one as well? Why, why, *why* would I mess up with the first person I have sat in front of who is interested in what I have to say and can kickstart me? I feel myself sliding down in the chair.

'Unfortunately, Belle – I can call you Belle, can't I?' I nod but fail to smile or make eye contact, my shame still washing over me in a tsunami. 'The run-up to Christmas is insane but if you have a free spot in um...' He pulls up his diary on his laptop. I sit up straighter. This is it, this is a booking. '...May of next year, we'd love to have you in then.'

'Oh my goodness, isn't this so pretty?' A woman next to the display I am close to holds a bauble aloft. 'It reminds me of how my daughter decorates her tree.'

I'm on my second job trial of the day and this customer looks like a mum, or at least how I always picture a mum should be. You know, like how grandmas are always supposed to resemble Mrs Claus, a little tubby, carefully styled but dated hair and a pair of pince-nez. This woman looks like she could knock up scones whilst bathing a grazed knee and still play Monopoly with a spare hand. Mothering 101.

'They're one of my absolute favourites,' I agree. 'I love how the different glasses all fuse into one another, and that colour, it's ice sprites, and snow fairies, winter balls in the ice palace. Magical.'

'Oh, she'll love this. It *is* all those things.'

'Isn't it lovely? It's so delicate. I think it goes beautifully with this one as well.' I pull up another bauble, this one in the same colour scheme of icy blues and greens but with little feather details on the inside of the glass, tiny, as if Jack Frost himself lived inside and had very lightly blown upon it.

'You're so right. She's going to love them.' She takes four of each – they aren't cheap either – and I'm shot through with a thrill I never had when I sold coffee or shoes or a sausage roll or two in that ill-fated month in Greggs. Mind you, the less said about that the better.

This is turning out to be a whopper of a day, I have cleaned a den of iniquity – who would have ever thought I could have added that to my CV? – secured my first school booking and now I'm selling Christmas decorations in the best ever shop in the world and smashing it. At least I think I'm smashing it.

A friend of mine, Sarah, who had gifted me the Dickensian evening tickets, had to suddenly fly to Australia, her mother being in some kind of accident. She had a seasonal job at the Christmas bauble shop and knowing I was out of work and that she wouldn't be back until at least January she pitched my name to her employers and called me to tell me to follow up with them. Which I did. On my super-industrious I-will-not-be-beaten-Monday.

And now I'm doing a couple of hours to see if I exude enough Christmas spirit to work two shifts a week in the most Christmassy shop ever.

I love it in here; it's actually part of my Make-Rory-Love-Christmas plan. But it has to be done carefully – this can't be pulled out the bag until he is practically converted and far more ready to enjoy the full Christmassy-ness this shop brings. It will have to be once all that nonsense about being scared of sparkling lights has been eradicated from his soul because this is sparkle and glitter and snow and Santa heavenliness all in one place. You can't move for rows and rows of baubles and trees, all set out in colour-coordinated joy.

The store is madly busy, as it always is when the Bath Christmas market is on. Traffic swirls out of the city like worms on a rod. People queue for miles and as the market throngs, the majority of shoppers can't fail to be pulled into this shop.

My customer seems content with her purchases and I help her carry the baubles over to the till. They're so fine and so delicate it seems sacrilegious to put them in a basket, to risk them being knocked in the crush of customers. I catch the manager looking at me, is he pleased? Or does he want me back on the shop floor? Is he cross that I'm guiding this woman to the till instead of making her browse her way to pay? Arrggghhh.

I'm not going to risk making any positive assumptions. I head back into the throng, only stopping when I see that someone has put a red icicle on the tray of pale gold baubles. Savages. That wouldn't do, oh no, and that blue one is meant to be all the way over the other side of the shop.

I can still feel the manager's eyes on me so quickly swish them back to their correct place. I must stop fussing, I need to interact with someone and quick.

'Excuse me...' Oh, thank you, Christmas Fairy Godmother.

'How can I help?' I turn around to face my saviour with the perfect I-know-everything-about-baubles smile on.

'I wondered what you knew about Christmases in days gone by. I'm looking for a traditional Christmas in my home this year, one with a historical bent, but these things are all so pretty it's hard to focus.'

'Oh, isn't it. I know exactly what you mean.' Thank you, CFG, I mutter up a prayer. 'I think as tempting as these are, if we head over here you can see the more traditional decorations. Back in the Tudor times they would bring in all the evergreen from outside, the fir and the pine, the holly and the ivy, mistletoe. In fact, the first recorded decorated tree in England was in the fifteenth century but it wasn't until the nineteenth century we adopted the German tradition of bringing the whole tree inside.' The woman looks genuinely interested. 'Up until the tree became commonplace most houses would have the kissing bough, a ball made from evergreens and mistletoe. I think if you go for a theme as green as possible and maybe don't use tinsel or too many baubles, then you should be fine. These pinecones here, and maybe these mini green decorated trees, would be perfect. And if you had the time and wanted to, you could thread popcorn for your tree. I do that and it's ever so soothing. Christmas movie on the TV, glass of wine and a bowl full of popcorn to thread. Although, of course we also have these pinecone garlands over here...'

'Oh yes, those would be perfect. And what about these here...' The woman points to more inside a little gift box.

'Yep, you can't go wrong with pinecones,' I say trying not to blanch at the price tag. I usually nip to Greenbank cemetery to collect my cones and then add a bit of ribbon saved from the beautifully wrapped presents Luisa gives me for my birthday and Christmas each year. But as much as I long to tell her this, I'm fairly convinced that will probably count against me landing the job. And this is clearly one of the best jobs ever. I've had enough self-sabotage for the day; this one I'm going to try and keep.

I like this place,
And could willingly waste my time in it

December Ninth.
Belle.

I thought I saw you selling Christmas last night in Bath. You
must have a twin. As frightening as that is.

I was so whacked last night that I didn't hear my phone
beep with Rory's message. I had arrived home and
fallen into bed, pleased with my efforts because before I had
left, the manager had taken me to one side, said I was a
natural and definitely had the job. Huzzah!

However, now I jump up and get dressed – still seven
layers, but not necessary as a safety precaution anymore. It
looks mild outside. A stark contrast to yesterday when I
nearly lost my ears to the freezing winds.

No twin. The world couldn't get that lucky I start to type
and then delete the last bit because what if he thinks I mean
it? I'm well aware that one evening being the Queen of
Christmas-decoration-selling did not really make up for my
many, many flaws. The world definitely does not need two
Belle Wildes.

No twin. If you mean you saw me in the decoration shop – I got
a new job! Two actually AND a school booking. Some elf magic
must have rubbed off because yesterday was a great day.

Two jobs. No way. Well done.

Shot straight back. Why is he up this early? Does he have a secret cleaning job too?

The phone beeps again.

This doesn't mean you'll be too busy to do the Shakespeare project does it?

Nope. That is still my number one reason for life. Do not fret. One job is a couple of hours a day, cleaning just around the corner from me, the other is in the shop two/three shifts a week so plenty of time left over.

Congratulations! Do you fancy meeting up for a celebratory drink later?

Ooh, I could. I'm not due in the shop until tomorrow. And now I have two jobs one drink isn't going to break the bank. Ah, but actually. How about...

I am free. But I have a better idea. As part of your Christmas project, I'm going to set you homework. I took you to a Christmas themed treat on Monday, you have to think of a reasonably priced, preferably free, Christmas activity we can do tonight.

My phone starts beeping so frantically I wonder if it's having a stroke.

Oh

My

God

We

Are

No

Longer

Friends.

See you at seven?

A huge grin crosses my face. He punctuates.

Damn straight. I'll bring you a hat.

———————

Sure enough, as I peek out the window at two minutes to seven, I see Rory's car pull up. That man is nothing if not prompt. It occurs to me that I have seen Rory more than anyone else this week, and each time has been kinda nice, bizarre considering how dull I thought he was at uni.

I grab my hat, scarf and gloves and run down to meet

him, to save him coming out into the cold, and as he opens the car door, there I am jack-in-a-boxing my way around the pavement.

'You're keen.'

'We're going on a Christmas adventure.'

'So you tell me. Are you imagining reindeer rides, penguins and icicles, that sort of thing?'

'Yes!' I bob my head up and down, aware that my answer is more of a squeak than a word.

'You may want to manage your expectations.'

'Never.'

'You've been warned. Do you wanna hop in then? And please, tell me you were joking about the hat.' I boing my way around to the passenger door. It's been a fab few days, I've zoomed from having no job, mad financial worries and being concerned that I wouldn't know what to do with myself now I no longer have my project to work on in the evenings, to having lots of jobs, a whole Christmas mission and what is appearing to be a social life, albeit only with one other person. Life is good.

'This is a nice car.' I slide my legs in. This car is what you're meant to drive when you're in your thirties. Luisa and Remi have one each. Whereas if my exhaust isn't hanging on by a bit of emergency wire and there isn't moss growing by my car's windows then it wouldn't feel like mine.

'It's a rental. I'm only here for a month but I wanted to be able to get between here and Bath easily and reliably.'

'What did you come back for?' Ouch, as soon as it's out of my mouth I realise that sounds bad. Blunt old Belle.

Either not thinking before I speak and pissing everyone off or overthinking and then never speaking. At what age are you mature enough to find a happy medium or am I going to be stuck doing this for ever?

Rory slides me a smile and starts the car. We coast through the Bristol traffic, out of Easton, across the city centre, up Whiteladies Road and over The Downs. All the way from my Bristol to posh Bristol.

Slightly embarrassed about my verbal faux pas, and aware of his lack of response, we put the radio on and I *fa-la-la* and *how-still-we-seeeee-theeeee-lie* until the Suspension Bridge comes into view.

It doesn't matter how long I live here, it always makes my heart happy. I love this city at night, all lit up and glittering. I point to it, wondering if Rory shares my awe.

He nods and I can see his eyes light up at this great big architectural wonder. Surely this mark of our city makes every Bristolian proud when they see it, conjuring up feelings of home, of comfort.

'I wondered if I could fly off that once when I had done too much acid.' I break the awe and wonder.

'Of course you did. Luisa is a saint among women. I assume she was the one who stopped you.'

'Uh-huh.' I nod my assent and look across at him again. He really does have quite a nice nose. 'I'm not going to do it tonight though. I'm more grown-up now. I'll never take that again. Last time, Dementors chased me up the stairs.'

'Glad to hear it. Not about the Dementors obviously, *that's* terrifying.' He pulls up by one of those old kerbs by the bridge, the ones that are super narrow and have two steps to them and also make my heart happy.

'Right? Proper scary. I had to choose between giving up reading or giving up LSD...' I pause and flick him a look under my eyelashes and see him grin quickly before composing his face into serious again.

'Mmm, I've heard reading can be like that. Makes you delusional and all sorts. Dangerous stuff.'

'Right.' We exchange a grin as we both unclick our seat belts at the same time and get out of the car.

'I think I'm going to like my Christmas surprise.' I'm genuinely enthusiastic as I glance over the roof at him, silvery in the glow of the streetlamp. He locks eyes with me and again I'm struck by the greenness of his. Even in the dark of a December evening.

'Good,' he says, the brilliance of his eyes not matched by his vocabulary.

He starts to walk away from the bridge. 'Hang on, aren't we going across it?' I squeak.

'Based on what you just told me, no. It's freezing cold, let's get somewhere warm.'

'Freezing. This is nothing. You should have been out at 5.45 yesterday morning. That was cold. I thought my nipples were going to freeze off.' What is wrong with my idiot mouth? Why, *why* would I say the word nipple to Rory Walters? God, just gobble me up now, free me from my stupidity. I raise my eyes heavenward, just in case he's listening and prepared to beam me up.

'You had your nipples out in this weather?' Rory doesn't seem anywhere near as mortified as I am; that's good.

'What on earth were you... No, don't tell me.' He holds up his hands. 'I don't think I want to know.'

Non-judgemental but with firm boundaries. I wonder if he gives lessons.

'So where are we going?' Changing the subject is a good move. He must be rubbing off on me.

'I thought we could have my work's night out. That's Christmassy, there's really only me so you're doing me a favour by keeping me company, and as my treat, it's free. You could go the whole hog and have a Christmas Dinner.'

I can't help myself, my eyebrow raises at a 45-degree angle. My body parts have always been disobedient. 'This is your work's night out?'

'Uh-huh. Although if you could keep the pity from your voice that would be great.'

'Sorry. Kinda slipped in there.'

'Said the bishop to the actress.'

'Oh my God, you make dad jokes.'

'But only the best ones. Will try not to do it again.'

'Right, come back into the 2020s.'

'Hmm, they've not been great so far.' That is certainly the truth.

'But tonight will be, come on let's get you to the food.'

'I do like food.'

The food is good, the view of the bridge is outstanding but the atmosphere a little stuffy. I itch to jump on the table and do a dance of the seven veils with the heavy linen napkins, but I practise self-restraint and Rory and I chat about what a nightmare Dad is – a subject I can blather on about for hours.

'I've never talked like this about a client before and it's so unprofessional of me, especially as he is your father, but he is driving me up the wall. He doesn't listen to anything...' I nod archly. That's the absolute truth. 'He's happy to pay for my advice but then refuses to take it, and I would love it if I could roll up my sleeves and just take the cash but it'll impact my professional reputation too. He tweets drunk...'

'Yeah, I'm not surprised. Drink is a real thing in my family. Drinking is fun and they despise anything they see as dull, like Shakespeare. They veer from telling me that I'm irresponsible one minute and too dull the next when I don't join in. I gave up trying to work it out years ago. But when they drink, they're not nice.'

'Uh-huh, I think I'm beginning to realise that. Your father has started an online war with a reporter by threatening to punch out his "millennial snowflake arse" the next time he sees him ... and have you seen the article he wrote for today's *Express*? I wrote a statement for him, accepting the blame for his behaviour and outlining the steps he was going to take to change, and then boom, I open up the article this morning and it's unrecognisable. He has blamed everything on today's society. No personal responsibility... Sorry. It is your dad I'm ranting about.' Rory calms his tone.

'Ah, trust me, you ranting about him is by far the least of my worries and you're not saying anything that's not true.

I'm sorry you took him on, but at the same time not sorry because now we're friends.' I don't pause there but speed up, so he doesn't have time to argue that last point. He feels like a friend and as I've never been someone with a wide social circle, I don't think I'd like it if he corrected me, told me or implied that I was merely an acquaintance. 'But I haven't seen today's piece. After the news that broke last month I adapted my news feed so I see nothing about Dad. I was so saturated, so ashamed, I couldn't bear another story.'

'I can't even begin to imagine what it must be like to have your family's business beamed onto everyone's phone, all the time.'

'Right? People think I'm lucky and I am. But Dad does have his downsides.'

'Yeah.' He places his hands on mine, I can feel that he means it, that he's trying his best to comfort me. This is good, it's kind. It doesn't feel like it comes with an agenda or that I need to whip my knickers down to keep his attention. Maybe I genuinely have a new friend.

'He's an arse, and I don't think he's capable of change as I genuinely don't think he thinks he's ever in the wrong. He's a shocking narcissist and he can't cope if people don't share his viewpoint or see him as anything less than perfect. I think that's why he lashes out at me, because I struggle to pretend I think anyone is wholly perfect. It's Mum I feel for; Rose and I, we're out. I used to wish she'd go too. She did once before, when we were kids, but she came back really quickly. And I can't see her ever leaving now, although she has openly cheated a couple of times. They're both as bad as each other, to be honest, and I think, despite how dysfunctional they are, they're kind of co-dependent. Each needs the other and dearly loves them in their own messed-up way.'

'She left without you?'

'Yeah.' He keeps his face straight but I wonder if he is thinking, what kind of mother leaves her kids? Truth is, when I was a child I thought that too but now I realise things are more complex than that. Women are their own people, not a homogenous mass of adoring motherhood. Some feel bound, restricted by their children; it doesn't make them less of a woman, any more than it does those who choose not to have children at all. I think it's unfair the way society condemns them just because they find their children a pressure or don't want to be defined by motherhood.

'I understand,' I say. 'Their relationship is bizarre; it veers from toxic to sort of sweet. She probably decided she couldn't be a great mother until she got herself strong, away from him, straighter in her head. When she learnt to love herself, only then could she love her children the way she wanted to. My concern, ' I say, rationalising it, 'is that rather than the fiery woman I remember from my childhood, these days she seems frozen and I wonder if she'll ever be able to find the fire to stand up to him again.'

It's funny how you can see all the reason, all the theory, laid out bare on the table, see why they are the way they are. You can see how much they are hurting as individuals and not want that for them but the impact still feels pretty personal and hurts badly. It's hard at times; adult me –

public me – may manage to be rational about it all but there is still a part of me, child me, that wants to scream and shout about the lack of fairness. I know it's the way that my parents have treated me – compounded by the fact that when Rose came along she slotted in perfectly, their behaviour making her a competitor rather than a team mate – that has shaped the way I view myself. That has made it difficult – no, impossible – for me to commit, for me to be attracted to anyone that I may want to commit to. I am forever haunted with the feeling of not being good enough, of knowing I consistently fail to please, and for all my adult perspective I don't know how to change that. I don't know how to dig inside deep and recognise that I am okay, I'm not that bad. That there are positives in who I am. I often wonder if I ever will.

'That's very reasonable of you.' Rory smiles a half smile and then changes it quickly as if he knows I do not want to be pitied, that being pitied is something I have no control over, rather like Mum leaving, and makes me feel small and by its very nature – despite the good intentions – pitiable. 'So, tell me, how did you get consumed by this overwhelming love for Christmas?'

God bless him.

'Well that's easy…' I start to tell of how Christmas had exploded for me since I was a teen and had been sent away to boarding school and met Luisa. One year she took me back to Germany for Christmas and showed me that her Christmas was fun, sparkles, argument-free, everything the adverts promise it is and that I had never seen.

As the waiter brings us our second course, I tease Rory

about how ordering seabass is selling out the whole Christmas theme and I realise that I have never been taken to dinner in a place like this by any boy I have ever dated. Sam had regularly dragged me to Kings Kebabs, which, if you could weave your way through the crowds of fighting Neanderthals, had been quite tasty, but linen napkins, crumbers and heart-pounding views have never been on the menu before. And it isn't the money spent, it's the sentiment, the implication that to Rory, as his friend, I am worth it. And as I look at those green eyes, that face as it roars with laughter as I recount one of my Christmas pasts, I realise there is a lot more to Rory Walters than I remember.

But come what may, I do adore thee so
That danger shall seem sport, and I will go.

December Tenth.
Rory.

'This is so dull,' Mum says as she lifts the corner of what I think is a perfectly acceptable nightgown in Marks and Spencer. 'Is this really all there is to life? Is this what it is all about? Shopping for nightgowns?' She sighs and rolls her eyes, giving both Kevin and Perry a run for their money.

Woah, I thought this was her idea of heaven. 'Mum, you've always loved Marks and Sparks.' When I was small, she would've shrieked with excitement at the thought of being able to afford to shop here. A cup of coffee and a slice of cake that we would share in the café on the top floor were a monthly treat for years, well before she could actually buy anything in here. Riding up in the lifts as a child with her would be the pinnacle of the month for the both of us. 'What about these?' I hold out something cotton and lemon yellow. I know nothing about nightwear for the post-menopausal woman but it looks okay. To be fair, I know nothing about nightwear for the pre-menopausal woman either.

'Oh my God, Rory! I'm not ninety.'

What is going on? When I offered to come, we were meant to be shopping for something nice for her operation.

A grown man shopping for lingerie with his mother is not a look I am going for, ever.

Desperately I pull out another – a cotton gown, quite short – and pray.

'Look, I don't mean to be ungrateful, I really don't.' She chucks me under the chin as if I am six, even though these days she has to reach up to do it. 'It's kind of you to come with me. I never dreamed I'd get to do this with you. You know, not once I realised you liked girls.'

'Eh? Mum. When did you not know I was straight?'

'Well, I wasn't sure there for a bit, there was that stage you had, you know with the black nail polish and the what do they call it... Ooh, excuse me,' she grabs a passing shop assistant, 'can you help me? What do they call it when men wear make-up, dear?'

'Drag,' the girl replies. 'I bet you look beautiful with those eyes. What's your drag name?' she asks me.

'Um...' What the hell do I say? Whilst I may enjoy the odd episode of *RuPaul's Drag Race*, I'm not in the habit of tucking and donning sequins on a weekend. No problem with it, just not how I spend my leisure time. That would be the correct answer. But all I do is stand here, mouth open and say um repeatedly. Clearly won't be winning any challenges for quick wit.

'No, no, not that. Just eyeliner?' Mum interrupts, sort of saving me, sort of not.

'Oh, okay. Guyliner? We stock it on the first floor.'

'Yes, that's the one, that. Thank you, love.' She pats the girl's arm, her early petulance disappeared and full-on mumness back in play.

'That's okay. That would look great on you.' She smiles and she heads to tinker with a display very nearby.

'That. Guyliner and the nail varnish. Then.' Mum nods with satisfaction.

'Mum, that was once, once when I was thirteen for Halloween. I don't think that is the perfect snapshot to assess sexuality.'

'Oh, I didn't mind. I mean Janet's son, older than you, he goes shopping with her all the time. He took her to Ann Summers.'

No.

I love her but I am *not* taking her to Ann Summers. I'll never be able to have sex again. I may have currently forgotten what sex is like, but I'm hoping one day in my future, when I feel less broken, I'll dabble again. Ann Summers is most definitely *not* happening.

'And now they can have children and go shopping, well, it's a win-win, isn't it?'

'I don't think "they" is a term anyone uses about *any* group in society these days, Mum. Pretty reductive and prejudiced.'

'Hmpf, the only thing I'm prejudiced against is these bloody things.' She flips through a rail at lightning speed, somehow managing to tut, flick and speak all at the same time. And I know that her words are true. I've spent my life watching my mum be open and kind and generous with every single person she has ever come into contact with. 'I just told you, I was quite excited about the fact that you may be gay. Mind you, that's old hat these days, isn't it? I watched a documentary on Netflix. It's all about pan these days, isn't it, love? Are you pan? Best of all worlds it seems to me.'

Dear Jesus Christ, I swear if there is anything worse than your parents becoming unintentionally but increasingly out of the loop as they get older, it has to be them intentionally trying *not* to be, over a nightdress rail in the middle of M&S. I can feel the whole department's eyes on me. It's clear that it isn't just my mum that wants to know.

'Tell you what, why don't we go and get a cup of coffee?'

'I've got a better idea…' she said. I close my eyes and pray. If she suggests what I think she will, I'm going to kill Janet's son.

'Let's go to House of Fraser.'

Now my mum isn't mean by any shot, she's the most generous woman I know. *But* she is the queen of frugality – she uses her teabags twice – and has always had very firm views on the sort of people that shop in House of Fraser. Views that aren't always very kind, which often reference Margaret Thatcher, and are another example of her lumping a whole band of people together in one box.

Normally the thought of even looking inside the three-floored department store in Cabot Circus would be enough to bring her out in hives, and now she wants to go there to buy herself something? This is most bizarre. However, if she wants to treat herself to something a little bit more luxurious for her op, then I am all for it.

This excursion has been triggered by her talking about her hospital trip – *'If they think I'm wandering around Southmead Hospital with my bottom hanging out, they've another think coming. There'll be men all over the place ready to take photos and load it up on the internet. Janet dated a porter from up there once and well, the things she said...'*

Janet has a lot to answer for.

Ten minutes later we're in House of Fraser and she's tutting at the price tags. Despite being in Beelzebub's den she seems full of the next-level joy that she usually only gets when her strawberry meringue sponge – a cake of a devilish nature – turns out right.

'Would you look at this – £120 for a sleep set. What's a sleep set? It's just pyjamas with less fabric.' She tuts.

My phone beeps and I pull it out and look at the screen. It's Chad Charles, the latest loud-mouthed boy to catapult to reality fame who had posted some stupid stuff on Twitter years ago. He can wait. This is Mum's time.

She grins. 'Ooh, but look at this...' She picks up a silk nightie. It's long and has proper sleeves – she's had concerns about the tops of her arms for years, even though they just look like arms to me – and is in the palest pink. 'Ooh, you'd feel like a princess in this. Imagine waking up with this on.' Then her tone changes, becomes less enchanted-garden, steelier. Hmmm. 'I'm going to try it on.' She hasn't even glanced at the price tag.

'Go for it. I think that's a good idea.' I nod encouragingly. She's still using a whole load of Timotei she stockpiled about the time I was born. This sort of unfettered spending is uncharted territory.

'Yup. And you're going to wait over there.' She points to the exit.

'Really?' Is she scared in case I see a slip of her in silk? Yeah, actually, I can wait over there.

I stand right by the side of the door – doing as I am told – when my phone beeps again. Honestly, celebrities and their need for constant hand-holding. I've already written a statement of apology for Chad and told him to slowly give out money to charities, pitch in, do some good and refrain from posting about it on social media. He should be doing good because he bloody can and somehow it will get known about. Self-serving, I know, but you have to work within the realities of life and human nature. And at least some charities get huge chunks of cash out of it.

It isn't Chad.

I've just got a phone call from Greenbank Primary School. They wondered if I could cover a cancellation for tomorrow.

A smile covers my face, ear to ear. This is great news. I can imagine how happy this must make her. I see her face in my mind, excited.

Wow. Can you?

Of course. I'll have to make it Christmas themed which is trickier than you'd think and somehow make it suitable for infants but yeah!

This is great news. I'm so pleased for you.

Thank you. I wanted to let you know.

Will you let me know how it goes?

Of course.

I start to type *Shall I come and help you research* ... which I know is stupid, there's hardly anything I can add to the discussion, but sometimes having company is fun. And then my mind flashes to this morning.

I delete the message.

I had a dream about Belle Wilde last night, not some teen dream but one where she had very much been in it and as my girlfriend. We'd been going on some wild goose chase and I couldn't remember exactly what for or where, or even the point of it; there was something about tinsel and chickens and cupcakes, but I knew from the way I felt that everything was all right because we were together.

Honestly, it freaked me out.

It still is.

I made a conscious decision after Jessica that I was better off on my own, even after allowing myself time for grieving and healing. That level of involvement is not good for anyone. I want to be by myself and I never want anyone to hurt as badly over me as I did over her. That way I can keep myself safe. I can keep everybody safe.

I carry a lot of guilt over her death. I know that I wasn't responsible for the weather that night, that I wasn't driving the car, but there is something that makes me feel that it all could have been avoided. That I should have stopped it, that it wouldn't have happened at all had I behaved differently. Either on that night or the months preceding.

Growing up alone with Mum, having been abandoned by my biological father, meant that I was a very responsible child and that carried on into adulthood. I'm proud of that, that's the type of man I want to be. But there are two edges to that particular sword and I never ever want to be in the position again where I can impact someone's life so badly that it results in such levels of pain. Jess was lashing out and trying to escape from me that night. So it is better for everyone if I just stay by myself.

Rational me reminds me that Belle Wilde is exactly what her name implies, she's beautiful and a little too feral for me to handle. We are far from compatible. The picture of a fox pings into my mind again as does an awareness that I may be being over-harsh, judging the Belle I once knew, not the one I've met recently. The mind is the most bizarre thing, it seems to be able to hold several conflicting opinions at once and be fine with them all. It's exhausting. The one thing I am sure of is that Belle Wilde and I might be best off with a bit of distance. It has to be safer that way. Stop my mind imagining it wants things that I really don't. Although I am pleased about her school booking, that is gr— What the actual…?

'Run, Rory, run!'

My mother streaks past me at speed and as she does so an alarm starts going off.

'Run, you daft bugger!' She hurls the words at me over her shoulder as she pegs it out of the House of Fraser, a silky-looking skirt billowing out from under her winter coat.

I run.

There's so much security in Cabot Circus, how the hell does she think she's going to get away with this? They're bound to stop us before we even reach JD Sports. I catch up with her and shout across.

'What on earth?'

'Don't talk, slows you down. Run!'

'Oi!' I turn my head and sure enough there are two Cabot security guards chasing behind us. They're still right by House of Fraser and we're dashing past Timberland. We might be able to do this, get out of the mall, but where then?

I'm careful not to outpace Mum; my heart and feet are pounding, my adrenaline in full flood. I need to hang back just a little so, worst-case scenario, she can get away and I can distract the guards. How has this become today's plan?

For a small woman who, as far as I know, never does any cardio or gym, she sure as hell can run in the moment.

She's ahead now, round the corner of the shopping centre, and then runs up to the number 5 bus as it's driving off, bashing on the door. The driver stops and opens the door, at which point she grabs me and hurls us both on, shouting,'Drive, drive' as if she's in some kind of heist movie. Within seconds we're down the road, sailing through the green lights as the red-faced security guards come out of Cabot, pausing to see which way we have gone.

'What … the … hell, Mum?' I pant, holding onto the pole on the bus to steady me.

'Now that, Rory…' she says, sat on the chequered bus seat, smoothing down a very expensive silk nightie, now fully out and hanging over her trousers, 'now that's what I call living.'

To business that we love we rise betimes
And go to't with delight.

December Eleventh.
Belle.

I stand on the stage next to delicious Mr Latham. The plan is to deliver a brief five-minute hello in front of the whole school and then get cracking. For all my social anxieties I had always thought that talking about Shakespeare was the one thing that could never scare me.

I was wrong.

I'm standing in front of a whole school and I'm proper terrified!

There are about two hundred and fifty pairs of eyes on me. On me! I'm not prepared for this. Shakespeare to secondary schools, bring it on. Primary school children, not so much. And Shakespeare and Christmas! Christmas is the one thing he *didn't* bloody write about at length.

'Let me pass you over to the woman that knows all things possible about the Bard, we're very lucky to have her at such short notice, Miss Wilde.'

I smile, take a deep breath, and go with bluff-it-don't-fluff-it.

'Thank you. Hello, school. I'm so happy to be here, with the lovely Mr Latham…' A titter runs through the children, some of the mums nod in agreement and I feel the blush spread up my neck, and across my face, matching the deep red of the Elizabethan dress I'm wearing today to give my talk. I plough on. 'When Mr Latham asked me to come and talk about my favourite storyteller of all time, how could I say no? The truth is, I'm not sure if any of you have heard of this guy. Hands up if you've heard of Shakespeare before, any of you? Okay.' All of Year Six have their hands up, with a woman sat to the side of them looking suitably, and rightfully, smug and about twelve others. 'That's okay. Truth is, he won't have heard of you guys either. Do any of you know why that is?'

'He's dead, Miss.'

'That's the one right there. He lived when people dressed like this so he has been dead for some time. You don't see people wearing this in Asda, do you?' I run my hands up and down my costume.

'You might in Bedminster, Miss,' a voice shouts out. I fight the laughter; that's true enough. All sorts goes on there.

'I'll tell you, it's not that comfy. It's easier to breathe in jeans and a jumper.' I love this dress, want to be buried in it, but Ariana had laced it so tightly this morning, I think she muddled me with one of her clients – certainly halfway through the lacing I wished I had come up with a safe word. 'And when Shakespeare lived he wrote thirty-seven plays, thirty-seven! And even more sonnets, one hundred and fifty-four of those, that's a huge number. Sonnets are poems and we're going to talk about those later but when it comes to Christmas, out of all those plays and poems he only mentioned it three times. That's all.' I hold up three fingers to reinforce the point and catch a glimpse of Mr Latham's really?-oh-I'm-sorry face and can't help but smile. 'But that is not going to stop us now. Oh no. We're going to spend the day looking at this amazing man, looking at some of the stories he told, looking at how people celebrated Christmas when he was alive, and generally have a day packed full of loads of fun. And I can tell you, I am so excited. I cannot wait to meet you all.' And I curtsy. Of course I do, because who wouldn't wearing a dress like this, having finished a speech whilst standing on a stage? Looks like my dad's sense of showmanship hasn't completely skipped the next generation after all.

A few hours later, I'm sat in the hall on one of those little PE benches, legs akimbo and not exactly looking the picture of Elizabethan decorum. It may be December but I'm as sweaty as a pig in July. I have spent this morning with the little ones; we dressed up as kings and queens, fairies, donkeys, bears, Roman generals, witches, soldiers, and put on plays. We made our own Tudor Christmas decorations from ivy and pine, we spiced and honied and drank our own communal wassail (apple juice – even with my slightly shitty adherence to social conventions I know ale in a primary school is a no-no) and we talked about *Twelfth Night* and watched the British Council's amazing short animation of it. This afternoon I have done a little more in-depth work with the older ones; we talked about themes in *Twelfth Night* and tried to do a scene or two with cue scripts, not an easy task but hilarious and a great insight into Elizabethan theatre. But right now, all that leaping about in this dress means if I sweat any more I'll be able to fit into those trousers I bought four years ago and so far have not managed to get more than half a thigh into. Do people still pass out from exhaustion in the twenty-first century? Are smelling salts kept in first-aid boxes these days?

I have an hour left to go and truth is whilst I'm dehydrated, exhausted and broken I am so high. This has been amazing. I'm literally living my dream and the kids are so receptive, more so than in my wildest imaginings. I'd worried like mad when I had been asked to deliver a workshop for each age group on Shakespeare with practically zero preparation time and the knowledge that Shakespeare didn't really ever reference Christmas, much to the dismay of modern-day directors looking for a sure-fire festive box-office draw. But I've done it. I don't want to get carried away but I think I've done it quite well.

'Are you okay?' Mr Latham kneels down beside me. 'Can I get you anything? A glass of water?'

'No, no, I'm fine,' I say, trying to sit up straight and knowing it would be deeply inappropriate to ask him to loosen my stays.

'I wanted to come and let you know how enthused the children are, they can't wait for you to come back, so I'll definitely be asking you to come and do more workshops in summer, if that's okay with you?'

'Oh, wow, yes, of course it is. I'd love to.'

'And I'm so sorry I asked you to do Christmas. I'm no expert, it didn't occur to me that Shakespeare didn't write lots about it.'

'No worries. It was just a matter of tying what I could to

the Christmas theme and bringing in Tudor and Jacobean Christmas ideas. I enjoyed it.' I don't mention I had been awake and anxious half the night .

'Well, so did the kids. And I have another proposition for you. Shift up.' He stands from kneeling and indicates he wants me to move along the bench for him to sit down. I try to control my breath, aware that the Tudor neckline means my bosom is heaving frenetically. The man is going to think I have some kind of sexual disorder at this rate.

'It wasn't just me that got caught out by the entertainer's cancellation today. We're part of an academy trust and all the other schools did as well. There's six of us in total and obviously I didn't want to say anything until I had seen you in action – I needed to be sure that you could deliver – but having seen your work today and chatting to other members of staff, I was wondering if you'd be willing to step into the breach again? Each of the schools had the same entertainer booked for a day next week as we did. That's five days, right up until the end of term. Are you free to take those slots too? What do you think?'

This is not helping my heartbeat. This is more exciting than the thought of a filthy proposition. I have two shifts at the shop next week, but they're lates and if I can get someone to cover me for the first hour I should make it. I'll be shattered at the end of the week and possibly never be able to stand again, but five full day's work, doing this. Oh yes!

'Oh, and I've told them all you charge £250 a day, which they're happy to pay because the insurance for the cancelled entertainer will cover it.'

'Oh ... wow ... oh ... of course.'

'Of course?' He doesn't look like he is convinced.

'Yes. Yes, of course!' I say, my enthusiasm clear now my initial shock is waning. 'Yes, that's incredible.' I want to high-five him but am too scared that the sweat patches under my arms will knock him out. Five days' work! I knew this dress would be an investment.

———

So how did it go?

Oh. My. God.

Good OMG or evil bad OMG?

So good. So, so good.

I'm glad. Want to meet up and do something Christmassy?

I can't. I think I may be dead.

Texting well for a dead person.

Dead any minute. Exhausted. But guess what, I've been hired for a full week for the rest of the schools within the Academy Trust.

No way. I'm so pleased. Well deserved. I knew you'd be brilliant.

Thank you.

We have to celebrate.

Can't, told you. Practically dead and I still have my other jobs. Need to be up at half five again tomorrow. But if you're desperate to see me, and I can tell you are, I'm spending the rest of the day tomorrow babysitting Marsha. You can come meet us at Luisa's if you like.

I can do that. Afternoon okay? Have to do mum stuff in the morning. And boy do I have tales to tell you.

Afternoon all good. And look forward to it. x

Cool. Go die in peace. Sees ya tmrw. X

You have dancing shoes
With nimble soles. I have a soul of lead.

December Twelfth.
Rory.

'Should she be eating that?' I'm at Belle's dining table surrounded by pine-tree-shaped sequins, fake snow and enough glitter to give Rudolph a stroke. All compounded by some kind of Disney Christmas sing-along playlist. Less than a week ago I would have sworn on my life this would not be how I chose to spend a weekend.

'Probably not. Don't eat the dough, Marsha.' Belle winks and rolls a tiny bit of dough between her fingers and pops it in her mouth.

'Seriously? You're shocking.'

Marsha takes a huge wodge of the stuff and licks the length of it as she holds my eyes and smirks.

A laugh bursts from Belle and she clasps her hand over her mouth before putting on her serious face. It's very cute. I'm aware I am not doing well at the keeping-my-distance thing. I have tried but I spent the whole of yesterday wondering how her first workshop in a school had gone. I couldn't not reach out and find out, that would have been mean, and then before I knew it I was here.

'To be fair, he's right. I promised your mum I wouldn't let you eat it again, she's worried you'll cease to have a working kidney after last year, and you promised me, 'member? We have a deal. It's naughty of me to tease Rory like that. Neither of us should be eating the dough.'

'Yes, I know. But it tastes good.'

'No, it tastes bad. You're just a little toad. I promise not to eat any more if you do too. Shake.'

'Shake.' Marsha reaches out and shakes Belle's hand. Belle winces and pretends she's being forced down onto the floor with the strength of it, as Marsha's glee at her power bounces off the walls. I can't help but join in with the laughter.

'Plus,' Belle says as she clambers back up from the floor, 'no one wants your spitty lick for Christmas. Especially not after last year. You best put that there...' Belle wiggles a finger at the bit of salt-dough in question '...right in the bin.'

Marsha shrugs and lobs it into the bin from where she's sitting before turning back to model another indecipherable shape and sing 'Frosty the Snowman' at the top of her voice.

'I know it's bad but it won't kill her. At least I hope not. I made the dough myself using cornflour and bicarb. I learnt my lesson with the salt after last year. Mind you, I used to eat bags of the real stuff. My nursery teacher used to double the salt in an attempt to stop me eating it and it still didn't work. My mum said that, along with my insistence on dancing with my skirt over my head, it marked the start of me embarrassing her.'

'Your mum really knows how to boost a child's self-esteem.'

'Oh yes, she's the queen of it, although, in her defence, I don't think she does it on purpose. It's kind of a chain reaction – Dad is vile to her, she passes it on. Luisa has always said that the reason I pick duff men is because I'm scared of long-term relationships and that I'll turn into my mother so I deliberately choose ones I know I will never commit to.'

'Interesting. Luisa is a wise woman – do you think it's true?'

She makes a funny shape with her mouth and shrugs her shoulders. I suspect that she probably does. She turns to Marsha. 'Hey, our song is coming up next. You almost done?'

Marsha wodges a vast amount of glitter on to her decorations, pummels it in and then grins up at her godmother as if butter wouldn't melt. 'Done. Ready.' She jumps down from her chair as Belle pushes hers back. Belle turns up the volume of her laptop that's feeding the speakers. What fresh hell is coming?

A very jingly version of 'Jingle Bells' starts to play as Marsha puts her two hands up in front of her and starts to bounce around the room. Belle shoots me a grin, one chock full of mischief, and raises her hands as well.

'Paws' is her one-word explanation and the two of them throw themselves into pogoing around the room, screeching tunelessly about one-horse open sleighs.

'Tigger!' roars Marsha as she bounce-bounce-bounces.

I kind of want to join in. Me – a grown-up who has never pogoed like Tigger before in my life, probably not even when I was five! I raise a paw to see how it feels when they both have their backs to me and it feels weird. There's no way I can propel myself off this chair and participate properly. I guess that's okay, not everyone can do the same things, and clearly pogoing like a Tigger at Christmas is something I'm a little too buttoned-up to do.

'That was so fun.' Marsha flops back onto her chair when the song is over, picks up a bit of salt-dough, looks at Belle and puts it down again. 'So fun. Phew. What are we doing next?'

'Well, I was going to keep it as a surprise but ... look out the window...'

'It's snowing!'

'It is.'

'You made it snow for me, you're so clever! Can we go outside?'

'I'm not that powerful, the snow isn't made by me, little bear. But we're definitely going to go outside.' For a moment there feels like there is no one in the room but her and Marsha; the air is thick with shared camaraderie, a love crazy, strong and intense as they look at each other.

The moment breaks as Belle turns to me and smiles. 'We're going to Tyntesfield to sit in a horse and carriage!' She turns her attention back to the child. 'I couldn't get you a sleigh but Marsha, a horse-drawn carriage does await. You up for that?'

'Oh my gosh, yes, yes! I love horses, loooovee them.'

'And you? Do you looooovvvvveeee horses, Rory? You're welcome to come and join us if you can bear this much Christmas rammed into one day?'

'Oh do come, come with us. It's gonna be so fun. There's gonna be a *horse*.' Marsha tugs on my sleeve and is still bouncing up and down, her eyes big.

'Do come. If you're not busy. It's Tyntesfield so no flashing lights, it'll be a Victorian Christmas.' She winks. 'We'll do the horse-drawn carriage thing and then we can have a quick wander around the house, what do you think?'

'I think you'll have me wearing a tinsel crown and raving to "Last Christmas" before the day is out.'

'Good call. Gotta love a bit of George. Do you know "Last Christmas" is the most remixed Christmas song? I tell you what, if you're still up for it we can drop into Lakota tonight and dance the night away.'

'I'm a smidge too old for Lakota.'

'Yeah, probably. I'm not though.' And she winks at me again. Cheeky cow.

'Horses!' Marsha screams from the middle of the living room.

'Yeah, okay. We're coming. You coming?'

'I'm coming,' I say with a grin.

'Can we go and see Temperance in the shop first? I like Temperance. She always stares at me really hard with this cross face on and tells me the devil comes for little girls who don't behave and then I promise to behave and keep the devil out and she gives me treats. I'll try and get you some mango this time, Belle. It's easy to do because Belle says the devil doesn't really exist so I just have to say yes, look good and get the treats.'

'Strong work, Marsha.'

'What's your favourite fruit? I'll see if I can get you one. Last time she made the sign of a cross, that's what Belle said she was doing. I reckon if I do that and promise to keep the devil out I'll get double treats. What do you think, Belle?'

Belle high-fives her as she finishes tying Marsha's scarf around her neck, plonks her hat on tight and then gets herself into her coat and mittens.

'Seriously?' I whisper as she opens the flat door and Marsha runs down the stairs. 'You're encouraging her to fleece the local Christians?'

'Yep, and next year I'll teach her how to rob a mosque. No, of course not. I'm teaching her to stare fear in the face. Local Christian Temperance may be, but she's terrifying, I tell you. That firm look Marsha told you about, she could flay human skin from every heathen within a five-mile radius with that stare alone. Terrifying. You wait and see. You'll feel like falling to your knees and confessing every possible sin you've ever committed. Trust me. I'm just teaching Marsha life skills and not to be scared by people that threaten children with the devil coming for them. The devil is not coming for my beautiful goddaughter!'

'Nope, nope, he's not,' I say. 'He's got his hands full with you.'

Belle.

We park at Tyntesfield and walk up to the house. The National Trust property is even more popular at this time of year and there are people everywhere.

'It's so busy,' Rory says. 'I haven't been here for ages, probably not since I was a kid and my grandmother brought me and mum here for my mum's birthday. A theatre company were playing and we sat in the grounds and had a picnic and I couldn't get my head around that a house this big was just for one family to live in.'

'That's pretty cute. I think I'd like your mum.'

He gives me a look. 'I think the two of you would get along. In fact, recently she has been showing some very Belle tendencies. Have I told you about House of Fraser?'

'No, you hinted but didn't tell the full story. Come on … spill!'

'It's snowing, you two – why are you taking so long?' Marsha interrupts us.

'She's her mother's daughter.' I smirk at Rory.

'I want to see the horses. Let's skip! We'll get there quickly then. Everything's better with skipping.' Rory doesn't look as if he's sure, but Marsha isn't taking any prisoners. She grabs his hand then mine and then skips, dragging us with her. I skip whereas Rory looks uncomfortable. So I give him a look that says he doesn't need to worry about it.

'Hey, Marsha, look at me.' I stop and stick my tongue out to catch snow. I may not be a parent yet but I already boss using distraction as a technique. 'It's melting on my tongue. It's melting. You try it, go on.'

Marsha stops skipping and sticks her tongue out too and nods to Rory with her fiercest do-it look on, brows furrowed. Rory immediately sticks his tongue out.

'It feels weird, doesn't it.' She looks up at his face, assessing whether he feels the same as she does. 'They don't last as long as ice-creams.'

'I think catching snow is even more magical than ice-cream. It whispers hello on your tongue and then poof, it's gone. Look, try again,' Rory says, poking his tongue out a second time.

Marsha is captivated. 'Poof, it's gone. I'm gonna catch more and more and more.' She runs ahead and Rory and I exchange a glance, both of us still with our tongues out. That thing about whispers was cute. He'll make a good dad. Strong, stable, kind.

Woah, where had that come from? I hope he can't read minds.

He waggles his tongue at me.

'Can I put it back in my mouth now?' is what I think he says but it's a little distorted.

'Probably best,' I say, hoping he doesn't know I'm currently having some very non-platonic thoughts. That needs to stop right now. I do not need to be harbouring a crush on Rory Walters. Not even the tiniest, weakest little flame. For a girl that avoids rejection, that would be a soul-destroying infatuation to develop. There is no way in the world this cosmopolitan, successful, kind man would be interested in my own unique brand of chaos.

He puts his tongue away and I breathe a sigh of relief.

Somehow, we're walking close, the gap left by Marsha has closed itself and I can feel him at the side of me. His presence. It's as if it's a being in its own right, hard to define but there, calming, authoritative, a little bit intimidating. Part of it is just the essence of him, I think, a man very much in control, a man who can be relied upon. A man most unlike the majority I have encountered across my life. But it's tied to his physical form too. Rory has always been tall but these days he is a grown-up, filled out, mature, looks like he can build a log cabin with his bare hands. Whoops, my mind seems to be circling back again.

When I first knew him, he was still skinny, boy-like. Although I hadn't noticed it so much at the time. I don't think you do when you're young, everyone looked so grown-up back then. But I had sneakily peeked at his Facebook last night – when I say sneakily and peeked, I mean after my full-on day I got lost in a wormhole that easily spanned ten plus years and took up the majority of my evening.

I learnt a whole lot.

Like how his mum's friend, Janet, is a bit of a wild card.

Like for all of his shyness at university, as a small boy he was really fond of dressing up. His mother has no shame about uploading photos of his childhood and tagging him. I can only imagine how cringe that must be.

Like how cute he was as a teen – he was really gangly there for a bit.

I had committed the cardinal sin of liking a post of him from twelve years ago. And then hitting unlike immediately after.

I swipe a side glance; he looks heavy in thought and I'm hoping that it's because of global poverty or something rather than him working out how to broach the subject of me liking his old pictures

'So, last night I was thinking … um … do you remember…?' Rory stops walking as he speaks. Oh shit, oh shit.

'Snow is so pretty isn't it?' I say gesturing at the picture-perfect snowflakes gently raining down on us, as I attempt to change the conversation.

He looks at me, considering. He is always doing that. I wish I had his powers. I wish I could see into the darkest deepest recesses of his mind, work out what exactly is going on in that big brain of his. Work out exactly what he thinks of me. What he's thinking right now. Rory is hard to read at the best of times, inscrutable. Why is he spending time with me? Can I trust him being here? What's motivating him? Is it tied to my dad or is it me? I realise again I am doubting his friendship, doubting my ability to make friends solely on my own merit. Honestly, at what age will I stop being so insecure? Is this me for life?

'Yes, yes, it is.' He answers the snow question.

'So even though you hate December...'

'Yep, still hate it.' But he says it with a smile rather than murderous loathing.

'You like snow? Your words about the whisper of a snowflake were damn near poetic.'

'Aha, your love for metre and verse must be rubbing off on me.' His eyes crinkle as he replies and I see the beginning of where his crow's feet will start as he ages. In this moment I feel like I want to watch them crinkle forever.

Argh. It's the snow's fault. It makes me all romantic. I'm blaming every Christmas movie ever for this complete misbehaviour of my hormones. Hopefully next week I'll be back to my usual uninterested self.

'But, poetry aside, do you remember, back when we...?' Aha, he's going to be persistent. Of course he is.

'Go on,' I say, wanting to scrunch up my eyes and put my fingers in my ears.

'That time I drove you home and we got a puncture and I thought it would be easy to fix and you buggered off and sat on a gate and smoked a joint whilst I wrestled with it.'

I laugh, relieved that this is his question. 'I do. I was bloody useless, wasn't I?'

'I would never have thought on that day that we'd be traipsing around stately homes together all these years later. And you weren't useless, just young. I imagine if it were to happen now you'd elbow me out of the way and try and get the wheel-nuts off with your teeth!'

'Probably.' I grin and he looks back at me and my tummy flips a bit.

'They're here, they're here. I saw it, there's a whole horse, a *whole* horse, and he's so big. Quick, quick, come on, before they go.' Marsha rounds the corner and pelts at us full speed, the words falling from her mouth neatly changing the conversation, and Rory and I start walking again. I hadn't even clocked that she had disappeared around the corner. How could I? I let her wander around a vast public space with millions of bushes. Millions of bushes that could easily have had murderers sitting inside them, sharpening their knives and practising their scariest looks.

Okay, so she was unlikely to have been kidnapped and killed in the three minutes I've taken my eyes from her, but still it's a reminder not to be remiss about my duties, which are making today super Christmassy for my goddaughter and *not* indulging in unattainable romantic imaginings about this man beside me. Bad, Belle, bad.

Rory.

'You're right, this horse is huge,' I say to Marsha as we round the corner and she stands there looking up at it in awe, its head topped by a weird feathery thing.

'Isn't he handsome, Rory?' Marsha answers me, her words breathless and slow as if she's been placed in front of some kind of magical castle. Which I suppose she has. For the horse is standing in the driveway of Tyntesfield House. A large Christmas tree stands out in front of the house and the pillars of the doorway are wrapped in garlands, interspersed with red roses, in keeping with the red ribbons we had seen bedecking the large shrubs as we drove into the estate. It is pretty Christmassy and, as Belle had promised, pretty Victorian. Tinsel and piped Christmas muzak nowhere to be seen or, thankfully, heard.

'Are you here for the pony ride?' a young woman dressed in Victorian attire, complete with top hat and scarlet tie, asks.

'Yes, we are,' Marsha says quietly, clearly still awed by it all.

'Okay, well then, if you and your family would like to hop up here...' The woman waves us up into the carriage at the back. She isn't addressing either me or Belle individually, but the three of us as a family unit. Belle's cheeks flame and she starts to stammer. I hold out my hand to Marsha to help her up the step and to give Belle a moment or two to stop feeling so embarrassed and then realise that I am just as stung by the words as she is. Not embarrassed – Marsha and Belle would be perfect family – but saddened a little.

As I grew up, I hadn't ever considered not being a father, my determination shaped by my own father's absence and the solidity of Dave to make sure that when I had children, I committed, I was there. For ever. That had been unswerving. And then Jessica. Jessica and I had planned a family; we were going to have three children and they would have golden hair like their mother and laugh and play in the garden of a house we would buy on the outskirts of... Well, that was a dream that never came to fruition. And after Jessica one of the things I have had to make my peace with is the fact that having a family may not be for me after all. If I can feel that much pain, that much hurt after losing Jessica, then how much worse would it be if it had been the woman who had also given me children, if it had been my child... No. That level of loss does not bear thinking about. It is a very good reason for embracing a solitary life.

I need to distract myself. Belle is her normal colour again and as the carriage fills up she pulls Marsha onto her lap. The two of us are now pushed up close together, our thighs touching, our bodies almost overlapping as we squish together.

'Are you excited?' she whispers.

'I am a bit.'

'So am I,' Marsha responds, and I realise the question had been for her. 'Do you think they'll go really fast? I want them to go really fast.'

'I think they'll go at a speed that keeps us all safe but is still quite exciting,' Belle answers. Both Marsha and I look at her, our eyebrows raised. That is not the answer I expect from Belle.

'That doesn't sound fast,' Marsha says.

'It's as fast as Santa goes,' Belle says, nodding firmly, 'and if it's good enough for Santa, then it's good enough for us.'

'That's true,' I say, wanting to back her up. 'Santa is very fast but very safe, wooahh.' We tip forward as the horses start to move off. Marsha wibble-wobbles and then rights herself, satisfaction all across her face.

'Yeehah!'

The ride only lasts five minutes, but Marsha is entranced as we trot through the snow, nodding her head to the clip-clop of the horses' feet on the tarmac.

'That was so fun, so fun,' she says after climbing down from the carriage, stroking the horses' flanks for what seems like an excessively long time as Belle stands staring at her with a crazy amount of love in her eyes and I find myself staring at Belle.

'We could go in the house, see what they have to do that's Christmassy. Get in and warm up for a while, what do you think?'

'Yes.' Marsha's answer is quick, to the point. Belle looks at me.

'Rory?'

'Yeah, I'm keen.'

'Keen?'

'Well, you know, happy to come along,' I say. It's true.

Dave has taken the day off and is taking Mum away for the night as a special treat, although she kept trying to cancel, claiming it was selfish to go away when I was in the UK. The only way I could get her to go was to admit that I was spending the day with a friend. The word 'female' had magical properties. The grin that spread across her face threatened to overwhelm me as she raced up the stairs to pack her bag, shouting over her shoulder that they would be away all weekend and if I wanted them to stay away longer then I just had to text.

I pointed out that I had my own flat in Bath but Mum was adamant that I might want to bring 'your new friend' back here, to see where I grew up, and did she have time to whisk around with the Pledge first? Dave doubling over laughing as she bleached the loo again – just in case – did not help. Neither did me repeatedly (at least five times, maybe more) shouting the word *platonic* up the stairs.

On the upside, despite the fact I will be questioned to death over her deliberate misunderstanding when she gets back, it does mean my weekend is free. And as Christmassy as Tyntesfield is, I've surprised myself with how much I'm enjoying myself today.

I hurry through the front door to find Belle and Marsha already in the large hallway standing around a grand piano with a small group of others whilst a young man in Victorian garb is belting out 'The Twelve Days Of Christmas'z in a deep baritone and with a huge amount of jollity, shaking bells with gusto as he does so. I don't think I could fake that for eight hours a day.

'...And a parsnip in a pear tree,' he booms out to his amused audience. Okay, that's it, I admire him but I can't listen to much more. I'm beginning to have murderous thoughts that include putting those bells somewhere illegal.

There's a great tree to the side of the piano which I examine in detail to avoid concentrating on the song. A song the guests are now beginning to join in with.

'Let me know if you need a silent, darkened room to lie down in,' a voice whispers in my ear and I turn my head to see Belle standing close, her Belle smirk on her face.

'I'll try to struggle through. Although a dark room shouldn't be too hard to find. The amount of dark wood in this house is quite a thing.'

'It is, isn't it? I love it. All those wood carvings and engravings. All this work was done by master craftsmen, the dedication, the excellence. I don't find the darkness of it suffocating, I find it comforting, like a duvet. I can imagine swanning around these rooms at the height of their glory, sighing Victorian heroine sighs as my one true love goes off to fight in the Crimea and I am forced to marry the local landowner who looks like a frog and has seriously impairing digestive disorders. Not that I would necessarily be the daughter of the house...' she adds in a rushed voice. 'I can also picture myself as a kitchen maid, scrubbing like mad on the floors but still sighing for my sweetheart, also off to the Crimea, and trying to avoid the handy nature of the under-butler, Rawlings, who is so greasy he looks as if he would drip on you.'

'You've put quite a lot of thought into this.'

We move away from the piano, following Marsha as her eyes fall upon a small table offering the chance to do colouring in. The girl is very fond of a crayon.

'No thought, that was all spontaneous. It's a gift I have.' She smirks again, and I can't help but grin myself. When she's comfortable with someone she's such a pickle, as my mum would say. Her naughtiness radiates from her, pulling her confidante into a special kind of world.

'Ha! You have the imagination of a doomed romantic,' I say.

'I am a doomed romantic,' she responds and then lets out a little half laugh. 'Although Luisa would say I am a doomed romantic with appalling taste and intimacy issues.'

'Oh, I'm with you all the way on the intimacy issues,' I say, surprising myself that such a statement should fall from my lips. I hadn't realised it was true until I said it. Let's face it, I hadn't even thought it until I said it. But now yes, it's a fair point to make. Maybe Belle Wilde is good for me after all.

'I drawed this for you.' Marsha presses a piece of paper into my hand. It's a picture of a reindeer. 'Ooh, what's that?' She says as her eye catches something and she's off again. I swap a smile with Belle as we trail after her into a large room where there's a woman, again in Victorian dress, with a gramophone playing behind her and a keen smile on her lips as we enter. Bar her, we are the only people in the room.

She is welcoming as she waves us in but I feel the hackles on my neck rise. This is not feeling friendly, this feels trap-like.

'Hello, hello, how are you today?'

'Great, thanks,' Belle answers.

'Christmassy, we've made decorations, done snow tasting, ridden in the horsey carriage and I've just done colouring in,' Marsha informs her.

'You have been busy. And how do you feel about learning to do a dance?'

'Oh, I like dancing, look.' Marsha breaks into some weird dancing style that seems to combine acid house and the Charleston.

'Ooh, yes. I see. Most unusual. Here we like to dance to celebrate Christmas.'

'That's what I'm doing.' Marsha pants, still free-forming with the whole of her heart.

'Yes, I can see. That particular style hasn't caught on here yet. Would you like me to teach you our dance?'

Marsha pauses, 'Hmm, my godmother Belle says you should always be willing to learn new things.'

'She sounds like a very wise woman. Your parents chose well.' She flicks a smile across at us. Oh God, she thinks we're the parents. I'm about to interject when Marsha speaks again.

'Yes, they did. What's this dance then?'

'It's the St Bernard's waltz. Would you like to learn with me? Then Mummy and Daddy can dance with each other.' The woman holds her arms out wide and Marsha goes towards her.

'Oh we're not...' I start to say.

'That would be lovely,' Belle says, that mischief back on her face, a complete reversal of her blushes earlier.

'You have to be joking me,' I mouth as she stands in the centre of the floor and holds her arms out waiting for me to join in, knowing full well that I won't abandon her.

'My mummy and daddy aren't very good dancers, they could probably use some practice. But my Aunty Belle, she is the best dancer, she taught me all my moves.'

'That explains a lot,' I say, reaching Belle who gently taps me on the arm.

'Be kind,' she admonishes.

'I was.' I laugh.

'Shhh!' Marsha shoots over her shoulder.

'Okay, ignore the music for now and we'll learn the steps. Three slide steps towards the window, one two three, then tap, tap, tap.'

I hold Belle and we do our slide steps and tap, tap, tap.

'Two steps back to here then I'll step forward with my left, if you do that as well, sir, and then you step back with your right.'

I step forward and so does Belle.

'Ouch!' I say, picking up my foot and waggling it in the air.

'Oh, you make such a fuss, put your foot down.'

'And two forward and then two more steps back.'

'Ouch! Are you doing this on purpose?'

'No!' she says indignantly. 'I'm not good at formal dancing. Honestly, they tried to kick me out of country dancing at primary because I kept stepping—'

'Shhhhh!' Marsha hisses at us again.

'Sorry.'

'Yeah, sorry!' Belle adds and gives me a fierce look.

'Don't go looking at me like I'm the bad one. You're the one with the rhythm of a demented otter.'

'A demented otter, that's very rude, how dare you... Ooh, what are we meant to be doing now?'

'Sliding, I think. Let me lead.'

'Let you lead, why let you lead?'

'I'm the man, I'm meant to.'

'Let me tell you what I think of the Patriarchy...'

'I don't think Victorian heroines had an opinion on the Patriarchy. Look, tap, tap, tap.' Somehow we're managing to do the dancing thing, with Belle only trampling on my feet periodically and giggling as we do so. The woman restarts the gramophone and we dance. Belle is clearly made for a slightly more modern era.

'You're meant to love dancing,' I hiss at her.

'I do love dancing but I can't find the beat.'

'Here, listen, one two three, one two three, one two three.' I count out the rhythm and she joins in, our feet sliding and stepping and tapping in unison once she masters it.

'We're getting quite good.'

'We are,' I say in return as we glide around the room, lost in the music and with me enjoying the feel of having Belle in my arms, her looking up at me as we both silently mouth the numbers. Half of me wants to pull her close and keep dancing. There's something about having another person so close to me, something I hadn't realised I had missed as much as I have. Somehow this crazy world I now inhabit means that I, Rory Walters, am waltzing around a

Victorian stately home with Belle Wilde in my arms and absolutely loving it.

We keep dancing, both of us caught up in each other's rhythm, only to be jolted out of our little waltzy trance state as I hear the woman who had taught us the dance say in an aside to Marsha, 'That's lovely, isn't it? To see your mummy and daddy so in love.'

Boldness be my friend.

December Thirteenth.
Belle.

Luisa asked yesterday if I'll have Marsha for a few more hours today, not having finished all the Christmas prep she had planned to do whilst child-free yesterday. I'm so keen and with the weather obliging overnight I have the perfect day planned for the two of us. We just need to get a wriggle on before the heat of the sun starts to melt the snow.

I still haven't fully processed how I feel about dancing with Rory yesterday, how I had to break the spell when I heard that woman saying we were Marsha's mummy and daddy to squawk that we weren't. Dancing with Rory, seeing the sinews in his forearms, the way the hair was sprinkled lightly up his arm, had made me feel a bit dizzy. A little bit too lustful for a celibate Saturday afternoon. And way too intimate for my head to be able to cope with. I'm fine being friends with Rory, I'm enjoying it, even. But being that close, that's a step towards a world that isn't going to work for me. The sheer Christmassyness of yesterday had caught me up and made me a little light-headed. Today I know that even the teensiest crush is not to be indulged.

I'm taking my vow of self-respect and celibacy very seriously; a lifetime of dating twats means I absolutely do not want to engage with anyone sexually again unless it's meaningful and the start of a happy, healthy adult relationship. I'm done with sleeping with men who have zero respect or consideration for me, and so far I seem to have failed to find any other type. My sexual judgement has proved itself time and time again to be seriously flawed.

Having said that, I don't want a relationship, not a long-term do-everything-together type of thing, matching anoraks on hallway hooks and so on. I can't begin to imagine how claustrophobic that would be. And certainly not with Rory, who is not my type – even though I recognise I need to break that type thing – but I wouldn't know what to do with a decent man. I'd be on tenterhooks the whole time, worrying that he would go off me real quick rather than *wishing* they would go off me real quick as I am used to. It would get way too stressful.

More importantly I am not his type. I can barely drag a brush through my hair most days and by no stretch of the imagination can I be considered well groomed. I'm not grubby or anything, *obviously* I shower every day – right now I smell like daisies, that's how good I've got with early mornings – I just really can't be arsed with that whole manicure, pedicure, regular hair appointments and matching underwear shite. Not really. I'd rather be comfortable and spend my spare time reading. One only has to look at my mother to see being impeccably groomed does not automatically bring happiness. And Rory, as Jessica was testament to, is a man fond of immaculate grooming. He himself is faultless.

Plus there's the Australia thing, that would mean leaving Marsha behind, twenty-three hours on a plane away rather than fifteen minutes in a car. Nah. Not in a million years could anyone take me away from that girl. She is the vessel into which I pour all my love. I sometimes wonder if I overstep but Luisa doesn't seem to object. It's just that I know Luisa and Remi – as adoring as they are – are busy, successful, a little bit like Rory. And as the daughter of a busy and successful man I know what it's like to be overlooked and I am never, never going to allow that to happen to Marsha. I am staying by her side until she is an adult and only backing off when she needs me to.

I realise I am getting carried away and remind myself of the pertinent facts of the case: it's not about whether I could cope with his lifestyle and the expectations that it would bring. A move to Australia, hah! Getting ahead of myself much? Rory will never ever fancy me, and neither should he. He has seen me at my absolute worst. He has seen me vomiting in the corner at parties, he has reminded me of my lack of practical use in emergency situations, like the day of the flat tyre, he has seen where I come from, the chaos and dysfunction that make up my genes. There is no way in this world someone as responsible, as aware of reputation as Rory is could ever, would ever consider me romantically. And I do not need that hammered home any further than it is by looking at him doe-eyed until he gets embarrassed and imposes distance. I am so much better off staying pressure-free and single. I am so much better off not devoting any energy to even thinking about this. I am so much better off not embarrassing the new friend I have made with this nonsense. And selfishly, selfishly I am far better off protecting myself from the inevitable rejection.

All this is running through my mind as I'm strapping

Marsha into her car seat and as if she is some freaky mini mind-reader and saboteur she asks, 'Is Rory coming?'

'No, I don't think so. Just you and I.'

'Why not?' she persists. And I admit it does feel weird going to do something Christmassy without him. It's funny how quickly you can get used to something new. It won't hurt to ask, I suppose. I'm hardly going to try and sleep with him this afternoon. I can rein in any leftover lust from yesterday and I would love to see him doing what we are about to do. I pull my phone out of my pocket as I slide into the driver's seat. Half of me doesn't expect him to answer, so I nearly drop the phone when he does. His voice is a little bit sleepy, and sexy with it. Damn. I can hardly hang up now.

'Hey. Sorry to ring so early but Marsha and I are off to do something fun. We've got the best day planned. It's not often we get this opportunity and … um … she … I … wondered if you'd want to join us. But it's early, and I imagine you've probably got plans so…'

'Okay. That sounds cool. Shall I come meet you?' sexy sleepy voice murmurs.

Oh shit. Okay, this is fine. It will be good. Good training not to act on lustful instinct. To be new, not-sexually-available Belle. I need to learn to manage crushes when someone is nice to me. It may happen again one day. This will be good for me. I can embed trying not to fancy him. Form new neural pathways and reinforce them with steel.

'No, no. We're in the car and we're going on a magical mystery tour. Our destination is not that far from you so we'll whisk by. Probably be with you in about half an hour.'

'Perfect.'

'Okay … um … wrap up warm. And wear old clothes!' I say, though I bet he doesn't have any old clothes. This can serve as a good reminder of why we would not be well-suited.

'On it! See you in a bit.'

Okay then. He's coming. Marsha cheers and I make a firm resolution to avoid any scenario that could prompt further daydreams.

We speed through the back lanes to Bath. My body is so used to early mornings now it isn't fazed by the fact that it isn't even eight. I feel well rested and alert.

We pull up outside his house, a beautiful Georgian townhouse in the middle of Bath, and I send a message to say we're here. I want to get moving before the roads get busy, the snow melts, or loads of people have the same idea as me and ruin the crisp virginity of the snow.

Rory comes out of his house looking dozy but gives me a heavy-lidded half smile that does weird things to my tummy. Balls. This man is so gorgeous and he is my friend. Seeing him in the flesh puts paid to all my 'I can't have a crush' nonsense. He is *super* cute first thing in the morning.

'Hey. Morning.' He slides into the car and smiles a hello. Marsha waves frantically at him and then pops her headphones back on to listen to her audiobook.

'I can't believe there's even more Christmas stuff to do.' He rolls his eyes and faux groans.

'This is the best, promise. Although those clothes don't look particularly old.' I give him a stern glare whilst feeling a little smug inside.

'The oldest I've got with me.'

'Hmm, I've got a hoodie that's probably big enough in the boot and some trackies you can borrow too.'

'You want me to borrow your clothes?'

'When you say it like that it sounds weird. I didn't mean it like that!'

'Oh, you want to lend them to me but for me not wear them, just carry them around. Hmm, little bit kinky for dawn on a Sunday morning. I may have to tell Temperance.' Rory had met Temperance in the mini-mart yesterday and the two had bonded ridiculously quickly.

'You're an idiot. You know what I meant.'

'Uhhuh, I'm saying what you meant. You want me in your trackies…' He giggles and then looks mortified. 'You know I'm just joking, right?' He uses both hands, flat out and down, to try and reinforce his message. He looks a bit panicked. Which I'm not sure is flattering.

'Woah, woah. We're good. I've known you, what, ten years? I think it's safe to say I wouldn't be comfortable inviting you to spend time with me and Marsha if you were some kind of predatory sex pest slathering to get in my trousers.'

Rory nods in a relieved fashion and then makes some freaky kind of laugh/groan/monster noise and pretends to dribble whilst rolling his eyes into the back of his head.

'Ha, ha, you look like the men I date when you do that.'

Rory laughs and then looks at me as I drive. 'Yeah but you've grown out of them now, right?' he says.

'Oh yeah, yeah, of course,' I reassure him. And then that whole not being able to lie thing kicks in and I can't not say it. 'Well, kinda. I'm trying, let's go with that. I am not going to date Lost Boys anymore.' He quirks an eyebrow. 'I want to keep my mind solely on getting the Shakespeare project off the ground, concentrate all my energies into that. I can't think of anything I want less in my life than some man trying to get in my pants, lessen my focus. I really have got enough going on at the moment as it is. Seriously, naked Idris Elba could turn up and declare undying love on my doorstep right now and I'd tell him to put some clothes on and leave me alone. I am off men for good, for good! Especially after my last boyfriend and that whole internet palaver…' I trail off and wince, shooting a quick look in the rear-view mirror to check that Marsha is still plugged in.

He stares at me. Shit. If I weren't driving I'd close my eyes. Instead, I fix my eyes firmly on the road ahead. If only I had one of those *Men In Black* zapper thingys. That would come in handy right now. I count to twenty and risk glancing across at him. He's still staring at me, a definite twitching at the corners of his mouth. He grins.

'So, the internet palaver?'

Argh! Eyes on the road.

'Please don't make me tell you.'

'Okay.' And that is that. Luisa would have pushed for detail. My family would have launched into a litany of you-can't-be-trusted. Rory just starts to chat about one of his clients, a Formula 1 driver, comparing him to me.

'How, how are you still alive?'

'No wonder walking on the edge of the Suspension Bridge held no fear for you.'

'Have you ever considered a career as a rally driver?'

These are just some of the comments he makes as we swing around corners and down lanes. 'Outrageous hyperbole, Walters. I did an advanced driving course the minute Marsha was born, to reassure myself I was competent enough to put that bundle of screwy-eyed, bawling treasure in the back of my car when I started godmother duties proper.'

'And you passed?'

'Aced it!'

Rory hmpfs and then grabs the dashboard as I come to a shrieking halt behind a van.

'Jesus!'

'Shhh! Marsha will tell Temperance on you.'

'I believe you. I reckon she'd sell you out too, if she got a good enough deal.'

'Yep, she would.' As the van moves off I have a flash of guilt. Rory's girlfriend died, *died* in a car accident and here I am driving super-fast, although as I believe I may have mentioned, competently. How selfish am I? How could I forget such a huge thing and drive at speed? I slow down and flash a quick glance at him. I really am a complete arsehole. He seems pretty oblivious, and his mild teasing appears to be exactly that, rather than some kind of PTSD call for help. But still, how could I be so thoughtless?

'Just a minute, are we going to your parents' house? Voluntarily?' Rory asks, recognition clear on his face as he clocks the village we're turning towards.

'Not exactly, no.' I check the mirror to make sure Marsha can't hear, and sure enough she's still lost in her story. I have never wanted her to meet the duo of toxic negativity that are Nick and Cyndi and today is no different. 'But we are stopping, just here.' I pull up outside a rundown, roofless stone hut. 'Wait a minute.'

'What the?'

'Where's Belle going?' I hear Marsha ask through the open car door. It's important I'm quick here, that I'm not spotted.

'I have no idea,' Rory says, 'but let's trust her and if she's not back in one minute we'll go find out.'

'Stop it, you two worrywarts,' I shout from inside the building. 'I'll be back before you can count to sixty.' I tug at the metal that I want, stashed behind some tumble-down rocks. Ivy has grown across and is proving a forceful deterrent. I haven't been here since last winter; I should have realised that it might not be as simple as I had hoped.

'Make that one hundred and twenty.' I grapple with the ivy and hear movement from the car. No one knows my hiding place, and although it isn't as if treasure is here or there's any great secret, it is another bit of me that only I know about. I had brought Luisa here years ago but she was made to wait in the car, and Marsha last year for the first time, but she was smaller and napping whilst I fetched what is currently hidden under greenery.

'Get back in the car,' I say as I tug even more. Honestly, this stuff! The irony that I will be using ivy next week – actually that's a point, I could put all this in the car for tomorrow – is not lost on me. Tomorrow it can be my friend, right now it's a pain in the arse.

I almost have them. One more tug! I can do this. I'm like an athlete, I place one foot back, the other foot slightly forward, both firm on the ground. I brace myself, deep breath in. One, two and pull. I pull with all my might, the ivy comes haring off way easier than my earlier attempts indicated and I shoot back, off my feet and across the hut, hearing the intake of breath as I do so from two audience members.

I look up from where I sit, my fall luckily cushioned by the soft snow, as Rory reaches out a hand and pulls me up.

'Are you okay?'

'Yep, all good.' I brush myself down as Rory and Marsha lend a hand. I bat them off. Marsha is walloping my arse harder than necessary and they feel like a little family of gorillas. They'll be picking bugs off me next and eating them.

'What were you doing?' Marsha asks, her little face scrunched up.

'Yeah, what's worth bodily injury? Surely not ivy?' Rory adds.

'Oh, no, the ivy is the added advantage. Here…' Triumphantly, I walk over to the uncovered pile of rocks. 'Here, look. We are going to have the best day.' Proudly I hold aloft the treasure I'd been searching for.

'Oh, I know what we're doing! I know what we're doing. Look, Rory, they've got our names on!' Marsha dances on the spot excitedly. Rory looks at us as if we were both bonkers as our treasure is revealed to be two slightly dented, tarnished but very well-loved tin trays.

'When you rang this morning and said in your princess fairy voice – you know, the one that sounds like you have cured all the world's ills and are about to sing me a lullaby...'

'I didn't realise I had that sort of voice.'

'Normally you don't, which is why this morning I was surprised to hear this gentle lilt tinkling in my ears. When that siren-like soothing voice whispered in my ear that it had the best day planned...' Rory says as he grips the sides of his tin tray, glaring at me. 'I didn't realise you meant risking life and limb. I *should* have realised you meant risking life and limb, of course I should. Yesterday was just part of this plan, part of the plan to make me think Belle is all grown up now, likes to flit around stately homes, doesn't engage with hare-brained schemes full of danger...'

'This isn't dangerous, Belle isn't dangerous, she's fun,' Marsha objects. I tighten my grip around her waist and she in turn tightens her grip upon my arms.

'She's right.' I nod knowingly.

'There's a tree bang in the middle of this field.'

'Yes, and unless you've been lobotomised in the night there is no way you're going to hit it from this angle.'

'So you say.'

'So I know. This will be fun. Look ahead, look how tempting that is.' From our position at the top of the hill I wave my arms over the rolling fields below, the snow soft, undisturbed. Snow is dotted across the rural landscape, the spiny trees wearing little snow caps on each branch, a snow-covered farmhouse with smoke curling from the chimney.

He looks forward, looking ahead at the beauty of the scene before him, nods slowly as a smile I haven't seen before plays at the corner of his mouth.

'Race you!'

And he is gone.

We must have climbed this hill ten times, with Rory carrying Marsha up all ways – a fireman's lift, Marsha slung under his arm as if she is a roll of carpet, a piggy back – all of which cause her to shriek with joy and declare this is the best day in the history of forever. I huff my way up the hill alongside them, tin trays in my hands and a breathlessness brought about by laughing so much in the cold air. We've made tracks through the snow, each of us taking turns to guess what the other person is meant to be: dog, snake, badger, horse.

Gradually other people start to appear on the brow of the hill, and crying with laughter and chilled to the bone, we head back to the car. I drop Rory back at his and he invites me over to spend the evening once I've dropped Marsha home. I want to say yes. Instead I find myself shaking my head as I say no, my fear of getting too infatuated stopping me from having the perfect end to a perfect day.

Thou sodden-witted lord! Thou hast in thy skull no more brain than I have in mine elbows.

December Fourteenth.
Rory.

'It is absolutely ridiculous that a fully-grown intelligent man...' Hmm, his words not mine. '...can't live his life as he pleases. And these ridiculous dictates of yours, I have no words. How am I supposed to repair my reputation by saying I'm an alcoholic? I'm beginning to doubt you have any clue about reputation management. My fans, of which there are many and most of them women, let me tell you, want to see me hav—' Nick Wilde continues to screech down the phone at me.

I have spent the whole day troubleshooting. People say never work with children or animals but honestly, they have it easy. That was life before *Love Island* was invented.

'And as to your suggestion that I cut back on my drinking, let alone need a residential detox, that is downright offensive. You name anyone of my age and level of success that doesn't like a glass of wine with dinner. Had I known you were part of this ridiculous, clean-living, no-sugar, no fun, virtue-signalling woke brigade I would never have hired you...' I hold the phone away from my ear. Today really couldn't be more different from yesterday, which I spent with Belle and then my parents, worlds away from this level of crazy.

Although when Mum heard that I had spent the

morning hurtling down a snow-covered hill she had clapped her hands like a performing seal and jumped around the kitchen as if I was about to gift her a bucket full of fish. When I foolishly confirmed I had been spending time with a female friend she practically cartwheeled over the kitchen table. I didn't dare add I had invited Belle over for the evening as well, even if she did turn me down. I'm half dreading the possibility of Mum making up a banner out of an old sheet saying *Please date my son* and parking up outside Belle's flat.

I feel really guilty for telling her about Belle; it had kind of just fallen out of my mouth before I had realised the ramifications of what I was saying. I need to talk to Mum, make her understand that I cannot just start dating, that it is important to honour Jess in my life and that flirting with every woman that happens to appear is the exact opposite. I'm going to have to schedule in some time to try and make her understand, but guilt – my very best friend these days – says it's cruel to upset her, and it will upset her, whilst she is so poorly, and has bigger things in her life to worry about than her son's deliberate celibacy. I switch my mind back to the call.

'Nick, I can understand why you are feeling like this…' I understand that your ability to believe you have never ever done any wrong is akin to a superpower. The man truly and utterly believes the world repeatedly deals him an unfair hand. 'And if you want us to cancel our current contract then of course that's fine. But if you undertake this detox, my contact has offered you a double spread in next week's Sunday paper alongside the photos of you going into The

Priory tomorrow. They'll then do lots of promo in the run-up to the weekend, for a piece where you to talk directly to your fanbase about your new clean living, how you are very grateful to be married to Cyndi and your determination to prioritise your family above all. They'll also promote your latest cookbook with a money-off coupon.'

'Make it look like I'm being repentant and proactive and put my side across, you mean? The media have been very reluctant to engage since that slapper—'

'I think the focus is very much on reflection, what you've learnt—'

'Yes, yes. And I could talk about consent, now there's a topic of the day.'

'Okay, good.'

'About how fucking blurry it is and how I feel for the young men of today. How exactly are they supposed to function sexually in this world gone mad, huh? Are they supposed to wrap themselves in goddam clingfilm, ask for consent before they make a move? Hardly the stuff of great romance...'

I know I've already mentioned it but children and animals would feel like a gift today, a gift.

'It's getting late so I'll send you a plan of the sort of thing they'd like to write. If you're happy to comply, The Priory are expecting you tomorrow Nick, and I do think it would be good for you to give it a shot. That's my professional advice. If you can send back the plan with suitable quotes and the understanding that I will take a large red pen to anything I feel may hamper your optics then that would be great. Doing it this way means you have more control of the narrative than if you aren't participating. Then you could monetise it when you come out, make a big thing of it. Have Cyndi do your social media whilst you're in there, make sure you show you're aware Christmas is a flashpoint, push a whole book on mocktails next year. You'd have a whole new market there, lots of young people are increasingly not drinking. I really think you should do this, but we'll talk again when you've had a chance to think it over. Thanks, Nick, bye.'

In my business you learn when to listen and when to get the hell away. Had it not been for Belle I would have ended my connection with this poisonous oaf ages ago.

I pop some food in the microwave and wait for the ping. I'm ready for my bed. Today may have been crazy but this weekend was good.

Really good.

I surprised myself and I can't remember the last time I did that.

I hurtled down a hill on a tin tray. Multiple times. And laughed as I did it. If you had told me this was how my UK trip would turn out I would have dismissed you as a lunatic. Yet somehow a little bit of lunacy is creeping into my life and I quite like it.

Bing.

Belle has psychic bloody intuition, she always seems to know when she's on my mind. At least I hope that's her, it better not be Nick again! I try to stop the grin that wants to break out all over my face as I pick up my phone and see it is Belle.

Hey, how's your day been? I swear I'm too tired to even speak but thought I'd check in.

That's cute. My day has been hectic too. You may have to bail me out on a murder charge at some point this week. How? How? How did I get into this as an industry?

I thought it best not to name names. Professional confidentiality and all. Although let's face it, her dad has been the biggest of my problems today.

Desperate need to control?

Ouch. But before I can respond—

Sorry didn't mean that. Don't know why I typed it. Forgive me.

She typed it because it's true. She does that. Speaks before she thinks. She will say you cannot rely on Belle Wilde for much, but that's not right. You can rely on Belle Wilde for so many things that she doesn't seem aware of. To have your back when it's needed. To make each day fun. To make the most miserable bugger – and yes, I include myself in this – laugh in the depths of winter. And she'll always tell the truth even though sometimes it pinches. Sometimes it pinches a whole damn lot but with my line of work, Belle and her unflinching need for truth is refreshing. However, I'm not telling her any of that.

Forgive you? Hmmmmm, I'll have to think about it. Go on then, best bit of your day?

The kids. I see why teachers get into teaching. Kids are so rewarding, engaging. They make everything fun.

Okay and worst bit.

The kids! They may be the best bit but my God they're exhausting. I can cope with Marsha, but thirty of them in each class, the younger ones always seem to need the toilet and are just one big mess of snot in winter and all of them are so jacked up simply because they're not doing maths or whatever they would normally. They're insane.

Hahaha. Was is just school you were in today?

I wish. Nope, cleaning job first thing, then school and then an evening shift at the shop. Hence nearly dead, and possibly currently asleep.

I wouldn't be surprised if you were texting and sleeping at the same time. You're a powerhouse. But more importantly, you were in Bath? When are you next in the shop?

Thursday. Why?

Let me feed you and look after you when you've finished. If you're getting the train I'll drive you back afterwards.

The fact that she does this is also testament to who she is. Belle will always walk or get public transport if she can. She only drives with Marsha or to places too out of the way to practically get to any other way. I know she'll get the train to Bath after her school workshop and then have the hassle of getting home on public transport too.

By Thursday I'll be too whacked to talk.

Which is why I'll feed you, not literally but with some of the best food Bath can provide. I'll even watch Christmas movies with you. No talking required. In fact no talking preferred.

Sounds good.

And you know how much you love free food.

I do love free food.

Brilliant. Go to sleep. 'We are such stuff as dreams are made on, and our little life is rounded with a sleep.'

Did you just quote Shakespeare at me?

Yup.

Do you know that one by heart?

I know it by google. Go to sleep.

Google, pah! And I don't know about the stuff dreams are made on. Feels more like 'Weary with toil I haste me to my bed.'

Well then, stop sleep texting, haste ye to bed and I'll see you Thursday.

I am going to cook her the best dinner known to man.

The web of our life is of a mingled yarn, good and ill together.

December Fifteenth.
Rory.

I'm sitting by the pop-up ice rink at Cribbs Causeway and the grin widens across my face as I see Mum approach. She sees me and her face does the same. Both of us have always been like this whenever we see each other, even when I was a teen. Although in the past I would fight really hard to stop my face giving my affection away, casting my eyes at the ground immediately and trying to think of something to make me cross so I didn't look like a complete twat.

She is laden down with bags and I jump up to take them. Both of us have come to do our Christmas shopping but we split up because she's terrified I might see what she is buying me and thus ruin Christmas for ever. Because obviously I will never be older than seven in her head.

I've managed to pick up some terribly swish-looking food processor for her. Hers is about thirty years old and when I was making the pastry for the mince pies it looked like it was trying to hurl itself off the worktop, pleading with me to allow it to die peacefully. The one I bought looks as if it could land a probe on Mars if you press the buttons in the right order. I've also found a signed copy of the latest book from her favourite author. I suspect she has already read it on her Kindle but still, I know it will make her smile. I've ordered a new shed heater for Dave online so he is taken care of but I did buy him a bottle of specialist whisky as well. You can't ever be too warm when dealing with important shed-based matters. But the hardest thing is not picking up anything for Belle. I have already seen something online that I feel compelled to buy for her but still, every shop I went in I saw something that I thought would be perfect for her. I can't get it all, it would scare the bejesus out of her. She'd think I was some crazy stalker type. But I did pick up a Victorian-themed snow globe for Marsha which I thought was a nice reminder of the weekend.

'Don't look! Don't look!' Mum fusses at me as I reach for her bags to carry them over to the car.

'I won't, honestly! Have you got everything you wanted to?'

'Yes, but … um … how much of a hurry are you in?'

'No hurry.' Any work I can more or less deal with from my phone. 'Why?'

'Well…' She casts a look back at the ice rink. 'I've always wanted to try ice skating. I mean I don't think I'd be any good at it. But I'd love to give it a try.'

'I've never skated before either.' I look at the ice rink and can imagine ambulances, me and Mum encased in plaster for Christmas.

'And as you know, I'm all about embracing new things these days. So let's do it. Let's both go learn how to ice skate.'

Ahh! This is not what I pictured happening today. But the eagerness on Mum's face, and the memory of how much good her latest, more criminal, new thing has brought her, means there is no way in the world I can say no.

'I'll sling these in the car and then you'd best lead the way.'

———————————

We lace up our boots and take to the ice, clinging onto each other like wartime orphans. Luckily it is pretty empty bar one overly loved-up couple and a gaggle of teenagers. When we let go of each other, I fall twice, and she falls once but goes down with such a squeal of joy it's clear she hasn't done herself any harm. Then, before I know it, we're swooping around the rink getting bolder, eventually doing all sorts of fancy things like skating backwards, attempting figure of eights and dancing to the Christmas music that is playing. Or at least Mum is. I'm just grateful to stay upright and keep throwing longing glances at the exit.

Mum whizzes up alongside me, cutting in front of me with some highfalutin zig-zag skating.

'Rory, this is so much fun, I'm loving this. Why have I never tried it before? Thank you so much for today and for coming home. Honestly, I've been beside myself with worry and seeing you is really helping.'

'Mum, I think that's understandable,' I say, trying to match her pace as she continues skating backwards so she can face me.

'I'm not scared of dying for death's sake. Cancer certainly heightens your awareness of your own mortality and I veer between sheer panic some days and resignation on others, but my biggest fear, my biggest fear is leaving you.' She stops and reaches across to touch my cheek. I grab her hand and hold it there for a minute. 'Now, I know you're an adult but still ... you'll always be my baby and I need to be here for as long as possible to see you grow up.' We're both static on the ice now, the teens whizzing by, and it seems an odd place to have this conversation.

'I'm grown up.' I laugh. 'Even got chest hair.' I quirk my brow at her and we both giggle, remembering the time I so despaired of ever having any that I drew some on with Biro. 'But I am all in with that plan. I'm a big fan of you sticking around for as long as possible.'

'Right,' she agrees, nodding enthusiastically. 'It's been a bit of a wake-up call, made me determined to do things I have always wanted to but never had the confidence to.'

'Like shoplifting.'

'Yes, and ice skating.' She waves her hand at the rink we're on. 'And when I get this operation out of the way and when everything goes well ... which it will ... then next year I am going to fill it full of doing things.'

'I am very glad to hear it.'

'I am also going to be more blunt.'

'God help us.' I mock groan.

'I mean it and I'm going to start right now. It is so good to see you doing so well. You even have a flash watch.' I do, it's true. 'When Jessica died I was worried about you, knew you needed time, but I never doubted you. And look at you, the perfect picture of the successful, loving son. But...'

'I'm okay, Mum. I am,' I lie through my teeth. I don't tell her that it's all carefully constructed. That I know people see me as polished. I have all the external trappings but it's a deliberate mask, a mask to hide that beneath the surface I'm still struggling with the guilt. They don't see me staring up at the ceiling at 4 a.m., they don't know that every single call I take I expect someone to say this man doesn't know what he's doing, why are you listening to him? He is nothing but an imposter, he couldn't even keep the woman he loved safe and you're asking him for advice?

'So you say, but the truth is I know you. I. Know. You. And I think your feet are paddling quickly under the surface and it worries me. I don't know who you have to talk to, to confide in. I hope to God there's someone but I suspect you keep everything all tightly bottled up, under control. I know you're here to support me but stupid cancer or not I am your mother, I will always be your mother, and if you need someone to talk to, then I am here for you.'

'Thanks, Mum, I know and I'm so grateful for it.' I squeeze her hand. The trouble is Mum's not objective; I could tell her I'd just set a dozen kittens on fire and she'd still find a way to tell me that I had good reason. I wonder if now is the time to broach why I want to remain single, that she needs to stop looking for romance for me, that it hurts me to my very core every time she brings it up. Jess is no longer here to speak up for herself, she only has me to do it for her, and Mum needs to respect the decisions I have made, the decisions I will continue to make for a good long time and with very good reason.

'Okay but I haven't finished. People say time heals all, and it's true, but grief doesn't always behave the way you think it should. It's not linear, it can come and hit when you least expect it. Neither is it always quiet, slow, depressed, sometimes it's angry and raging and directionless and that's alright too. The one thing that is true is that in order to heal you have to face your emotions, and if I can help in any part of that then please let me. One day, I promise you, the memories will bring you peace not pain.' She is so genuine and I am tempted to open up, I am. I want to tell her I am still pulled apart, torn in two with grief and disappointment in myself every single day. But to do so, at this time, would be selfish.

'You've always been a boy with so much heart, so much love to give, so listen to me now and then I'll leave you be.' Her voice takes on her stern tone. 'This is guesswork but you need to stop blaming yourself for something that was not your fault, was beyond your control. You did not make the decision to get behind the wheel that night, no matter what you think about how you shaped things, and you are not in charge of the weather. It was an accident, love, an accident, and you need to stop looking to the past, you need to look to the future. Both of us do. I am, will you?' The sincerity is cracking her voice and I nod my head, grip her hand, look her in the eye and agree. I wish it were that easy.

Mum takes a deep breath, puts on her brave face, grins, does a massive figure of eight, shrieks with laughter, and says, 'Right, well, let's get skating, race you to that side.'

That I know I can do.

'You're on!'

And we're off.

We reach the other side, her leading a little – she's so much better on the ice than me, a natural – and as she turns the joy beams from her face. Her cheeks are rosy red from the cold, her ears also scarlet. She has a bobble hat perched atop her head, her hair sticks out from underneath it and her eyes are alive, bright. She has aged since I left for Australia, and these last couple of weeks she has been looking tired from the worry of it all but in this instant, she is vibrant, vivacious, joyful, and I make a conscious decision to snapshot this moment and keep it in my memory for ever.

But if the while I think on thee, dear friend,
All losses are restored, and sorrows end

December Sixteenth.
Rory.

I stand at the fridge door, double-checking. I'm fairly sure I have everything I can possibly need for tomorrow. Okay, I'm beyond fairly sure, I'm certain that unless I actually have some real-life turkeys wandering the flat and Father Christmas and Mrs Claus sat on the sofa drinking Gluhwein and gently reprimanding wayward elves, I cannot make this place any more Christmassy.

And truth is I have quite enjoyed myself. I mean I'm not going to turn the lights on now and sit with the tree all lit up whilst I'm by myself but it has been nice, going out and picking out things that I think Belle will like, that I think may put the smile on her face that makes everything in her shine.

The smile I'm picturing in my head is a different smile to the polite one she flashes at people, to the polite one she usually flashes at me. The one where she's truly happy and comfortable is one I've seen far more rarely, really only around Luisa and Marsha, or the night she saw how genuinely interested I am in her Shakespeare project.

When that smile is on her face she radiates, the happiness shines out of her, capable of melting the frostiest day. There's something transformative about it; not only does it transform her face and the way she holds her body but it transforms those whom it is bestowed upon, the warmth of it lasting long after its first flash. It could easily become addictive.

It's becoming more frequent as she relaxes into being around me. She had it on when she caught my eye the other day whilst we ate salt-dough. And it had been glowing from her, bright as a beacon, as we had raced down that hill on those rickety old trays, as she and Marsha had clung to each other and shrieked with laughter as they hurtled down, her face occasionally turning back to mine to see if I was enjoying myself as much as they were. And I was. I really was. It had been liberating, that adrenaline rush of letting the this-is-stupid-maybe-we-shouldn't feeling be overwhelmed by the we're-doing-this-and-it-feels-amazing rush, a feeling I haven't had, haven't allowed myself to have, in a long time.

I have a feeling Belle Wilde is teaching me lessons that could be very good for me. And I feel safe with her – well, obviously not physically, as the sledging testified to, but emotionally, which is far more important to me at the moment. The safety comes through knowing that she is deliberately avoiding romance to concentrate on her work, that there is no risk of mixed messages or misread symbols. She is safe and happy with friendship and *nothing* else. I could, if I was of the mind to – which I Very Definitely Am Not – wave red roses or engagement rings or even my boxer shorts at her and be met with nothing other than a tut and firm request to sod the hell off. She will never have any idea of how grateful I am to her for that. The pressure is off, I don't have to worry about what she may be thinking and she doesn't have to worry about me hitting on her. And in her company I feel more relaxed than I have for years.

I need to repay that somehow. I figure after the hecticness of this week that her shininess might be waning. If I can help her feel a glimmer of pleasure through the exhaustion, then that I will do.

I'm aware, now, that socialising isn't always an easy thing for Belle. She's been honest enough to say as much, that the outgoing social persona she had at university was fuelled by stimulants rather than by her being naturally comfortable around people. Her ability to interact or enjoy herself fully without social anxiety is limited; she worries about every little thing she's said or done. What's been left unsaid is that it comes from a place of not feeling good enough, that *she* isn't good enough.

I can remember that feeling. I had it when I first started university, surrounded by all the rich kids. The kids, like Belle, that I had assumed had everything gifted to them on a silver platter. The students whose mums hadn't had to clean four different houses a day to put food on the table, who hadn't skipped meals when the rent was due. The students who could tell from a glance that I was poor, that I didn't have the right clothes, that my laptop had been bought refurbished from eBay rather than brand new from the Apple store.

I had grown out of it quickly though, as it hadn't taken long to realise that with my mother – and then later with Dave and my mum – I had grown up richer than most of those children with their Antibes holidays and designer clothing. I had been loved and nurtured and encouraged. And, as yesterday had proved, still am.

When I think about Belle and how she scared me then, intimidated me and yet compelled me, and when I think about her now and that lunch I witnessed at the Wilde house, her adolescent behaviour is no surprise, textbook in fact. A child constantly ignored or put down by parents grows up not feeling good enough, turns to substances to mask feelings of inadequacy. Not that she has ever blamed her parents for that in my hearing; she takes full responsibility for all of her decisions. That evening with Luisa, she didn't hesitate to admit it was her who cocked up all the time, none of the blame-shifting she could easily have done.

I can't help but admire her for that. In fact, the more time I spend with her the more I realise there is a complexity to her I may have guessed at before, but never fully understood. When I was younger, categorising people and putting them in boxes made me feel better, more in control, superior even. I realise now that it wasn't just unkind but unfair, misrepresentative. It did both them and me a disservice.

I realise I'm just standing staring mindlessly in the fridge as I have damascene moment after damascene moment, but I can't help where my thoughts are taking me. That's a lie; I can. I'm good at control. That I'm A-star in, medal-winning. I don't want to control where my thoughts are, not right now.

I'm enjoying thinking of Belle, I've been enjoying thinking about Belle. I enjoy doing things for her, repaying the kindnesses she has shown me since I turned up at her parents' house.

I pull a bottle of beer and the leftovers of last night's takeaway with it out of the fridge and shut the door. If I were in Oz now I wouldn't be drinking mid-week but I'm having some difficulty sleeping over here, with replays of that last argument with Jess going over again and again and again in my head. Mum's words about it not being my fault were too simplistic. I can't help but think how I should have behaved differently, how I should have recognised that I was an irritant and changed myself accordingly, how I should have kept my cool. As the thoughts throttle through my mind I hear that bloody Christmas album on repeat, providing the background noise to the scene as it played out. The Christmas tree lights flickering in the corner of my eye as my speech, Jessica's speech, became more and more disjointed, emotional, fractured.

I take a deep breath, place the food and the drink on the work-surface and pull open the drawer to grab the bottle opener. With a swift jerk, I have the cap off the bottle and the glass to my lips. I drink deeply.

I'm thankful, I guess, that it's only at night that my demons resurface, that in the daytime I'm normally able to carry on as usual. It had been my fear that I would be triggered the minute I landed back in Bristol, especially in winter with all the seasonal celebrations blaring out of every building, through the high streets and the villages. That I would be paralysed, unable to support Mum and Dave, contribute in any way.

I had been scared that every blonde woman I saw

wrapped up in a camel wool coat would jolt me, shake me and trigger flashbacks to that night. Of me shouting, raging even. The only time in my life I have ever lost my temper like that. Flashbacks of the drive to the hospital, Dave's face set and grim, Mum sat next to me in the back as if I were a child again, stroking my arm as I stared forward, dreading what was coming. I didn't need telling, I knew. I could feel it.

Another glug of beer.

But it hasn't been too bad, coming home at Christmas time. It isn't that the demons haven't come haring back, tracking me down. They have, especially that first day or two; as I landed, as Mum and Dave tried to make everything normal, as I escaped back here to my Bath-based cocoon every night so I wouldn't hear the sounds of *the* city, just a city.

But the month has progressed and it's no longer every night that I lie awake, staring up at the ceiling, beating myself up as the memories come flashing back. If I'm entirely honest, the days I spend with Belle are the ones when I get into my bed and fall asleep almost immediately, and I know I'm guilty of seeking out her company because of it. I am using her as a kind of therapy, a survival method to get me through. And her well-intentioned plan to get me to love Christmas may not make me love this season, but it is helping in a way. As I look around my flat and see all I have done to try and make Belle smile tomorrow evening, I know I am creating new Christmas memories, frequently daft ones that make me feel something very close to happy.

Small cheer and great welcome makes a merry feast.

December Seventeenth.
Rory.

T he rain is hitting hard and fast, and the city's lights –
of which there are bloody hundreds – are all blurry
and jagging as it hurtles down in the dark evening sky.
Little stingy spikes of rain jabbing at you, targeting every
part, making everyone hurry as fast as they can to their next
destination. Back in Australia, people will be firing up
barbecues right now, with hand-held fans and suntan lotion
crammed into their overstuffed beach bags.

I watch Belle come out of the shop, laughing with her
colleagues as they pull their coats and their scarfs tighter,
their hats down on their heads, and all saying goodnight as
the manager turns the key in the lock before they turn and
speed walk to safety.

'Hey,' I call, and her head bobs up. When she spots me
her mouth turns upwards. The smile polite but genuine all
the same.

'Hello. I was just about to walk to yours.'

'Here, get under the umbrella.' I wave it towards her,
opening my own head up to the sharp, cold drops. 'You
can't walk in this, and besides, you know what a warren
this city is. It made way more sense to pick you up.'

She looks tired, and I'm not surprised. I remember back
to the start of this month – hard to believe it was only a
couple of weeks ago – when I thought that Belle had grown

up to be an underachieving stoner. Now I know she is one of the hardest workers I have ever known. She has dark circles under her eyes and even the brightness of her smile is not enough to fool me now I know her. Running three jobs this week would be enough to kill anyone; it's a miracle she's still standing.

She ducks under the umbrella and sends me a little smile of gratitude and for a second, I wish we were walking home, the two of us in this small space protecting us from the elements as they attack, just me and her as I lead her to safety. God knows what that says about me. Ever needing to be the bloody hero. Instead I walk her around to the passenger side door, and open it for her.

Whilst the work ethic is all her own, I feel a little bit responsible for the crazy effort she is demonstrating at the moment. If Jamal had come through then she'd be doing the school stuff, working with app developers, and wouldn't have to be killing herself to make the rent. I still haven't got to the bottom of what had happened but I have scheduled in time to catch up with him over Christmas when he'll be back in the city again for a few days.

'I'm not used to this,' she says.

'What? Being treated like a human being?'

'Nah, I'm fairly sure human beings just have to get on with stuff, you know, get wet in the rain, open their own car doors. This is being treated like royalty.'

'Behave! I'm just not letting you touch the car cos you'd have the handle in your hand and a helpless look of confusion on your face if I did,' I say before I shut the door on her and walk around to the driver's side, shaking the umbrella out before I put it in the back.

'True,' she says turning to face me as I get in and turn the engine on. 'Although I am behaving. For example, I haven't teased you about your non-existent lights phobia. You're parked in front of the glitteriest most light-flashy shop in the whole city right now and seem perfectly fine.'

'How dare you suggest my phobia is made up.' I laugh as the car purrs out of town, up the hill and towards the flat. She doesn't know yet that not only have I been outside the shop this evening, I was also inside it earlier in the week.

'Oh, I dare. And lights in the rain are fab. Squint and then shake your head, it's so much fun. You should try it.'

'You want me to drive the car, squint my eyes and see if I can make things look trippy as I drive?' I say. 'I'm willing to try new stuff but I think careering down that hill the other day on something that looks like it was stolen from a school dining room in the Fifties is probably my limit. I'm going to keep these bad boys fully open until we get ourselves to the flat.' She laughs but it's clear her energy is not full Belle.

'You look shattered, do you want me to run you home so you can go straight to bed?' I offer.

'Tempting, so very tempting, but you promised me free food and a Christmas movie. I reckon I can last a little bit longer.'

'Okay, but if at any point you hit a wall and need to get home super quick then say and I'll take you straight back. Here we are.'

Belle's face is a picture as she looks up at the Georgian townhouse.

'It's so beautiful, you're lucky to live here.'

'Renting for the month and only a flat, not the whole thing. But yes, it's pretty special.' I understand her wonder. Child me could never have dreamt of renting somewhere like this. Somewhere that sums up the affluence and the history of this city as perfectly as the housing in the centre of Bath does. It was Jessica who had helped me expand what was usual for me, embrace the more chi-chi elements our success brought.

'Can you imagine the sights this building has seen? Jane Austen herself could have stayed here, or nipped in to have tea before taking the waters.'

'I imagine if she had, there would be a blue plaque and the rent would be twice the price. Here.' I dash around the side of the car to open the door for her, umbrella aloft.

I hold out my hand to help her up. She looks at me as if I am mad and then decides to play along and takes it.

The touch of her hand in mine sends my head into a tailspin and I call on all my years of self-control not to make it look as if thirty thousand volts are racing up my arm at her mere touch. What is this? It certainly isn't how my friendship with Belle is meant to feel. Part of me wants to drop her hand and part of me wants to act as normally as humanly possible. Dropping her hand would imply things. This isn't some budding romance, I'm not an adolescent boy, this is me thanking a friend who's making my stay back in the UK far more bearable. I'm not going to indulge my brain with any other scenarios. I'll be back halfway across the world in no time, two weeks to the day, and then I probably won't ever see her again.

When we were dancing at Tyntesfield I had had a similar reaction but assumed that it was because it had been a long time since I had held a woman's hand, and my body was getting confused. But this is twice now. That excuse can't play twice, can it? Yes, it can, I tell myself. It's been years, to be fair, and you're not the most tactile guy. This is just friendship, the fear of anything more is nothing but your anxieties coming to the fore, the perpetual fear that you are being unfair to Jess. I keep rationalising, reassuring myself, and she keeps hold of my hand.

'I'm going to play Georgian heroine this evening,' she explains, bobbing a curtsey once I've locked the car, led her up the steps and let us both into the dry.

I shut the door with my back and still holding her hand twirl her around the tiled floor of the hallway. We're getting good at this dancing thing.

'It seems to me, madam, that you are very fond of playing the historical heroine, as this is the second time you've done it in a week,' I say, relieved that a sense of normalcy has returned to my body and that my voice isn't giving my momentary doubts away.

'This is true, it is my one natural calling,' she acknowledges. 'It seems a shame to rob you of the chance to do the same. I know deep down you really want to be a villain.'

'I do, I do,' I say, twirling an imaginary but very villainous moustache. 'Welcome to my lair.' I unlock and throw open the flat door and usher her in with a particularly nefarious sweep. 'Do come into my parlour.'

'My mother has warned me about men like you,' she says, picking her feet up daintily and role-playing her way into the flat.

'And yet still you came in.'

'I did. Like a fly to a spider's den,' she says with a big grin and then she stops short as she takes in the scene in front of her. 'What's this?'

'This, madam, is your carefully curated sofa spot. Let me lead the way.'

I have worked quite hard. I put up a Christmas tree in the window and have decorated it with sparkling white lights and baubles I bought from her shop. I tried to get some of the ones she had talked about. The ones she said she had fallen in love with but openly admitted she couldn't justify buying. I plan to gift both the tree and baubles to her when the evening is out, because although she's certainly making my December a lot more fun, I still feel no need to have a permanent flashing reminder of the season in my home, not even my temporary one.

I lead her to the sofa, two snowflake cushions one end and two blankets neatly folded at the other, one silky smooth and the other so fluffy that it's a miracle it's not mewing. There's a small table to the side where I've popped the remote control for her and a small bowl of nuts to snack on.

The room does look pretty and I have pinched one of Mum's millions of scented candles, one designed to smell of Christmas – pine, clementines and eucalyptus. To me it smells like loo cleaner but I hope that the scent wafting through the room will please Belle. It certainly sent my mum into a paroxysm of joy when I asked if I could pinch it.

'I knew you'd be shattered after your insane work week so I've made you a Christmas nest from where you can eat your Christmas dinner...' She looks at me with wide eyes. 'Yep, it's just a roast really but with pigs in blankets and a couple of extra bits. Don't get excited, I can't compete with your dad,' I say and shrug my shoulders.

'I ... I don't know what to say,' Belle says, her eyes casting around, lighting on one thing and then another. 'I really don't. It even...' She stops and sniffs. 'It even smells of Christmas in here.' She starts to move forward and for a minute it looks as if she's going to launch herself onto me but she stops at the last minute and instead runs her uplifted arms through her hair, looking at me intensely as she awkwardly brings her hands back to her side. 'This is insane. You've done all this for me?'

'Of course.'

'It's ... it's amazing. The tree is so gorgeous, all those baubles, and they're the ones I told you I loved. You've got me Christmassy snacks *and* a Christmas dinner too. I could cry. You have no idea how hungry I am. I swear I've been living off sandwiches, samosas and toast this week but...' She pauses again. 'Why? Why have you done all this? Apart from the fact that clearly you're a saint and have completely become my best Christmas angel of all time.'

'What do you mean, why?'

'Why would you go to all this effort?' she questions.

'Most people wouldn't ask that.'

'Maybe not but I bet they'd all think it.'

'No, I'm fairly sure most people would just accept it as their due. Why? I guess I want to say thank you for being my friend. Honestly, I expected this to be a difficult trip. The past, you know … and the fact that I'm here to—'

I realise I haven't told her why I'm in the UK, about Mum's diagnosis, and I assume she knows about Jessica, thanks to the invasiveness of social media and our linked past. I'm so used to keeping everything to myself, not seeing a need to share personal information, that she couldn't possibly know *why* I am here. In fact, I know that I have very deliberately swerved the question when she has asked before. I sit myself down on the sofa as I debate whether I want to tell her and realise that it isn't a case of whether I want to or not, it's more that it feels weird not doing so.

She comes and sits next to me and looks as if she's going to rest her hand on my leg but, again, stops herself and places her hands back in her lap. I look at her and we hold eye contact as if she's silently acknowledging that she's here, ready to listen and she wants me to know that. Then she pops a handful of the nuts in her mouth without once taking her eyes from mine and that smile sparkles at the corner of her lips, mischief peeks out of her eyes as she rolls them to show me how heavenly she thinks they are. I'm not unaware that she has deliberately not spoken. She's waiting for me.

My mum would love Belle, although they probably couldn't be trusted together. Together, the two of them would end up on the modern-day equivalent of wanted posters, the length and breadth of the land. My mum is a good judge of character though and I know she not only won't mind me telling Belle, she wants me to talk to someone.

I take a deep breath.

'I'm here because my mum was diagnosed with breast cancer.' I can feel tears from nowhere suddenly prick in the corner of my eyes. I blink rapidly, pushing them back. *This is not me. I do not cry.* I'm good at many things but salvaging people's reputations and supreme self-control are the things I excel in. Excel in. This is just the first time I've said those words out loud to anyone other than Mum.

Belle opens her mouth and, in an attempt to make her realise the truth of the situation, to see that I am a rational adult not an over-emotional child and that I know things are probably, no, *are* going to be okay, I quickly add, 'It's stage two but they've caught it early and the differences in prognosis, in a woman's chances, are so different now to how they were ten years ago. I'm fairly confident that this time around she's going to be okay.' This time around, I say. I know that the chances of it recurring are high, that another time she may not be so lucky. Nope. I am not going down that road.

Belle makes a move just a fraction forward and I can see that she's seeking to reassure me, to comfort me. I move away. In the back of my mind a sneaky voice warns me I'll fall apart if she touches me. I'm scared of the torrent that a little bit of sympathy could unleash.

I shake my head to dispel such an unsettling thought.

I'm not going to get caught up in emotion right now. Facts are what matter. 'The surgery is next week, just before Christmas, and her consultant says she has high hopes of it all going well. Mum will have a lumpectomy and they'll get anything left and have a good look around, see what's happening to the lymph nodes then decide on next steps. We don't know at this stage if she'll need radiotherapy or chemo or anything like that but like I say, the consultant is hopeful. They've moved really quickly; Mum says since the diagnosis it's like being on a carousel as everything whirls around her. So, they're being speedy, which is good, and we'll know much more after the first surgery.' I force a smile to my face, to reassure Belle there's nothing to worry about.

'That's a lot. Of course you came home. I'm so sorry that is why you've had to fly back but it sounds like your mum's got a lot going in her favour.'

'She has.' I'm glad Belle understands what I've been trying to say. That she appreciates my need to stick to the practical.

'But you know that doesn't mean you can't be upset.'

I gulp.

She ploughs on.

'You're an only child, aren't you?'

'I am.' And then all semblance of holding it together vanishes, a seawall finally washed over by the incoming tide, ferocious in its attack. Words spill forth. 'And the thing is, the thing is that the thought of losing Mum as well, I just … I just can't…' I pause as I try and collate my thoughts that are now rushing at me in a fury. 'Mum and Jess rooted me, they made me feel tethered. Secure.' I sniff and take a deep breath but it's as if now I've started talking I can't stop and something in me, something I can never remember feeling before, something is encouraging me forward, reminding me that I am safe with Belle. That she will understand, that there will be no judgement.

'Jess was my everything. The love she had for me, the love she chose to have for me, made me feel like a king. She was the most remarkable woman I have ever met and to this day I cannot quite believe it was me she chose to be with. Me she saw a future with. I know you knew her, Belle, but you didn't, not really. No one got that close apart from me. I was the one she chose to let in. I saw her, the whole of her, and she was perfect. Even in her flaws she was perfect. She made me feel I could conquer the world.' I hear myself release a short, sardonic laugh. 'When I was little I struggled a bit. I'm not alone in that but having my dad walk out before I was even born, to know that I wasn't even worth holding once before he rejected me, to know that he didn't feel that any good could come of his life if I was in it, that makes a child feel lost, unworthy. And the ridiculous thing was it didn't matter how much love Mum poured into me, it was his absence that I dwelt upon.'

'He didn't know you, Rory, if he had he would never have walked away.' Belle rubs my arm as she says it and I look at her face. It's hard to read but I don't believe she thinks that it's that simple for one minute.

'He did search me out once. I remember it so clearly. A primary school football match. This man no one recognised was there, some flash woman on his arm. Mum couldn't watch that day, she was working, and I never gave this new guy on the sidelines a moment's thought, why would I? Then he came and introduced himself as my dad with this woman cooing all over me as if I was some mystical creature. I must've been about nine. And he never came back again. That was it. Poof!' I feel the tears streaming down my face and I move to brush them away.

'Rory, that is not your fault. That speaks to the kind of man, the fool, that your father was, nothing about you at all. Do you hear me? At all.' Her tone is fierce, and I know on one level she is right but there is a huge difference between rational self and emotional self and right now emotional me is taking a turn.

'I know, but I think it's made me wary of men, does that make sense? Still to this day I don't trust them until they've proven their worth. I trust women, I trust women like my mum who are there, who are staunch, honest and put the work in. And I've already lost one of the two women who has shaped me, the one that chose to be with me, and I will never ever get her back...' I am choking the words out now. 'I'll never get her back, and now I am terrified that I am going to lose the woman who I have not lived a single day of my life without being secure in her love. And I have wasted all this time, I abandoned her, and now it could be too late. It could be too late.' Belle remains wordless as my tears dry and my rant finishes. As I stop talking, she pulls me towards her and wraps me in her arms, squeezing me and stroking my hair. She does not say a word. She does not reassure me that all will be well. It's as if she knows there are no words that I can have faith in and, in this moment, I want to nestle here and be protected for ever.

I last two minutes before embarrassment takes hold of me. I have just sobbed like a baby in front of someone that I have invited around for dinner. My heart had calmed but now it starts to beat real fast, the humiliation threatening to take control. I sit up, look Belle square in the eye and try to remind myself that she of all people can be trusted.

'Hey, we should eat. Let me just go get everything ready.' I take a deep breath, stand and pull out the blanket and make a show of laying it across her and tucking it in, my hands running down the sides of the couch, down the sides of her. Tucking *her* in. I feel a shiver at the intimacy of it, and a flash of how my mum used to do the same for me when I needed to rest. For God's sake. My friendship with Belle is meant to help me escape my emotions, not intensify them. This evening is not going as I planned. I give her my biggest grin as I straighten up and try to wrestle back a semblance of normal.

'Now you rest up, don't move and I'll be back in a minute with your dinner.' But as I start my sentence she raises her brow and I know she now knows more about me than I am comfortable with any person knowing.

Take him and cut him out in little stars,
And he will make the face of heaven so fine
That all the world will be in love with night
And pay no worship to the garish sun.

December Eighteenth.
Rory.

'Hey, what are you doing awake?' I ask Belle as she stumbles into the kitchen bleary-eyed but fully wrapped up in coat, mittens and scarf. 'It's half past four.' I am embarrassed after my outpourings last night but am determined not to mess this friendship up by hiding away. I need to face this morning, and Belle, as if nothing happened. And maybe we can go on as we are, both pretending that I never said a word.

'I could ask you the same.' She is her usual self and instant relief fills my body.

'After you fell asleep on the sofa last night I took myself to bed as well and fell asleep way earlier than normal, so consequently I'm awake now instead. Your turn.'

'I'm sorry I fell asleep on your sofa, but I need to be back in Bristol for six, half six at the absolute latest, for work.'

'No apologies necessary, you needed to sleep. You looked pretty cosy under that blanket. I'll run you home. Oh, and you must take the tree.'

'Oh, it was so good, no sofa should be that comfy. But honestly, don't be daft. I can get home and I am not taking your tree. We can discuss that after Christmas!'

'Seriously, you're planning on getting a train home now and walking across the city in the dark to go straight to work?'

'I checked, no train till six so I was going to get a Lyft.'

'You're mad. I'll give you a lift home, no arguing.'

The drive didn't take long despite going extra carefully. Overnight, the rain had turned to snow that battered the windows and the wipers were on full pelt to clear it. All of which is accompanied by Belle singing along to the Christmas songs on the radio.

'*They've got rivers of gold…*' She is giving the song her all.

'How on earth do you manage to be this happy in the morning?'

'This cleaning job has made me see the joy in early mornings. Before, I would have scowled at anyone who dared to talk to me before nine, now I love the early mornings. There's a magical quality about the city as it wakes, and the streets are almost deserted.'

'Did you want me to drop you at work or at home?'

'Oh, home, please, although…'

'You're very secretive about this cleaning job. I'm still not sure you've told me where it is.'

'No, I very probably haven't but seeing as it's only quarter past five now, do you want to do something proper lush and magical?'

'That could be agreeing to anything.'

'Uh-huh. Trust me?'

'I must be mad.'

'In that case let's go to Eastville Park. I can easily walk to work from there, it's literally three minutes away, and I've been itching to do this but not on my own in the dark.'

'Eastville Park, here we come.'

Before I know it, Belle and I are walking through the park, in the dark, with the snow still falling heavily. Like the morning we sledged down the hill, everything around us is white and untouched bar some paw-prints running across the wide-open space.

'I haven't been in here for years, and I don't think I've ever explored it properly.'

'Okay, well, it's pretty ace. It's got a disused lido that they sometimes use for theatre but I'm hoping they'll turn it back into an open-air swimming pool, and you're going to love this.' She grabs my hand, her mitten in my glove, and starts to pull me along at speed.

'Woah, it might be icy,' I say

'It's not icy, come on.' She pulls me down a wooded path, the trees snow-topped and Narnia-like, and then we are at a huge lake.

'Look, isn't that something? I love the reflection of the moon on water but a few years ago Luisa made me promise to not walk here alone at night. I've missed it. Isn't it beautiful?'

'It is.' It's eerie, quiet but quite special. Ethereal.

'I love it here, I half expect fairies to tiptoe out for moonlit winter balls, but also, on a more practical level, it's such a haven for wildlife.' She encourages me down onto a bench. 'Loads of people use this as a photography spot. You get herons, and kingfishers, and otters. I love otters. Not to mention the more obvious foxes and badgers, swans and ducks. It's amazing. Teeming and bang in the middle of a city.'

'I didn't know you were into wildlife.'

'Yep, for sure. Although I'm not very science-y about it. I tend to think about them all as having mummies and daddies and brothers and sisters.'

'Anthropomorphise them?'

'Yep, isn't that the best word? Anyway, I know more than you'd think about wildlife.' She looks at me quizzically as if she is deciding to say something or not. I hope she isn't going to reference the conversation we had last night. I am pleased that I opened up a bit but it was definitely a one-time deal, I can't do emotions again today, and certainly not before dawn has even broken. 'Let me tell you about wood frogs,' she says. I grin; that is not what I expected. 'They're so interesting, although we don't find them here, but in cold, cold places like Alaska, where in winter they freeze almost completely solid. But they've evolved so they make glucose, which acts like an anti-freeze and keeps them alive. They live in this frozen state for weeks and weeks and then as the temperature rises their hearts start to beat again, they gulp for air, have a little wriggle and off they hop to look for a mate. Kinda cool, isn't it?'

'Yeah, that really is.'

'I always thought so.'

'But they don't live in Eastville Park?'

'Nah. But otters do and they're awesome. Let me tell you some amazing facts about otters.'

'Whilst I would like that very much, I'm bloody freezing. You must be too.'

'Yeah,' she admits, 'I am a bit.'

'Here.' I grab her hands, even though they're encased in wool, and blow onto them in an attempt to warm her. She looks at me funnily but doesn't pull her hands away.

'Come on then. I need to get back but I want to make sure we've got time to do one more thing first.'

'One more thing?'

'Yes!'

'Go on then, Wilde, lead the way.' We weave our way back through the Narnia trees and she runs off the path right into the middle of the large expanse of snow-covered park, stops and plonks herself down, waving me over with a huge grin on her face.

'I'll get wet!'

'Damn straight. But you have a seat warmer in your car so you'll be toasty before you're even on the other side of the city. C'mon.' It strikes me that I have been very easily bossed around this month but nonetheless I am trying to be more Belle so I sit down next to her. The damp snow is three inches thick, soft and not as cold as I anticipate.

Then she drops herself back so she is lying flat out.

'You too,' she commands. I do as I'm told, unable to stop a laugh at the ridiculousness of it all.

We lie there looking up, the moon shining bright and the stars twinkling in the blue-black sky. I've never done this before and I wonder why. I feel the vastness of the universe, the smallness of me and the joy of companionship as I look across to the nutty girl lying by my side, who makes me do these crazy, life-affirming things that I would never have even dreamt of.

'You know what we have to do now, right?' she asks.

I haven't a clue.

She moves her arms up and down and her feet across from side to side at the same time.

'You're bonkers!' I laugh.

'Do it!' she shouts, the laughter in her voice cutting through the threat, and, of course, I obey.

We thrash around on our little spots next to each other, laughing so much I'm convinced we'll wake up the whole district, until she jumps up, pulls me to my feet, turns me around and wraps her arm around my waist, holding me tight to her as I look down at the grass.

'You and me, Walters, we are dawn-beating snow angels. Night-time stealth-attack snow angels. Almost as cool as wood frogs, huh?'

I do entreat that we may sup together.

December Nineteenth.
Belle.

Phew, I can't believe it but my crazy week is over and I have a shiny thousand pounds in my bank account. A thousand and two hundred and fifty pounds to be precise. I have never had that amount of money to play with in my life.

In My Life!

Which is insane considering I'm thirty-one and that's less than a month's minimum wage these days. But if my cleaning job and the shop hours cover next month's rent and if I put half of what I've earnt in the schools this week to cover me for January once the shop work stops, in case I can't get something else to tide me over, that still means I have a lot more money this Christmas than I'm used to, even once I pay Luisa back. A bit of me wants to reach for my phone and let Rory know all about my new-found financial whizzery, and my very sensible idea of saving half. He'll definitely like that bit. I bet he has savings. He probably had an ISA in uni.

However, I need to retrain my brain from dwelling on Rory. My crush is no longer a little one, it's a major one. So major it has epaulettes and a flag. On the upside it means I've broken my dreadful Lost Boys pattern and now I have taste that I can be proud of. Taste that doesn't make me feel like I need to sign up for therapy or shower myself in bleach.

On the downside there is nothing, *nothing* I can do about it. The man is still deeply traumatised and in love with Jessica and everyone knows you can't compete against a saint. Secondly, he's only in the UK to care for his sick mum. You cannot jump the bones of someone when they're only here for their sick mother.

It just isn't appropriate.

I may have been queen of the inappropriate before but I'm actively trying to change and even I know there are lines one should not cross. Rory is one of them. He has enough to deal with without having to fend off passes from me. I seem to be giving him something other than his mum to think about over here, I'm not going to complicate that by overtly panting over him or trying to ram my hand down his pants. No, my crush on Rory is going to have to simmer down and I'll allow myself the treat of sobbing about what might have been when his plane takes off on the first of January. The fact that he opened up about his grief, his fears for his mum and his ongoing love for Jess reinforces the fact that I need to step right back and dial this crush down.

But honestly, it's not going to be easy. As I drift off at night I see the green of his eyes as he looks at me, usually laughing. It's his face I see when I wake in the morning and the biggest smile crosses my face as I open my eyes. I can't ever remember that being a thing in my life before. I think of all the things he has done for me and know that no one – no one – has ever nurtured me with such tenderness. In my head he has become the perfect man and the thought of us having a future together is akin to Cinderella finding her prince.

And just as likely.

I have no chance with Rory, none at all. When he talks of our relationship he uses the word 'friend'; it seems to stand out in his sentences and be said in a very firm tone and it makes me feel like he is saying it specifically to make sure I don't get any ideas. He is saying he has no interest in me. And I don't blame him for that, I really don't. I wouldn't have interest either. The truth is, life shouldn't be about levels or leagues, but it has them. And I am not on his level.

My eyes light on the salt-dough gifts on the side. Marsha and I had worked hard and tried to personalise them in all sorts of ways for the people they were intended for. My dad has a snowman with a chef's hat on – part of me is desperate to give it a wine bottle and a restraining order but I want to be a good daughter. My mum and Rose have intricate snowflake decorations for their trees. Marsha has made more snowmen for her mum and dad with a muffin in one person's hand and a phone in the other. Fair representation. I've known Remi for seven years and not once have I seen him without his phone in his hand.

I can get Chardonnay a proper present now – she would never have appreciated a salt-dough creation although I can't quite stretch to sound-proofing her bedroom.

I'm going to write a shopping list right now. I'll get something for Luisa and Remi, Marsha obviously, and I saw some lovely mini Jesus pictures on Etsy the other day – I have no idea how I stumbled across that, it was a late-night thing – the ones with the light all above and around him, Temperance will love that. And Rory. Rory is definitely having something special, not to represent my crush but to signify how much I appreciate his belief in my Shakespeare project, his attempt to help and all the little things he does wordlessly for me since he's come back into my life.

I'm midlist when my phone goes.

It's still face-down on the sofa next to me and I have butterflies in my stomach as I turn it over. It could be anyone, but I have that slightly sick, slightly wavy, fully trepidatious feeling in my tummy as if I'm twelve and the grown-up boy from down the road has flashed me a smile on the way to school.

This is ridiculous.

This cannot be healthy.

It probably isn't him anyway.

Mum wants to know why I stole that god-awful Christmas candle.

It's him and my butterflies are doing backflips of joy!

I'm not surprised. She's probably scared you've turned to crime.

She would have been the one that indoctrinated me into a life of criminality. But considering her recent behaviour and the fact I am now too scared to go back to Cabot's Circus I think that's unlikely.

A laugh springs from my lips. He'd been so funny when

he was recounting that story back to me this week. It had
made me *really* like his mum.

*That somewhat upsets my next Christmas elf plans. I was
hoping you'd help me hold up Santa's grotto at the garden
centre. He's charging twenty pounds per child. I thought we
could be like the Robin Hood of Christmas, stuff him in a sack
and dole out the presents for free.*

*For God's sake don't tell Mum. She'll make you upscale it to all
the overpriced grottos in the nation and then drive around the
country righting wrongs through crime.*

Aha, I knew she'd be more willing than her lily-livered son.

*Rude! Anyway, what I'm trying to ask is that if you can promise
not to corrupt my mother any further than she already is, would
you like to come to lunch tomorrow? If you don't have plans of
course.*

Would I like to come to lunch tomorrow? The only plans
I have this weekend are to rest after this mammoth week,
and today has been a full day of lying on the sofa watching
Hallmark Christmas movies and eating mince pies. I'm
fully rested now. Would I like to meet his mum and step-
dad? I know I should really try and avoid Rory until I have
this crush under control and can manage it well enough not
to embarrass him in any way but would I like to see the
woman who has managed to successfully bring up a son
who is a complete gentleman at all times?

Um ... yes!

Of course I want to meet her. How can I answer so it's not overtly effusive? As I'm taking far too long pondering, I see the dots appear indicating he's typing another message, then nothing. The dots appear again and then again stop. What is he trying to say but keeps changing his mind about?

I realise I haven't answered yet. What am *I* going to say?

Yes, please.

Succinct and to the point. I know I should stay at home but I won't be missing tomorrow for the world.

How far that little candle throws his beams
So shines a good deed in a naughty world!

December Twentieth.
Belle.

I t's clear and dry and sort of sunny this morning. I've checked the forecast and put a great deal of thought into my outfit for today. I want respectable, respectful and me all in one.

I think I have it down. I have a little patterned dress that just skims above the knee and if you look really closely you can see that the pattern is dancing reindeer. Luisa bought it for me a couple of Christmases ago when I had fallen so deeply in love with it that I had flopped around town sighing with desire for weeks. It is my absolute favourite dress ever. And it makes my eyes pop. Or so Chardonnay said once.

I never thought I would want my eyes to pop, it always sounds messy rather than a good thing, but maybe today is the day. I even spent time last night learning an eye make-up tutorial on YouTube. Three hours I practised and I still can't do it. No matter how hard I try I still look as if I've been attacked by an angry chimney sweep.

Luckily Hope House hadn't been very busy this morning and Ariana did my make-up for me once I finished cleaning. I've been almost too scared to move my face since. Getting the dress on without smudging any once I was home was not an easy thing. But I'm happy with the result.

If Chardonnay were here she would be proud. She might not recognise me but she would be proud.

I team the dress with my only decent leather boots, a present from my mum a couple of years ago that are beginning to border on tatty. But after work I shined them as my Nana had taught me as a child and I have to admit they look ten times better than they did. I should have done that aeons ago.

I have a spare outfit on the bed, a little bit more casual should Rory look at me as if I've gone overboard when he arrives. I know I should just be comfortable being me but it's hard to break down three decades of feeling inadequate overnight and besides I don't want to let Rory down.

I hear Rory's car pull up outside and my breath starts to speed up. This is ridiculous. Then the doorbell rings and my heart starts pounding. Oh My God! I'm going to meet Rory's mother.

Rory.

Oh my God, Belle is going to meet Mum! And I don't really know what to do about it. I should have said no the minute Mum asked, not even indulged the thought of it. But the woman is having surgery tomorrow. Surgery for cancer. And if meeting a friend from uni that I happen to be spending a bit of time with is going to help her relax and enjoy today rather than panicking about tomorrow then obviously 'no you can't' isn't a choice.

I stand in front of Belle's front door and ring the bell. I should probably warn her that my mum is going to be all sorts of crazy. She seems to have got the completely wrong idea about Belle and me and is swooping around the house humming 'Love is in the Air' and dusting. Belle will be chill, I know she will. If anyone understands how family can occasionally be a little bit nutty, it's her.

I hear Belle buzz me in and I start to rehearse my speech as I climb the stairs to her flat. 'My mum may have got the wrong end of the stick and I don't want you to feel—'

She opens the door and my breath leaves my body. Her eyes are enormous, warmth pouring out of them although her smile is tentative, a little scared and she reminds me again of a little fox.

She is absolutely breathtakingly beautiful and I lose the ability to speak.

Belle.

Lunch has been lovely, a great big bowl of comforting stew and hunks of crusty bread and real butter.

'I can't believe you're Nick Wilde's daughter. Fancy. I would have had something more ooh-la-la prepared had I known that. Although to be honest, I didn't make this. Rory did. He is such a good boy.'

'Oh my God. I'm thirty-one,' Rory says, faux rolling his eyes and completely sending up his teenage response. I can't help but laugh.

'And you'll always be my boy. It's so good to have you home, especially as you can celebrate Christmas with us.'

'I can indeed. You know Belle is as potty over Christmas as you are. I'd even go as far as saying she may be worse!'

'I do love Christmas. All the sparkle and anticipation and joy of being able to take time out to celebrate the love you have for the people in your life,' I say.

'Yes! Yes! Exactly that. You must come to our pub's festive quiz, it's a couple of days after Christmas and is all about the season itself.'

'She'll smash it,' Rory says.

'I would love that.' I grin, this family is so cute. 'Something extra to look forward to. Are you all ready for Christmas? Is there anything I can help with whilst I'm here?'

'Oh my goodness, aren't you a love? Truth is, Belle, I've been in a bit of a state today…'

'I'm not surprised, tomorrow is a big day.'

'I know. But it's not that. Obviously, I'm nervous about *that*, but it's all out of my hands. I have no choice there but to go along with things, that's the sensible thing to do, I've got the best surgeon in Bristol, so all I have to do is turn up and pray that they're on the ball first thing on a Monday morning.'

'Of course they will be.' Rory leans over and rubs her shoulder. She turns her head and smiles at him. The love between the two shines. This is what family should be. She turns back to me. 'No, my thing is a silly thing…'

'Oh love, we've talked about this,' Dave says at the same time Rory says, 'Mum, you need to let it go.'

'Right. Out, the both of you! Go sit in Dave's shed and do whatever it is men do in sheds,' Alison says firmly.

Without thinking it through I waggle my eyebrows at Rory and giggle before backing his mum up and saying, 'Yes, out!'

Mortification kicks in. I've just ordered him and his step-dad out of their own house. On my first visit. What is wrong with me? No wonder my own parents never take me anywhere.

Rory smirks at me, thank the Lord, before he turns to his mum again.

'I'm not sure that's a good idea.'

'No. I love you, Rory, but of course you don't. You've not brought a girl home since Jessica, and yes, I will mention her name, because she wouldn't have wanted you living in this self-imposed purgatory, and I want to get to know Belle a bit, not have you stepping in and controlling everything. So do as you're told.'

Savage. I can't meet Rory's eyes. That's a lot to unpack. Alison doesn't take prisoners. And whilst Jessica probably would want Rory to move on I'm not convinced she'd be happy that *I* am sitting at the kitchen table. And that aside, I definitely am not here in any capacity other than friend. Maybe I need to make sure Alison knows that. Although I sort of wish Rory would take that burden of responsibility from me.

'Mum, I—'

'Love, you don't have to take the whole world and all its machinations on your shoulders so...' She makes a shooing gesture.

'They are nice shoulders though.' The words just fall out of my mouth as memories of Rory playing football topless at uni and him dancing at Ashton Court festival one baking hot summer day kaleidoscope through my mind.

'They are.' Alison nods in agreement. 'Really lovely. He's got great legs as well.'

'Oh my God!' Rory exclaims as Dave laughs.

'Shed now! Both of you. Go!' The men turn and leave, both shaking their heads – one chuckling, one mortified, and I wish with all my being that I'd been born into a family like this. A family that laugh and tease each other, that are honest in the things they say, that speak out of love and respect.

'You said you were worried about something? Even though you said it was a tiny thing, I am a good listener.' I lean forward and place my hand on her arm.

'I feel a bit daft.'

'Oh, trust. I am The Queen of Daft. I'd give you a few examples but I'm wary of making a bad impression.'

'Impossible. Rory's smile in recent weeks is all the impression I need. Besides, I don't know if he told you but I'm a hardened criminal these days.'

'Ha, he did. I would have loved to see that. It sounds hilarious.'

'Honestly, I don't know what came over me in that moment. I just really wanted to do it. Actually, maybe I do know. The cancer diagnosis, it shakes you. It certainly has shaken me, made me reflect on how I've lived my life, the choices I've made and the things I've done. And at the risk of sounding big-headed, I think I've done okay. Rory is my proudest achievement...' I nod my head. I may not be a parent but I can understand her pride. 'And I've tried to live a life where I've done no harm to anyone, but I've never been naughty, not really. I'm outspoken about my views so I'm no shrinking violet and I was a cool-ass punk in my youth but that naughtiness, that thrill of mischief, I've not felt that since I was a child and you know what? It was magnificent. I still don't feel any guilt about it. That moment of not believing I had dared to do it, my heartbeat as I ran – I never run! – through that shopping centre, it was the most exhilarating thing I've done in decades. It was amazing. And after this surgery I'm going to make sure I fill my life with such moments again.' She grins at me and I get it. 'Not theft, that's not really okay and honestly, Rory returned to the shop and paid the next day. He didn't really approve of me sticking it to The Man.' She winks. 'But special heart-racing moments – I want those. I'm thinking I'd like to do a parachute jump. Dave and Rory will go mad but I'm going to give it a go. Maybe work up to one of those flying squirrel suits, have you seen them?'

'Oh yes! I so want to do that. Imagine how that must feel, just flying through the air.'

'Yes! I thought you'd get it.' She pauses for a minute, looks at me, considering. I don't know what to do with my body so just hold my smile and hope she hurries up. 'My son is quite tight-lipped about his emotions, you know.' Oh wow! Is this what she does? Pulls you in and then blindsides you. 'I don't know what's happening between the two of you. I'm nosy, I want to know, he's my boy, my only baby and I adore him. I'm biased but I don't think you could meet a nicer man in the world.'

I nod in agreement. I've certainly seen the evidence of that.

'I should probably tell you, we're just—' I start to say but she holds her hand up, interrupting me.

'You don't need to tell me. Just cos I want to know doesn't mean I should, he's an adult and has the right to some privacy. But whatever you're doing, if you could just keep doing it I would be insanely grateful.'

I don't know how to respond to that. I know my face alone is chucking out enough heat to melt any remaining snow between here and Bath and that inside, parts of me are squealing with joy.

Even just by being his friend I am helping put a smile on this gorgeous man's face.

And his mum likes me. I don't think that has ever happened before. My heart is doing cartwheels ... no, scrap cartwheels, my heart is a full-on acrobatic circus.

But today isn't about me. Today is about Alison.

'I'm so glad to hear that Rory is more relaxed but ignore your boys for a minute and tell me what's been bothering *you*. They mean well and are obviously only trying to shut you down because they care; they probably just don't get it.'

'Let you weave some of your sunshine magic on me, you mean?'

'Ah, I'm more of a Christmas elf at this time of year.'

'In that case you'll like this. It's a little bit Christmas elfish and it's been so much fun.' Alison grins and in her I see Rory at his most playful. I rub my hands. I am so here for this.

'Oh wow, go on then.'

Alison recounts her worry, claiming it's the closest she has got to naughty before her crazed House of Fraser dash, and I fall a little bit more in love with her. It is the cutest thing I have ever heard. I can see where Rory got his caring side from – always going further than he needs to – from his role model right here.

Her face is a picture as she sits telling me how every Christmas for the past five years she has made batches of chocolate and then crept into her workplace super early and left a bag on everybody's desk, including her own, as a surprise anonymous gift. It's clear how much she loves doing this and I can see flashes of the mischief I occasionally glance in Rory's face as she explains how exciting it is tiptoeing around the building, the adrenaline building if she hears even a merest snippet of noise, terrified she'll be caught. She is proud that so far no one has worked out the secret Santa is her.

'I've been itching to make them over the past couple of weeks, and yet I know how stupid it is. When I got the date of my appointment through I was so relieved that the surgery would be happening so soon and before Christmas, that they were going to cut this, this thing, out of me quickly. But when the relief had simmered down a bit there was a real pang that it was on the Monday of all days. But I guess that's the universe for you, a little bit of give and take.'

Isn't that the truth? I smile. She pauses and looks at me

and I nod lightly, indicating that I'm more than happy to listen as she starts to trace a shape with her finger on the table.

'I am so grateful for my boys, for the fact that Rory flew home so he could be here and spend time with me before and after. That Dave is, well, Dave, the kindest, most supportive man on the planet. I know how lucky I am to have not just one but two of them determined to drive me to hospital, to sit with me, wait for me. I can't ask them to do a quick flit across to the other side of the city at the crack of dawn to deliver secret homemade gifts to indulge me. It's too much. It's taking advantage. But the trouble is now that I'm not doing it this year and I'm out on long-term sick leave, everyone's going to know it's me. I don't do it for the attention, for me the joy is the secrecy, that little bit of Christmas magic, and if I start it up when I am well enough to go back … touch wood, then that magic will be lost. Everyone will know I'm the anonymous gift giver.'

'I can understand that. I get it completely.'

'Right. And I understand the boys' point. It's not life or death. Cancer is … cancer *is* life or death and I'm lucky to be in the position I'm in. We caught it early thanks to all those awareness campaigns and the mammograms. I'm guessing Rory told you.' I nod but stay silent so she can continue. 'And this secret Santa thing, I need to let it go. And I thought I had but now today is my last chance to do it and I'm in a bit of a panic. I know I should calm down, I know how silly I'm being. But our brains are crazy creatures and boom, it's at the front of my mind and won't stop niggling me, even though you're here and providing a beautiful distraction. You must think I'm so daft.'

'Hell no. I think you're freaking inspirational. And that it speaks to the sort of person you are. I think it's a lovely thing and you're right, our brains *are* crazy creatures, they don't always behave the way we want or expect them to. Mine definitely doesn't. Where do you work?'

'Daltons.'

No, surely not. 'Daltons on the Bath Road?' I can't believe it, of all the coincidences!

'Yes, that's the one.'

'And what section are you working in?'

Alison looks at me oddly but bless her, answers. 'Accounting and payroll.'

My brain is click-click-clacking. 'Do you have the ingredients?'

'Not for the chocolates I would normally make. But I could probably gather up the ingredients to make rum truffles.'

'Enough rum truffles?'

Alison gets up and checks the fridge, then wanders over and opens a drawer which from where I'm sitting I can see is crammed with chocolate. Life goals right there. She turns to face me, a grin as wide as the Avon gorge across her face, and nods.

'Alison, if you feel well enough and strong enough to help me make the truffles you need, I think I may be able to help you perform a Christmas miracle.'

'Belle Wilde, you are something else. Will you really?'

'Of course! I'd love to.'

'You know what, they've been saying awful things about your dad recently in the papers but I don't believe any of it. He can't be *that* bad, he has to be good at his core to have made you. He must be so, so proud to have you as his daughter. You're just lovely.' Alison walks around the table and wraps me in a huge hug. I blink back the tears that suddenly threaten to fall and let myself breathe in the warmth of her embrace.

Love alters not with his brief hours and weeks,
But bears it out even to the edge of doom.

December Twenty-first.
Belle.

As I run down the steps into the basement at Hope House, I cannot keep the smile off my face. This is the sort of Christmas mission I love, the sort I was born for. I just have to hope that today is not the day that Fat Alan has broken his madly unhealthy addiction of sleeping in the dungeon.

I asked Ariana if she minded me asking her client for a favour, but she laughed and gave me some tips. Tips I'm hoping I can ignore. I've raced through the cleaning and now I need to get down there. I push open the door and hear his gentle snore fluttering up from his very large body huddled on the two pallets in the corner.

For this next bit, I'm going to have to play a character and not one I'm madly comfortable with. In fact, not one that I would ever, *ever*, have played if this wasn't about making Rory's mum smile today, on her most scary day.

More than a little bit nervous, I walk over to Alan, crouch down and gently rock his shoulder.

'Alan, Alan,' I whisper into his ear.

He rolls over a bit and makes a nestling noise. 'Mmmmm.'

'Alan, Alan.' A gentle snore comes from him. I try again. Nothing. This is not working. Ariana's advice is in my head:

be tough with him. He's here because he likes mean, likes to be told what to do. Shout at him a bit and he'll be putty in your hands.

I'm not keen. I've been hoping to avoid that.

I remember back to my first couple of days on shift when he was waking up and seemed quite fond of my feather duster. I take it out of my cleaning basket and brace myself.

'Alan, wake up.' I make my voice steely, commanding and prod him with the tip of it, although how he's going to feel it through his full-on latex suit is a mystery. 'Alan!' I prod him again. His eyes shoot open.

'Alan.' I wallop him with the duster. I don't know if he is smiling, you can't see facial expressions through the mask but he seems receptive.

'Alan. I need you to wake up and do as you're told,' I bark. This is ridiculous. 'I need your help.'

Silence.

'Alan. You are going to wake up, get dressed and take me to Daltons and let me in. I'm going to be ten minutes and you'll lock up after me. You're not going to tell anyone I was there and in return I won't tell anyone about this. Snip snap. Quickly. Do as you are told, right now, right now,' I shout, my tone as firm as it has ever been.

He jumps to his feet.

'Yes, mistress.' His words are muffled but his head is nodding up and down frenetically.

'Right away. I don't need you to talk to me. Just do as you're told.' This feels so odd.

'Of course, mistress.' He bends at a funny angle so I bat

his bottom with the feather duster a few more times, not quite believing what I'm doing, the thought of Alison's face if I succeed motivating me.

Rory.

Today is the day. Hopefully after this we will all know if the cancer has spread to the lymph nodes, if Mum is going to need chemo or radiotherapy or if it's contained and they have it all out. The consultant said she believed there was a good chance of the latter being the case but until Mum is on the table and she can look around properly she can't be sure. I'm trying not to be nervous, to keep it in, but I'm scared of what we may hear, that we won't get the news we're hoping for.

My phone bings with a photo from Belle. When Dave and I returned from the shed yesterday, the kitchen had been a fug of cocoa powder with the most delicious smell of rum and chocolate emanating from a huge saucepan. They were rolling small ball-shaped chocolates and singing 'White Christmas' at the top of their shamefully tuneless voices. Both had turned in unison and waggled their chocolatey hands at Dave and me, as we walked through the door, their glee at their unspoken threat mutual. In fact, scarily mutual and scarily unspoken. It was quite possible that they had developed some kind of freaky Christmas telepathy in the hour we had left them alone.

Mum had been determined to make those chocolate

things and even though both Dave and I thought that she should concentrate on her health and the events of today, the grin on her face yesterday told me that we had been mistaken. A chocolatey mess was what she had needed and Belle was the one who had listened and made it happen. A couple of hours later I had dropped Belle home with a huge cardboard box full of pretty cellophane bags secured with reams and reams of curly red, gold and green ribbon.

I open the message and lean over to show Mum, who is out of Recovery now, with all of us waiting on the consultant for an update. She's still a little groggy but was so happy to see me and Dave that tears pricked at the corners of my eyes when they wheeled her through.

There are two photos. The first is of the beribboned bags sat upon desks at her workplace. How Belle had managed to get in there, I don't know. Then there is a second photo of her, mask on and with exaggerated tiptoeing across the car-park, bags in hand. She must have an accomplice, someone who took that picture, maybe someone who had helped her break in. I knew Mum wouldn't have given her the keys, and Belle breaking and entering at dawn is not beyond possible.

'That girl is an angel. An angel, you hear,' Mum says.

'You may be right,' I concede, not mentioning the likelihood of forced entry being one of the angel's skills.

There had been something special about seeing her amongst the mess yesterday, my mum and her happily working alongside each other, giggling as they did so, as if they had known each other for years. A pang hits as I realise my mum had always been kind to Jessica, always made her welcome and yet in all the years we were together never once had I seen her so relaxed, so at home with Jessica as she had been with Belle yesterday.

I don't want to dwell on it too much, but I can't help but think how odd it is, the way life pans out. Never had I thought when I used to stare across our tutorial group at Belle – on the rare occasions she turned up – that that wild, untamed hedonist of a girl would one day become my friend and would end up sitting in my mum's kitchen making her Christmas wish come true.

I would my father looked but with my eyes.

December Twenty-second.
Belle.

The bite of the wind means I burrow my face down into my scarf and pull my hat a little further down my ears as I hurry down the street. I can picture them turning red, then blue then snapping off at this rate. It is *cold*.

I play Puff the Magic Dragon all the way down to St Marks Road to make me smile. It was a favourite game of mine and Rose's when we were kids on days like today, huffing out big clouds of hot air into the cold weather and pretending we were dragons. We'd follow it up with the loudest dragon roars you could imagine, but these days I keep those inside my head. There isn't much you don't see in the community in which I live – my mother can't bear to visit the area, squishing up her nose and saying things like 'I don't know why you can't live in Clifton, or Cotham, somewhere a bit more civilised, darling' – but loud dragon roaring all the way to the shops is possibly still a step too far.

I love this community, probably for all the reasons my mother doesn't. Its vibrancy, the mish-mash of people that you come across and make friends with. The fact that right now it is Christmas means there are decorations everywhere, up in people's windows and spilling into the street with unfettered joy. Just as there had been for Diwali last month and the Grand Iftar earlier in the year. Everyone comes together, shares food and music and celebrates each other's cultures. I love it.

I wave at Temperance as I walk past the minimart. She has Innocence on his knees spray-painting a nativity scene onto the front of the whited-out window. She stands behind him waving her arms with force as she barks at him, 'You must use the talents God gave you to make people understand the *power* of his word. Hallelujah to his word!'

The timing is perfect, I'm able to high-five her on the Hallelujah and carry on my way. I turn onto St Mark's Road now, heading to SweetMart where I plan to pick up some of the spices that my father loves to use at home. I'm making him a little ingredients hamper for Christmas now I have some money in my pocket and am looking forward to selecting things I know he will appreciate and that aren't easily available elsewhere.

There is a box of Christmas baubles out on a wall, so I stop for a minute and root through until I find one with a little painted reindeer. It looks ever so old, and as if it has been much cherished. I fall in love immediately and pop it in my bag. It will look perfect on my tree. Then my eye catches one more, again very old – a fox made out of some kind of old wool, like an ancient teddy bear. He has patches where his fur has worn away, is a little scrunchy to the touch and one eye has fallen off and somehow, and I do not know why – apart from an unhealthy obsession – I am reminded of Rory. Why I think he will love this scritchety old thing I don't know, but convinced I am. I pop it in my bag alongside the reindeer bauble.

Mum had called this morning to let me know Dad was home, that he had responded well to alcohol detox at The Priory and had already seen the psychotherapist that Rory had engaged for after-care. Had I seen the pictures the press snapped of the two of them deep in conversation? Hadn't he looked serious? She felt like this was a really positive step forward.

I haven't told her I block stories about Dad from my news feed. Neither did I comment that I thought the process of alcohol detoxification should have been longer than he had stayed for – by my reckoning, he shouldn't be out until Christmas Eve.

A quick look on Google and it was clear to me that Mum – not the press – had hidden behind the stile at the end of the garden to snap the photos. Who went for a walk with their therapist, especially in December, if not to get a picture? Honestly. Those two are as bad as each other.

I'm thankful to Rory for trying; the guy he engaged has qualifications and recommendations coming out of his arse, plus a CV that includes a brief stint with at least two of the Rolling Stones, and that sort of stardust impresses my dad. I know that had it not been for Rory's advice he would never have engaged with sobriety and a detox programme at all, although truth is I still doubt his commitment and I'm not convinced our family's issues can be resolved that simply.

But it's a start, and there's a chance he may actually listen. I'm hopeful for a damascene moment where he decides that he (and the whole female population of the world) will be served best if he stops drinking altogether. I don't hold much hope but I indulged in a brief fantasy when I woke up this morning of me handing him his Christmas present as tears spring to his eyes and he realises he's been a bit of an arse. Self-indulgent, sure, but you know, who doesn't want their dad to approve of them. Especially when that approval has been withheld for so blooming long!

Hence the guarded enthusiasm behind my shopping trip now.

I walk around the corner of the road, the old church looking picture perfect for Christmas with its stone walls and ancient trees, and the mosque right next door, golden and ornate. As I walk past Thali, Rory pops into my head a second time and I pull my phone out of my bag, texting with my mittens on. Not easy.

How's your mum doing today?

I figure that's all right, just a friendly thing to do. Plus, I want to hear what the surgeon found. I don't bother putting my phone away as the minute I send the text I see the dots that indicate he's writing. Of course he is. I can't think of a single time that Rory has kept me waiting, not once.

He's shown me that decent, caring and honourable men do exist. Even though I can't have Rory – and I know I can't – he's helped me make this monumental step on a path to a healthy adult future.

Luisa will be made up when I tell her that bit.

Which I won't do until Rory has left the country again. I love my friend but I don't trust her not to meddle. She won't be able to help herself. And for Rory's sake I need to let him concentrate on his mum right now. Not deal with the embarrassment of having Luisa try to fix him up with her loony friend who is so far from his type that it's laughable. Jess and I are incomparable. It would be like putting Cousin Itt in a room next to Gigi Hadid and asking someone to choose who to date.

Bing.

Mum is doing well, thanks. The surgery was a complete success. It's such a relief although tbh I've not processed it properly yet, and I'm not sure she has. It's almost as if she's waiting for someone to say, we're really sorry Mrs Walters but there's been a mix-up. The consultant did say that it seems that there has been no spread to the lymph nodes, which I was really worried about, and she has booked Mum in for a full mastectomy in January along with reconstructive surgery. Mum's so positive usually but the thought of a mastectomy has knocked her and she's finding it hard to process. But no chemo, no radiotherapy needed and a final operation will mean there is no way it can reoccur in this breast. So fingers crossed, a brilliant outcome.

I can only imagine how hard that must be to process, the mastectomy thing. That on a rational level you know it's the right thing to do, sensible, but on an emotional level it must be hard. Must be. Maybe I can visit over Christmas and see if she wants to chat.

Bing.

Oh, and she's still talking about you and how on earth you got into that building and got her chocolates delivered. She's got a friend coming over this evening with her bag so she's overjoyed that her secret is safe another year.

I answer immediately.

I can't tell you that. I'd love to, trust. I think you'd giggle. But I just can't.

That's what I was afraid of.

As I read his words I can hear his laugh, see the crinkle of his eyes. Jesus Christ. I have it bad.

The phone rings and I hit the green button quickly, images of Rory still flashing through my mind and I assume it's him.

It isn't. A split second after I hit answer I realise it says Dad on the screen.

'Nice of you to check in and see how I'm doing, Belle.'

'Oh, hi, Dad. Good to hear from you. You sound well. How's things going?'

My heart is racing as I try to keep my voice jovial, as I prepare for the inevitable imminent attack. I feel a sudden need for a cigarette. How does his voice trigger such a physical reaction? Still? Thirty bloody one!

'Well, I'm home. Getting ready for a booze-free Christmas. Waiting to be wrapped in the warmth of my loving family.' Sobriety hasn't dimmed his sarcasm.

'Ah, okay. It will be lovely to see you.' The lie falls from my lips. For someone who struggles to lie most of the time – it makes no sense to me – it seems that as a defence mechanism when speaking to my father then I have no qualms about mendacity. That or my willingness to please, to gain his approval, trumps my desire for complete honesty.

'You could have seen me at any time. I was in Bristol for the past week.' It has started.

'And I would have loved to, Dad, but I've been working. Really hard. Otherwise I would have done. Did Mum and Rose come over?'

I don't know what's wrong with me. Why do I veer from protecting myself to baiting him? I know that Rose won't have visited.

'Of course your mother did, and Rose is very busy, you know. She can hardly leave Jack and come racing down, the work they do does make a significant impact on society.' Society, eh? Maybe he has learnt something from all the therapy.

'I've spent the last week working full-time in schools across the city as well as running two part-time jobs, Dad.' Surely he can see how hard I am trying to make things work? That I've been properly professional. That I'm right to be proud of what I've achieved this month, that after years and years of prep I've managed to make some money from my Shakespeare work.

'Pffft!' Okay, maybe not. Suddenly, even though I'm now bang outside of SweetMart, my desire to buy him a delicious range of unusual spices and herbs has dipped somewhat.

'Tis a night of revels, the gallants desire it!

December Twenty-third.
Rory.

'No one throws a party like Luisa, prepare yourself!' Belle laughs as we pull up outside Luisa's front door. The sage green door clad in a wreath feels welcoming to me now and I have a secret weapon at my side. I turn and smile back at it. Her.

'I don't doubt it. I'm expecting roller-skating elves serving me that delicious mulled cider.'

'See, it's so good isn't it? It sounds, Mr Walters, as if you may have changed your tune a little. My Stockholm syndrome approach to making you love Christmas seems to be working.'

'It might be. Although I'm disappointed that you're not wearing that oh-so-colourful flashing hat.' This is the first Christmas party I've attended since that night five years ago. I've avoided them ever since, fearful that the combination of jollity, Christmas music and people drifting about wearing their sparkling seasonal best will be one trigger too many. That I'll lose hold of my carefully constructed current reality and go spinning back to unendurable grief, to self-reproach and incessant blame.

I close my eyes for a second as I get out of the car. The memory is back now. Staccato snapshots: Jessica and I screaming at each other in the dining room whilst our friends and family party in the next room, the loss of control, that feeling of bewilderment of not understanding what she was saying to me, what she meant, of being powerless as she stormed out of the house, car keys in hand. Me screeching that she wasn't safe to drive. Her composure so shaken that she had turned around, still for a moment in the pounding rain and shouted, 'Fuck you, Rory, fuck you!' with all the passion that could be in one body. Me racing out of the house to stop her and not being quick enough. Her driving off into the insane rain. The car around the tree; the coroner ruling accidental death.

I take a deep breath and another one.

'You know how I feel about that hat. I'm not brave enough to actually wear it in public. Hey, hey. Are you okay?' I can feel the gentle tug as Belle pats my arm, catching on my coat as she checks in on me.

'Yeah, of course,' I reassure her, her face reminding me this is a different time, a different period of my life. Belle has a tricky couple of days to get through; she has supported me through the last three weeks and now I need to be grounded, I need to return the favour for her. Her dad is out of rehab – way too early – and I know how Christmas Day is already playing on her mind. My Christmas is going to be lovely this year, as long as I can continue banishing my demons back into their boxes – the first one spent with Mum and Dave in person rather than on Skype in years and celebrating her clean bill of health, the fact that she is seemingly cancer-free. I'll cherish this Christmas now, and I have no doubt I'll be returning home far more regularly at Christmas now I know I can cope with it, and, thanks to Belle, have some stand-out moments of enjoyment too.

'You sure? We don't have to go in.' We're standing on the doorstep now, the throb of the music reaching us outside, interspersed with the laughter. She's such a trouper; the people she loves most are behind that door celebrating her favourite time of the year and I sincerely believe that if I ask her to, she will walk away and support me. The girl doesn't stop giving.

'We're going to have the best night.' I link my arm in hers. 'Ready?' She nods and we rap rap rap on the door in unison.

———

I glance at the clock in the corner, a great big old grandfather clock, and am surprised to see that three hours have already flown by. I hadn't expected to spend more than one here, two at the absolute max if I was enjoying myself.

I have drunk far more cider than I should have done and am remarkably unbothered by that fact. It will be a Lyft home for me tonight. I watch Belle, who has been dancing nearly all night. She started off being pulled in circles by Marsha and then after all three of us danced, a lot, she had grabbed her sleepy goddaughter and with a nod to Luisa we'd carried Marsha up the stairs to bed, given her the snow globe, which she delicately placed next to her on the pillow. She had fallen asleep before we had even got to the end of *Mog's Christmas*.

And now Belle is back downstairs and completely lost in the music. It's moved on from Christmas songs in the background and decks have been set up in the front room where Luisa's husband, Remi, is proving a master. Belle's hands are above her head and she is in perfect rhythm with the bass. I'd forgotten how good a dancer she is. She definitely spent more time dancing than studying from what I remember in college. It makes me happy that she hasn't lost her love as she has grown older.

'Hey, now that's a big ol' grin.' Luisa slides into the space next to me. 'Not a dancer?'

'Not so much.'

'You used to when we were younger.'

It's true, when I first got to uni and before I started to get serious with Jessica I would dance with wild abandon and love it. Why had I given that up?

'We were younger,' I answer.

'We're hardly over the hill.'

'I know.' She's right. I suddenly feel as if I *have* been living old for a while. In fact, I can't remember the last time I danced, actually danced. Threw my arms up into the air, lost myself, let the music take me for a bit. That used to feel *so* good.

'I hear you've been spending a fair amount of time with our Belle.' Luisa leans against the wall as she speaks. She looks as if she's had a little too much Christmas Cheer as well.

'I have. She's remarkable.'

'She is. It was a shame your contact didn't come through.'

'It is. Still don't know why but you know, she didn't need him. She dusted herself off and went and banged down doors until she got her foot firmly in one, which then naturally led to more work.'

'Yes, she would. For someone who has very little faith in herself, I find her pretty inspirational.'

'Yes.' I let out a short laugh. That is the perfect word, the way she goes through life, constantly up against it and refusing to give up, battling forward to make her dreams come true whilst supporting those around her, those she cares for, making their lives sweeter. The way she is with Marsha, the way her presence has revolutionised this visit, the way she had put a smile so wide on Mum's face on the morning of her surgery. Remarkable. 'She really is inspirational.'

'She is.'

Belle dances her way over. 'Hey what are you two whispering about so conspiratorially? Oh, let me grab some water.' She leans over me and grabs a nearby glass and whacks it under the tap.

'You,' I answer.

'Nothing in particular,' Luisa jumps in. 'I was just telling Rory about our new BBQ hut in the garden, it's the most perfect little Nordic lodge, complete with a fire pit.'

'That's sounds really nice,' I say. I do love a fire.

'Oh, I'm so glad you got it, you've wanted one for ages. Is it all kitted out?'

'We have and it is. You must go and check it out,' Luisa says enthusiastically.

'Okay, we will,' I respond – it seems the least I can do given her hospitality – as Remi starts playing a remixed version of 'Last Christmas'.

Belle and I look at each other.

'Noooo!'

'It's our song.' Her face is the picture of every mischievous elf ever existing all rolled into one being.

'You have a song?' If Luisa's ears could physically prick up like a dog when he thinks he's heard a cat, or an intruder, then they would have.

'We don't have a song,' Belle bites out quickly, realising her mistake.

'The rave version of "Last Christmas". We knew it had to happen.' I laugh.

'We did.' She holds out her arm, holds it halfway. Not grabbing me, not forcing me. Then she waggles her eyebrows. 'You know you want to.'

I guess I do.

GPs should probably prescribe dancing. I had forgotten how much fun it is. How releasing it can be to lose yourself in the music, to just let go. My hair, those damn curls, are sticking to my forehead and I feel as if I'm dripping with sweat but my face is aching from smiling and I just don't care. Luisa's living room has taken on a magical quality. The huge mirror behind the decks doubles it in size so it feels as if we're dancing with twice the number of people in twice the amount of space. I'd found myself double-looking as I caught sight of Belle next to me in the mirror. We have danced and danced and danced. We have danced beside each other, both lost in our own worlds, and we have danced together, losing ourselves in the other's. It's been bloody magical and even though my breath is coming hard and fast, I'm exhilarated and so, so happy.

Happy!

'Wanna grab some water?' Belle smiles up at me as she pushes her own damp hair from the front of her face. She looks beautiful.

'For sure.' She grabs my hand and pulls me through the throng back to the sink where we both take great big glugs of liquid and great big gulps of air.

'Shall we head out and check Luisa and Remi's Nordic heaven?' She nods out of the kitchen window to a little hexagonal log cabin at the end of the garden, all lit up and sparkling with white fairy lights.

'Good plan.' I lead this time, my hand seeking hers, my fingers curling around hers as we both clasp each other tight. Our grips speaking of all the affection we hold for each other far better than any words ever could. Or at least I think so, but I'm riding kinda high. We weave through the people in the kitchen, through the open door and out into the bracing cold of the night air in the garden.

We exchange smiles as we reach the door and I'm grateful that whilst I can hear party noises coming from the house, there is no sound at all from the cabin. I fervently want it to be empty. I use my shoulder to push open the door, still holding onto Belle's hand, and the door opens to the most perfect space. In the centre of the cabin is a fire pit, almost burnt out but with some softly glowing embers lighting up the hut. The rest of the cabin is lit only by a string of muted white fairy lights around the top of the building, which is interspersed with mistletoe. A lot of mistletoe. With the building shaped with its six walls, each point, each bench, has a great big clump of ancient greenery hanging above it. Belle follows my gaze, looks up and laughs.

'Ha, I've known Luisa for years but never thought she'd be planning an orgy in her back garden.'

'It does look a bit like that, doesn't it? Like this hut is made for kissing couples.'

'Uh-huh.' Belle heads towards the seating opposite the door and takes me with her. Is she going to kiss me? My heart speeds up, galloping even faster than it had on the dance floor. If she leant over now... The thought of holding Belle in my arms, kissing her, feeling the warmth of her against me... I can imagine my hands tangled in her hair, my hands caressing down the length of her body, pulling her close and ... I quickly try to gain control of myself. The last thing I need right now is my body showing signs of what I'm thinking and it's not far off. *What* is going on in my head? I haven't thought this, *felt* this for so long it is shocking to me, but also a comfort, a feeling that an old friend has returned. I know this, I know how attraction works. I had just forgotten how lush it is. I smile as I realise I even use her language now.

'As much as I hate to thwart Luisa's orgiastic plans, I'm no longer that girl.'

Of course she isn't. Belle has always been clear about how she is not doing men at the moment – her words. It brings another smile to my lips and reminds me in a timely fashion of what is likely to be happening in this hut tonight and between us. And that is nothing other than a whole load of alcohol, an overflowing bucketful of mutual friendship, gratitude for all she has bought into my life and a quick reality check for my mounting … um … desire.

Belle.

'…I'm no longer that girl.' The words fall out of my mouth as I seek to make Rory feel safe, make him realise that even though we've fallen into some dastardly trap set by my best friend – I don't dare look out the door of the hut, she'll be at the kitchen windows, looking smug and doing a thumbs-up – that I'm not going to start ripping his clothes off his body just because he's drunk, vulnerable and … so fucking hot! The way he dances! Someone save me.

I have always believed that the way a man dances tells you a great deal about him sexually and although I remember Rory at one or two freshers' events – yes, I had clocked him fairly early on – and he had danced well, it wasn't long before he settled into dull domesticity and wasn't out throwing shapes with the rest of us. Or if he was there, he would be at the sidelines with Jessica talking about, I don't know, Hansard or the situation in the Middle East. But tonight, tonight has been a revelation, the boy can *move* and he does so with a fluidity, grace and confidence that makes me think of nothing but him moving over me, under me, beside me, in every single way imaginable.

I lean over and chuck a log on the fire and then make a

great show of huffing on it and trying to get it going full pelt again, although making this shed even warmer than it is isn't such a good idea. The last thing this poor boy needs right now is the sight of me stripping off to cool down. The last thing *I* need is thinking about stripping off in front of him. But building a fire is better than giving him even an inkling of what is going through my mind, how much I want to feel his hands between my thighs.

I cannot look at him, not for a minute. Compose yourself, you dirty bitch, I tell myself shrilly.

'So, I want to talk to you about Christmas,' he says. I blow on the fire one last time, give myself one last little tongue-lashing and decide I'm better off at this point just trying to have a conversation like a normal person.

'Uh-huh.' I pull myself up on the bench and attempt to look him in the eye whilst giving myself a lecture on consent and inappropriate behaviour. I've just got Rory to manage to enjoy a little bit of Christmas; best not tarnish that and scar his memories of the season further than they already are by hurling myself across the wooden benches at him like some kind of festive marauding sex-pest.

'Mum says if you want to, you're very welcome to come spend Christmas Day with us, although she imagines you wouldn't want to. She thinks Christmas Day with your dad must be awesome.'

'Yep, all festive bunting, and perfectly stuffed goose.' I smile to show I'm teasing rather than bitter.

'Right. I didn't want to blow her preconceptions or your confidences by telling her the truth of it...'

'Dad being pissed from the minute he wakes up and

then verbally berating us for the entire day, whilst my mother tries to compensate with saccharine sweetness and I sit watching the clock hands move so slowly, wanting to shout at her, shake her into seeing that we all should leave. That truth?'

'Yep, that one. No one would blame you if you wanted to escape that for one year, and you would be very welcome to come to ours.'

'Your mum is lovely and Dave is cute, you're all so normal.'

'You're just biased.'

'A little bit, yes,' I admit.

'And I'm a bit scared of what the two of you might cook up.'

'A life of crime I'm thinking, proper Thelma and Louise shit but, you know, minus the dying.'

'Yeah, she's already beaten death once this week.'

'Shit, Rory, I didn't mean—'

'I know. You worry way too much about what you say and how people will react. And I'm in reputation management so if I'm saying this then that means something. You know, you're tonnes wiser than me but maybe you should work on a "fuck them" principle.'

'My dad has accused me of working that way my whole life.'

'Yeah, and in his case, you most definitely should. But look, if people know you they love you, it's impossible not to…'

I don't know where to look now. I know I'm drunk but waves of gratitude are rolling over me. I feel tears at the rim of my eyes. This is what Rory thinks of me? That I'm impossible not to love?

Rory carries on speaking. 'And they know your intentions are never anything but good, pure...' Oh, I definitely am not finding the courage to look back at him now. Pure? Trust me, boy, the last thing on my mind this evening is purity! 'So if they don't value you and think the worst of whatever it is that comes out of your mouth then fuck 'em, well and truly fuck 'em.' His arms are waving with the emotion of it on each 'fuck'.

I start to giggle. He really is quite wasted. I don't think I've ever seen him like this. He starts to giggle too and before I have time to think he has swept me up into his arms, both of them wrapped tight around me, my face buried on his chest by his shoulder. He holds me there and squeezes once then twice and doesn't let go. I feel so good. Safe. Loved. Like nothing can touch me. Like nothing on this earth I have ever felt before.

Fuuuuucccccccckkkkkkk!

He's going home in a week, Belle Wilde, *he is going home in a week.*

I should feel liberated knowing that it's only a week I have to hold it together, keep my feelings in check, and that after seven days I can let all the emotion out, knowing that Rory won't be around to see me. That my emotions won't make him feel guilty for being the object of my affections, or repulsed – I'm still not sure what his dominant emotion would be. Instead I am filled with overwhelming sadness that I have found the perfect man and I fall so far short of him that I can't just cling to him in this perfect moment and make all my romantic dreams come true.

And then I decide to turn my mind off and enjoy what is happening in this moment. He is just holding me. In no way has he made it sexual. I sure as hell am not going to. I'm going to enjoy the friendship offered. We turn a little and sit in silence watching the flames flit and spit and crackle and lick.

'Hey, Wilde...' He speaks into my hair, his chin resting on the top of my head. 'I get you not coming for Christmas but I've got a shit-hot present for you, or I think I have. Will you give me the whole of Boxing Day instead?'

Who could refrain
That had a heart to love, and in that heart
Courage to make's love known?

December Twenty-fourth.
Belle.

I t is clear this morning as I walk to work, though still bloody chilly, but then what do you expect at 5.30 on a December morning? And not just any December morning but Christmas Eve.

Christmas Eve! I'm so excited. It's also possible I'm still a little drunk after the party last night. But what a party! I can't remember the last time I had such a good night. There had been something special about last night. So special I hadn't been able to stop grinning from the minute I woke up. I'm like a twelve-year-old with a crush so enormous that I may well faint if the object of my affection ever addresses me.

But I'm not twelve, I'm thirty-one, and me and the object of my affections danced until the wee hours and then curled up last night in that hut with an intimacy I don't think I have ever experienced with a man. Ridiculous to think that a cuddle, a chat and a bit of hair stroke can feel more intimate than sex but it did and my body is trying not to explode with sparkles and glitter and excitement. My mind is far more sensible and trying to shut all that down. It's not doing very well and there is a spring in my step. I can't remember the last time I indulged my heart over my head. My vagina, yes, but not my heart.

I cannot wait until Boxing Day and in the meantime, I'm going to daydream all day. I shall revel in the daydreams, respect his desire to honour Jess and keep everything wrapped up tight in my head. That doesn't mean I can't enjoy the odd wallow.

This afternoon I have one final shift in the Christmas decoration shop and then work drinks in Bath. I was toying with giving Rory a shout afterwards but seeing as my thoughts tend to go to dirty places whenever my brain says his name, or pictures his face, then calling him may not be helpful right now. If I want to draw a protective bubble around him to make his last few days here safe and enjoyable, then keeping my distance until Boxing Day is sensible. He doesn't need my lust-filled stares piercing him after the pub. Daydreams may be abounding but as intimate as yesterday was, he couldn't have been clearer the other night about how he is still very much in love with Jessica.

'Hey,' Dorothy greets me as I get through the door at Hope House. 'Happy Christmas.'

I rifle in my bag and dig out a bag of the rum truffles. Alison insisted I take several bags to give as gifts myself. 'I know I'll probably see you in the morning but here, this is for you. Happy Christmas.'

'Thank you, that's kind. I wanted to talk to you today.'

Oh shit, that's the phrase that has led to every sacking I have ever had. I rack my brain desperately to think of what I could have done to screw this one up. She'd okayed me talking to Alan and I really couldn't think of anything else. Unless it's the time I'd walked in on Angel last week with a female client – that had been an eye-opener, the fact that women used Hope House too. I like that.

'Everything okay?' I say, wishing I could close my eyes and not see the face she makes as she builds up to the inevitable.

'Yes, of course. I just want to say thank you...' Wow! 'And to tell you to take a few days off. Do *not* come in tomorrow morning, in fact I don't want to see your face until Monday. Do you hear me? Enjoy Christmas.' She uses her firmest voice. I'm not going to argue.

'Are you sure?' Why can I not just say yes and thank you like a normal person and leave before she changes her mind?

'Yes.' She gives me a wrapped bottle. 'You're the best cleaner we've ever had.'

'I am?'

'You turn up every morning with a smile and get the job done. The girls really like you, and you have never brought drama to my door. You don't know how rare that is. So, take some time over Christmas, relax and thank you for these. Now, what are you standing here for, there's work to be done. Chop chop.'

'On my way, ma'am.' I head down the hall to see Fat Alan coming up from the basement.

'Hey, you! Tell me who the secret Christmas chocolate giver is,' he says as he reaches me. 'We've been trying to work that out for years. Go on, whisper in my ear and I promise not to rat you out.'

'Ha! No way, Alan. I am a great keeper of secrets and I ain't telling you shit.'

'Thank fuck for that,' says Innocence, coming out of one of the adjoining rooms. I put my finger to my lips to promise secrecy and then nod towards the door. I'm going to pretend I haven't seen him because I cannot begin to imagine what his mother will have to say about this. But I'm fairly sure this is not the early morning service I had heard her referring to yesterday.

Rory.

My head is still pounding as I drag myself onto the sofa but yesterday was so worth every bang. I had the best night. But the oddest thing is that my attraction to Belle, which I thought last night may be a thing of a moment, is revealing itself to be more than that. It seems as if someone has imprinted her shape, her mannerisms, the flick of her hair, the way she pulls her sleeves over her fingers as she speaks – all of it on my eyelids, in my brain. She is what I was thinking about last night as I fell asleep and again when I awoke. Awoke sober with nothing to blame my thought processes on. And those processes are very definitely no longer merely platonic.

I accepted last night that I am very, very attracted to her and my mind went into freefall. I had been happy to have her as my friend, she is the most remarkable woman, and although I have felt odd flutters of attraction in the last five years – of course I have, I'm human – they had, to my embarrassment, been for women not involved in my actual life. You know, like Emma Watson. Women that are safe.

This is not safe.

This is Belle Wilde. She is firmly in my life. I can't imagine a world in which I don't check in with her most days, even when I'm back in Australia – when, if, I go back. I've decided to stay and see how the mastectomy goes with Mum in January; it seems foolish to leave before everything is finished. I'm also – tentatively – toying with the idea of relocating back here permanently. Loads of my clients are UK- and States-based so I'm up half the night when I'm in Oz to stay in tune with the time differences and truth is, I don't have a huge life over there. It's largely work-based. Australia was a means of escape and I love the lifestyle but I don't really take advantage of it. I'm almost as much of a hermit now as I was when I first moved there, looking for escape. And Mum is not getting any younger.

I reach out to gulp the water I had brought in from the kitchen and my mind switches back to Belle – as it frequently does. I admire her. The way she sets a goal and goes for it, the way she got knocked down and got straight back up again, and the way she manages to support people without trying to take control – something my far-too-honest mother is fond of telling me I need to learn how to do. I had never really understood her point until I watched Belle do it and do it without thinking. She is remarkable.

However, I cannot mess this friendship up. She has had more than her fair share of shitty relationships and from what I can see, new celibate Belle is a whole heap more together than uni Belle ever was. And I can't help but think some of this is because of the choices she has made, particularly the ones about valuing herself. The last thing she needs is this broken, messed-up bloke suggesting that our friendship might not be the stable platonic relationship she thinks. I worry if she thinks I am attracted to her she will decide that *all* of our friendship has been a ploy, that I was never interested in her Shakespeare project for its own merits, that this was nothing more than me playing the long game to satisfy a long-held teenage crush. That I am no better a man than her father and our friendship has been built on deceit. None of which is true.

Nevertheless, I'm excited about Boxing Day, I can't wait to see her face when I deliver her gift and I want it to be given and received in the spirit of friendship. Images of last night have been flashing through my head all day and I can see us as we sat around the fire, remember how it felt as I cuddled her in to me. That feeling was something I hadn't expected to feel again, like I was keeping her safe, providing for someone. I've missed that. I think it's an instinct deep in all of us. I'd been fighting the desire to tip her face up and place my lips on hers, lose myself in her. This morning part of me wishes I had been bold, but the other half is relieved that I hadn't. The alcohol may have relaxed me, made me realise that I am capable of being attracted to someone again, but thankfully it didn't make me lose all my inhibitions and put our friendship on the line.

I need to take some time and work out what exactly is going on in my head. Has there been some battle between my conscious and subconscious mind, my desperate constant reiteration of the love I have for Jess that's making me block the feelings I may be developing for Belle?

Just sitting here, all of this swirling around in my head and combining with my hangover is a little overwhelming. I can feel myself getting in a fluster. My heart is beating faster than it should, and when I bring my hand to my face I feel that I am clammy.

Today may not be the day to overthink this. Stick to the basics – hydrate, get food – then consider the thoughts in my head. Even if Belle and I do remain friends, which I cannot help but think is the very best option, then I maybe need to re-examine where I slot in with Jessica right now. Do I have to take advantage of being in the UK to make my peace with her? Maybe that's what's needed before I can move on properly.

That thought comes as a bit of a jolt. The phrase in my head is a fact rather than a question and now recognised, I know that it is true. I want to move on. I do. I hadn't thought this day would come so soon and certainly not whilst I was here, not now. But today it's clear in my head – about the only thing that is – making my peace with Jess and finding a way forward feels like the right thing to do both for the past and future.

I don't know if I want to move on with Belle specifically – okay, I would really, really like that – but I recognise that getting to this point has been made possible only by her help. Her presence has opened my eyes to the life I could still have. With Belle or without her, this is a huge step. I know that at some point in the coming weeks, before I leave, I'm going to make a trip to our old house, and spend some time saying goodbye to Jessica.

Bing.

Hey! Back in Briz for Xmas. Hit me up.

Damn straight. I smile as I hear another Belle phrase now embedded in my own vocabulary as I pick up my phone and hit Jamal's number.

I'm going to make the most of this Christmas with her.

Belle.

I am in a pub in Bath. It's loud, raucous and proper Christmassy. As well as my colleagues from the shop and half of Bath, I am surrounded by bags full of gifts, all lovingly wrapped with brown paper and green ribbon, teamed with some teeny-weeny pinecones I found in the cemetery, ready for my family tomorrow. I also have Rory's present, which is considerably less wieldy and proving a monumental pain in the arse, as well as the battered little fox I found on the wall.

A god-awful hangover kicked in mid-afternoon so I am knocking back a gin but largely because it's socially expected. I'm not a massive drinker and as soon as I've finished this I'm going to high-tail it out of here, head to a taxi rank and get me and all this stuff over to my parents' house.

I pull out my phone to check the time; I don't want to get there too early and have to converse with Mum and Dad. Mean, I know, but I know myself and would like to tiptoe in once they're in bed, rather than peak too early with trying hard to be the perfect daughter tonight and not have enough patience left for tomorrow.

I see a missed text from Rory.

I've had a word with Santa and he's promised to make this your best Christmas ever. What you up to tonight?

Cute, probably not true, but cute. Really not helping my crush though.

I'm in The Hat and Feather but just about to grab a taxi back to my parents' place. And thank Santa for me. I need all the help I can get.

Don't get a taxi, that's madness. I'll give you a lift.

Thank you but don't be daft. Really is no need.

Practically in the car already. See you in ten.

I didn't expect to see Rory today and after the sexual tension of yesterday feeding my crush I'm giddy at the thought. I pick up my bags, all nine million of them, and try not to injure too many people as I balance the big box for Rory – it had been such a good idea at the time – and head outside to stand by a parking spot.

In a matter of minutes, he pulls up beside me.

'Hello, beautiful.' He winds down the window and speaks with a mock-European accent.

'They still arrest people for kerb-crawling, you know,' I say, trying to calm my heart. He called me beautiful. Rory Walters just called me beautiful. To all of us girls with low self-esteem out there, we really need a higher bar, but it feels so good.

'And how do they feel about full-on kidnap?' He jumps out of the car and immediately frees me of all packages.

'Yep, definitely still an offence but if you want to kidnap me, I'm willing,' I say. Oh God, is that too flirty? Rory doesn't run up the hill screaming so I figure I'm okay.

'What on earth is this?' He mock-topples under the size of the box.

'That's yours.'

'No!'

'Yeah.'

'That's insane. What have you got me, a small army? A baby elephant?'

'It's big but it's not heavy. Do you want it now?'

He moves the weight of the box from one hand to the other and grins. 'I kind of do, but let's wait, shall we? Wait until Boxing Day and we can both do gifts then?'

'Yes. I like that. It will be something to look forward to after tomorrow.'

'Perfect.' He slides the box into the boot and then puts all my other bags in too.

'But you can have this now.' I slide the fox out of my pocket and hand it to him.

'You've bought me a Belle-fox,' he exclaims and looks way more joyful than I imagined.

'It's a Rory-fox!' I say.

'No, it's definitely a Belle-fox. Thank you. I love it,' he says and I know I am bright red so try to concentrate instead on the bells of the Abbey, ringing out for the late-night carol service. A siren call for all lovers of Christmas.

'You know, for all our Christmas activities we haven't set foot in a church,' Rory says, changing the subject to spare my blushes. I'm desperate to ask if that's a proposal but it's a little too close to the bone to be funny.

'We did visit the chapel at Tyntesfield and there were carols around the piano. But you're right, it's a shame. I love carols. Love, love, love them. I think it's because we all learn them when we're so little and they make me feel warm, secure. Like all is right with the world.'

'Yes, I'll admit I do like carols.'

I look at him assessingly and say, 'I would love to go. I haven't had the chance this year, it's all been so busy. What do you think? Are you in a hurry?'

'What, go to the late-night carol service in the Abbey?' he asks. I nod, trying not to get too excited. This is not how I expected my evening to pan out.

'My choices are drop you at your parents' or go to the carol service with you and then drop you back?'

I nod, unsure which way he's going to land. He locks his car, pops Foxy in his pocket and holds out his hand.

Rory.

Even I have to admit the Abbey looks beautiful all lit up. The huge stone building towers over Bath lending it both gravitas and beauty. It may be late at night and the market is all closed up but people are packed into the Abbey and we are singing our hearts out. Belle is curled under my arm, sharing my carol sheet although she knows all the words. Her head leans against my chest as we stand and sing and I can't think of a time – for a long, long while – that I have been so content.

After working our way through 'O Little Town of Bethlehem', 'We Three Kings' and 'Come All Ye Faithful' we stumble back outside into the square and both of us stand staring up at the Christmas tree, imposing by itself but lending its festive twinkle to the majesty of the scene. We are holding hands and Belle is leaning into me and I am aware that since we left the car we have been touching in one way or another the entire time. I like it, I don't want it to stop. What I really want to do is make sure this night never ends. I want to turn her around and bend my head down and kiss her, feel her mouth open under mine, feel her hands snake up around my neck and pull me down to her, I want to keep her as close to me as humanly possible and then take her back to my flat where we will undress each other, in the brief gaps our mouths can leave each other alone. And then I want her to spend the night, spend all the nights, and wake up with me, turn to me in the morning and wish me a Happy Christmas.

My tongue will tell the anger of my heart,
Or else my heart concealing it will break.

December Twenty-fifth.
Belle.

I snuggle into my pillow, then flip over and try to snuggle again. A yawn comes and I try to ride it, remind my body that I'm super tired, that it's Christmas Day and I can have a lie-in, a little morning nap due.

My body is disobedient. I spend a good ten minutes snuffling and snuggling and trying every sleeping position known to man, but my body clock has well and truly changed into that of a grown-up who wakes with the lark.

Not that there are many larks to sing a greeting to me in late December. I lie in bed listening to the silence. It isn't often this house is silent, and lying here now as it is, staring up at my pictures of icons of a bygone age, I feel at peace. It feels the way this house used to be many moons ago when it was Nana's, my mum's mum.

There is no way I'm going back to sleep now; my parents won't expect to see me until at least noon but this is going to be the year that I break the pattern of truculent child the minute I'm in their house. This year I'm going to be fully adult, I'm going to try really hard to bond with them, make them see what I'm achieving, what I hope to achieve, that I love them.

But first, tea. I can't begin such extraordinary tasks without tea, and then a good couple of hours here to lie in bed and catch up on some journals I've been looking forward to but which this crazy month has afforded me no time for. There's one on Patriarchy and *The Winter's Tale* – always relevant in this house and at this time of year and of particular interest because it's my favourite. I think it's one of the most overlooked plays. I wanted to be Paulina when I was growing up; the woman has no fear. My dad is *so* Leontes with his bullshit and need for control. Leontes ultimately repents and I'm hoping this stint in rehab is the twenty-first century's equivalent. I'm very keen on the thought of my dad's repentance and then remind myself that this is the year I'm letting go of baggage and accepting him as he is, flaws and all. I will only ever have one dad and I should be mature enough to try and make the most of it.

Tea, I need tea.

I go downstairs and patter across the empty kitchen, catching a glimpse of Charlie Brown on my pyjamas. I'm in the same pyjamas I was wearing when I met Rory again, at the start of the month. And what a month it has been. At that moment in time I was in debt to Chardonnay, had just lost my job and was wondering how on earth I would get as far as Christmas. Yet here I am, gainfully employed and with a budding reputation as a Shakespeare educator for local schools with bookings already in my diary for next year. It has flown by and I can't believe all I have achieved in the space of a mere three weeks.

And even more than that, I have a new friendship, a friendship that has opened my eyes a little bit to my value, I think. Although of course the minute I think it, I doubt it again. I don't want to be big-headed, but I'm definitely beginning to feel that I *do* have stuff to give. Rory's brought an awful lot of positives into my life, and I'm pretty chuffed with myself for not trying to get him into bed, despite being in the midst of a searing crush.

Mind you, after the carol service last night, we had held hands and stumbled out of the Abbey and stood in front of the huge, twinkly tree and for a moment, just a moment, I was convinced he was going to kiss me. I swear I saw a flash of desire in his eyes so strong it nearly knocked me over. I know how much I want that but it came to nothing. We walked back to the car, hand in hand – so cute – but that was it. Friendship. It is apparent that is all he wants. I can live with it; I don't want to but I can.

I tiptoe up the stairs, huge mug in hand. Right! Back to bed for a good couple of hours and a browse on JSTOR as a special Christmas Day treat.

By ten o'clock, I've thoroughly submerged myself in academia for hours, updated a bit of *The Winter's Tale* on my project, showered and am now ready to tiptoe down the stairs to surprise my parents.

I haven't bought their salt-dough snowmen and snowflakes, as I know they don't really want them, and my school money meant I could buy another Jo Malone goody for Mum, a silk scarf for Rose, a tie for my brother-in-law, and a book on addiction for Dad, alongside his bag of spices. I want to show that I am here for him, that I support him on his journey and that I'm proud of him for this.

'Hello.' I wander into the kitchen all bushy-tailed as Mum is plating up pancakes. She always does Christmas breakfast although this is the first one I've been awake for in years. The table looks amazing. There's a huge bowl of berries to go with the pancakes as well as poached eggs, smoked salmon and hollandaise, currently sitting in my nana's favourite jug and oozing creamy yellow richness. I've been a fool missing out on breakfast all these years. My eye catches the champagne coupes.

'Ooh darling, what a lovely surprise. Merry Christmas. Have you just got in?'

'No, I came over late after work drinks yesterday and snuck upstairs for a good night's sleep. I didn't want to disturb you. Happy Christmas.' I move towards her and plant a peck on her cheek. Usually I don't go in for small gestures of familial affection but I'm determined to demonstrate my love for them today.

'Where's Dad?' This is unusual. Dad is usually up, swooping around the kitchen, reprimanding Mum about the angle of her eggs or some utter nonsense whilst scrolling through Instagram looking for likes. His addiction to social media validation is akin to that of a thirteen-year-old.

'He'll be down in a minute. He's been a bit tired the last few days. I think rehab took it out of him.'

'Yeah probably,' I agree. I imagine after years of drinking, the body may have the odd twinge or so that without alcohol is no longer being masked.

Dad gets downstairs, he's a bit breathless and sits rather than stalks around the house looking for faults. I'm worried about him but he still manages to criticise at every turn so that's a good sign – Mum's hollandaise is lacking (it's not), I'm not peeling carrots the correct way (I am) – and starts his 'you've always been a bitter disappointment' chat even earlier in the day than usual. Happy Christmas.

As the morning progresses I know I'm being irritating, coming across as smug – 'Perhaps we should have virgin fizzes for breakfast, Mum? Dad?' – but my intentions are well-meant. There's something off, he's not right and I'm not convinced getting plastered before noon is going to help.

I try to talk to Mum about it but her 'don't be such a stick-in-the-mud, darling' combined with 'you know how hard your dad works, I think he deserves a treat' defence means she's chosen her side. But, to be fair, she has been successfully petrified into obedience by my dad over the last two decades – she's hardly going to change her stance now.

Again, the scene playing out in front of me reminds me of Hermione and *The Winter's Tale*, though the hope my mother will also one day turn from stone into a woman with opinions and rights and resolutions is probably never going to materialise, no matter how many times I re-read the play. I know my parents love each other in their own way and just because I struggle to accept the behaviour in their relationship doesn't necessarily mean that they do.

A couple of hours in and half an hour before lunch is served, Rose arrives with her golden husband in tow. My dad adores Jack and is frolicking about in the hallway like a spring-born lamb, albeit one heavy on his feet and with slightly swollen ankles.

'Oh Cyndi, look! Our daughter is here, come in, come in. There's nothing like family to put a smile on your face.' Our daughter. *Our daughter.* I mean, I don't want to be an arse but... Hello, I am right here.

'Who in their right mind would expect people to be sober on Christmas Day?' Mum queries as I wave the bottle away at lunch, still trying to keep to my plan, prove sobriety is possible, and bite my tongue from replying, 'Ones straight out of rehab, I would have thought.'

My intention to be kind, loving and non-judgemental is beginning to wear a little thin. I hold firm but this had better get me a sainthood, or at the very least guaranteed entrance to heaven.

'So, how's work?'

Oh my goodness. Dad is looking at me as he says this. Straight at me. Is it really happening? Who needs heaven? This is reward enough. I start to tell him all about my project. 'Really good. I'm actually quite proud...'

'I was talking to Jack. The world can't always revolve around you, you know, Belle. She spent the night last night, isn't that what you said, Cyndi?' My mother nods, no attempt from either to engage me, to look at me, instead speaking to Rose. 'That's two nights in one month, we're a bit worried she's homeless and just not telling us.'

The table explodes with laughter as I look up at the clock.

We make it through lunch, watch the Queen's speech

and are just about to play board games, the final point of the day before visitors can withdraw home – i.e. Rosie and Jack can leg it out of the front door with me not far behind.

I'm proud I've bitten back any responses to the constant pitter-patter of put-downs from my father. So far Armageddon has been averted at least fifteen times and Rose has even taken me to one side as we were clearing the dishes to say that she's impressed with how I'm not biting today. I gloss over the fact she's eight years younger than me and try to appreciate the sentiment. She'll no doubt be doing the royal wave as she drives off as well.

As we huddle around the Monopoly board – I had mildly suggested Buckaroo or KerPlunk, both of which seem less likely to result in murder when my father objects to paying rent or going to jail – the atmosphere gets more tense.

'So Jack, I was wondering if you had any openings for Belle here, you know, just basic entry-level work. I'd give her something myself but don't want to be accused of nepotism...' Clearly, he doesn't understand what that is. 'Always having to watch the what ya call them, optics these days, or so my reputational management guy would say. Ha.'

'Dad, I've got work.' I keep my tone peppy.

'I mean, obviously nothing important, we wouldn't want Belle involved in government...' The whole family laugh for a full three minutes at this, stopping then starting again as they catch each other's eye – my sister actually clutches her sides – as I sit there and try not to roll my eyes at my dad's humour. 'But even she can make tea. Anything?'

'Dad, I've got work,' I repeat. Surely when they hear I have bookings for next year, surely that will shut them up? I just need them to listen. I've been meek and mild all day but this is important, all I want from him is some recognition that I have finally managed to make a go of what I love. I can shelve the mild, albeit ever-diminishing, hope that he would be proud.

And if not him, then maybe Mum. Mum's mum gave me the Shakespeare bug, surely, she can see that my love of the Bard, all of the work I put in, is testament to the love I had for Nana, and the pathway she set me on?

'Well, you hadn't when you were here for your mother's birthday. Rose told us you had been sacked again,' he shoots back. I look over at Rose. Seriously? She gives a hands-up don't-blame-me gesture.

'I'm sure with your watchful eye she won't be any trouble. After all you have Rose in good shape,' my mum reassures Jack. Yeah, cos he's the one sitting here desperately seeking reassurance. I swear my parents are somehow completely unaware of anything about the twenty-first century, I'd go as far as to suggest most of the twentieth as well.

What had I been thinking this morning? Leontes. I swear if Dad could order me from his life then he would. He would have loved it if I had sodded off to grow up on a mountainside as an orphaned shepherdess. Quite frankly, even in December, it is pretty appealing right now.

'I don't need a watchful eye, Dad.' I can feel my temper

building. Come on, Belle, you've done so well. You've almost got through the day. It's early evening. So close.

'Why don't I get us a nice cup of tea and a slice of Dad's amazing Christmas cake,' Mum trills.

'I have been working in schools teaching the children about Shakespeare, making him relevant to today's kids,' I say as Dad sniggers dismissively, swapping looks with everyone else in the room.

How I wish I could say Jamal is funding me and backing me up. That would shut Dad up – there's nothing he loves more than a bit of external validation from another man – but really, I should be enough. I am not going to let Dad's stupid, outdated, overly unfair assessments of me carry on shaping me anymore, shaping the way I view myself, the way I present myself – apologetically and always expecting to be a disappointment. I have done well this month. Alison's words came back to me. *He must be so, so proud to have you as his daughter. You're just lovely.* And maybe, maybe instead of thinking *not really, I'm a bit of a disappointment*, maybe I should think *damn right he should be*. Maybe if I had had parents who told me I could do anything if I tried hard enough, who told me I was good enough ... maybe I wouldn't be so permanently bloody lost, always looking to see if I have made anyone cross because that was my default setting growing up.

Today I have had enough. Today I will speak out. I need to, for me.

I stand.

'You may be disappointed in me because I am not like you, not a tiny bit, but you know what, what you fail to see is how much that is a good thing. You think if it's not made in your image then it has no merit. Rose looks like you and also fulfils the role you think suits a female best – sorry, Rose – and I don't. She is quite literally the golden child and I have never had a chance in hell. You see no good in me at all, you're genuinely disappointed in the person I am.'

'Yes, I'm disappointed. You are nothing like me,' he fires back. 'You don't have a practical useful bone in your body. Shakespeare, for fuck's sake, that's about as much fucking use to the world today as, I don't know...' he looks around the room to find something worthy of his insult and lets out a laugh, '...as your mother is to brain surgery.'

'How dare you? What on earth has Mum done to be brought into this? I'm so done with your stupid worldview on what has merit and what doesn't. You should idolise Mum, have her on a pedestal so high she towers over you. Because that's what she does, she towers over you. She is still here, decades on, opportunities no doubt missed, and still by your side. I don't know why, I don't know if it's because she loves you *that* much or if she's here because she's scared of anything different. But she's still here, and quite frankly after just this last year alone you owe her for that. You owe her for a lot and—'

'Belle!'

'Well, he does. And I don't ever think I've heard him say thank you.'

'Jack, Rose, I'm so sorry. I don't know what's got into her,' my mother says.

'Stop apologising for me. I do plenty of things wrong, but I can apologise for myself because I am not Dad. I can accept that I fuck up, that when I do it's my fault, not the fault of every single person around me so yes, Jack, Rose, I am sorry I am making you uncomfortable, and on Christmas Day, but seriously, Dad...' I turn to face him again and see that something isn't right. I should have known something isn't right by the very silence of him. The power of my words isn't what is keeping him quiet. Somehow, when all eyes were on me, no one had noticed him sitting back down on his chair, a stream of sweat upon his brow, his skin greyish. He isn't dripping wet or anything, but he isn't right.

I cross over to the chair and sink to my knees; he feels clammy to the touch.

'Dad, Dad. Are you okay?'

'Yes.' The word comes out, but it's slow and breathless.

'Are you in any pain? Your chest? Your arm?'

'I have had a bit of a sore throat all day, that's it though.'

'I'll get him some honey and lemon. Nip of brandy, that should do it,' Mum suggests.

'No, Mum, get him an aspirin, and hurry. Do it now.'

'But he says he's not—'

'Please, Mum, now.' There's a firmness to my tone and she turns on the spot to do as I ask. 'Rose, call an ambulance. We're probably okay but let's err on the side of caution.'

'I say, I'm sure we don't need to—' Jack starts to bumble.

'We do!' I snap back. 'Rose, please.'

'I've nev ... never heard anything...' Dad's words are slow, laboured.

'Here.' Mum is back and passes me the small pot, the childproof lid already undone and balanced on the top.

'Dad, I want you to chew this. Just humour me, okay.'

'I don't need…' he starts to quarrel. Of course he does.

'Oh, you bad-tempered bastard, just do as you're told!' I don't want to scare him but I do need him to chew on the aspirin. I'd had first-aid training earlier in the year when one of my colleagues had a silent heart attack at work. This looks suspiciously similar.

'How long are they going to be?' I call over my shoulder to my sister.

'I'm doing the whole name and address thing. What am I to say is wrong, sore throat, slightly slurry speech? Over-dramatic daughter?' She laughs at her own humour.

'My speech is not sl-slurry.'

'No, suspected heart attack.' The room erupts.

'But he hasn't, he isn't…'

'He doesn't need to have chest pain or arm pain. Yes, it's the most common symptom but not there in a quarter of all heart attacks. For once just trust me, huh?' I shoot over my shoulder. 'Now Dad, crunch down on that aspirin. I know it tastes foul and I'm sure it's not needed but humour me, huh? Just today. You can tell me what a waste of time and space I am again tomorrow.' I smile at him as I finish undoing the top button of his shirt. I hope to hell he *can* tell me off tomorrow.

Beshrew that heart that makes my heart to groan
For that deep wound it gives my friend and me

December Twenty-sixth.
Belle.

'Hey.' Rory gives me a big smile as I open the door of his car and I slide in, as well as I can with his present in my hands. 'I half expected you to cancel today.'

'Yeah, I nearly did but I went down to the hospital earlier and he's doing okay. Told me to sod off again so he could enjoy Mum and all the nurses flapping around him. He's loving being on all the front pages with a "nearly died on Christmas Day" headline. It was only a mild heart attack, if there is such a thing. A wake-up call. Turns out it's pretty common amongst diabetics and when they ran the tests in hospital they discovered that's exactly what he is, so that's a lucky catch. They're keeping him in to observe today and he's talking about starting a new healthy eating trend, seems to think he's invented it and has come up with the idea of a Nick Wilde mocktail book.'

'He came up with it?' Rory arches his brows and I giggle.

'Right? Anyway, he's very happy to be trending on Twitter and in the most read section of BBC News. Best Christmas present ever and apparently, he never needed to spend a penny on you because this was all he needed to win back the public's heart.'

Rory arches his brow. 'Near death is the preferred option to working hard to become a better person?'

'You have met my dad, haven't you?'

Rory laughs. 'No killing the fatted calf for you? The papers say that it was the love and attention of his eldest daughter that saved his life, Paramedics claiming it was your quick thinking that stopped the situation being a tragic one.'

'Pah. Not exactly, but, get this ... Mum told me today I had done well and told Dad he should thank me.'

'Wow.'

'Right! He didn't and she pushed him a second time. That is such a win. Mum took my side over his. I can't think of a time that has ever happened. And eventually he did do as he was told, like a truculent schoolboy, but he did it. We might not suddenly become the closest family in the world but to have her stand up for me, twice, and make him acknowledge that I did something good yesterday is huge. Huge! As dysfunctional as I think they are she does love him and the way he's been with her this morning reminds me that he loves her too. I mean, he keeps making stomach-curdling jokes about her being his favourite nurse and sponge baths but I guess they're cute in their own way. Plus, it means I don't feel at all bad about coming out with you today as promised and leaving the patient to the tender ministrations of his wife. Here.' I pass him the huge box I am carrying.

'Ah, my ginormous gift,' he says and I nod excitedly. I've been very careful with the wrapping of this gift. I didn't want to give it away so it is currently sat inside several boxes, like pass the parcel, and wrapped in brown paper that I had printed myself with Marsha – reindeer-face potato prints – with a giant bow that Temperance had given me when she gave me the boxes earlier. She has taken a shine to Rory, it seems, and declared that he was here to do God's work and then kept giving me meaningful stares that left me no clearer about what she was talking about.

He leans over and takes the big box. 'Shall I open it now?' he asks.

'You can try.' I smile back.

He sits and unwraps it, taking care to preserve the paper. In days gone by this would have irritated me – *just tear the paper off and do it* I would have wanted to scream. Now I see a man who is careful, shows respect for the gift and the work that has gone into the paper. He isn't dull, it isn't boring or lacking in verve for not ripping it off, he is just more measured than me, careful, and that is a good thing.

'Eh? Why have I got a giant box of frozen pizzas? I mean thank you, I love pizza.'

'Ha! You haven't, you have a letter attached though. Look.' I gesture to the envelope that is attached to the top of the box, sealed with brown tape.

'Hmmm.' He holds my gaze as he takes the envelope from the top, building into the mystery and I feel a shiver run down my spine. Just under a week and he'll be gone. I'd best bank these looks. I'd thought he may stay a bit longer, especially when he told me Alison would need more surgery, but so far he hasn't said anything.

'Rory,' he reads out loud. 'Okay, definitely for me then.'

'Yep.' He turns it around and opens it carefully.

'Happy Christmas to you, here's a Christmassy clue... What is one of the best things about Christmas and rhymes with the arachnid family?'

'Arachnid, nothing rhymes with arachnid. Pan lid ... um ... stranded ... um ... kid ... um...' He scrunches his face up in panic.

'No, you need to think a bit harder. It'll come to you and when you've answered the clue you can open the box.'

'Or I could just cheat and open it now.'

'But you won't.'

'No, probably not. Arachnid...? Argggh. I wish I had made your present more complicated now.'

'I'm glad you didn't. What is it?'

'It is a magical mystery tour. Today, Belle Wilde, it is your turn to be whisked away to somewhere special, or so I hope.'

'Really?'

'Oh, yes.'

'Well, why are we still here then?' And I wink at him cos I like his face when I do so.

***

Rory.

It has taken a while to get to where we are going, Belle asking every fifteen minutes or so if we are nearly there. Her face as she started to see the signs for Stratford-on-Avon was super cute. That is the best Christmas present I could have asked for, regardless of what lies deep within the pizza box.

'Are we going to Stratford-on-Avon?'

'Are we going somewhere close to Stratford-on-Avon?'

'Oh my God, we are, we are!'

'You're turning! You're turning! Rory, what have you done? My favourite place.'

I smile and remain non-committal until we have driven through the town, past the turning for Anne Hathaway's cottage, past Shakespeare's place of birth.

'Oh my goodness, we're not?' As we pull up in the small road beside the theatre she starts to wriggle her fingers in her lap, such is her excitement, and it makes me feel like Father Christmas 'We're not? Wow! I've always wanted to come but have never been able to afford the tickets. Are we really here for...'

'Yup and it's *The Winter's Tale* this season; how could I not buy you tickets to see this?'

'Oh my God, Rory.' She has the beginnings of a tear in her eye as she looks at me, the whole of her shining, and I fill up with pride. I made this happen. Belle Wilde sitting in front of me looking like she is about to burst. I lean over and wipe the tear from her eye and she stays still, staring at me as I do so. I feel prickles all up my neck and remind myself of all the reasons I can't spoil this by leaning in for a kiss. How Belle deserves me respecting her desire to be man-free.

'*The Winter's Tale*. In Stratford-upon-Avon. On Boxing Day. I swear I have never believed in fairy godmothers before but something special has brought you into my life, Rory Walters, I swear it has.'

'It certainly has,' I say, holding in the thought that it is her, Belle Wilde herself, who is the special thing that has brought me into her life and kept me there. I'm a confident man in many ways but saying that is too cheesy for words and I can't bring myself to do it. Apart from embarrassing her, it would embarrass me as well. This evening is meant to be a treat, not me pushing things past the friendzone and making her feel awkward. I have a feeling I may have to remind myself of this frequently today. 'I'm glad you're pleased. I hoped you would be.'

'Pleased!' She flings her arms around my neck and holds me, her head close to my head. Close enough to hear her breath. I breathe in. She gives me a strength I didn't realise I had before. She makes me feel like I can do anything, be anyone.

A thought pops into my head but I don't want to speak, or pull away. I just want to enjoy this moment a little longer and we sit there for a little while. Arched over the handbrake, our heads resting against each other's. I give it a couple more minutes and then I move my head just a little to whisper in her ear.

'Spider.'

'Finally,' she whispers, neither of us moving just yet.

'What rhymes with spider, and what did I learn to love this Christmas? That must be...' I pause for effect and move away. She moves backwards too and we exchange a smile that is so intimate it makes me dizzy.

'Yes...' She draws out the word, anticipation in her voice. She looks more excited than me about opening the box. I can't think for a minute what could be in it.

'Luisa's cider!' I say triumphantly.

'Aha. Yep, open the box, open the box.'

I use my nail to cut the tape, carefully lift the flap and find there is another box with another envelope.

'You're joking me,' I say and she claps her hands with excitement.

'It's pass the parcel for grown-ups. Next clue.'

Again, I carefully open the envelope. 'The very next day…' I read aloud. 'She gave it away,' I say without thinking

'That's not fair, you're supposed to take longer.'

'How could I? That song is now etched into my brain.' I push my hands in the air and start to act out the rave version of 'Last Christmas', complete with chugga chugga beat box noises.

'You're a fool. Okay, go on then, next clue.'

'There's another bloody layer, how many boxes are there? Am I going to go through all this and find something tiny like a pea or something?'

'Maybe, maybe. But what time is the show starting? Shouldn't we get in there?'

We wander around the theatre, Belle oohing and ahhing and looking at all the pictures of performances past, chattering about things that are way over my head with a couple of members of staff and occasionally turning around and patting me with a mix of excitement and gratitude. Her happiness bounces from her. Finally, we take to our seats.

'How well do you know the play?' she asks.

'I was going to ask you for a quick précis. I'm a bit rusty and you're my walking Wikipedia. It's not one of the more well-known ones.'

'No, but it's an absolute beaut.' She gives me a quick rundown of the plot but refuses to give the end away, smiling enigmatically. 'The great thing is this play is so full of themes, about recognition, about inequality, country versus city, jealousy, all sorts of things, and I just love it. It's one of his later plays and is hard to be categorised as anything other than late romance—'

The woman in front turns around to shush her, cutting her off. We have both been so caught up we haven't noticed the curtain coming up.

'Oops, sorry,' Belle says and lowers her head. I scowl. There was no need to be arsey; no one is even on stage yet although there is a huge Christmas tree in the corner.

'Look.' I point it out to her. 'You didn't mention Christmas in your précis.'

'Because it's got bugger all to do with Christmas, that's just stagecraft and a director trying to find a link to help ticket sales.'

'But it's *The Winter's Tale*, I thought it was partly your favourite because of Christmas.'

'You *know* Shakespeare wrote very little about Christmas!' She gives me her cross face as if I am a naughty pupil who hasn't paid attention to his lessons. Far too cute and I bow my head in acceptance of the telling off. She's right, I do know that, she told me back when she was preparing to go into the schools. 'It's a winter's tale because it is a good old tale with lots of morals which is perfect for drawing up around the fire and telling on a winter's eve, or at least I think that's why…'

'Shhhhhh.' The woman in front turns and hisses at us again, whilst rustling so many sweet wrappers she could be a one-woman orchestra. Belle grimaces an apology, settles back, ready to get caught up in this retelling and I sit back to watch Belle.

Belle.

The time whooshes by and I am so happy. It was magnificent, *such* a good production, and I can't believe that Rory has thought of this as a gift. In the first half I had found myself leaning into him over the seat arm as the play began and couldn't help but notice how a tear welled up in his eye at the courtroom scene as Leontes' fury rolled out across his life and caused him to lose everything he had previously held dear. After the interval, I reclaimed my position, as close as can be, and in the final scene – the unveiling of the statue of Hermione as the father is reunited with his daughter – I felt him sit straight, caught up in the anticipation and emotion of the moment. But then as the statue moves and Hermione reveals herself as alive all along he stiffens. Shit!

Shit!

Shit!

Shit!

Of course, it had never occurred to me that Rory would buy me tickets for this play, let alone sit and watch it with me. And then once he had my joy took over and I forgot to factor this in. I forgot that for a man carrying the burden he does – the loss that is etched into the brow of his face – witnessing a play where a lost love is revealed as living, back from presumed death, would be hard.

The audience stand and clap and clap; the cheering is thunderous as the actors stand and take their bows, blowing kisses to their audience. I stand and clap as Rory does too but the cheers I want to hurl are silenced as I watch another tear trickle down the face of the man I know I have fallen in love with.

I want to wrap him up, make my arms a secure web in which to keep him safe, free from further hurt, tell him it will all be okay. But how can it be? Jessica isn't coming back.

'I shall never have the words to thank you for bringing me to this,' I say as people slowly begin to file out and I gently squeeze his arm, hoping the words I don't say are conveyed.

'It was a pleasure. Was it as good as you hoped when we walked in?' he asks with no mention of his own response to the play, the tears pushed back behind his eyes with iron Walters self-control.

'Oh my goodness, yes. It was amazing. I really will remember tonight for ever. For ever.' And I will. He has taught me so much. He has taught me how a man treats a woman he respects. He and his mum have taught me that I am good enough. They showed me what I had suspected was the case all along, that normal parents – good parents –

put their children's needs before their own, that they use their strengths to build their children up, not allow their weaknesses to dictate the constant tearing down of their kids. That maybe, just maybe, it isn't me that is the only failure in my life, maybe my parents have let me down a little, our failure to have a healthy relationship may not all be on me.

Just because nothing I do is good enough for them doesn't mean I'm not good enough for me. That lesson had come roaring in full force when I had finally snapped at Dad on Christmas Day and leapt to my mother's defence but also to my own. I had, quite literally, saved my dad's life and still he struggles to see any merit in the person I am, so sod him.

I have always seen myself as Perdita, and that is the only flaw of this play, this winter's tale – her ready forgiveness of a father who was willing to leave her to die on a mountainside. Maybe I'm not Perdita, maybe I shouldn't be aiming to be quite so forgiving and meek. Maybe I am kick-ass as well. In all my years I have never seen anyone stand up to my dad. And I had done so, in the lion's den with all the other lions there, ready and happy to rip my throat out.

I *am* Paulina!

We head out of the theatre into the bright winter sun and I notice Rory is not fully present, the conclusion of the play presumably hanging over him. I try to change the mood; it's obviously best not to mention the play anymore. *The*

Winter's Tale may be beautiful but the fact that Rory will never have his loss made whole is breaking my heart a little, so God knows what it is doing to him.

'Shall we go see if you can work out any more of the clues?' I ask brightly, aware that my silly little present is no remedy for the deep grief this man must feel, flashes of which I have seen in him on this visit, my mind flicking back to the sight of him in the hospital that day all those years ago. Details of which he told me the night he made me Christmas dinner and opened up about his grief.

'Yes, let's. Now I know it's not twenty-four pizzas but my interest is piqued.'

We buy coffees and sit on a bench just outside the theatre with his gigantic box.

'So the next clue…' He opens the envelope but his heart isn't in it. The distance that dawned when the curtain fell is still there. A chasm I don't think I can bridge.

'Yes,' I say forcing jollity. Such a generous gesture on his part has led to the opening up of a wound far from healed. I could kick myself. Why had I ever mentioned the damn play to him in the first place? 'This is your final clue. Are you ready?'

Even if he is, I'm not sure I am. What seemed like a sweet idea last week now pales into insignificance compared to his gift but there is no turning back, I will sit through the unwrapping and the drive home and then go to bed and try and recall the magic of today, how spoilt and how lucky I am, rather than dwell on the hurt it may have caused the man sitting next to me shaking his Christmas gift box.

Rory stops shaking and opens the last envelope. 'I was scared, I was petrified but now I know what fun it is to be alive...' He reads the last clue and looks at me, eyebrow cocked. Jesus! What had I been thinking when I wrote these clues? I remember cackling as I wrote this one out, the memory of his face on the day that had prompted this present making me laugh time and time again.

But not now. Now it feels stupid, self-absorbed. I'd been so pleased with myself when I had written and wrapped this and now I wish the ground would open up and swallow me whole. Seriously ... what fun it is to be alive? After he had opened up to me about his grief and the worries about his mum? Straight after this play has bought Jessica to the forefront of his mind?

'I have no idea what this means. Give me another clue. I can't work it out at all. This is the final clue?'

'Yep, the final one.'

'And this clue means something I have done that I was scared of and now am not.'

'Yes,' I say, determined to pull myself together and make the best of this. Rory has done a wonderful thing for me today, I am not going to make it any worse by getting inside my head. 'Not that you, great and brave he-man that you are, are a scaredy-cat, not that at all...' I quickly make strongman arms to show I'm teasing. I try to pull it back. 'You're definitely all man.'

Jesus Christ. Gaffer tape my mouth shut now!

'Look, this present seems silly now but at the time of getting it I wanted something you could take with you back to Oz – if you want to, obviously, you can bin it if you don't,

I won't mind – and hopefully think of me whenever snow falls and you want some fun.' I mean I would mind, obviously, I would. This present means heaps to me but that doesn't mean it will to Rory and he may not want to use up precious baggage allowance.

'I think it's safe to say that when snow falls I'll always think of you and … oh, I think I may have it. No, surely not. Hang on.' His fingers tear at the tape this time, his decorum lost and, if nothing else, that is gratifying. I offer up a little prayer that he won't be disappointed.

'Oh wow. Oh wow. You didn't. But this is your special thing. Yours and Marsha's.' He unwraps the final box to see an old tin tray nestled in a bed of tissue paper.

'It was, and now it's yours too. Look.'

He picks the tin tray up and turns it over, a little gasp coming from him as he spots his name. Like mine, it is scratched in with my old school compass, the letters spiky and childlike, but done with love.

'You've put my name on it.'

'Yep, that's yours now you are a permanent member of the hill-sledging tray club and this is an open invite anytime you see snow to race down the nearest and hilliest hill at super speed, a little bit scared and remembering us.'

'A permanent member.' He is still turning the tray over in his hands, running a finger alongside the bevelled edge and looking as if he has won the lottery. It's my turn to well up. This beautiful man likes my gift.

Carefully he places it back in the box, grabs my hands and squeezes them and then lifts one of his hands to my face, to cup it, stroke along my cheek line. He is going to kiss me. I can feel it. I've read everything wrong. Rory Walters is so taken with the gift he wants to kiss me. I can see it in his eyes, feel it in the pace of his breathing. He's going to lean in any minute and all my worries about him being upset or my gift not being meaningful to him vanish. Rory Walters is going to kiss me! My heart is pitter-pattering in my chest as he looks into my eyes and I try not to close them in anticipation.

'Belle, this gift, this gift … it means the world.' And he slowly starts to lean in and I start to think of the life we could have together – I know, skipping ahead a bit – and I can't believe today is panning out like this after all. Best Christmas ever. I close my eyes and tip my head and feel him coming closer and closer and then his lips graze my cheek.

'Thanks, Belle. You really are the best mate any man could ask for.'

Give sorrow words. The grief that does not speak
Whispers the o'erfraught heart and bids it break.

December Twenty-seventh.
Rory.

I'm sat at on the grass of The Downs, the rolling greens that span Clifton, staring at the flat Jessica and I lived in. I am aware I may look a little deranged but right at this moment, I don't care. It's cold and damp and that suits my mood entirely. I have come here to wallow, to wallow and ask advice, permission maybe, I'm not sure. I'm not sure of anything right now other than my desire to reconnect with Jessica. Not in a woo-woo seance kind of way but my thoughts are so muddled, especially after that play yesterday, and I think she can help. All the problems surrounding her death, the issues I anticipated would be raised by this visit, had more or less become non-things, but new ones have taken their place.

I had braced myself for the fact that being home, or near to Bristol, for a month would trigger all sorts of hideous anxiety, flashbacks. It's as if I had expected people to approach me on the street and shout abuse in my face for letting Jessica down.

Obviously, that hasn't happened.

Instead I have started to consider my return here permanently. Being around Mum, and the fear that sat in me about her mortality, has made me realise I want to spend more time with her. *Far* more time with her. Be in her life more. Make the most of all we have. We have been lucky this time, I hope. We'll know better after the mastectomy. Cancer has a way of rearing its head again. This next operation makes that less likely but if that happens I don't want to be on the other side of the world. I'm not sure I want to be the other side of the world at all. Somehow confessing all this and talking about my mum to Belle the other night cemented it in my mind. It was as if once I had said the actual words out loud, my brain then knew what path I had to take. For the first time since Jessica's death, nearly five years ago to the day, I can see myself living a life here. I had needed to get away, create a new life for myself, but now, now I think I'm ready to come home.

And on this visit, instead of memories upsetting me on every street corner, I've found that the majority of my memories of Montpelier – now hilariously swish compared to when I was growing up there, when it was definitely more working girls and gunshots than specialist coffee houses and Italian delis – are from childhood, not uni or Jessica. If I venture into Clifton or even across to the Cotham side of Stokes Croft, that is where I am reminded of her.

Which is why I have come here, to the place where we'd lived, where we'd shared our lives, our aspirations, were honest about our insecurities and would curl up together at the end of the night, legs entwined as we slept, my arm slung over her torso as I curled around her.

I have come here because I want to ask her forgiveness. I feel no less for her now than I did when she was alive – she will be a part of my heart until the day it stops beating – but I'm beginning to realise I had made life-changing decisions soon after her death which helped me through the subsequent years but had hurt those that loved me. Decisions I am ready to revisit, to change.

And the old guilt has a brand-new layer added. Not only do I feel as if I have short-changed her because this trip hasn't been the hell pit of internal torture I expected, but also because this trip has been filled with Belle Wilde.

Nothing could have prepared me for this development, for Belle becoming my friend and for me developing feelings for her. Somehow our lives have woven together over these last few weeks. The woman I assumed she was is so different from the woman I now know her to be. She's good all the way through and her ability to find joy in the little things when the bigness of life is steamrolling over her is admirable. She has taught me that there is always joy to be found if you look for it.

A robin bobs over towards me, interrupting my thoughts as it stops, cocks its head and looks directly at me. I look at the robin, marvelling at its resilience, its feet seemingly comfortable on the frost-patina'd ground. Joy in the little things. I nod my head at it.

I'm meant to be sitting here trying to say sorry to Jessica and my mind keeps falling back to Belle.

I look around The Downs, the huge green expanse of space that surrounds the house in which we used to live, and I let out a little laugh.

We lived in Clifton because this was where Jessica thought we should live. And I understood her thinking, it was certainly the most affluent part of the city and where we had been based when we were students. But still, despite both of us bringing in good money, the rent for this house in front of me used to make me wince.

I understood her need for the symbols that shouted to everyone else how well we had done for ourselves. Such a contrast with Belle, born to money and completely unbothered as she dots around in a car that has moss on it.

Jessica worked in the BBC and I had started my business whilst still in uni. The rapid and massive expansion of Facebook had made me see there was a potential for reputations to be made or broken through social media. In school, I helped friends set up a positive online presence, and curate the way they presented themselves years before it became a mainstream awareness. This was back when people were sharing everything willy-nilly, without thinking through the consequences. When companies were only just beginning to check out profiles and make hiring decisions based upon them. Jessica had been proud and supportive of me as I set up the business, she really had. She hadn't minded me working all hours then; it was only later she had begun to complain. The same time as other parts of her behaviour had changed to the point of awakening a jealousy within me that I had never thought myself capable of. A jealousy I was reminded of yesterday in the theatre.

The robin is still here and is looking at me quizzically. It doesn't seem to want to fly off. I'm not going to shush it away but I am a little unnerved as it fixes that unblinking black eye upon me.

'Yes, you're right,' I say out loud. 'I'm here to commemorate Jessica, not raise the doubts I had about her. That's unfair. She can hardly answer back.' I know this is why I eulogise the relationship, why I never say anything about the way things were beginning to fray at the edges at the very end. The robin looks a bit more satisfied when my phone buzzes.

I pull it out of my coat to see a video call from Jamal, the Belle fox from Christmas Eve falling out of my pocket as I fumble for the phone. Do I really want to be interrupted by Jamal right now? I had meant to see him and so far hadn't got around to it.

I hear Jessica's voice in my head saying, *Don't put off until tomorrow what you can get done today*. The robin nods. Bloody hell.

'Hey,' I say as I answer the call.

'Hey, how you doing? Sorry I didn't get to see you over Christmas, it's been mad busy. But I've got plans to make that right, I'm back again for New Year's Eve, will you be about? Hang on. Where you at?' Jamal's face looms large on the screen. 'Isn't that where your old house used to be?'

'Yup,' I say.

'Long way from the badlands, what you doing there?'

'Trying to talk to Jess.'

'Fam!'

'Honestly, I know that I've deliberately put distance between us and right now, I'm back and I want to say sorry to her. Here seems like a good place.'

'Okay, okay, and how's that going?'

'Honestly, not quite as I'd imagined.'

'And why's that?'

Because I keep thinking of Belle and remembering the good bits with Jessica, and how I couldn't believe how lucky I was she picked me and how anything to do with Belle feels like a betrayal. Made worse by the fact that they knew each other, and it's fair to say Jess was not a fan, that she dismissed Belle as an overindulgent hedonist.

I want to try and explain all this to Jamal but don't know how to say it, or even if I should. My eyes alight on the fox, which bizarrely the robin has hopped over to, as if it thinks they can be friends.

'Don't know, mate,' I say instead.

Jamal gives me a look but stays silent. Belle would have just said it.

I take a deep breath and tell Jamal the truth of where my head is at. We've been friends since Pokémon came into being.

'Woah, look, I never got to know Jessica very well but you loved her, no one could ever doubt that. You wouldn't have loved her so much without good reason. But if you want to be true to her, you need to remember her as she was, the truth of the relationship the two of you had, otherwise you'll be putting her on a pedestal that no human can live up to and then how are you supposed to move on from that? Remember her as she was, flaws and all. You'll be doing her a disservice if you remember her any other way. And if you want to talk to Jessica just talk to her, man, it doesn't matter where you are. If you're uncomfortable talking out loud in public, put your headphones in and pretend you're on the phone, tell her all the things you want to say.'

'That's pretty good advice.'

'There's a power to words. Thinking through things is great obviously but sometimes the act of saying things out loud, somehow that makes it more real in our minds. Try it. And as to Belle, I've been wanting to talk to you about her.'

'Yup. I was a bit surprised when you didn't get behind her project.'

'I like the project, I really like the project but, you know, you didn't tell me she was Nick Wilde's daughter. That threw me. She don't need my money.' Jamal's brow furrowed and he shook his head to reinforce his point. 'I'm not giving her 75k.'

'I can see what you're saying, but just between you and me her father is an arse-ache, and he is never going to give her a penny – they don't help her out with anything – and what's more, she wants to do it on her own.'

'She didn't tell me that... I'm not surprised you're keen, she's got some spirit.'

'Woah, I'm not. We're no—'

'But you like her.'

'Yeah, I like her. But that's not fair on Jessica, you know.'

'No, I don't know. Jessica is gone, the only people you aren't being fair to right now are you and Belle. You shouldn't be playing with her if you don't mean it.'

'I'm not playing with her.'

'How many days have you spent with her since you landed, hmmm? Anyway, taking your personal feelings out of it, I wanna talk about mine. And mine are that my nephew, you've met him, Mark, he hasn't got no time for books, he's all about the football and that. Fair enough, I can see where my man is coming from. But he's only eight and turns out your Belle rocked up to his school soon after I knocked her back, like *soon*, and Mark loved it. Something she did really connected with him. He made his mum go and get him some of the plays in graphic novel form and he's eating them up. I don't know what she did but she did good. So, I want to talk to her again, not about money for app funding, but maybe about how me and her can team up, get her into schools doing this regularly, use my name, work together, get things done.'

'That sounds very much like a plan she'd like. To be honest she's all about the schools, the app thing she thought would be her starting point, and I pushed it, trying to monetise the sheer volume of work she has done.'

'Well, that work serves her well and I can help her get more established, if she's interested. Her knowledge and my rep should be a bold combination. And I'll make sure she knows it's not because of who she is, who she knows, but because she's worked hard and all that knowledge that's her own. So, can I have her number?'

'Oh, yes!' A huge smile spreads across my face. Belle recognised for who she is, what she knows and does, is exactly the lift she deserves.

Hey, hope you're doing okay? You'll never guess who I've just heard from. Jamal. Jamal wants to work with me. How amazing is that?

'Amazing and well-deserved,' I type out and then delete. I need to put space between us. Even if I am staying in the UK, Belle needs a man in her life without my issues. She's had enough of those to last a lifetime. She doesn't need me and my over-emotional head dragging her down, not when she is about to fly. I need to break these bonds now. She hadn't seen me as I was in the run-up to Jess's death, eaten up with jealousy and doubt. I need to make her see me for the arse I am – jealous, controlling, the Leontes-in-training rather than the man I suspect she sees now. I need to cut the cords, make sure she frees herself up for a future she deserves.

Her passions are made of nothing but the finest part of pure love.

December Twenty-eighth.
Belle.

Hey, I don't want to be a freaky stalker but are you okay?

I send another message to Rory. I spent most of yesterday evening watching my phone, waiting for him to answer. More than a few times, I watched those dots move, indicating he was typing a response but nothing came through.

It makes it harder somehow, knowing he's on the other end of the phone and that whatever he has to say to me is so bad he can't bring himself to send it. I've been spoilt by his company this month and know he'll be going back to Australia soon and it will hit hard when he does, but this I'm not prepared for.

I don't know whether I should worry about him or be hurt that he appears to be ghosting me. I resolve to give it one more day before I get really panicky. All sorts of things can come up. Christmas is a difficult time of year for many people and it's quite possible that he's run off his feet professionally. I hope his absence doesn't mean something has come up with Alison. There are lots of reasons for him not answering and all of which mean it will not be helpful for me to be pestering him. Plus, it's probably better for my crush if I don't spend as much time with him.

It's just that it bites. And I'm worried.

His very personality type dictates that it's unlikely he is ghosting me. If I have done anything to offend him, it's far more likely that he'd tell me directly, in a slightly apologetic manner, that he thinks it will be best if we don't spend time together.

Ghosting is very definitely not a Rory Walters thing.

And as Daddy dearest frequently likes to tell me, the world does not revolve around me.

However, knowing it may have nothing to do with me doesn't stop me feeling all those emotions you get when someone ignores you. The inadequacy, the paranoia, the anger. I'm spiralling through all of those feelings so I do the thing I always do in times of trouble, I curl up in my bed – to my shame with my phone right next to me so when he does get in touch I can see it – and pick up my well-thumbed copy of *Antony and Cleopatra*. I figure it's time to throw myself back in again from the very start. After all, I may have missed something the first few times around.

I'm at the bit where Antony has had Caesar's messenger whipped when my phone beeps. I'm so tangled up in my bedding I jump an inch or two in the air, the phone goes flying and I catch my foot in the duvet and land thwack on the floor, the phone hurtles into the air, I change my direction, shape my body into a preposterous angle and reach ready to catch it and ... miss.

Thwack.

I always was shit at netball.

Untangling myself from the covers before I trip myself over again, I grab my phone, right myself on the floor and look at the screen.

Still mad excited about the Jamal thing. You so deserve this. What you up to today? If you not mixing with mega-stars or working one of your zillion secret jobs obvs. Wanna come play?

It's Luisa.

Ding dong.

'Belle, Belle! Come in.' As Luisa opens the door Marsha propels herself through it and barrels into me, hugs my legs super tight and then grabs my hand and tries to drag me through the hallway.

'Woah.'

I dig my heels in to try and slow her down. Almost-five-year-olds may not be very big but don't ever be fooled into thinking that they lack strength.

'Mummy and Daddy bought me a pony for Chrissmas!' she shouts as I pull her back towards me.

'You bought her a pony?' I ask Luisa.

'Fuck no!' Luisa mouths over Marsha's head. 'Yes, we did, you're going to love GeeGee,' she says out loud.

'You'll love her and love her and love her,' Marsha declares, tugging on my hand again.

'And you keep the pony in the kitchen?' I ask, the corners of my mouth twitching. 'Does it try and get in the fridge?'

'We do. And of course not, she's very well trained. She's very happy in there,' Luisa replies.

'Oh my goodness, she *is* magnificent,' I say as we enter

307

the kitchen and Marsha pulls my arm half out of its socket in her quest to get me to see GeeGee, her beautifully old-fashioned rocking horse. 'And what a wonderful name.'

'Yes, we're going to get her a stars and stripes bikini and give her a pole for her birthday.'

'Don't be silly, Mummy! She wants hay for her birthday. Horses don't wear bikinis!'

'No, they don't. I thought you would have known that, Luisa,' I say in my most playground ner-ner voice, trying not to giggle. 'So with GeeGee here, I guess you won't be interested in any presents in my bag?'

Marsha stops lovingly stroking GeeGee and boings over to my side. 'What is it? What is it?'

'I tell you what, if you have your present from Belle now and we give her hers, will you go and watch a movie whilst we catch up?' Luisa asks and Marsha looks at her mother suspiciously.

'If I don't watch a movie will I still get presents?'

'No,' says Luisa firmly.

I open my eyes wide at her. 'Look, it's day five of the Christmas holidays, I've forgotten what adult company is, Remi seems to been superglued to the office chair and I need half an hour with my best mate and preferably six dozen Christmas cocktails,' she explains.

'Well, in that case...' I crouch down to Marsha. 'Let's make Mummy happy. How about we do the presents then I'll chat to Mum a bit whilst you watch any movie you want and then we'll have fun. What do you think?'

'Okay.' She gives me her cutest look.

'Go and get Belle her present first,' Luisa says to her

daughter who flashes a grin and turns to run from the room. Luisa pulls open the fridge door and takes a glug of wine from the bottle.

'Nice.'

'Seriously. It's medicine.'

'It looks like it's medicine that should be shared.' I grab a glass for myself and another for her from the cupboard. 'Fill, then we'll chill and do twixmas stuff.'

'Twixmas stuff like lying on the sofa drinking and binge-watching TV?'

'Oh yes, baby, that is how we are spending today.'

'Oh my God, can we? Can we really?'

'Yep!'

Remi wanders into the kitchen and heads towards the coffee machine. 'Hi, Belle, how's tricks?'

'All good. Are you mad busy today?'

'Nope.' He slips his arm around Luisa's waist and pulls her towards him.

'Excellent, then you are on Marsha duty whilst wifey and I have the day off to talk all things gal.'

'Yes.' Luisa smiles. 'We'll be curled up in the living room, drinking and watching romcoms and action movies, maybe talking about willies.'

'Nice.' Remi says. 'Mine's huge, by the way. Like a tree trunk.'

'It is.' Luisa nods and I faux gag.

'Seriously, me and Marsh will have the best day, won't we?' he continues, addressing his daughter who has come bowling back into the room.

'I'm having fun with Belle today.'

'Have fun with your dad instead? We could go try out the ice rink at Cribbs?' Remi counters.

Marsha looks conflicted.

'Hey, you go with your dad today, and I'll come back another time and make sure we have a me and you day then. What do you think?'

'Two fun days, yay!' She jumps up and high-fives me and then hands me a scrabbled together wrapped present that looks as if she has used an entire roll of Sellotape to wrap it. 'Look, I've got you your present. You're going to love it.' I do love it immediately. I can picture her, tongue out the corner of her mouth, as she wrapped this.

'I don't want to cut it.'

'I think you're going to have to,' Luisa says, fishing a large pair of scissors from a drawer.

'Yes, don't be silly, Belle. You can cut the paper. It's a salt-dough snowman and Mummy says you're very fond of them.'

'Oh I, am,' I say, willing myself not to look at Luisa, whose smirk I can see out of the corner of my eye.

'Well, I knew that, cos we make them every year,' Marsha replies. 'So here is one just for you.'

'Brilliant.' I cut through the masses of tape, far from easy, and unwrap myself the most perfectly imperfect salt-dough snowman I have ever seen, with an adorable lopsided grin.

'So, spill!' says Luisa who, after giving me another present – Tudor style pottery, God love her! – has made us both get into pyjamas to make sure we maintain the correct mood for the afternoon. And then she insists we do a couple of Jägerbombs, to take us back to our student days and get fully into twixmas. 'I haven't seen you since the party and I know you have news. I want to know what happened down the end of our garden.' She nods in the direction of her hut. 'And what's happening with Jamal? I thought he had binned you?'

'Ouch. Nice. Not really binned, more never even bothered to take me out of the packaging. But we can forgive him for that.'

'We can forgive him if he's going to give you several thousand pounds.'

'Always little Miss Business.'

'It's far easier to have morals with money in the bank.'

'Disagree. Anyway, he's still not going to fund my app.'

'Well then, why message you?'

'Because he has an even better idea, and one that I much prefer. But I do want to talk it through with you, you being my number one business mentor person.'

'I'm glad to hear it. Don't want that Rory Walters waltzing in and stealing my crown.'

'Honey, no one can steal your crown.' I lean across the duvet covering us as we lie at opposite ends of the sofa – just like we did as students – and deliver a great big sloppy kiss on her cheek.

'Hmm, I love it when you kiss me like that,' she says in a weird vampy voice straight out of the Hammer School of

Horror. 'But I love it more when you make me money. So, what is his plan?' Her voice reverts back to normal for the question.

'It's that we join forces to roll out a Shakespeare programme to schools. He gives his name and his support, ties it in with the fact that the RSC are having him in *Coriolanus* next year – Tullus Aufidius, although that's on the DL for now. It's not been announced and he wants to do it as Jamal Clarke not as Jamal, if that makes sense. But I love that he recognises that his celebrity doesn't entitle him to dethrone actors who have worked for decades perfecting their craft to get the top roles. That his ego understands. I think that bodes well for us working together, what do you think?'

'Yep, but he has a reputation for being pretty sound, doesn't he? My understanding is he wants to get involved but not dominate. Something lots of people could take on board.'

'Yes they could...' I stage wink and double point at my best friend.

'Maybe. So, he supports your schools programme? The one you've already set up?'

'Yes. I've had a small degree of success and word is getting around Bristol, but his name attached would give me immediate kudos, and kids will be eager to engage once he's given it his seal of approval. From what he has said so far, I do all the work on the ground, go into all the schools and deliver the actual programme, he promotes it all over his socials and on any media he does, and occasionally he'll come and join me presenting the workshops, give it a bit of star appeal. On top of which, he'll write it off as a charitable expense and pay me a salary so I can roll the programme out to schools who don't have the budget to fund workshops, which is exactly the kind of schools I want to target but can't at the moment because I need to feed myself too. It's going to be immense.' I'm so excited my voice is high-pitched, the words are pouring out at speed. Having Jamal on board is a game-changer.

'And did Rory have anything to do with this?'

'No. In fact, Jamal made a point of it. He said he was grateful that Rory flagged me up but it was my work in the schools in the run-up to Christmas that turned his attention to me. He heard about me speaking at Mandela City Primary and apparently, his nephew loved it. Told him all about it and that prompted him to have a rethink about the best way to use me—'

'Don't suppose he wants to use me?' Luisa says filthily. 'He's my celeb pass. Those shoulders!'

'I think he's good on that score, he's taken. Anyway, as I was saying ... use *me* and my knowledge in a way to benefit the community. He says that whilst he initially agreed to meet me because of Rory and the Shakespeare link he had decided not to get involved because he felt I could easily source the money for an app in a more traditional way and he was worried about the whole apple-fall-from-the-tree thing, so thanks, Dad. But when he saw how enthused his nephew was he thought I was worth a gamble. He wants me to know...' I have a grin as wide as the Pacific at this point, '...that my merit got me back on his radar and nothing else. It was as if he knew how important that was. I appreciated it. I really think this is going to work.'

'No doubt. Look back to where you were less than a month ago, no job and me bitching at you to monetise this thing, and now here you are, in league with the biggest superstar this city has seen since Massive Attack and on your way to realising your dream. So, now you build upon the dream. What's your next step?'

'Seriously? In an ideal world, I'd hire a couple more people who really know their stuff, expand my work into a handbook for them and get this rolled out nationally. I think it could work; I really do.'

'Excellent. This is awesome.'

We giggle and she leans forward again and envelopes me in a huge hug, kissing the top of my head.

'I'm so proud of you, Bells, I always knew you were going to make this work. Bloody superstar.' We sit like this for a minute or two. I love this woman. She lets me go and sits back down her own end of the sofa. 'Now, we've taken care of the important stuff, let's talk the fun stuff.'

'And what's that then?' I say warily.

'That? Why, Rory Walters of course. What is going on there? I like him. I always liked him but I saw a whole new side to him at the party. He was relaxed, so at ease, really good fun. And we did good, didn't we?'

'Oh yeah. You always do good. Your Christmas Eve Eve parties are one of my favourite things about Christmas.' I breathe a sigh of relief. The thing with Luisa is that she knows me so well, sometimes I'm scared she can actually read my mind. And then I would be in trouble.

'Mine too, but I hope you appreciate the effort I went to on Cupid's behalf this year. Poor Remi spent most of the evening banning people from the Nordic hut so we could keep it for the two of you. He wouldn't start his set until everyone there knew the hut was out of bounds. I hope to God you made a good use of it.'

I thought back to that evening, so recent and yet feeling like worlds away and know I have another silly grin on my face. But I can't help it. It had been such a special evening.

'Oh my God, you did! You did! You had sex in the Nordic hut. I'm putting those rugs in the bin now, but so well deserved. I can't remember the last time you had sex.'

'Neither can I, but you can keep your rugs. We didn't.'

'What do you mean you didn't? You didn't what?'

'Didn't have sex with Rory in your hut with a party full of people in your house that could come in at any point.'

'Why not?'

'I refer you to my previous answer.'

'We worked so hard on that for you. We turned it from family central into sex space extraordinaire.'

'Which I greatly appreciate but still, nothing happened. Thank you for trying though. Very sweet and all that.'

'Oh, girl, you know I've got you. You ever want a sex palace prepared for you again, then you know who to call.' She nods, channelling Snoop Dogg in the knowingness of her smile.

'Thanks. I'll bear that in mind.' I am definitely not doing that.

'Cool. So, what were the two of you doing in there all that time?'

The silly smile comes back. 'We cuddled up. Talked. He um ... he...'

'Oh my God, look at your face. You have it *so* bad. He what?'

'He stroked my hair,' I admit, in a very quiet voice because I'm embarrassed. I shouldn't be. But I feel like such a fool now because of how special it had felt that night, the bond I thought we had developed. I thought in that moment that we had something. What an idiot.

And now he isn't returning my messages. I'm used to being the one that disappoints people, the one seen as flaky in her shitty choices. I had expected to disappoint Rory from the very beginning, from when he came to my flat bearing my favourite take-away. The last thing I ever expected was for him to disappoint me.

And for it to hurt so fucking much.

Nope, stop dwelling.

'Ooh, hang on, what happened there?' Luisa pounced.

'Eh?'

'Your face just fell a country mile. One minute you're beaming like a lunatic and then boom. What the fuck happened between him stroking your hair and Little Miss Sad Face.'

'Honestly, Lu. I don't know.'

'You don't know?'

'There's some kind of freaky echo in this room,' I say, casting a look around, trying to distract her and then realising that I want to talk about this. Need to. 'Honestly, Luisa, it's all been a bit of a weird thing. We've practically spent this last month together. If, for whatever reason, normally work, we can't see each other then we're texting, sending each other stupid memes and threads. Otherwise we see each other every day. I've been to lunch with his parents in their home, for Christ's sake. He's gone from some guy I once knew in uni to my ... um, second best friend.' I smile at her. I may be soppy ga-ga in love with Rory but Luisa is my best friend and isn't getting robbed of that cos of some man. But everything I have done, felt, this month I have confided in Rory. We have our own jokes, our ways of speaking. He has become my go-to-guy in a very short space of time and I am missing him.

'I knew you two were spending time together but nearly every day? You've been to his parents' house? There's way too much here to process.'

'You're telling me!'

'So, okay, you've done some kind of fast and furious relationship shit and condensed a year of dating into a couple of weeks, yet you didn't have sex in the love hut?'

'We haven't had sex at all.'

'No!' Luisa bangs her drink down and sits bolt upright. 'No sex at all? I know I've had harsh words for you in the past but you have revolutionised your sexual behaviour in the last few years. From only sleeping with people who look like they're incubating every STD going or have the ability to steal your purse with one hand whilst stroking your face with the other...' I spit my wine out; she isn't far wrong. Funny, harsh but pretty accurate. '. . . You now sleep with no one at all. Ever. Finally, this perfect man comes along who is so into you and you still don't have sex? No sex at all? Little bit of hand play?'

'No! Ewww. Nothing. We've been strictly platonic.'

'Why?'

'Well, he's only here for a month, he doesn't like me like tha—'

'He likes you like that. I've seen him look at you. I've seen him dance with you. He likes you like that.'

'Nah, it's complex.'

'Complex how? You're an adult, he's an adult. You're single, he's single, I'm guessing. So, two consenting adults who like each other like that.' She puts a firm stress on her last six words, just to hammer it home.

'He still has a whole lot of feeling for Jessica.'

'Ahhhh. Okay. But he has to move on at some point, and he may well love Jessica – I imagine he'll love her for ever – but he can still have feelings for you. He needs to pull his...' Luisa whistled and makes nonsensical gestures with her finger '...out and take care of the present and the future, not keep living in the past.'

'I don't know if it's as easy as just saying it.'

'Saying it is a bloody good start. Maybe you could harness that Belle Wilde honesty and do so.'

'I could but I won't. Besides, he's ghosting me at the moment.'

'He's fucking what?' Luisa is bolt upright again.

'Yeah, he normally messages me back within seconds but I haven't heard from him since he took me to see *The Winter's Tale*. It was both beautiful, wonderful dream-come-true stuff and a little bit horrific. It's changed our dynamic, it looks like for good. Not a peep since. Not even when I got in touch to tell him all about Jamal. Dots for a bit but no actual message.'

'What the…? Nah, nah. We're not having this. Ghosting is the height of rudeness. No reason for it other than weak-willed cowardice. Just tell a person how it is and move on. Much better for everyone. That has changed my opinion completely. Com-plete-ly! Twat. How dare he?'

'Well, it's understandable, I think.'

'Of course you fucking do. Because you will excuse everyone's bad behaviour towards you until the end of time. Okay, look at it this way. Imagine Marsha is a grown-up and has spent the best part of a month with someone she really likes, who appears to feel the same and then from nowhere they stop answering her messages or whatever freaky futuristic thing people do then…'

'Hell no!'

'Right. Right? Not okay.'

Beep.

Both of our heads spin as my phone screen lights up.

'Noooo! Is it him?'

I screw my eyes up as I reach for my phone then gently relax them to check the screen. I shoot a look at Luisa.

'What? What!' she says.

'It's Alison.'

Luisa shrugs, of course she doesn't know who Alison is. Why would she? I have been rubbish at keeping her apprised of my life since Rory became my late-night confidante. Have I turned into one of those women, one that dumps her friend for a man? I hope not. I think I just got caught up in the joy of having Rory, hugging it as a secret close to me, maybe scared to share the intensity of my feelings, the speed with which they were changing. 'Um … Alison is Rory's mum.'

'Well, what does she say? Has something happened to him? Is that why he's not answered?'

'Slow your roll. She's reminding me of her invitation to a quiz night at her local pub. Would it be weird if I went? Yeah, it would be weird if I went.'

'Do you wanna go?'

'Nah.'

'Are you lying?' She wrinkles up her nose and pushes her face very close to mine.

'Yah. I like quizzes. And this is a special Christmas quiz. And Alison is sound.'

'And are you an empowered woman who does what she wants as long as it hurts no one else?'

'Well, yeah. I think so. Definitely empowered since I told my dad where to stick it.'

'Something he had coming for a long time. So, empowered woman who does as she wishes whilst causing no harm, are you not going to the quiz night cos you're worried you'll be judged by or upset a man who has ghosted you?'

'Yes.'

'I guess *that's* the wrong answer. Just be you. Tell Alison the truth, say you'd love to go but you think it could be a bit weird. If she doesn't respond then you know where her shonky-assed son gets it from and if she does and says it's cool, then it's cool. Belle it. You've always worked that way, just been straight with people. Sometimes too straight with people. Be straight with her and see what she says. Fuck Rory.'

Yeah, I agree with the sentiment. I do. Sod him. I never want to go out and now I have an invite to somewhere I'd like to go. But deep inside I know it's not that simple.

The course of true love never did run smooth

December Twenty-ninth.
Rory.

I know it will do me some good to get out but I have been struggling to find the motivation. I have been struggling full stop to be honest. Since taking Belle to see *The Winter's Tale* I have been plunged into a really low mood. It's been a long time since I found my emotions to be this overwhelming, this incapacitating. What started out as guilt towards Jessica has morphed into guilt towards Belle, so now I am paralysed with self-loathing over the both of them.

This afternoon I had resolved to dig deep and find the strength to stop prevaricating and message her to say I need space. I have to push her away. I care so much for this woman and I'm beginning to suspect it's reciprocated. But it's because I care so much that I know she deserves better. She needs to be kept away from me, my trajectory. She needs to find someone without my damage, have a full and normal loving life with someone who is able to meet her needs, not with someone who has so much to work out. I need to be a better man to deserve her and I'm not there yet. This plunging into depression after seeing a play is the perfect illustration of why. It's not a rational, normal response and yet for me it is the only one I can manage.

I care for Belle, there's no getting around that. I suspect I'm in those very first stages of falling in love. The attraction has always been there. I remember the first time I caught a glimpse of her in Freshers Week. It was the welcome rave and I saw her as I entered the club, and the breath swooshed out of my body. She had been on a podium and I stood there for a minute or two, entranced as her arms and hair flew around, captivated by her movements, her confidence. I know now that the confidence was a sham; that she was as young and desperately insecure as the rest of us.

As Belle had caught my eye, I had caught Jessica's and she had pursued me with an intent and a determination that turned my head. And I was glad of it. I had fallen in love with Jessica, the love deepening over time. I had been bowled over by her then; she was blonde and polished, articulate and intelligent, and she had wanted me.

Me!

With Jessica I learnt what it was to fall truly in love. Not an attraction from a distance. Not an adolescent school-based crush, proper everyday love where I loved her because of the realities, the flaws, the everyday living with each other, loving each other. The freedom to see her flaws and to be vulnerable and expose mine. Two humans that went on to determinedly build a life for ourselves, together. With every passing day I fell more in love with her, every day I thought it was impossible to love her more and yet every day I did. She had been The One, she really had.

We rarely bickered or argued, not until the few weeks leading up to the accident. I had started to notice and then worry that she was behaving oddly, staying out late claiming it was for work, coming back with the smell of cocktails on her breath, a high in her eyes, showering before she left the house and again the minute she would get home, going to yoga classes twice a week when before she had always said she liked to do it on the bedroom floor with me, watch me watching as she stretched and bent and flexed. I began to fear I was losing her, that she was looking elsewhere. There was such an overwhelming sense of something I did not know. The night of the party I had become so jealous I had accused her of cheating, I lost my temper and I ranted, I became a man I hadn't ever seen before, and she had left. Eyes bleary, vision further impaired by the driving rain on that furious New Year's Eve night. To this day I do not know where she was going.

And now with Belle, if I accept my attraction, accept I am not cheating Jessica and that she is gone, has been for five years and would want me to move on and not grieve for ever, I can't shake the feeling that if I pursue my feelings then I'll be cheating Belle. She lifts me up and helps me see myself through her eyes. She brings out the lighter side of me. The side that laughs, makes stupid jokes, hurtles down a hill on an old tin tray. I try to do the right thing, to move through life with honour, and Belle gets that. She's the same. I like who she sees, the whole man that she pictures. I want to be him. I wish that was all of me. But what she doesn't see so clearly is the dark. The side that I saw, was reminded of, the minute I sat with her in a darkened theatre and watched *The Winter's Tale*; when I saw myself as Leontes.

Was it not my jealousy that had sent Jessica sobbing out into the night? Was I not guilty of the last few years of grasping the control of my environment even more than I had before? Of shaping everything the way I want it to be, need it to be, to allow me to get through life as unhurt and unscarred as is possible? Belle thinks that I am the shining opposite of her dad. But what if I'm not? What if I am very, very similar? The saying about girls falling in love with a man who represents their father is not a cliché for nothing, it is rooted in truth.

I need to put distance between us. No matter how many circles I spin in, I always come back to this same point. Belle may make me feel great about myself but the only thing I know for sure is that I am bound to disappoint her.

Belle.

It's the night of the quiz. I have picked my outfit carefully, washed every single tiny millimetre of me and then spent the afternoon talking myself silly, convincing myself that I am doing the right thing. I have veered back and forth, back and forth, but have come to the conclusion that this decision is the right one.

But now, as I stand outside the pub, I wonder: what the hell am I doing here? I mean really. This is so awkward. I remind myself that Rory hasn't called me for a reason, I can't force my company on him. On his family.

A noisy group of people, all about my age, are laughing and jostling each other across the cobbles. They reach the front doors of the pub and push past me into the warm. As they all pass by me one stops, smiles and holds the door open.

'Here you go, sorry. You were here before us. After you.' He makes a swooshing forward motion with his hands and now I really am stuck.

'I don't know if I want to,' I say. Of course I do, because that's not at all weird. He smiles.

'Ahh, it's toasty in there, look!' And he gestures towards the fire burning in the long narrow pub, chucking out warmth. 'It's brass-balls cold out here. You know you're going to have fun, come on.' He cocks his head and like some conditioned woman of decades past, I smile meekly in thanks and walk through the door. He grins, pleased with himself for 'helping' me and leaps off to join his friends at the bar. He was well-intentioned.

I stand in the doorway of this pub, the smell of mulled wine arising from a great big warmed copper pan on the bar, which runs along most of the narrow room, with a fire blazing in the grate at the very end of the pub, its flames licking the inside of the fireplace. As welcoming as it is, I know I shouldn't be here.

Now I'm inside the door my realisation is even more intense. This is a shit idea. I've got it wrong again. Just because I like the thought of what this evening could bring doesn't mean it is a good idea.

'Belle! Belle! Over here!' Alison stands up from where she is seated three tables down. 'Look, everyone, it's Belle! You're going to *love* her.'

I smile, at least I hope it's a smile but I would bet money that it may have been a grimace, and walk towards her table. I grudgingly acknowledge that half of me has been hoping that Rory would be here and see me and that grin would cross his face, reassuring every part of me that he hasn't gone off the idea of spending time with me. Yet at the same time a little part of me is relieved to see he is not at the table.

'Hello, love, get that coat and scarf off before you bake, it's crazy warm. Budge up, Dave, Belle is going to sit right here.' She pats the banquette cushion next to her.

'That's all right. I really only nipped in to say hi but I really…'

'Nonsense, we need you. Belle is the queen of all things Christmas. There is nothing she doesn't know.'

I definitely grimace at that.

'We need you on our team. Usually I've got sports covered…' Dave says, 'geography and politics is Eve…' A woman of similar age to Alison smiles and nods '…we have Janet on popular culture—'

'There's nothing I don't know about *Celebs Go Dating* and *Naked Attraction*,' says the woman sat next to Eve and wearing a Christmassy sweater that says 'Like A Virgin'. Of course this is Janet. How could it not be?

'And Ally has literature and history but we need you onside,' Dave continues. 'Even if Rory makes it, we know he's … well, not madly into Christmas even before … um… Anyway, he's got caught up with something work-related and we really want to beat Steve's team over there.' He nods towards a table that looks very serious, with one member even sharpening pencils. I look back at this table, everyone with festive jumpers on – I should have bought that hat – and a look in their eyes like I may be the one to save Christmas for them. Shit.

'So we *need* you.' Alison pats the cushion again and Dave beams at me. Eve and Janet are nodding to back them both.

Rory is caught up. He isn't going be here. My stomach dips with disappointment at the exact time my brain reminds me what a relief this is. I can stay, not hurt Alison's feelings, have a nice evening and then leave and by the time Rory knows that I was here he will be heading back to Australia anyway and I won't have to see the pity on his face.

I sit down and squidge on up.

The bell rings and the quiz begins, with questions coming in thick and fast. I am amazed at how competitive the lovely Alison is, and the breadth of her knowledge.

'Dominican Republic,' Alison hisses with the ferocity of a stage villain as she answers a question about where people begin their Christmas Celebrations in October. She has almost jumped out of the seat with excitement that she knows and that the pencil-sharpening team looked bemused by the question.

'How do you know that?' I ask.

'My old neighbour is from Santo Domingo but I've been reading up for this.'

'Definitely a tradition I can get behind. Shall we move? Little bit of Caribbean sunshine for our Christmas next year.' I giggle.

'Next question…' The quizmaster, who is dressed in a beautifully cut three-piece wool suit, silk tie and matching artfully angled handkerchief and has dreadlocks so long they are doubled up, shoots us a look that manages to combine both the widest grin and eyes that firmly say, 'Shut up for a minute.' I like him. 'What was the traditional Christmas meal in England before turkey became popular?'

'Ooh, I know this. It's a pig's head and um ... um ... mustard, it's mustard,' I hiss at the team. I'm loving this and learning tons of stuff.

Although how anyone is supposed to know how many houses per second Santa has to visit to get all of his deliveries done, I don't know. The quizmaster gives us a margin of error of twenty, not enough, and there is some very irritating fist-bumping coming from the other table. I don't want to wish them ill – although Alison's filthy looks are sending bubonic plague levels of ill over there – and the results haven't been counted yet but they really do need to dial down their levels of smug.

Somehow Dave knows it was twelfth-century French nuns that started the tradition of putting an orange in the bottom of the stocking.

'He may not know much about history but he seems to have the habits of nuns ingrained in his brain!' Alison confides in me with an arch lift of her brows.

'Very niche.' I waggle mine back.

'She gave me one of those novelty books one Christmas about nuns when she was threatening to leave me for a convent!' Dave immediately responds.

'You were going to become a nun?' I ask, interest piqued.

'Of course not, but it's best to keep him on his toes, make him think I may have a better offer.'

'She's always been very comfortable in a costume and on her knees!' Dave jokes and Alison hits him with a coaster.

'She's not the only one.' Janet guffaws.

'Forgive him, Belle. He hasn't learnt that we live in the twentieth-first century and his humour hasn't been acceptable since the seventies.'

'My friend Temperance would say there's no better offer than being a Bride of Christ!' I giggle.

'And she'd be right. I hope you're listening to this, Dave, no better offer! I've heard about this Temperance, Rory says that she … ooh, Dave, go!'

The dapper quizmaster has rung an old-fashioned bell to signify that the quiz has reached half time. Dave practically leaps out of his chair and, taking our orders, hotfoots it to the bar. Eve and Janet get up with equal speed to peg it to the loo.

'I'm so glad you're here, Belle.' Alison reaches out and puts her hand across mine.

'Me too. But tell me, how are you?' I say quietly, so to escape earshot of anyone at neighbouring tables. I haven't see her since her op, though Rory has filled me in with a lot of it. But as supportive and empathetic as a son can be, or a husband, I don't think they can truly empathise with what it must feel like to be preparing yourself to go under the knife like that. I know now is neither the time or place but I want her to know I care and am an ear should she ever want it.

'I'm okay.' She looks at me and I can see that she understands my intention. That, like me, she doesn't want to waste this moment with small talk.

'Honestly, I'm scared. I don't want it. I know I have to, I know not doing so would be beyond stupid. But the thought of walking into that hospital, actively putting one foot in front of another so I can lie there and have a surgeon take such a big part of me away... I'm terrified and don't want it.'

I put my hand over hers before I speak. 'Look, I know you have a lifetime's worth of friends, and you have Dave and Rory, but if you want to rant at someone, say all the nonsensical stuff you're scared to confide in people who know you really well, I'm here. I listen, I don't judge and I won't ever tell a soul. Call me the minute you want or need a rant or a sob or just a whisper, and at any time, day or night. Honestly, I keep the strangest hours so you won't be disturbing me. Call me.'

'You're a love and you're right, I'm very blessed with the people around me—'

'Like attracts like,' I say quickly

She smiles. 'But an ear outside my social circle, that would be nice. I have the Macmillan nurse too and they are wonderful but there's something about you, Belle. I may well take you up on that. In the meantime, I am so grateful that you are in my son's life.'

'Ahh,' I say and then am unsure of what to say next. I don't know if I am? Your son seems to have booted me out of his life. Luckily the need to fill the gap is relieved as Dave comes back to the table, a tray of drinks precariously balanced in his huge hands.

'Ooh, would you look at that! There he is now. Rory! Rory!' Alison screeches with excitement and my forehead crinkles as intensely as a Klingon's. I'm too scared to raise my eyes from the table and all the doubts I have about coming along tonight resurface. However, there is no escaping. I slowly – very slowly – raise my eyes up towards the door and as I do so I see Rory standing there, staring right at me, and as he looks at me the expression on his face freezes my heart.

Shit! He's going to think I'm a right weirdo and he'd be right. Whilst I may feel very comfortable sat here with his family, it definitely looks a bit stalkery. I should never have come.

I look under the table for an escape and then picture myself crawling across the flocked carpet on my hands and knees like all heroines in all ;movies ever. Although without the rom and on my part not really feeling the com. Plus we all know how that move would pan out, I'll end up looking completely bonkers.

What am I going to do? Shit, shit, shit!

I have no option but to stay put. I raise my eyes again to meet his. A small seed in me – okay, a giant avocado stone of a seed – hopes that when I see his face this time it will be flooded with the pleasure it has been all month. That I'll see the obvious joy at being around me weave through his mouth, his green eyes, that look that is so, so addictive, that it seduces me into thinking of future possibilities. Hope is fluttering all the time whilst my inner voice is saying to me in a firm, dismissive and slightly patronising tone: if he's not answering your calls or returning your messages it's because he doesn't want to. None of these 'he's lost his phone', 'it's out of charge' excuses are valid. People don't answer because they don't want to. There isn't going to be any joy in that face to see you sat with his mum and step-dad.

I look and see horror is flooding his face like armies on a dawn-flushed plain. My heart freezes even further as the ice of his alarm slowly fills my veins, cracking them one at a time as all hope seeps out of me.

'Rory's here,' Eve trills as she darts back to the table, unaware of what is unfolding, the subtext. Janet is trying to pull the quizmaster in the corner. Alison and Dave both look from Rory to me and back to him again, recognising that there is something going on that they don't know about. That I am a cuckoo in the nest.

Rory gives Alison a sad little half smile and then wordlessly turns and leaves.

My face is burning and I am filled with mortification, with shame. My selfish desire to take part in this quiz, experience a normal family Christmas activity, to try and force Rory into talking to me, the embarrassment of all of this floods through me. I feel as if I have betrayed Alison's trust and I make a lunge for my coat, hat and scarf. I need to get out of here. It is no longer important how many bloody stops Santa makes in a second; the heat from the fire combines with my humiliation and something is stuck in my throat, I am getting hotter and hotter and hotter and feel like a volcano trying to force the lava back down, knowing its spill and the torrent of destruction it will unleash are inevitable.

I wind my way around the table.

'Belle. What's going on?' Alison asks. I shrug my shoulders because right now I cannot make words come. If I open my mouth and make a sound I am scared of what will rush out.

I push my way through the still crowded bar, through the door, and the cold of December blasts my face. I don't dare cry; each tear will freeze as an icicle and I may be stuck this way for ever. I cannot be this way for ever. I am a mess.

I see Rory walking down the hill towards the corner of Picton Street. Once he turns onto Stokes Croft I will lose him; the swirls of people that populate this area will be out in full force tonight. I can hear them even from here.

'Rory.' I force my mouth open, to call him, to stop him. For all of his new-found dislike of me I need to hear him, I want him tell me why he cannot face me anymore. What has caused this shift from friends to enemies. This could be my last chance. No sound comes. I try again and this time it bellows out of me like wind filling sails, like Blanche in *A Streetcar Named Desire*.

'Rory!' I watch as he pauses. He stands still for a minute and I take advantage of his lack of movement, running helter-skelter down the hill, praying that I don't hit an icy patch, that my ankle doesn't turn, that I catch him before he begins his walk away again.

'Rory!' I shout a second time, to keep him there. This time he turns and under a streetlamp I see his face lit up – drawn, sad. *Wait for me, wait for me* runs through my head;

I'm telepathically willing him not to turn and walk away again. I race towards him, my feet slowing to a running stop as I approach the lamppost.

'Rory!' My breathing is heavy now and I bend slightly to catch my breath before looking up at his stony face. 'I can explain.'

'There's no need. Go back in, win that quiz for Mum.' His tone is dulled, a robot just before the batteries run out. He smiles a little wan smile and suddenly instead of wanting to make everything right I am filled with anger. How dare he? He doesn't answer my messages, he walks out, away from his family when he sees them – presumably to avoid me – and now his sad little smile is fully infused with a pity-me martyr tone. Nah, bollocks to that.

I know this glorious man in front of me has his issues, I know that something has occurred to turn him from Technicolor to washed-out sepia and I strongly suspect that somehow he has mixed me up in his misery and now he needs to escape. I get that. I understand a need to escape. I spent most of my late teens embracing that. But understanding he is grieving, that he has things he needs to process, doesn't mean he gets a get-out-of-jail-free card. It doesn't mean that he can't be held accountable for his actions here and now. His mum has had to go without having him around for years and now he's in the country, what? He can't sit in a pub with her and her friends, make her really happy for an evening, because of *what*? Because he is having some kind of tantrum, some kind of crisis about me being present. So, stand like an adult and ask me to leave, don't silently walk out and leave your mum there confused and abandoned again.

And actually, what about me? We've been good friends now for a month, a sped-up whirlwind of a friendship that may not see December out, fair enough, but that doesn't give him the right to go from being my closest confidante to someone who won't pick up the phone. Nah, nah. I'm not having it. I deserve a little bit more respect than that and I'm going to bloody take it, not thinly smile and accept that being treated like bullshit is all I deserve.

'Do you know what, you can stop that. Stop that right now. *You* go back and win that quiz for your mum and then you can come find me and talk to me, tell me why you've suddenly turned into someone whose behaviour lacks any kind of merit. Who thinks it's okay to ghost his mate, not give a shit about how it makes her feel.' I am standing tall now, one hand on my hip, the other waving about with the ferocity of an Italian mama when her boys have let her down.

'Look, I get that you and my mum get on and I'm happy about that. But I'm a grown man, I know what I'm doing. I don't need you to tell me what to do right now,' he snaps back. I raise an eyebrow.

'Yeah, you think? I beg to differ. Nah. Not beg, I do differ. I think that's exactly what you need. Your mum wants you in there next to her. You've flown halfway across the world to spend time with her and what now, cos I've done something to piss you off, upset you somehow, you're going to let her down? I know you're more of a man than that. I know you are.'

He breathes deeply and shakes his shoulders a little before standing and staring at me, the lost look temporarily gone from his eyes.

'Yeah, you're right. I need to go back.'

'Correct. Now I'll get myself home so you don't have to put up with me looming over the table but you kinda owe me an explanation later. You can't be all you-deserve-to-surround-yourself-with-people-who-respect-you and then go and undermine that at the last minute with your own behaviour. I need to know what I've done to cause this flip of attitudes. You owe me that.' His face softens and I fight everything inside me to stop doing the same. His absence has hurt me.

'You haven't done anything, Belle. Really, you haven't. It's me…' He reaches out to touch me and I flinch back. I can feel the tears coming now but unlike before when I felt frozen, this time they are hot, washing down my cheeks, melting tracks as they go.

'Don't you dare. Do not dare pull that line out.'

'But it's—'

'I don't care how true it is, you can find a better way to say it. You're an articulate man. And you know that I wouldn't have believed you a little while back, I would have assumed it was me at fault and that you just didn't know how to say that. But something's happened recently, shifted, and it's thanks in part to you that I don't feel that way anymore. I have been wracking my brains for days, trying to work out why you can't celebrate the Jamal thing with me, a thing *you* set up the meeting for, and I don't think I've done anything wrong, I really don't. I think you have. Regardless of whatever you're going through, and I am here for you if you want me to be…' I pause to draw breath; that is a lot of words tumbling out at once. 'Nothing will change that, I am here to hear you, but nothing stops you sending a frigging text to say, "You know what, I need a bit of time, my head's a bit of a mess but I'm pleased for you". And expecting that from you doesn't make me egocentric and self-centred. It makes me someone worthy of a fucking explanation when you fall off the face of the earth!'

'You're right.' He shrugs his shoulders and I am infused with a mix of emotions – pity, empathy, irritation, anger – but I hold them back, let him speak. 'You've been a good friend to me this month and I shouldn't have ignored your messages and of course I'm pleased for you with the Jamal thing. You deserve all the support in the world. It's a good business decision for him as well, adds more to his profile, and pleases his heart. Don't see it as a favour; he didn't do it because you're likeable, although you are, he did it because he can see it makes sense to have you on his team. You can be trusted to deliver his vision in an honourable and effective way. Your merits won this. I do owe you an apology and probably an explanation but Belle, right now, right now you're right, I need to get in that pub and spend some time with my mum, put a smile on her face. And truthfully I don't know how to say what I need to say to you.' He flashes me a smile, a brief fake one and I have a vision of me putting my hand in his mouth, pushing it down his throat and pulling out these words he is having difficulty saying. I don't want to hear about how Jamal feels about me. I need to hear how Rory feels.

Rory nods in the direction of The Mont and we turn to walk back up the hill. Our feet falling into a rhythm together, ironic symbolism. This time the warmth of the pub isn't scaring me off but now tempting me as a symbol of what I can't have. We'd been having fun before Rory turned up, I wanted to be part of beating smug team quiz-winny face but also I need to deal with those words – he needs to say stuff to me and doesn't know how.

'Okay, you may have things you need to say to me and don't know how to. I'm going to gloss over the fact that that in itself is a little hurtful, as you've grown to be someone I feel I can talk to honestly. Be me. In fact, I've confided more in you in the past month than I have practically anyone else in my entire life. I let you in and I'm thankful for that, you have been doing a good job of teaching me to have less walls, be more open rather than merely pretending to be. It's a shame that you've fucked me over at the last minute.' I pull myself back, remind myself that my words need to be constructive not merely reactive and coming from a place of hurt. Although it's hard. My emotions want to scream at his face right now, jolt him into having an emotional reaction. A purge.

'Sorry. I'm not trying to be aggressive, or judgey or blaming. I'm trying to be good here, honest, but I'm hurt.' Even this admission isn't enough to make Rory say anything in response. He is still matching my pace but his eyes are very much focusing on the pavement. I take a deep breath. I'm going to push forward; even if I receive no answers it may do me some good to say it. I need to say it. I've spent years biting back my feelings with my dad, avoiding confrontation and uncomfortable moments, I'm done with that now. Now I want to speak but do so in a mindful way, not ride roughshod over the person I'm talking to simply because I have found my voice. We reach the square archway that leads to the entrance of The Mont and both stop. I don't have much time before he heads back through those doors, leaving me out here.

'What I am trying to say is I'm sorry you don't feel you can talk to me like I have learnt to talk to you—'

'No, that's not it, Belle.'

'Well, what is it?' I pause, my breath held in my throat as I telepathically plead for him to open up, tell me what is causing this look in his eye, what has changed us so drastically from that couple that had cuddled up in front of the fire on Christmas Eve Eve, him stroking my hair, the desire between us palpable and, I had hoped, mutual.

How had we gone from that to this? Luisa always talks about how I'm blunt and just say things, and it's true. I ask the questions that I need the answers to but that doesn't mean it's easy for me. I don't have some forcefield of courage, I still have all the inhibitions everyone else does, more than many. It takes a lot to reach deep inside and vocalise it. But I need to ask this question.

'Is this because of the Nordic hut? Are you worried I have some kind of mad crush on you and you don't reciprocate it? That's okay, that can be said here, now, and I'll walk away, leave you to go see your mum, and our friendship will survive that bombshell.'

'No, no, it's not that.' He laughs but it's a bitter laugh, one completely devoid of joy or positivity. It is not a laugh I have heard from him before.

I decide to bite the bullet. If he's leaving in a couple of days and determined to ignore me then this may be my only chance and suddenly I want it said.

'I do, you know.' Argh! So articulate.

'Do what?' He looks at me.

'I do have a crush but I don't need you to feel the same. I just want you to know that spending time with you means I've changed my type, and that's a good thing. You've taught me what I'm looking for in a partner, the values I wish for. That's a massive reset.'

'Ha. You've moved from self-serving arseholes to completely broken. Good move, Wilde. You may want to reconsider that.'

'No. No, I don't. And broken? I don't think so. I think everything you have done since Jessica's death is really human. I don't think you're broken, I think you're normal. Actually, scratch that, you're not normal, you're remarkable. You are a kind man, a gentleman. You put others first, you don't see the bad in people apart from in yourself, which from my biased view is somewhat misguided. You have brought a confidence and a security to my life just by being in it and that will be more valuable to me than you can ever know. In this short space of time, Rory Walters, you have taught me how to love properly, with boundaries and self-respect and toe-curling lust. I thought I'd be stuck with the bad boys for ever and now I have no interest at all. None. I want a man like you, not a Lost Boy. Sure, it's a shame you don't reciprocate my feelings but I'll survive. Don't think I'm standing here offering to fix you, heal your wounds. I'm not. Partly because that has to come from you, but also because I don't think you need fixing. I think you're more than worthy of my love and I think deep down somewhere you must know that.' I take a breath. I have been hoping at some point he might interrupt me, especially at the toe-curling lust bit that had fallen out of my mouth but he has remained silent and is now looking at me, shaking his head slowly.

'I know I said I don't need an answer but I was lying. Right now, I really need you to say something, talk to me. I've just laid everything out for you and this silence is torture. Please. Anything.'

'Look, Belle, you are an amazing woman and if things were different, if I were the man you think I am, not the man I know myself to be, then, well then, we'd be living a very different life. But I can't do this now. I can't.'

'I know you need to get inside before the quiz is over, I get that. But we could talk tomorrow?' I gesture at the door and feel a little bit ashamed of myself. It feels a bit like I'm begging, throwing dignity to the winds but I need to know I've given this my best shot. And if the timing is the issue I can wait until tomorrow. I just want an honest conversation.

'No.' He says this firmly, holding my eyes as he does so. 'No. Belle, you and me, it's not going to happen. It will never happen. Not here and now, not tomorrow. There is too much you don't understand.'

'I can't understand what I'm not told.' I immediately cringe. Oh shut up, walk away. Why am I still talking?

I watch him close his eyes, draw in a deep breath, open his eyes and fix me firmly with his gaze. Another deep breath. What is probably only a matter of seconds feels like forever.

'Belle. Go home. Go to Luisa's. Go live your life to the best it can be. There is no place for you here. I'm not interested, it's too much and you need to leave me alone now. I'm really sorry if I have led you on but you need to go.' Giving me a look of firm resolve he nods abruptly at me and turns on his heel, opening the door to the pub, a wave of laughter and voices streaming out into the night. He does not look back, not once, as I stand there and my heart, my hopes, my love are smashed into tiny weeny pieces on the cobbles.

Words pay no debts, give her deeds.

December Thirtieth.
Rory.

Bing.
    I reach out from my bed and grab my phone. I'm extra groggy this morning; I couldn't sleep at all last night. The self-loathing and the guilt are eating me from the inside out and rightfully so. The enormity of the impact of my words is making the guilt I felt before seem tiny. I have truly caused hurt and damage now. I can see Belle's face as I broke all of my rules and lied to her. Lied to her to protect her was what I told myself at the time.

Fool.

Cruel fool.

I imagine I will fall asleep at night with Belle's face seared onto the backs of my eyelids for the foreseeable future. Only from now on it won't be her laughing as we tear down that hill at wildly irresponsible speeds or as we lie in the park making snow angels. It will be her standing opposite me outside the pub with the hurt I have caused shaping her whole face.

Bing.

Seriously?

I check it and see it is Mum. She had a fair few things to say to me last night when I came back to the pub minus the woman that she had fallen in love with almost as much as I had. Self-indulgent, cruel, misogynistic and bullshit were but a few. She clearly feels the need to add some more this morning.

I really do not want to open this message.

The fact that I am a thirty-one-year-old man seemed lost on her last night as she gave me a dressing down in front of the entire table – the entire pub – that would have been more suited to a nine-year-old boy. I don't need my mum to tell me what an arse I have been. I know that. I knew that I had made a mistake the minute I had turned and walked away from Belle and I was too much of a self-righteous, self-indulgent twat to turn back and chase after her.

You've had all night to think. Now, what are you going to do?

When I ask what are you going to do it's a rhetorical question. Obviously, you are going to go find her, apologise and see how you can make this right.

Bing.
Really, a third?

I know you meant well, but you need to let her make her decisions herself. Making them for her is outdated and an example of your need to control destroying your life.

Harsh! But nothing new. This had been another overall theme of last night.

I know you can love again. Belle knows you can love again. It's just you who needs to convince yourself.

As had that.
Bing.

And quickly. Very quickly.

Jesus Christ, I need coffee. But she's right. I know she is. I need coffee and a plan.

———————

'She is not there.' Temperance pokes her head around the door of the mini-mart.

'Any idea where she could be?' Stupid question, as if Temperance has some kind of superhero vision or psychic skills. Both of which I am fairly certain she would view as occult and worthy of God's righteous and cleansing flame.

'Mmmmmhhmmmmmmmm.' She draws herself up and looks me up and down, hand on her hip, her cheeks sucking in.

My brow furrows and my shoulders rise.

'She gone off with that friend of hers, you know, the child's mother.' She flips her hand around. 'She did not look happy. She did not look like the Belle I know.'

'She looked...' Innocence comes out of the shop behind his mother, arches his brow, folds his arms like his mum. 'She looked like someone has proper upset her, you know what I mean?'

'Yeah, I know,' I say. 'Thank you.'

'She look like *all* the demons from Hell have come up here and danced around her, pinned her down and then the

devil himself has risen up and twisted out her soul...'
Temperance explains.

Innocence nods as his mother continues.

'She look like someone has laid juju on her and she did not have enough love in her heart for Jesus to know that these things are the preserve of witches and conmen.'

'She didn't even wave,' Innocence adds.

———————

I toy with the idea of going to Luisa's but in each scenario I imagine I end up getting punched in the face. Sometimes by Remi, usually by Luisa and occasionally the both of them. None of my imagined scenarios involve me being allowed to speak to Belle and I think they are probably accurate. I need a better plan than turning up on Luisa's doorstep.

Obviously, I have tried to call her and she has not picked up. That's unlike Belle. She always answers her phone; I've seen it. Even when she really doesn't feel like talking to anyone, even when it's her father merely ringing to have a go. Although of course there is always the possibility that Luisa has kidnapped it and locked it in a steel box. That is way more probable than Belle letting it ring out.

I think I need some help. I do not want to sit in this car and dwell on all the ways in which I've messed up, all the ways Belle could be feeling right now because of my knee-jerk reaction to seeing her and panicking. I need action not overthinking. I look out the car window and see Temperance putting up a new display outside the shop to entice customers in. Hmm, maybe not her. Not that I'm doubting the power of prayer – oh, actually, good point. I'll take *all* the help I can get at his moment. I wind down the window.

'Temperance, I need your help. Will you put me in your prayers? And Belle too?'

'That sweet girl is always in my prayers. Now move on out of here. Sitting there, scaring away my customers. They're going to think you're police. Go on, begone.' She flaps her hands at me as if I'm an errant chicken.

I drive towards Eastville Park. I don't want to go all the way back to my flat, and I'm not sure that I want to go to my mum's. Sitting by the lake will be the perfect place to think.

As I drive I cast my mind back to the times Belle, Marsha and myself have driven around in this car, and how much we have giggled. I've not had such carefree feelings in a long time. That is what I want in my life. I want a family of my own. Funny what one month can do to your life. One month and a glaringly sharp moment when you hurt someone you care about deeply because of pig-headed stubborn control-freakery. There is nothing I want more than to recreate that family feeling at Belle's side. But right now, the only thing that matters is to make her realise how much I regret hurting her. To make her see that I think she is a miracle.

Enough daydreaming. I need to act, formulate my next steps. As much as it pains me, Mum is going to have to be part of my crack team. She'll bring ideas to the table, she devours romance books on her Kindle – Dave used to joke they could have had a tropical holiday every year if she just stopped buying every romance book that was ever published. Plus she will make sure I never hear the end of it if I don't give it my best shot.

And Jamal, I could do with him on board too. He is super busy, yes, but he knows me well, has met Belle and likes her. He'd been great for talking through things the other day and he's a master of creative thinking. That, and he has a way with romantic partners. I've seen him in action, it isn't just his sculpted jaw and millions in the bank that win him his success there. Ever since he was eight that man has been able to cast a spell.

This is the start of a plan. Now to implement it.

Mum, you're right, I need to do what I can to apologise and try and win her back. Wanna help?

Oh yes. Glad to hear it. What are you going to do?

Ummm. That's the thing, I'm not sure yet.

Okay, you need to make a big romantic gesture, like those in Love Actually. *Is she going to an airport at all? Oh and a speech, you definitely need a speech, like Jude Law's in* The Holiday.

I haven't watched those movies in years.

Well go watch them today. Get tips from the masters. You can fast forward to the main bits.

Okay, any other advice?

Preferably some that doesn't involve watching movies that I remember being quite long and which are bound to make me feel wildly inadequate...

Hmm, make sure you tell her you've been a fool. That she's the one for you, that she is not second best to Jessica. I mean don't say that if it's not true, but if it is, then say it. And music, definitely you need to think of music. Look at that lovely Andrew Lincoln with the flip cards.

Love Actually *again?*

Yes! See, you do know. Just watch Love Actually *and then do that.*

Great, thanks.

No need for sarcasm. Oh and those nice jeans, the ones I said I like, wear those. With some of that nice citrussy aftershave you have.

Okay. *Love Actually*, clean clothes, wash. Got it.
Which boils down to a big romantic gesture that will terrify me and basic personal hygiene. Time to see if Jamal has anything to add.

Ooh ... 'The Tide Is High' by Blondie. That's a song you need to use. 'Number One'. That tells her she's the centre of your world.

She is quite literally your number one. And she looks a bit like Debbie Harry as well, you know, but with dark hair.

Okay … that isn't a bad idea. I can see where Mum is going with it.

I send Jamal a quick message and hope he has the time to come back to me.

Hey, I'm reaching out for some personal advice. You were so helpful the other day. Hit me up if you have a minute.

His reply is immediate.

Always time.

I listened to what you said. And you were right but when I saw Belle – funnily enough at The Mont with my mum – I flipped a bit and told her to sod off and leave me alone. I was caught up in the guilt, the Jessica thing, the not being good enough thing. But then the minute I walked away I realised I'd cocked up, that like you said, Jessica is past, always loved but past. Belle, I want her in my future. Now she's in hiding, she's hurt and I'm an arsehole. I may have made the biggest mistake of my life. You're an emotionally intelligent man, any advice on how to make it up to her? Feel free to be blunt.

Jamal comes straight back.

Grand gesture. Make her feel special, step out of your comfort zone and do something that is completely for her. It's about love languages. Work out what hers is and then communicate to her that way. Making a bit of a twat of yourself won't hurt either, especially if you've made her feel silly for her honesty, you be sillier, show her you'll do anything to apologise, and tell her your truth, man. Be honest. Stop bottling shit up cos it doesn't just damage you, it radiates out, you know, like a pebble in a stream. You've been honest about how your choices have hurt your mum, and now they've hurt Belle so you need to look at that. Oh and sort this shit out quick. Do not let it fester, the more time she has the more time she will build that hurt into the core of her. Get it out as quick as you can. Blunt enough?

How he does this in no time at all I don't know. I do know he's right though.

Brilliant, cheers, mate. I may come back to you in a bit for more. I'm going to try and formulate something now.

Cool cool.

Okay, so mum's list is big gesture, aftershave, nice jeans and the song 'Number One'.

Jamal's is a big gesture – so I guess that I am definitely going with that – something I find uncomfortable that Belle loves and doing it quick. Plus, something about love languages. I do a quick google and decide that makes sense. It really does.

I pull in, sit back in the car and close my eyes. Forget the lake, I'm going to sit here for another ten minutes and see what pops into my head. I've solved some of my biggest work problems this way, now I just have to solve my life problem too.

It doesn't take ten minutes and I have a great idea … I think. I am absolutely terrified. It's going to need Jamal to risk his professional reputation for a bit, and I'll have to get Belle in place. The thought of carrying out this plan is so anxiety-inducing, so out of my comfort zone, that I'm sweating merely at the imagining of it. If this doesn't make Belle see how sorry I am, how serious I am and how much I want to spend my life with her then I don't know what will. As long as I don't collapse with hives and terror beforehand.

If Jamal says yes, I'm going to need to pull back every skill that my English degree gave me, and all in time for tomorrow. This is going to be tight!

They do not love that do not show their love.

December Thirty-first.
Belle.

'Go pack a bag then, babyface. Oh, no. Ah-ah-ah-ah!' Luisa does her staccato machine-gun noise as she guides Marsha from her stool towards the sink and flashes me a look that says I should know better. We've been sitting pulling out melty marshmallows, one at a time, from our hot chocolates and dropping them dripping into our mouths. Our hands and faces are a little sticky. 'You are both gross.'

I puff out my cheeks and tilt my head at an angle to epitomise my grossness. Luisa shoots her eyebrows up and purses her lips. I love her.

With Marsha dispatched upstairs Luisa sits on the stool next to me and ripples her fingers across my knees at speed. 'So Marsha is going to Remi's mum's for the night, I have given up being a good mother and you and I can spend New Year's Eve in style!'

'Hmpf,' I say as I gulp down another sticky drippy marshmallow and then start to swirl patterns in the foamy top with my finger.

'No, you have to do better than hmpf. Much better. This is my first New Year's Eve out since my pre-pregnancy days and I only called on Remi's mum so I can cheer you up, so you *are* going to make me feel young again.'

'Can Remi do that? I'm not feeling particularly fresh and youthful right now.'

'Remarkable seeing that you're behaving like a bloody three-year-old.' She scowls, in jest. I think.

'Look, I wanna go dancing. I may feel far too old when I get there as students trip around us, we look wildly out of place and then throw a hip out. But still, I want to try. So come on, gee up. Where we going to go?'

I deep breathe and roll my eyes at her.

'I guess we could go to Lakota. Jamal has guestlisted me,' I say, my tone deliberately nonchalant. He had messaged me yesterday afternoon and whilst I hadn't really felt like it, I know a return to the stomping ground of our youth will make Luisa's day.

'What?'

'Lakota.'

'Did you say Jamal has guestlisted you? What the hell? Why, *why* did you not mention this before? Are you seriously shitting me? Guestlisted for Jamal's homecoming set, tonight? New Year's Eve. Like the most sought-after sold-out New Year's event this evening. One of the big last nights in Lakota before they shut it?'

'Yeah.' I snap my mouth shut like a baby bird, another marshmallow down.

'I'm going to take that bloody mug away from you if you're not careful. No, you can stop doing that with your mouth, I am not going to kiss you. Tonight, baby, we *are* going dancing.'

I love Luisa, and it's great to see her so enthusiastic, but to be honest, the last thing I feel like doing tonight is dancing. Hiding under a quilt and feeling the heaviness of my Norton Shakespeare on my legs, that could work. Staying there for a year, maybe. I could get behind that.

Rory.

Things are going well. Although my mother is determined that I find a way of getting her in to the club. I tried to argue that Lakota may not be the best place for her, its finest hour has passed, and that clubbing isn't the same now as it was in her day. She clipped me around the ear, muttered something about how that wasn't illegal then either and reminded me that it was not my job to make decisions for others, has this week not taught me this? And if I don't find a way to get her in she will make such a scene outside that the bouncers carry her in, naked on a palanquin, just to get her to shut up.

I believe her.

Everything else seems lined up for tonight, although I have a strict timetable. I need to run into town and pick up some props. I'm hoping there will still be some places selling these things, it could be a case of finding them at knock down prices or finding them all sold. I have the music primed, I've chosen three songs – just snippets of each – and hope she understands what I'm trying to say with them. Then I have the biggest job of all to do, but Jamal reckons I just need to have faith in my feelings, my natural abilities and to let it flow. Easy for him to say. He's promised if I mail it over he'll scan and tweak it, if he really feels it needs it. I can't really ask for more than that, although obviously I had to. Cos I had to ask for mum to be guestlisted as well. Jamal's laugh is still echoing in my ear. Main thing is, plan seems a go-go.

Belle.

My phone rings and I see it's my dad. I shoot a look across at Luisa. I have been ignoring calls from Rory but I can't ignore this one.

'You don't have to answer that, you know,' she says.

'Apart from I do,' I say. 'What if something has happened again?' I take the call, bracing myself to hear whatever it is I have done wrong this time.

'Belle!' His voice booms down the phone and in a jovial tone I am not used to. 'My first-born daughter.' My eyes widen and I look across at Luisa in shock and mouth, 'He's being nice.'

'Mum and I wanted to ring to wish you a Happy New Year.' I hear Mum's voice in the background echoing his sentiment. What craziness is this? 'And to tell you how proud we are.'

'Dad, are you okay?'

'Yes, yes. Mum has been looking after me since that … you know … incident and I know I thanked you before but the doctors told me how differently things could have been if you hadn't rung for an ambulance. But listen, your sister just called...' I hold my breath; he's buttering me up for something. Something to do with Rose? '...and told me your news. We wanted to say congratulations, amazing news.'

'Eh?' As I say it I remember that Jamal was doing an announcement on his Insta today about us working together. I had forgotten completely even though he had told me of his plan yesterday when he invited me to Lakota. But my swirling self-pity had pushed it to the back of my mind. My brain only wanting to concentrate on how I had been rejected rather than the things I had made a success of. Was that what has caused this? It would make sense.

'I've always said that your love of Shakespeare would take you places...' I don't have time to counter this revisionist bullshit as he continues. 'And now it has. I don't know why you didn't tell us that you were going to be working with Jamal. That's huge. My little girl working alongside one of the UK's biggest stars.'

'We're so proud of you, Belle,' Mum pipes up into the phone as Dad adds, 'We couldn't be prouder.' I can't help the daft grin that crosses my face. I had given up any hope of those words being said a long time ago and now, in this crazy new world I am living in, my parents have rung me to tell me they are proud of me. I know I am beaming as I thank them and wish them a Happy New Year. They stay on the phone for a bit longer, pressing me for details and reiterating that they had always known how clever I was and I choose not to call them out or suggest they had never made it particularly clear. I merely revel in their praise and hug their words close to me, just in case they never say it again.

Finishing the call, I relate this strange turn of events to Luisa, who high-fives me, puts on some Lizzo and gives me free rein in her wardrobe. There are some gorgeous things in there. We aren't identical body shapes, I'm taller for a start, but every now and then we can get away with it. And the combination of Lizzo and the offer of the most divine, if very, *very* short, green velvet dress combined with my parents' call is cheering me up no end.

The fact that she then makes me drink two of her Lollapalooza cocktails also helps. As has her relentless verbal soundtrack which focuses on how I cannot let one man stop me having fun. How it is okay to mope for a day or two but then I have a duty to womankind – I think she's overegging it a bit there – not to mention myself, to pick myself up and move on with my life. By the time we get around to 'Like a Girl' for the second time we're both on our knees screeching into a hairbrush and straighteners respectively and then jumping up and bouncing around the side of the bed, dancing like we are eighteen. There is hair swirling, twerking and full-on shoulder shimmying.

She is right, Rory was a chance at happiness but he wasn't *the* chance of happiness, that is all on me. I have to make life choices that make me happy and fulfilled and not rely on other people to do so. Luisa reminded me yesterday that my life's dream has come true this year, in these last few weeks, and that I need to embrace all I have achieved.

I have been able to make the break to being a self-employed educational consultant on Shakespeare. And I am doing it with someone with one of the highest profiles in the country, a partnership I've achieved by my own merit. My parents have made the effort to reach out to me and tell me they are proud.

She adds that if I can't get dressed up and celebrate that this New Year's Eve then I need to take a serious look at my priorities.

I know she's right.

And to be fair to her she had sat with me into the wee hours yesterday, and the night before, as I sobbed about how rejected I felt, what a fool I was, when was I going to learn and so on and so forth. The soliloquy of every broken heart the world has ever seen. It is time to pull myself together and get my moves on!

Oh.

My.

God.

Luisa is so right, sometimes you just need a splurge. After the cocktails at her house I stayed relatively sober because it may be New Year's Eve now but it's Marsha's birthday tomorrow *and* I want to go to work in the morning. For a start it's the only way I have of paying my rent for sure until the Jamal alliance fully takes off and it's wrong to leave the Hope House girls in the lurch. So drinking I'm not, but dancing I can.

Jamal's set is outstanding, he has us all in the palm of his hand, lifting us up and twirling us around with the music he plays. I haven't danced for so long. Tonight I dance on a podium, I dance with my head in the speakers, I dance with Luisa and Remi and I dance with strangers. I dance and dance and it feels magnificent.

High on life, I pull out my phone to see how close we are to midnight – ten to, so not long – when my eye alights on someone sliding off the stage and into the front of the crowd. He is all lit up with fairy lights and from a distance his frame is similar to Rory's. My heart pangs. We could have been so good.

I turn to look for Luisa and Remi to make sure we're together as the New Year is counted in when Jamal takes to the mic.

'Ay. Ay. Ay. Thank you, Bristol, for coming out tonight. It is so good to be home and to be playing to my people. It is extra special because as we know this iconic club, one that has seen decades of music history being made, one that I may have had a moment or two in myself in my much younger days...' Innocence is there, I see him in the crowd as he whit-woo's loudly and Jamal raises an eyebrow and nods with a damn-right look on his face. 'Anyway, this place is being shut down soon...' The crowd gentle-boos and Jamal holds his hand up for quiet. 'However, I'm going to ask for all of your patience whilst we create another very special moment in this seminal club. One of my oldest friends from back in the day, who came up with me all the way from Mandela City Primary, has an apology to make. Tonight, as the old year bows out and the new one swooshes in seems like the perfect time. So please, a bit of quiet for my boy, and I promise we'll have the music back

on in a few minutes.' Jamal stands to the side and claps his
hands in the direction of the man who had slid down from
the stage. A man now enrobed in Christmas tree lights with
a spotlight fixed right on him. *Rory!* Rory stands there all lit
up and looks straight at me.

It's the first time I've seen him since he left me outside
The Mont, since he broke my heart. I'm frozen to the spot
for a minute and then shake myself out of it, casting around
for Luisa or Remi. Both walk up behind me, and Luisa rubs
a circle on my back, reminding me that she has me for ever
and that whatever is about to unfold is going to be okay.

I'm not so sure.

What *is* going to unfold? Dear God, I hope Rory isn't
going to apologise in front of the hundreds of people,
paused and clustered into groups and watching. I hope he
isn't going to reveal to the world that he's sorry for hurting
my feelings and please can we be friends.

I want to die. That whole hole-opening-up wish that
people have in situations like this is not strong enough, but
death will probably do. I look around for a fire exit. There it
is, the lettering lit in neon green, I can run out there if
needs be.

The bars of a song come on and Rory throws his arms
out wide. Before I know it he's dancing towards me singing
Blondie's 'The Tide Is High' – shouting rather than singing,
to be accurate – whilst thrusting a solitary digit into the air.
He is making such a fool of himself but my God is he giving
it his all. People stand all around us chuckling good-
naturedly, captivated by his very personal and public
humiliation. He is right in front of me now and I can't help

but smile, beam even, anxiety disappearing as I look at this man, this man with the kind green eyes and strong shoulders and fear of making a tit of himself in public, who is currently covered in fairy lights and murdering Debbie Harry.

He hurt me badly the other day but right now he is here, doing this for me. Telling me, and I hope to God I have interpreted this correctly, telling me he wants me to be his number one. Am I being wildly optimistic? What else can it be?

The music changes suddenly to 'Careless Whisper', at which point he falls to his knees as he mouths, 'Waste a chance that I'd been given.' Mortifyingly cringe but tears of laughter are streaming down my cheeks – he was born to overact eighties dance moves – and I feel a little tap on my shoulder. Alison has somehow snuck in and is beside me nodding and pointing with pride. I look across the circle that has formed around Rory and see Innocence punching the air and shouting, 'Go boy, go!' and I see the beam of joy across Luisa's face. Chardonnay has appeared from nowhere, her pilot standing behind her and holding her close. Everyone is here and sharing this moment with me.

The music changes again. I recognise it immediately.

No, surely not?

Jamal comes across the mic again, 'Rory is going to teach us a new dance, guys. You never know, it may well take off. Feel free to just let go and join in.'

Rory is a foot in front of me now and gives me the biggest smile. Surely he isn't going to … oh yes, he is. He brings one hand up to his chest, then another and then drops them into paws. I can't stop laughing now; it spills out of me like waves over a beach. I literally have to clutch my tummy as he starts boinging around the dance floor, spotlight still on him, paws held high and singing Tigger's version of "Jingle Bells".

He is insane. This is insane. Utter public mortification.

I hold one paw up, then another and boing over to join him, singing as loudly as I can.

'Oh, what fun it is to ride in a one-horse open sleigh.'

He shoots me a look, a look that says so many things, the most obvious being gratitude but the deepest being love. No one but him has ever really looked at me this way before and I know I will follow this man to the ends of the earth.

The place lights up – for some bizarre reason Rory's dance seems to tickle people and they all start to join in. I don't think Lakota has ever seen its club alive to Winnie the Pooh music before, but tonight it does. Everyone is Tigger bouncing. Remi and Luisa are boinging and from the passion Alison puts into it I can picture her as a young woman with some seriously impressive punk moves. I even see Innocence boing past at one point and my heart swells with love for these people, this city, this man in his stupid lit-up Christmas hat and jumper, making a fool of himself to get my attention.

The music comes to a stop and Jamal holds up his hands,

'Now my man has one more thing to do, and I thank you for bearing with us. You are amazing. Ready, Rory?'

Rory nods and Jamal starts to beatbox. Rory turns to me

and looks straight into my eyes. 'I know I have been a complete fool, Belle. An absolute arse. So I have written you this to make it clear how bad I feel, how sorry I am, how much love and respect and, well, awe I have for the person you are and how much I would love you to let me start again.'

He takes a deep breath and then…

'Shall I compare thee to a Christmas Day?
Thou art more merry and bring far more joy.
Thy smile, thy voice, the truth of what thou say'st
Maketh my soul less brok'n, my hope less coy.'

This is a sonnet, he has written me a sonnet! My mind flashes back to the time we had sat talking about them in my flat, how he had confided then that he thought there could be no greater love letter in the world than someone sitting down and writing a sonnet.

I am dumbfounded.

'Thy faithful loving caus'd all fear to flee
From my heart, froze solid and stuck in time.
Ribbit…'

He makes a frog movement with his shoulders as he says this word and I quite literally don't know what to do with myself.

'… Thy patience truly thaw-ed me
Thus, I stand here asking thee to be mine.

I want us to plan a life together
And can see us, our future shining bright
Let me cherish you, love you for ever
And hear this heartfelt vow I make tonight.
As long as I have breath, true I will be
And dedicate my heart, Belle Wilde, to thee.'

He feels like this? He really feels like this? About me? Wow.

He finishes and looks at me and I nod my head. How can I not forgive this man, this wonderful man I have already given my entire heart to? Can I live this life he envisions, a life with the two of us building a future, here in the city we love and surrounded by the people that mean the most in the world to us? He comes and takes my hand and just as he does so, 'Auld Lang Syne' comes through the sound system.

'Oh my God, Rory. You wrote all that? For me? When did you find time?'

'Of course for you. Yesterday and today, I was up half the night, it's not as perfect as I wanted it to be. But will you forgive me my stupidity? I was scared and I was stupid but I know how much I want you in my life. Will you give me another chance to prove that I am a man that deserves you? Let me show you all the ways I can.'

'Rory, sometimes you talk too much.' I lean forward and touch my lips to his just as the first boing of twelve strikes, but for me right now, right here, the New Year is not uppermost in my mind. The man who has closed the distance between us is returning my kiss and making me feel very, very squirmy indeed. I love this man and I love his dreams of our future together. There is nothing in the world I could want more than to have him by my side for ever.

Who would have thought it all those years ago? Rory Walters is *my* perfect man.

Acknowledgments

I loved writing this book. Belle and Rory have been sitting on my shoulder and demanding I write about them for a while now so it's great to have been able to tell their story, it really was one of those that grew legs and ran away with itself, so there's an argument that Belle took over and wrote this one, but I certainly enjoyed the ride.

However, regardless of who was actually in charge, none of it would have been possible had it not been for my agent, Hayley Steed, who fully supported my plan to write a novel where each chapter is one day of December and a true celebration of all things Christmassy. She is a wonderful cheerleader, and I am very grateful that I have her.

This is my first book that has not been part of the The Cornish Village School series and was written especially for One More Chapter, my new publisher. I landed on my feet with my editor, Charlotte Ledger, who has been absolutely fantastic every step of the way. So a huge thank you to her for being welcoming, supportive, thorough and generally fabulous. I can't tell you how much I appreciate it.

Because I had been planning this book for a while, I managed to get out in November/December 2019 and scour Bristol and Bath for Christmassy things that Belle and Rory could do together as their romance developed and I am so grateful that I did. I love these two cities and had no shortage of things to write about. My partner and I learnt the St Bernard's Waltz at Tyntesfield and I went on their horse and carriage ride. If you want to immerse yourself in a Victorian Christmas, Tyntesfield House is definitely the place to do it. I also dragged my partner to the SS Brunel for an improv theatre evening, so much fun, where just like Belle I hid myself behind a pillar so I didn't have to participate.

One of my best friends in the world, Janette (who this book is dedicated to), let me use her experience of breast cancer when I was writing Alison and put up with endless video chats where I asked question after question about a truly harrowing time to make sure that what I wrote was as accurate as could be. I hope that I have handled it sensitively and that by using the real-life story of someone I love deeply I have managed to avoid causing offence to anyone who has been touched by this dreadful, dreadful disease. Obviously, any mistakes are entirely my own.

I'd like to say thank you to Scott, who also put up with a barrage of questions to make sure that the signs of Nick's silent heart attack were authentic. Again, any errors are because of my inability to understand anything science-y and my own responsibility. And a shout out to the lovely

Barbie, who let me steal her surname because it so beautifully suited my character.

Then there is Jane Cable, my writing buddy and fellow OMC author, who checks in every day and helps me iron out niggles, congratulates me on successes and cheers me along. She is a thoroughly wise woman, and I am grateful to her daily.

And finally, a huge thank you to my family. My children, who make me as proud as any parent can be. Namdi, who good-naturedly endured me dragging him to Christmas events under the guise of research. And to my own parents for not being as horrific as Nick and Cyndi and supporting everything I have ever done. Also, one final mention for my late Great Aunty Kit, whose name I stole at the start of my writing career and who instilled a lifelong love of Shakespeare that has never left me.

YOUR NUMBER ONE STOP

ONE MORE CHAPTER

FOR PAGETURNING BOOKS

One More Chapter is an
award-winning global
division of HarperCollins.

Sign up to our newsletter to get our
latest eBook deals and stay up to date
with our weekly Book Club!
<u>Subscribe here.</u>

Meet the team at
<u>www.onemorechapter.com</u>

Follow us!
 <u>@OneMoreChapter_</u>
 <u>@OneMoreChapter</u>
 <u>@onemorechapterhc</u>

Do you write unputdownable fiction?
We love to hear from new voices.
Find out how to submit your novel at
<u>www.onemorechapter.com/submissions</u>